JUST THE TRUTH

GEN LAGRECA

Winged Victory Press
Carmel, Indiana
www.wingedvictorypress.com

Available in print and ebook editions

Just the Truth
ISBN paperback: 978-0-9744579-5-6
Library of Congress Control Number: 2019920107

Published by Winged Victory Press
www.wingedvictorypress.com

Cover by Watson Graphics

Printed in the United States of America
First edition 2020

Quality discounts are available for bulk purchases of this book. For information, please contact Winged Victory Press.
Email: service@wingedvictorypress.com

OTHER NOVELS BY GEN LAGRECA
available in print and ebook editions
NOBLE VISION
A DREAM OF DARING
FUGITIVE FROM ASTERON

ADVANCE PRAISE

AUTHOR'S NOTE

 I want to thank David Lips, Russell Burge, and Cynthia Noe for reading the manuscript and offering valuable comments. In addition, I owe special thanks to my editor, Marcia Eppich-Harris.

 In the words of the fictional judge Daniel Redmond in *Perry Mason*, "The Case of the Witless Witness":

> *If we refuse to fight for the dignity of truth,*
> *we have substituted expediency for justice.*

PROLOGUE

His teacher had told him to stop asking so many questions. They disrupted the class, she'd said. Although he asked them in earnest, and she tried her best to reply, his questions too often pushed the bounds of her knowledge. She squirmed, and the children laughed. The little schoolhouse he attended in rural Virginia eventually became like a shoe that no longer fit the growing footprint of Julius Taninger's intellectual curiosity.

At age ten, he'd decided he'd had enough of the place. Instead of going to school, he worked on his family's small farm. On days when his chores were light, he walked the four miles of dirt road to town, where he borrowed books from the library of a local lawyer who took kindly to him. Julius devoured the titles he'd selected and returned them promptly, without so much as a smudge on any page, never wearing out the books—or his welcome. In 1948, with the country still recovering from the Second World War and his family nearly destitute, he read the histories of nations, the tomes of philosophers, and the classics in literature. These books lured him away from the dull landscape in which he chopped wood, fed hogs, and planted crops, toward a fresh canvas on which to paint his future.

At age fifteen, his fascination with the printed word drew him to the office of the town's newspaper. He made himself useful by sweeping floors, emptying trash, filing papers, and doing other odd jobs without asking for or receiving any pay. The boss noticed his initiative and taught him how to set type and operate the press, which earned him a small salary. Soon he was contributing articles and making more money. After a hurricane struck the town, he set off another storm with his investigative reporting into a no-bid contract approved by the mayor for debris removal. He discovered that the contractor had a checkered past and the mayor was getting a kickback to ignore it. He also found that the mayor's real talent lay in smearing anyone he perceived as an enemy. After the mayor and his friends launched a campaign to discredit the young reporter—"He's a fool kid," "He's looking for attention," "He just wants to make trouble," "He lies"—no one believed Julius's story. When the town turned against Julius, the editor pressured him to retract his accusations. When he refused, the editor fired him. Vindication came a year later when more evidence was uncovered, and the mayor and others involved in the scheme were tried and sent to jail. This experience spurred Julius's drive to have his own paper—one that would never compromise the truth.

At age twenty, Julius Taninger's footprint grew larger. He moved to Washington, DC, where he obtained a loan to buy his first newspaper, a struggling broadsheet named *The Pulse of the People*. He changed the name to *Taninger News*. The owner had a motto, which he never stated to his readers but shared with the young buyer: *Capture the crowd at any price*. Remembering how his former community had formed a gang of sorts that tried to crush him when he was a young reporter, he realized that his passions lay in capturing something else. He changed the motto to: *Find the truth wherever it hides*. Instead of keeping his slogan to himself as a marketing scheme, he printed it on the front page as a declaration.

Within a decade, he had increased the paper's circulation to a national readership of millions, transforming his modest local daily into one of the highest-ranking newspapers in the country. He broadened the newspaper's scope by adding top-notch reporters and correspondents in key cities around the country and the world. When he acquired thousands of acres of timberland in Canada, along with paper mills, power plants, and a fleet of ships to transport megatons of newsprint to his giant, never-still printing presses in Washington, DC, he developed a corporate empire spanning two countries. In subsequent years, he ventured into sports and entertainment and had a building erected to house his growing company's headquarters. His holdings expanded to include television stations and a professional football team. *Taninger News* became part of a larger corporation, Taninger Enterprises.

Julius Taninger was tall, handsome, and rich. His quiet self-confidence gave the appearance of calm, except for restless gray eyes like two steely perpetual-motion machines that took in everything and missed nothing. His straight black hair fell of its own will across his forehead as the only part of him not subject to rigorous self-control. He was the town's most striking bachelor, but no woman wanted him. His reputation for making enemies of the city's most influential people kept the women away.

He kept his office on the newsroom floor, at the epicenter of the daily hurricane of activities that spewed the news, while the office suite designed for him on the top floor of his building sat idle.

When one of his major corporate advertisers was caught in a scandal, and his editor asked him if they should cover the story or ignore it, Julius replied, "Run it."

When a powerful businessman-turned-politician tried to buy advertising space for his companies in exchange for favorable coverage of his political adventures, Julius replied, "We put our advertising columns up for sale, but we never sell editorial pages."

When a small newspaper in Philadelphia was shut down by a new law spearheaded by a local politician to silence his enemies, Julius financed the publisher's battle through the court system to get the law declared unconstitutional. He won.

When the president of the United States, in the heat of a reelection campaign, sent an aide to implore Julius to end his newspaper's relentless attacks on the incumbent, and in exchange *Taninger News* would receive priority access to his administration and exclusive interviews with him, Julius replied, "No deal."

When his fiery editorials excoriated the local mayor for proposing regulations and taxes harmful to business, Taninger Enterprises became victim to a truckers' strike and a plant fire. After doing his own investigation, Julius discovered that the mayor was covertly driving the actions as retribution against a political enemy. The mayor feigned ignorance, claiming that coincidences happen. One actually did, and it was not to his honor's liking. Julius had finally found a woman who admired him for the very qualities that scared off other prospects. She was the mayor's daughter. To the indignation of her father, they eloped.

Julius refused invitations to the parties, golf games, and country clubs of the city's social elite. He kept a chair's length away from the fangs and claws of the powerful, whom he oftentimes lashed in editorials printed in his newspaper. He signed those pieces with his iconic initials, affixed like a dare under his column: JT. Everyone called him JT, even his wife and the son and grandchildren they were to have.

His business and his life were inseparable. Other men would take their families on vacations—JT took his family along on business trips. Sharing the excitement and fascination for his work was JT's version of family values. He took his son and later his grandchildren to corporate meetings with him, on trips to explore his vast properties, and on tours through his plants, explaining the business to them. When they grew up, they joined Taninger Enterprises.

Sometimes JT could be spotted by the newsstand outside his office building, where he found a quiet satisfaction in observing customers buy *Taninger News* and in seeing the stack of his newspapers dwindle on the shelf. Once, a father and child walked up to the newsstand while JT was there. The man took a copy of *Taninger News* from the stack. It had a photograph on the front page of the president of the United States with the leaders of the Senate and House of

Representatives. As the customer paid for his purchase, his daughter, who looked to be about five years old, noticed the tall stranger watching them.

She pointed at the stack of papers and asked him, "What does a newspaper do?"

With the glower of a teacher reacting to delinquent students, JT gestured at the photograph of the nation's leaders on the front page and replied, "It watches these rascals and keeps them in line."

The years never softened Julius Taninger; instead, they hardened even more his crusty patina. Competitors feared him. Politicians smeared him. His wife revered him. As his son and grandchildren grew up in changing times and joined the business, they tolerated him, except for one granddaughter, who adored him. When other family members accused her of being just like her grandfather, they meant it as a criticism, but she took it as a compliment. Her name was Laura Taninger.

CHAPTER 1

Find the truth wherever it hides.

Laura Taninger glanced at the motto as she walked into the office building. Years ago, her grandfather had arranged for his words to be engraved in stone and placed over the arched entrance to the granite and steel building that housed Taninger Enterprises. Walking under the motto every day reminded Laura of passing through the gateway of a temple she had toured in an ancient city. JT's words reminded her of why she was there—why they all were there, she and the staff who came through that doorway each day.

The cool air inside brought her relief from the oppressive August heat. Was the weather in Washington, DC, more stifling than usual this summer, she wondered, or was it the heated politics of the town that tested her stamina? She wondered if her meeting later that day with a whistleblower in a key agency would turn up the political heat—and form storm clouds over those in power.

Laura greeted the security guard at the reception desk and glanced at the wall behind him, where a large metallic sign with block letters announced the building's owner and resident: Taninger Enterprises. Under the sign, two rows of photographs displayed the corporation's executive management. Laura had always thought of that wall as her family album. Her late grandfather, Julius Taninger, the founder, and her father, Clark Taninger, the chief executive officer, were featured on the top row. Her sister Irene, brother Billie, and she were shown on the second row. There was room next to her portrait for her younger sister, Kate, now attending a local college, who would join the family business and become part of the executive management after graduation.

Laura took the elevator to the television newsroom of *Taninger News* and walked past the electronic blur of studio sets, cameras, lighting tracks, and workstations wallpapered with monitors. She smiled at the staff members who noticed her arrival and greeted her with a hurried wave or a quick, "Hi, Laura," as they performed the daily miracle of ferreting out the news and broadcasting it across the country and the world. The small local newspaper business that Julius Taninger had founded seventy years ago had now grown into a corporation consisting of a major television news network, an online news service, and a still-vibrant national print newspaper, with sister companies in sports and entertainment.

Laura entered her office and opened the blinds so that she could see the newsroom from the expansive window on one of the walls. Even though she was president of the news division of Taninger Enterprises, like JT, she kept her office adjacent to the cyclone of the newsroom, rather than in the distant calm of the executive offices on the top floor. Her office, like her home—and her life, in general—contained only a few essentials. A desk, a couple of chairs, a couch, and a coffee table were the only furniture. A map, a calendar, a clock, and two rows of television monitors occupied much of the wall space. Only one wall had the distinction of holding just a single item, a large poster of her on the set of her prime-time television program, *Just the Truth*. In the poster, the show's flamboyant logo, the initials JT, shone in the background. Two years ago, when her grandfather had died, she created *Just the Truth*, which she envisioned as a mixture of breaking news and commentary. As a tribute to the past and a promise for the future, she had taken Julius Taninger's lifelong attachment to the truth, as well as his iconic initials, and repurposed them in the show's name and logo.

That morning, like many others, she tossed her purse under her desk and her suit jacket across a chair, then sat at her computer to check her email. She glanced at the clock. It was almost time for the weekly executive meeting of Taninger Enterprises, held every Friday.

She looked comfortable and poised in her expensive business clothes, as though her job as president of Taninger News fit her as well as the clothes matching it. Her silk blouse over soft breasts and her above-the-knee skirt over shapely legs defined the boundary where fashion and business meet. At twenty-nine, she displayed an intriguing mix of intelligence and beauty that gave her the look of someone who could be brilliant at work, lighthearted at play, and seductive with a man she wanted.

Laura scanned her computer monitor, her auburn hair falling to her shoulders, its shiny tendrils like a mirror catching every light. Her brown eyes—large, direct, inquisitive, thoughtful—dominated her face. The simplicity of her makeup was like the openness of her expression, giving those who knew her the sense that they were seeing the real person without pretensions. She seemed ready to smile if the occasion arose; otherwise, her face remained neutral, neither smiling nor pouting, but quietly assessing the world.

"Laura, we did it!"

A man with a broad smile and an energetic voice entered her open door. It was her producer, Tom Shiner, wearing his headphones around his neck like a doctor with a stethoscope. He waved a printed article at her.

Tom said, "*Stone Media Research* has a story out today on our ratings. *Just the Truth* is now number one in television news!" He read from the article, "'In just two years, Laura Taninger has taken her prime-time program from an experimental start-up to the most-watched news show in the country.'"

He tossed the article on her desk.

She skimmed it.

"This is really great, Tom!"

They paused to smile at each other in a shared victory.

She rose to go, and took the article, saying, "I'll bring this to my meeting!"

Five people sat around the oval conference table. The plush carpeting, leather swivel chairs, and wood paneling gave the conference room a formal setting, but the similar facial features of the attendees gave it the air of a family gathering. The closed door provided the executives of Taninger Enterprises with seclusion from the outside world, while television screens on the walls and laptop computers at their places gave them instant access to information from around the globe.

At the head of the table, Clark Taninger faced his four children. They sat in their usual places, with Irene and Billie on one side, Laura and Kate on the other. Planning to join the family business after graduation, the youngest Taninger, Kate, came to as many of the executive meetings as she could while attending college.

Clark nodded to his administrative assistant, Caroline Davis, as she entered, took her place next to him, and opened her laptop computer, ready to take notes. He preferred her minutes of these meetings to a verbatim audio recording. After years of working with him, the efficient, discreet Caroline knew what to note and what to leave unofficial in the sometimes heated debates among these family members who were also business associates.

When everyone was seated, Clark began, saying, "Friday, August 18th, the executive management meeting of Taninger Enterprises will come to order."

His custom-tailored suit and gold cuff links gave him the air of a diplomat while he studied columns of numbers on his computer screen with the attention of a businessman. He looked up from his monitor to announce, "Taninger Enterprises is doing very well!"

The others smiled.

Although he was announcing good news, Clark looked tentative. His smile was modest, as if he could reverse himself and frown on a moment's notice. His peppery gray hair mirrored his ambivalence, as if a contest between black and white strands had ended in a stalemate. At fifty-nine, his face still looked young, although a furrow on his brow kept deepening with the years, giving him a questioning look, as though the world had changed and was confusing to him.

"Okay, Irene, let's hear from you first."

He turned to his first born, the president of Taninger Entertainment.

At age thirty-six, Irene Taninger looked as glamorous as the celebrities that dominated the newscasts, reality shows, and other programming on her network. A short-sleeved, figure-hugging satin blouse with the top buttons open, blond hair pulled back in a stylish braided bun, large earrings ornamenting her perfectly made-up face, and glasses sloping down her sculptured nose defined Irene as a woman in the entertainment business. Her long red fingernails tapped her keyboard to bring up a screen.

"This year, Taninger Entertainment will get a big, new contract. We'll be broadcasting the Pinnacle Awards."

"Excellent!" said Clark.

"Here's the letter from Pinnacle's CEO, Mort Bennett." She read from the document on her screen, "'Dear Irene: We at Pinnacle are delighted to be partnering with Taninger Entertainment this year to bring the industry's most vaunted motion picture awards to our growing television audience.'"

"Congratulations!" said Laura.

"Good job, sis," added Billie.

"We're set to sign the contract at a formal signing ceremony that'll be a big media event. And there's more," she teased.

"What's that?" asked her father.

"*Ken Martin* will open the program," Irene said and paused for their reactions.

Kenneth Martin was the president of the United States.

"Wow!" exclaimed her youngest sister, Kate.

"He'll be there *live*. The sponsors, ads, and money are rolling in. Viewership will set a new record for Taninger Entertainment."

"How'd you swing that?" asked Billie.

"I figured that the president could reach his voters through the event, which would be important to him in this reelection year. And Pinnacle's CEO . . . well, I know he's wanted to get in tight with the president since the proposed Fairness Tax on Movie Theaters has been under consideration in Congress. This tax would raise ticket prices and have a huge negative effect on the movie industry, so Mort Bennett has been trying to get the president to say he'd veto the bill if it passed through Congress and ended up on his desk. When I told Mort my plan for Ken to appear live at the Awards Ceremony, he jumped at the chance for face-time with the president to lobby him about the bill in a friendly setting," she boasted. "That's how I enticed Mort to sign on with me, and I reeled Ken in."

"Now we need to get President Martin to sit down for an interview with Laura," suggested Kate.

"Wouldn't that be nice," said Laura. "I've made numerous requests, but so far I haven't heard back from his office."

"I don't think he likes Laura," said Kate, smiling as though she were delivering her sister a compliment.

"I rather think Ken prefers *me*!" Irene boasted.

Ignoring their quips, Clark said, "That's very good news, Irene. Now, let's move on."

Clark turned to his son, the president of Taninger Sports. The Sports division of Taninger Enterprises owned a professional football team, the DC Slammers.

"Billie, what've you got?"

At thirty-four, Billie looked like a sports figure himself, with gym-tightened muscles and stylishly messy, light-brown hair. An open shirt, loosened tie, and rolled up sleeves with no jacket gave him the look of a hands-on executive, impatient with meetings that took him away from his work.

"In less than five weeks, the DC Slammers will be playing their home opener in our *new* stadium."

"How's it coming?" asked Clark.

"We're ahead of schedule. Ticket sales are through the roof, and with the increased seating capacity of the new venue, we're on target for a record year in sales."

"And the inspections, are they in order?"

"No problem. I've got good relations with the local and federal regulators. We're in compliance with everything they've thrown at us. In fact, we're at the cutting edge for professional football stadiums, with bells and whistles that exceed environmental and public safety rules."

"That's big news!" said Irene.

The others smiled approvingly.

"In two weeks, the old stadium will be imploded. I set up a huge media event to cover it. That'll generate fantastic publicity."

"We're all looking forward to the home opener," said Clark.

The others nodded.

"Now, Laura?"

"I just got some news."

"Let's have it," said Billie.

In a sudden flash, Laura thought of the years she had spent learning the business—covering assignments, reporting on them, writing scripts, choosing graphics, selecting stories to put on the air, shooting segments, editing them. She thought of the past two years of grinding work to develop her own show—of battling the skeptics and critics, of gathering a top-notch team, of being on the vanguard of news reporting, of building an audience that trusted the clear facts and straight-talking commentary she offered. Those years at Taninger News congealed into a lump in her throat that made her pause a moment before she could talk.

"*Just the Truth* is now the number one news program in the country!"

She sent the article around the table.

"That's great, Laura," said Clark.

"Very nice!" Irene added.

"Good work," said Billie.

"Laura, you did it!" Kate gave her older sister a hug. Then she turned to the others. "And you all told her it would never work!"

Like a miniature canine that barks at the big breeds daring to approach its turf, Kate, the youngest and most outspoken of the children, was unaware of differences of scale when it came to defending things that mattered to her. Ten years ago, when Laura was nineteen and Kate was only nine, their mother had died, and Laura, the sibling closest to Kate in age and temperament, became a surrogate mother. The two sisters were not only uncanny look-alikes—both brunette, with similar features and tall, lean figures—but they were also alike in how they thought and reacted to things. Hence, a bond developed between them, sometimes to the exclusion of the other family members.

"Katie, dear, you needn't reprimand us. I dare say we're all glad Laura's show worked out," said Clark. "On the other hand, it is *edgy*. We want to keep building Laura's fan base without having her stir up the entire world."

"Maybe the world needs stirring up," Kate persisted.

Laura looked at Kate, amused. She reached over, as she did when Kate was a child, to brush back strands of her sister's hair that had fallen over one eye.

"And what's *your* news," Clark asked Kate, "now that you're about to start your junior year in college?"

Although Kate was not yet a voting member of the company—her stock was being held in trust for her until she reached her twenty-first birthday—she showed great interest in the business.

"This year I'll be editor-in-chief of the *Collier Voice*."

"The third Taninger to be editor-in-chief of Collier University's oldest campus newspaper, after Laura and me!" Clark smiled. "So, tell me, does your interest in newspapers mean you'll want to join Laura at Taninger News after you graduate?"

"Maybe I'll take *your* job, Daddy. Won't you be retiring by then?"

"Don't get your hopes up!"

Irene and Billie laughed, but only halfheartedly, wary that Kate may have meant what she said. Laura laughed wholeheartedly, hoping Kate did mean it.

Clark turned to his laptop, calling up screens of data.

"The numbers look good," he said. He rolled his chair back, folded his hands behind his head, and looked contentedly at his brood.

"I have to tell you," Clark went on, "I had my doubts about JT's will. I was afraid it would put us at each other's throats. We've had our rough spots," he glanced at Laura, "but it's worked out pretty well."

Laura remembered the day they had sat in a lawyer's office hearing the surprising terms of Julius Taninger's will. JT had left equal shares of Taninger Enterprises to each of them so that each heir owned a fifth of the privately held corporation.

Clark smiled at his four children.

"Yes, JT's plan has worked, at least so far—"

His mobile phone rang in his pocket with the special tone he used for only the most important calls, which he handled personally.

"Yes?" he answered. "Hi, Darcy. What can I do for you? . . . Oh, really? . . . I see . . . Yes, of course, Darcy. I'll take care of it. Don't you worry, now."

He hung up and faced the others.

"That was Darcy Egan."

The others waited, with a hint of concern on their faces. The caller was the chief advisor to President Ken Martin.

"Laura, what's this about you trying to stir up trouble at the Bureau of Elections?"

"I'm trying to get information."

The faces of the others were blank, except for Kate.

"Don't any of you watch Laura's show?" she asked. "Laura's covering a hot story about the Bureau of Elections. She's trying to track down money they're spending in implementing the new Voter Fairness Act. She has some suspicions about that. Right, Laura?"

Laura nodded.

"I may not be the only one," Laura said. "This afternoon I'm meeting with a source involved with the project."

"Who?" Clark asked with a sharp voice.

"A high-level person. That's all I'll say."

"Hey, that's the president's signature program," Irene warned. "You don't want to poke your nose into that."

"Don't I?" Laura asked.

"Laura looked at the Bureau of Elections' posted list of contractors that were paid to design and implement the new voting system we're going to have. But the list was incomplete," Kate explained. "See, *I* watch Laura's show!"

"The list of contractors and expenditures that the Bureau of Elections posted doesn't add up with what the Department of the Budget shows Elections is spending," Laura added.

"Don't you have better things to do than weave through agency budgets and try to stir up problems for Ken?" asked Irene.

"There's a $400 million line item—money that the Department of the Budget shows the Bureau of Elections is paying out, but Elections hasn't accounted for it, and Budget lists the item only as 'Other,' without a recipient," said Laura, "so there's a mystery about what that money is for and who's getting it."

"It's chump change," said Irene.

"Who cares, besides just a few policy wonks?" Billie added.

"Is anyone else covering this so-called story?" Clark asked. "Who in the media thinks this is important?"

"*I* do," said Laura.

"Why should *Taninger News* be the only media outlet sticking its neck out to fence with the administration?" asked Clark. "We don't want to seem antagonistic to the president."

"She's always attacking him," Irene complained to her father.

"But I defended him when his political opponents spread nasty stories about his tax returns, stories that turned out to be false. I was the first one to find out the truth and report it. Remember that?"

"It's not just the way you report on Ken," Irene continued as if she hadn't heard Laura's response. "It's your show in general. Why are your stories such downers?"

She paused for a reply but received none.

"You need more uplift," Irene said. "You need entertainment spots on *Just the Truth*."

"And sports coverage too," said Billie.

"We mustn't be too suspicious, Laura," Clark warned. "We don't want to appear to be against this new voting system, do we? People will think we're against voting rights."

"But we're not against *disclosure*, are we?" Laura countered. "By law, these agencies have to disclose the money they spend and where it goes. I've contacted them with my questions—and been ignored. That raises my suspicions."

"I'm sure they have better things to do than cater to you," said Irene.

"But I'm the *press*. Do you think the administration shouldn't have to answer to the press?"

"You've always been against Ken's Voter Fairness Act!" Irene charged.

"I have," Laura replied.

"Now that it's passed, can't you accept it and go on to other things?"

"No."

"Why not, Laura?" her father asked. "You remember how the media smeared us as being against the poor, the minorities, the immigrants, the disabled, the elderly, the needy—all because you attacked that law."

"I said the Voter Fairness Act was a ploy to make people feel as if they were victims of a terrible injustice, and Ken Martin was their savior. It was a ploy to drum up votes for the president and his party. I stand by that."

"It was a law to protect everyone's right to vote, to make it easier for the disadvantaged, to make sure everybody's vote counted," Irene said.

"Then why are they hiding a big expenditure of the program from public scrutiny?"

Looking bored with the meeting, Billie, who avoided politics, checked his phone for messages.

Clark looked irritated.

"Your whistleblower may be nothing more than a disgruntled insider looking for attention," Clark said. "It wouldn't be the first time somebody played the media for fools."

He pointed a finger at Laura.

"I don't want any more calls about you from Darcy. Watch your step."

That afternoon Laura stood on the curb outside the Taninger building, the mid-August sun burning her face. Steam rose from the hot pavement to wilt her clothes. The cab she hailed pulled up, and a burst of cool air greeted her as she entered. When she gave the driver the address, he turned around to face her, eyeing her expensive clothes.

"Sure you wanna go *there?*"

"I'm sure," Laura said.

She was headed to a place called Bailey's, an eatery in a neighborhood—and a world—removed from the stately buildings, expensive shops, and trendy restaurants around Taninger Enterprises.

She followed the instructions of the man she was to meet: *Leave the cameras and crew behind. Arrive in a cab, and pay the driver in cash.* Two years ago, when the Voter Fairness Act had passed, she had interviewed the man she was to meet. He was a leading member of the team tasked with its implementation. At that time, her interview with him was on the record; this time, he wanted secrecy.

She watched as the view outside her cab window changed. The iconic monuments, classic buildings, landscaped thoroughfares, and tourist-packed museums faded behind her, replaced by meager stores with walk-up flats, parking lots with makeshift signs, sidewalks strewn with trash bags, and empty lots bound by chain-link fences to keep the squatters out.

The driver's radio, tuned to an all-news station, droned back to the passenger compartment. She listened absently.

"I'm Diane Harris with *National Report.*"

Music played, and a cheerful voice came through the airwaves.

"Our segment today is on the new voting system that's being developed by the Bureau of Elections. Earlier today we caught up with the man who's supervising the project, the assistant director of the Bureau of Elections, James Spenser."

Laura's attention piqued. James Spenser was the informant whom she was traveling to meet.

The radio host continued her introduction, "Following the Voter Fairness Act that was passed two years ago, our nation is getting a complete overhaul of its voting practices with a new national voting system that guarantees a fair and honest election for everyone. Isn't that right, Mr. Spenser?"

"That's the idea. A completely new electronic voting system will be ready to roll out in time for the November elections," said Spenser.

"I love the name you gave it: *SafeVote*. It inspires such confidence!" Diane Harris sounded as if she were nearly swooning. "Describe SafeVote for us, Mr. Spenser . . . "

Laura snickered at the name: *SafeVote*. She remembered how President Ken Martin had chosen to revamp voting in America as the key issue of his first term. The president and his surrogates launched a campaign to correct what they claimed was a grave danger threatening the country. Citizens were being denied the right to vote, they charged. Many of the states had requirements that a person prove citizenship or show official identification before voting, which the new law's proponents said discriminated against the underprivileged. Moreover, the new law's supporters claimed that most of the states had voting machines that were outdated and could be hacked, and state coffers lacked sufficient funds to update them. There were also instances of voter fraud, which the advocates of revamping the system claimed could only be rectified by the federal government's intervention. These claims of injustice, inaccuracy, and fraud were widely publicized by the president's party, the groups that supported him, and sympathetic reporters.

Whether the problem was alleged to be discriminatory state laws, outdated voting equipment, or outright voter fraud, the solution proposed by the president and his surrogates was always the same. The voting system needed a thorough makeover. It needed a massive influx of funds and good intentions that only the federal government could provide.

Before anyone realized, the tempest generated by the interested parties had funneled into a crisis. The public was swept up into its vortex. Demands intensified for the federal government to step in to ensure the modernization, uniformity, and integrity of the voting process. The Voter Fairness Act was created, and the president's party successfully pushed its passage through Congress.

The Voter Fairness Act gave the federal government the power to develop a single new system to replace the multiplicity of voting systems used by the individual states. Going forward, the individual states would be able to program the new system to enter the candidates and tally the votes for local and statewide elections, maintaining control of those contests. However, it would now be the *federal* government that would program the system and tally the votes for elections to *national* office, beginning with the upcoming presidential election, then in subsequent years expanding to include the contests for the House and Senate, which for the time being remained under state control.

There were those who had misgivings about the new measure, but they were harshly criticized by the bill's advocates. The critics were accused of being anti-suffrage, bigoted, unenlightened, and part of the privileged class—the Got-ins, as they were called—who were unconcerned about those who were disenfranchised—the Left-outs.

Opponents of the bill questioned the legitimacy of giving the federal government control over voting when the Constitution clearly gave that power to the individual states. But there were many precedents in other areas—from schools, to housing, to healthcare, to buildings, to energy, etc.—where the federal government had stepped in to oversee areas previously left to the states and the people. In so many cases Congress had passed laws and issued rules to the states, had given them funding to comply with the rules, and had withheld funds if they failed to comply that many in Congress had seen nothing wrong with granting yet another power of the states to the federal government. With the advocates of the new bill relentless and the opposition put on the defensive and ineffectual, the Voter Fairness Act passed.

A group of concerned citizens challenged the new statute in court, but the judges, hesitant to undermine a law passed by Congress, put their stamp of approval on it.

"Americans can now rest assured that our elections are fair and honest, thanks to SafeVote," Diane Harris told her radio audience. "Isn't that correct, Mr. Spenser?"

"That's the idea."

Was it her imagination that Spenser sounded *half-hearted?* Laura wondered. From private conversations with him, she knew he had his doubts.

"Thank you very much for talking with us today on *National Report.*"

The program's theme music returned as the segment concluded.

Laura pulled up a map on her phone's screen. She saw that the cab was now only a few blocks from her destination.

She wondered if Spenser trusted her enough to speak candidly. He had not contacted her directly but had been discreetly passed on to her by another journalist who had declined to pursue the story. Spenser had reluctantly agreed to speak to Laura.

On the phone a few days ago, he had shared his misgivings about her, saying, "I hear so many crazy things about you—the attacks on you by other newscasters, by the president's party, by my own boss. I don't know what to believe. They say you want to skewer the president to boost your ratings."

"They could skewer me in a minute if they put my suspicions to rest," she replied. "Why do they attack me instead of answering my questions about matters they're required by law to make public?"

"Look, if I talk to you, I could be risking my career and possibly committing a crime."

Laura couldn't deny that. There were laws to protect informants, but there were also laws to punish those who revealed internal information harmful to their agencies—and there were too many partisan players in the system to try to dissuade Spenser of the danger he sensed.

"I'm not sticking my neck out so that you can boost your ratings. I work for the administration, and I have a certain loyalty to it."

"What about working for the *truth*? Do you have a loyalty to *that*?"

She sensed in his pause that he was wondering whether he could trust her.

She went on, "I don't pursue stories in order to get ratings. I get ratings because I pursue stories—important ones. And the name of my show tells you what I look for." When he still didn't reply, she continued, "It's a pretty big deal that for the first time in our history, the federal government is taking control of the voting process for the presidential election. Don't you think the Feds—the people you work for—should be absolutely transparent and ensure that no suspicions are raised about their activities?"

"We wouldn't be having this conversation if I didn't."

"What do you know, Mr. Spenser?"

"First, tell me what *you* know."

For what seemed like minutes, she heard only his breathing over the phone. She decided not to press him when he was hesitant.

"Okay, I'll go first," she said.

She described the story she was investigating on how the Bureau of Elections was using the money allocated to it for implementing SafeVote.

"I discovered that the Bureau of Elections received $400 million that can't be traced. It's not included in their list of contractors and fees. For the way the government spends money, that may seem like a small amount, but for some of us, the unaccountability raises suspicions. I want to know who is receiving that $400 million, and what work is being done with that money."

"I may have information on that, Laura," he said.

She noticed his softer tone and use of her first name. Perhaps he was willing to trust her.

"What do you have, James?"

Again, there was silence.

"James?"

"Our agency finished the programming for SafeVote. As a final step, the program was tested for accuracy and security by a reputable outside company. It passed inspection and was certified."

"So what's the problem?"

"Sandra said another company is going to be brought in to do some last-minute programming, what she called updates and patches."

"Sandra Frank, the director of the Bureau of Elections? Your boss?"

"That's right. I thought it was odd to be planning more work on the program because the final check on everything had been done. No modifications are allowed after that, or else the program has to have another certification. I asked Sandra about that, and she said there won't be another certification."

"Did she say why?"

"She said the changes will be minor. But it's against the law to modify the program after it's been certified. I asked her who will be doing the modifications, and she brushed me off. She said the whole matter was trivial, and she would handle it. I also asked if this extra programming was her idea, and she said no, but she wouldn't say who was behind it."

"Does that mean someone above Sandra is ordering this work?"

"It could be. Sandra's a good soldier; she follows orders from higher-ups. When I looked at the records, there was no mention of this work, no line item for anyone to come in at this point to do any updates and patches."

"Do you think the $400 million that's unaccounted for will be going to the subcontractor doing these modifications?"

"Could be."

"Can you find out the name of the company and let me know?"

"I can ask questions and check around, but . . . " he trailed off, hesitating. "Sandra's been looking at me funny these days. I wonder if they think I could be . . . disloyal. Outliers tend to be watched closely here. I wonder if they . . . "

He sighed.

She waited for him to continue, feeling a quiet battle going on inside him.

Finally, he said, "Okay. I'll meet you on Friday and let you know what I find out."

Did James Spenser learn anything new? she wondered, as the cab turned onto a side street. An awning over the door of an old brick building bore the name Bailey's. Next to the restaurant was a parking lot that was less than half full at that midafternoon hour, too late for lunch and too early for dinner.

The driver left Laura in front of the restaurant and drove away. She looked incongruous in that setting, a businesswoman wearing a costly skirt and blouse, with a white linen suit jacket tossed over her arm, in front of what looked like a tavern with a restaurant tossed in as an afterthought. She looked inside a large bay window to see a sparse number of customers sitting on bar stools, amid a dirty tile floor and unkempt shelves where liquor bottles, glasses, and menus had been haphazardly placed. Sports banners papered the walls, and television monitors hung from overhead. About to open the door, she was startled by a loud noise that sounded like a gunshot. The sound seemed to be coming from the parking lot.

She hurried toward the lot. She saw the back of a man as he ran to the far end of the lot, jumped over the fence, and disappeared onto the street behind the restaurant. She heard a moan and saw what looked like blood trickling along the ground from between two of the parked cars. She walked toward it and saw its source. By the side of a parked car, she saw a man's body lying face up on the pavement with blood pouring over the front of his shirt.

"James!" she cried, her voice coarse with horror.

She crouched down to help him, to cover the gash on his chest with her suit jacket to stop the bleeding. The white fabric quickly turned red.

Two employees came out of the restaurant's side door, heading to the dumpster with bags of trash. As they gazed in horror at the blood-soaked scene, their bags suddenly dropped.

One of them pulled out a phone and called for an ambulance.

"I'll get the manager," the other said and ran back into the restaurant.

"Laura . . ." Spenser's face was twisted in pain. His head rolled, eyes half closed. He had bruises on his face and his clothes were rumpled, showing signs of a fight. His pants pocket was ripped. *Had his wallet been stolen?*

"James!" she gasped. "Who did this?"

"Don't know."

"Why would someone do this?"

"Don't know."

"James, hang in. Help is coming. Hang in, now!"

He grabbed the collar of her blouse to pull her closer.

"F . . . Fox . . ." He wheezed, struggling with every breath. His voice was barely a whisper.

"What? Fox? Fix? What did you say?"

"Fox," he whispered.

His eyes shut, and his head fell to the side.

"James . . . James!"

There was no reply.

CHAPTER 2

Patrol cars with flashing lights and blaring sirens descended upon the scene. The police weaved their way through onlookers and cordoned off the area. Crime-scene investigators examined the body as a stunned, blood-splattered Laura Taninger waited to be questioned by two detectives.

She overheard a patrolman who was first to arrive give his impression of the crime.

"The victim was assaulted, and his wallet was stolen by an armed assailant," he said. Detectives Andrea Stone and Glen Boyer listened, their faces somber, their badges prominent on their plain clothes. "There were blows to the victim's face and body, signs of a struggle that indicated he fought back. That's when, I'd say, the attacker panicked, took out his gun, shot the man in the chest, and fled the scene." The patrolman concluded, "It looks like an assault and robbery that turned into a homicide."

The patrolman gestured to Laura standing nearby. He introduced the detectives to her and told them that she was the first person to reach the victim.

"Did you know the victim?" asked Stone. "Who was he?"

Laura told the officers Spenser's name and that he was the assistant director of the Bureau of Elections. She added that she was a journalist who was about to meet with him to obtain confidential information about what he believed were anomalies in the SafeVote program being developed by his agency.

"What kind of anomalies?" asked Boyer.

"I don't know."

"Did you see the attacker?"

She told them what she remembered.

"I saw him, but only as he was running away with his back toward me. He was racing toward the fence at the far end of the parking lot." She pointed in the direction of the fence. "And then he jumped over it. He was a tall, heavyset white male, about 250 pounds, with short brown hair; he was wearing jeans and a gray T-shirt."

The detectives took notes, their eyes darting from their pads to her face. They continued to take turns questioning her.

"Did you notice anything unusual about the attacker? Anything about his appearance that stood out?"

She shut her eyes, trying to visualize the fleeing man. As she replayed the scene in her mind, she remembered seeing something as the man grasped the top of the fence. "Come to think of it, when he reached up to climb over the fence, I noticed a large tattoo on his right forearm."

"What did it look like?"

"It was a human skull, with black eye sockets and a full set of teeth."

"Really?"

"That's what caught my eye."

The detectives looked at each other, questioningly, as if wondering if the description jogged a memory, but neither one seemed to recognize it.

"Was Mr. Spenser conscious when you reached him?"

"Yes, barely."

"Did he say anything to you?"

"I asked who did this to him, but Spenser said he didn't know. I asked why he was attacked, and he repeated that he didn't know. Then, he said a final word that sounded like *Fox*, and he lost consciousness."

By the detectives' blank expressions, she knew that Spenser's last word puzzled them as much as it did her.

"Does that word mean anything to you, Ms. Taninger?" Stone asked, jotting it down on her pad.

"No, nothing."

Laura mentioned Spenser's concern that his superior might have suspected him of being a whistleblower.

"Maybe others suspected him, too. Maybe someone was monitoring his communications and knew about his meeting with me. What I mean is, maybe Spenser was not assaulted by a thief trying to steal his wallet. Maybe he was roughed up by someone who wanted to send him a message—to scare him into silence—and his wallet was stolen to make it look like a robbery and divert the police from the real motive and attacker."

"And who would this attacker be?" asked Boyer, his tone sharper, as if he were questioning Laura's hypothesis.

He and his partner paused from their note-taking to study her face.

"Someone who didn't want James Spenser to talk to the media."

"Like who?"

"Maybe someone on the outside who's working for a contractor, or someone inside . . . the agency or . . . higher up."

"Do you have anyone specific in mind?"

"No."

The detectives looked increasingly skeptical, as if she had an overactive imagination. They thanked her for the information and moved on.

Later, on the set of *Just the Truth*, Laura took her place, with printed notes and a laptop at her fingertips. She looked pale and tense, still reeling from the events of the afternoon. She sat at a striking glass table that seemed to be floating between brushed nickel columns on each end, its top curved like a crescent with sharp, pointed edges. When she had begun the show two years ago, she had chosen that table design because it was transparent and edgy, like the clear facts and incisive opinions she planned to give. On her laptop, she glanced at the websites of the leading news outlets to see how they were covering the murder of a high-level federal official.

Man killed in random robbery.

Man fatally shot in D.C. parking lot.

Man robbed and murdered.

The murder was covered as a common crime story on the local news sites. *It barely made national news.* The fact that James Spenser worked for the Bureau of Elections was mentioned merely as an aside and not treated suspiciously.

She had decided to handle the matter differently. She began her show each night with a monologue that she called her Daily Memo. She wrote these pieces herself and gave them to her staff to enter into the teleprompter. She had written that night's opening in the frenzied aftermath of the shooting. Her monologue would address James Spenser's murder.

She took a final look at her notes for the evening's broadcast. Although the lights on the set gave off heat, she had the chills. Spenser's final moments stained her memory. She could still see the blood seeping from his body and the life draining from his face. She would make it her cause to find out what he was going to tell her, to learn the information that could have cost him his life. When she did find out, would she, too, be in danger? She glanced at the studio set, and her eyes paused on the logo for her show, the bold initials of her grandfather, JT.

For a moment, she thought back to how he had described the work of *Taninger News* to her when she was a teenager learning the business: *We will always report the truth. Then we'll take a stand on it.* To JT, obtaining the facts was the first step. Commentary came next. *We will never be neutral,* he would tell her. For her grandfather, to be alive was to make judgments. *How do you make them?* she had asked him. *Not through partisanship. Political parties aren't sacred. Only facts and principles are sacred.* Like a scientist, he'd examined the people, policies, and events of his day through powerful lenses that revealed their essence, the lenses of justice and liberty. Did the objects of his scrutiny preserve or destroy these essential principles? Because his commentary was based on the facts and on the moral code that a free nation depended on, a wide audience considered his opinions to be well-reasoned and persuasive.

Those were his tenets, and now they were hers. She did not accept them uncritically, which would have been an insult both to her and to JT. She believed in them as wholeheartedly as he did. They powered her spirit as much as they did his.

She thought of the fierce pride he took in his verbal duels with those he believed were the purveyors of corruption, injustice, and unchecked power. She thought of the calling that was the newspaper business to him, and it somehow gave her the courage to pursue her story as she saw it, regardless of how others were treating it, regardless of the ridicule—and danger—it might bring her.

An attendant adjusted her hair and whisked a powder puff over her face. Another crew member announced the two-minute warning to air time. She thought of her father's order to drop the investigation of SafeVote, following the phone call he'd received from President Martin's aide, Darcy Egan. *Why was he so willing to do their bidding? Would JT drop it? Never.* Then, in the control room, she saw a hand raised with fingers counting down, and she heard through her earpiece: "Five, four, three, two, one."

The raised hand pointed to her. They were on the air. She managed a cordial smile for her viewers.

"Good evening and welcome to *Just the Truth*. I'm Laura Taninger. The subject of my Daily Memo tonight is: *Give Us Justice*."

Her smile faded, her face looking suitable for a funeral. Her voice grew somber as she continued, "This afternoon, yours truly was at the scene of the murder that's shocked our nation's capital. The victim was the assistant director of the Bureau of Elections, James Spenser. He was killed just moments before he was to meet with me to report his concerns over what he believed were anomalies in the programming of the country's new SafeVote system, which is being developed for use in the upcoming presidential election. Our calls to the Bureau of Elections and to President Martin's senior aides for their comments have so far gone unanswered."

She stared into the camera, her eyes wide and questioning, her face still showing the sadness, shock, and horror of the day's events.

"While we await the police investigation into the killer and the motive, I can't help but wonder if James Spenser was targeted. Could it really be a coincidence that he was gunned down moments before he was to speak to a member of the press? Other news outlets aren't mentioning this important fact. Instead, it has been reported that the man with inside information about suspicious activities surrounding the controversial federal takeover of our election system has been murdered at random by a street thief looking to lift a wallet." She paused to let her viewers digest her implication. "What was James Spenser about to reveal to me? *Just the Truth* will find out. We will pursue this story until we have answers."

After her show, Laura returned to her office. She turned on one of the television screens on her wall. She'd already seen the online coverage of the story, but she wanted to observe how network competition had covered the case of James Spenser's murder. She called up a replay of the flagship program of the Miller News Network, which had just finished its live telecast. It, too, broadcast from the nation's capital, and it aired at the same time as her show. *The Nightly News and Views with Sean Browne* began with its handsome eponymous host covering the political scene in Washington, DC. Laura fast-forwarded to the point when Sean Browne addressed the murder.

"Police in Washington, DC, believe that a robbery went terribly wrong today when the victim attempted to fight back and was fatally shot by his armed assailant. The victim, James Spenser, who worked for the Bureau of Elections, was in the parking lot of Bailey's bar and restaurant in the southeast part of the city when the attack happened."

Sean Browne had two guests on his show whom he questioned about the incident. One was a crime stopper, who cautioned the audience against resisting an assailant.

"It's better not to fight back," he said. "Just give up your wallet, or purse, or whatever else the attacker is after."

The other guest was the spokesperson for the Bureau of Elections, the woman who had left Laura's multiple messages that day unanswered, but who was now appearing on the program of her strongest competitor.

"We mourn the loss of our colleague and friend, James Spenser, who was killed during a robbery today. He was a man of integrity with a strong record of public service."

Sean informed the audience that the police would provide extra patrols in the area where the murder was committed until they found the perpetrator.

Was Spenser the random victim of a perpetrator on the loose who remained a danger to others? Laura wondered. That was the story Miller News and other media outlets were spreading. *Surely, that isn't true.*

She observed the demeanor of her college classmate, Sean Browne. He was a senior when she was a freshman at Collier University. Today, at thirty-two, he was considered the town's most desirable bachelor. Even in close-ups he was flawlessly handsome in the style that people described as clean-cut, with perfectly proportioned features, dark brown hair and eyes, and an engaging smile. Yet something was missing—a spark in the eyes, a vibrancy to the face. Sean's eyes were calm, and his face was static. Reading his lines off the teleprompter, his manner was pleasant without being critical. Interviewing guests, he questioned without probing. He was like a pristine ship that sailed only in calm waters, never battling the gales and swells of raging storms.

Not a hint of James Spenser's suspicions about the SafeVote program appeared in Sean Browne's report, although Laura knew he was aware of the matter. Just how much did Sean know? She was determined to find out.

The smiling maître d' came out from behind his stand to show Laura and Sean to a table.

"Good evening," he said, cradling two menus in his arms. "Follow me, please."

That Sunday The Waves, the city's trendy seafood eatery, was quieter than it was on other nights of the week. *Good,* Laura thought, *it'll be conducive to conversation.*

The couple was escorted into the dining room, with its famed walls of aquamarine glass, laced with curved metallic strips to simulate the ocean and its currents. Rippled daily by schools of journalists, lobbyists, and politicians, The Waves had seen more than its share of tsunamis.

The maître d' recognized the diners.

"My daughter loves your show, Ms. Taninger," he said, as he extended a chair for Laura. "And my other daughter loves *your* show, Mr. Browne."

"Do your two daughters speak to each other?" Laura quipped.

The three of them laughed as the maître d' handed them menus and left.

"Why do *we* speak to each other?" Sean asked. "We're supposed to be fierce rivals, aren't we?"

She smiled in reply.

"Never mind, I know the answer. It's because I like seeing you, and you like getting my leads," Sean said. "And nobody admires you more than your arch rival."

"I do like the leads, and I'm happy to be admired."

"Even if you don't admire *me* as much in return," he said. He looked hopeful that she would deny it, but he received no reply.

"Now your show's number one! I saw the Stone Media ratings. Congratulations, Laura!"

Reaching across the table, he squeezed her hand.

She returned the gesture. His genuine admiration for her and pleasure at her success, with no touch of envy, reinforced her feelings of friendship toward him.

"But thanks to me," Sean continued, concern sweeping his face, "you've witnessed a murder. I never should have given you that lead."

"I wanted that lead, Sean. I want every lead I can get about SafeVote and what happened to Spenser."

"Still, I wish I could have spared you the horror of what you witnessed. Are you okay?"

"I'm fine, Sean, really. But I could use help investigating this thing." She paused before asking, an edgy tone in her voice, "Why was your report on Spenser's murder such a . . . whitewash?"

His eyes dropped, looking hurt by her remark. "I'm just reporting what the police are saying. Considering the neighborhood, the murder was likely the result of a random street robbery gone bad."

"Why are you so trusting?"

"Why are you so suspicious?"

"Oh, please . . . " Laura said.

Sean replied, "I have no reason to think that the authorities aren't being forthright and trying to do their best."

"Spenser's death raises questions that need to be answered."

"Like what?"

"For one thing, with the robber being armed, why would he need to strike so many blows to the victim? I'm sure you saw the police report. Spenser's mouth and eyes were bruised. His clothes were disheveled. There was too much roughing up, I think, for a robber whose only motive was to steal a wallet."

"Maybe Spenser resisted more than the attacker expected. Maybe he had to fight Spenser for his wallet. Maybe he didn't want to be nailed for murder, so his fists were the first resort and the gun was his last. That would explain the blows."

"So much violence to steal a wallet? Really?"

"So, what's your theory?" Sean folded his arms, assuming a skeptical posture.

"Maybe the attacker's real motive was to rough up Spenser, to send him a message to keep quiet. The guy stole Spenser's wallet, so no one else would guess the real motive. But Spenser fought back, and when he did, the thug pulled his gun, rather than risk being caught. That's when he shot Spenser and ran away. That would make the *beating* the real purpose of the attack, not robbery. A beating to send a message—without words, just blows. Spenser was a smart guy. He would've figured out the point of the attack."

Sean shook his head.

"Look at the obvious. James Spenser chose a terrible neighborhood for his meeting with you. Right?"

"He didn't want us to be seen together."

"I'm just glad *you* weren't the one attacked."

"I didn't have a secret to tell."

"Come on, Laura." Sean persisted in dismissing her claims. "James Spenser was well-dressed in a rough part of town. He looked as if he had a few bucks, and that made him a prime target for a street crime. That's the most likely explanation. That's what the police are saying, and it's what Darcy Egan said when I called her for the administration's comments."

"Why does she take *your* calls, but not *mine?*" Laura said with indignation. "Never mind, I know the answer."

"How do you expect her to react? You practically interrogate people. Should she make it look like the president is on the defensive?"

"I'm the press. I'm supposed to question them." Laura said, feeling anger creep into her voice. "The president's chief advisor can't cherry pick press that's favorable to the president. I expect Darcy Egan—and the Bureau of Elections—to deal with me, not to blow me off!"

Sean smiled, embracing her with his eyes.

"You look so vibrant when you get angry, Laura. Controversy becomes you!"

Don't change the subject, Sean, she thought.

"And what about *you?*" she asked. "Why aren't you angry?"

"I like to think I left my wide-eyed fantasies in school. Isn't that what we're supposed to do as adults? Drop the youthful idealism and grow up?"

"Grow up to be what? The living dead? Soulless?"

He laughed.

"You are fascinating. Somehow you never got the message to be more realistic and practical. I hope you'll never let anyone kick sand on that wild fire that lights up your face."

Laura sighed.

"I don't understand you, Sean. If you like a wild fire in me, why do you keep only a . . . pilot light . . . burning in yourself?"

"I stir up plenty of fire. I give you leads, don't I?"

She thought of the scoops he had given her—a kickback scheme involving a governor and the state's key contractors, the tax evasion of a senator, the misuse of campaign funds of a congresswoman, and other scandals—which turned out to be important stories that she'd pursued successfully, while Sean chose not to lock heads with the officials involved.

"Why do you give me stories that compromise our political leaders, instead of breaking these scandals yourself?"

"Your positions give me something to counter on my show," he teased.

"Is that the real reason you pass on some of the most important stories to me? Or is it to allay your conscience?"

"Allay my conscience for what?"

She smiled in a friendly manner but spoke bluntly.

"For having such a cozy relationship with people you're supposed to be objectively reporting about."

"I enjoy a decent relationship with the people in power," he said. "It helps me in my work. What's wrong with that?"

She didn't reply.

"You think that makes me a coward? Don't you?"

A waitress approached to take their drink order, sparing Laura the necessity to answer immediately.

When the server left, a plaintive tone colored the newsman's voice, "That's what you think, isn't it? That I'm a coward."

She paused to select her words carefully.

"I think you're on the short list for an exclusive interview with President Ken Martin, and you don't want to rock the boat. I think that's your latest excuse for giving the people in power a pass."

He laughed and said, "And I might get that interview, if I play my cards right. Sometimes it's best to be *prudent*."

"You mean *unethical*," Laura corrected.

He shook his head at her. She could see she'd wounded him, yet his eyes were tempered with his affection.

"How is it that getting along with people and advancing my career make me soulless in your eyes? I'm being shrewd and practical."

"So am I," she said. "Here's something practical: Why are $400 million unaccounted for in the Bureau of Elections' expenditures on SafeVote?"

Sean waved his hand dismissively.

"Come on, that's a rounding error."

"A rounding error? With whose money?"

"Or somebody approved a contract that the agency doesn't want to reveal publicly, probably an award to a contractor for a political donation," he added. "But that doesn't mean the contractor isn't qualified to do the work. That kind of stuff is as old as time, Laura. Give me a break."

She leaned toward him, her elbows on the tablecloth, her hands outstretched, her eyes intense.

"It would help if another journalist—a popular, respected news host like yourself—joined me in investigating this, in writing and talking about it, in keeping the story alive."

The waitress arrived with their drinks. Sean seemed to welcome the interruption, but Laura wasn't finished with her plea. As the waitress left and Laura stirred her drink absently, she stared at her companion.

"Sean, we're not talking about a little program with no significance here. We're talking about a revamping of the country's entire election system. There are anomalies in SafeVote that James Spenser noticed. Now he's dead. I see anomalies in their accounting. Instead of quietly giving me leads and sitting on the sidelines waiting to do a puff piece on the president, you have a chance to join me in pursuing a really important story."

Sean's smile contracted under her attack.

"Why shouldn't I want that interview with Ken Martin? He rarely grants them, and an interview with him would blow my show's ratings through the roof. Every journalist would kill to get it—except you."

"I put my name in for the interview. I'd love to have it, if he'd sit for probing questions. But I'm sure he'd rather have softballs thrown at him."

"That's not fair, Laura. I ask questions that interest my viewers. Besides, my boss wants me to do my job the way I'm doing it. You remember my *boss*," he said sarcastically, "the man you most admire in the world?"

She dropped her eyes at the mention of Reed Miller, the head of Miller Communications, the parent company of Miller News Network where Sean worked.

"The man I *used to* admire," she said.

Laura's pain was palpable, and Sean seemed to retreat when he saw her expression.

"I'm sorry," he said, regret in his tone. "I didn't realize—"

"Forget it."

Reed Miller was the innovator and entrepreneur who had created Miller Communications, a major player in the retail sales, news, and entertainment industries. He had developed a winning formula for combining and transforming the way consumers obtained a wide spectrum of products. If you shopped with Miller Communications, or sought the news, or subscribed to one of the company's entertainment packages, you also received ample incentives to utilize the other services. Through its one-stop portal, Miller Communications made purchasing goods, obtaining the news, watching the latest movies, accessing major sports events, and hearing a virtually unlimited selection of music quicker, easier, less expensive, and more satisfying than other companies had done, and it rose to dominate the markets it served.

Two years ago, Miller Communications got caught in the crosshairs of the Martin administration's Bureau of Fair Trade, one of the most powerful federal agencies that regulated corporations, including their allegedly monopolistic activities. Fair Trade sued Miller Communications to break up the large conglomerate, which the government considered to be a monopoly that crippled the competition by causing disruptions in the marketplace—and by becoming too powerful a player in the news industry, a player critical of the president.

Laura had defended Miller Communications, the strongest competitor of Taninger News, against the action of the Bureau of Fair Trade. She fiercely supported Reed's company not just because of her professional integrity, but she was also romantically involved with him. Despite the fury unleashed on her by her father and siblings, the affair continued for a year, the most glorious year of her life. Then Reed ended it. He reached a deal with the Bureau of Fair Trade, and they dropped the lawsuit against him. In turn, he dropped Laura. The pain of it was like a wound that refused to heal.

"Laura, that bastard, Reed—"

"Forget it."

"I can't ever forgive him for what he did to you—even if he did give me my big break."

The terms of Miller Communication's settlement with the Bureau of Fair Trade were fortunate for Sean because Reed Miller agreed to restructure his news organization to reflect what the agency called more "diverse" and "even-handed" news; hence, Sean was hired to help accomplish that.

"I'd like to body slam him—"

"I said *forget it.*" She swept back a ribbon of hair that had fallen onto her face, wishing her memory could be so easily dispatched.

Reed is a distraction, she thought, and returned to the topic at hand.

"Sean, how is it that James Spenser came to *you*? I mean, you're not the kind of journalist to run with his story."

When he didn't answer, she pressed on, "He confided in someone else first, didn't he?"

"I can't say."

"I think the ideal person for Spenser to have gone to would've been someone with authority in voting issues, someone in government who would be involved with the new voting system, and yet would also be sympathetic to an insider's suspicions."

"I can't—and won't—confirm that."

Which seems to confirm it, she thought.

"Sean, I think that the ideal person for Spenser to have contacted first would be someone on the Senate oversight committee that oversees the Bureau of Elections and the SafeVote project. That committee is led by members of the president's party, so normally they won't buck the administration. Except this time, there's one senator who did oppose Ken Martin, a senator from the president's party who at first was highly skeptical of the new voting system and tried to stop it, but who had to relent because he's running for reelection too, and he needs his party's endorsement and financial support for the campaign. This senator just happens to head the Elections Committee. I'll bet James Spenser went to him. And I know that you happen to be friendly with this particular senator. *He* passed the lead on to you."

Sean's mouth tightened. His eyebrows arched. He squirmed in his chair.

"I can't say!"

"Your face tells me I'm right! Senator *Bret Taylor* was the first to know about Spenser's misgivings."

Sean leaned forward and grabbed her arms.

"You can't ever reveal that!" he said. "I'd be toast. I'd never be trusted again in this town."

"Sean, come clean!"

"Look, I told Spenser and his . . . ally . . . that this kind of investigative journalism was your specialty, and you'd do a better job of it. They gave me permission to pass the lead on to you, but only after I swore to them that you could be trusted unequivocally."

"Of course, you can trust me. I've never betrayed you, have I? Your sources are safe with me."

"Then keep them safe and forget about this issue!"

"But I need to know something."

"What?"

"Did Spenser ever mention someone, or something, called *Fox?*"

Sean looked genuinely puzzled.

"No."

"Did the senator mention—"

"I never admitted—"

"I mean, did Spenser's *ally* mention the word *Fox* to you?"

"No. Why do you ask? What does that word have to do with anything?"

"You're sure?"

"I told you all I know."

When Sean drove Laura home later that evening, there was a last, lingering glow of daylight in the summer sky and a lingering smile of contentment on his face. Despite their differences, he looked like a man who savored the time spent with his companion. Although he was a local celebrity and bachelor, with ample dates and sexual encounters, he treated other women differently than he treated Laura. Despite his public support for women's groups that rejected the customs and manners of the traditional male-female relationship, Sean acted in quite a contrary fashion with Laura. He instinctively opened the door for her, pulled out her chair, helped her on and off with her coat, engaging in the niceties that stressed his awareness of her not merely as a friend, but as a woman. Laura instinctively enjoyed the courtesies that expressed his masculinity and caring. They were not simply two people who were friends, but a man and a woman who were friends.

For dinner dates, Sean met other women at the designated restaurant, but he picked up Laura at her home or office. If he wasn't spending the night with one of his other dates, he put the woman in a taxi to take her home, but he escorted Laura to her door.

That night was no exception. He drove Laura home, passing the shops and eateries on the main thoroughfare of her neighborhood; then he turned onto a quiet side street of old row houses. He parked his car and walked with Laura to the renovated brick house with the turret, bay windows, and surrounding wrought iron gate, where she lived. He walked with her through the gate, up a few steps, and to the front door.

It was here that he stopped and waited, allowing her to make the first move, never pushing her. He knew he would not be invited in. She usually gave him a quick embrace, kissed him on the cheek, and said goodnight. This time he gently grabbed her arms. He had something to say.

"Laura, I want you to drop the Spenser case."

"But if, as you say, there's no basis for my suspicions—"

"But what if there *is* something to them? If what you suspect is true and there's something sinister going on—even if there's just a one-percent chance that there's foul play—I wouldn't be able to live with myself if anything happened to you because of a lead I gave you."

She looked up at him, smiled, gave him a hug and a kiss on the cheek. He slipped his arms around her slender waist and breathed her perfume, his hair-trigger desire ready should she ever . . .

"You're a dear, Sean, but don't worry about me." Pulling back, she rested her arms on his chest. "Goodnight."

His phone chimed. He grabbed it from his shirt pocket and looked at the text identification on his screen.

"Sorry, I have to read it," he said.

She could see the sender's name, too. It was Darcy Egan, the chief advisor to President Martin.

"Darcy's working late for a Sunday," she remarked.

"Apparently."

Laura read the message as Sean did:

> Interview with the president is yours if we can suggest a few questions and see the final cut before you air.

Sean's face lit with excitement. He quickly texted back:

> Yes to your conditions.

He slipped the phone into his pocket and turned to Laura, saying, "I got the interview!"

"Yes, I saw."

He reached his arms out to her to resume their hug, but she stepped away.

"Aren't you happy for me, Laura?"

"You're going to let Martin's people feed you questions?"

"No, not at all. They'll just make suggestions. I can work in a few of their ideas."

"And you're going to let them *approve* the interview before you air it?"

"I said I'd let them *see* it."

"That's their word for *approve* it."

"It's a good idea to have them look it over. That way I can correct anything I may have gotten wrong."

She didn't reply.

"Go ahead, say it. You're disappointed in me."

"JT would *never* allow—"

"Times have changed."

31

"Goodnight, Sean," she said, with a touch of resignation.

A subtle nod of his head accepted their impasse. He smiled and left.

Back in Sean's car, the scent of Laura's perfume left a sweet memory on his shirt. As was his habit, he had parked so that he could see her row house from his windshield. That way he could linger a few minutes, watching lights go on in her home and thinking about her as she moved around beyond the drawn drapes. Was she watching television? Showering? Curling up in bed with a book? After evenings spent in her company, he felt an intimacy with her—or was it with something inside himself? His thoughts would wander inexplicably to events locked long ago in a backroom of his mind, and he'd get a sudden urge to revisit them briefly, wistfully, as he sat in his car after seeing Laura home.

That night, what came into his mind, seemingly out of the blue, was a trip to a museum that he had taken with his class when he was seven years old. The children had received money from their parents to pick up souvenirs at the gift shop. The other children gravitated toward games and toys; however, he was drawn to another item. It was a small live cactus, with a bright red ball of a flower atop its prickly stalk. The delicate beauty of the plant fascinated him, so he selected it. During the bus trip home, the other children excitedly played with their action figures, toy cars, coloring books, and other items they had purchased, while he sat alone, holding the cactus. Some of the children began laughing at him; then others joined in. They jeered at his peculiar selection and made him feel like a misfit. Why did he pick such a silly item? Under his class-mates' mockery, he questioned his choice. Why was he the only one who liked a prickly little plant with the big red cap of flower? Why was he so different from the other children? Why was he so . . . sensitive? When his stop came, he rushed out of the bus red-faced, anxious, and embarrassed. Before reaching his home, he tossed the plant in a trash bin.

The story of the plant made his mind wander more. That incident was some-how connected to other painful memories. It reminded him of a piece of music he loved but rarely played. In his childhood, his older brother had made fun of him when he played it, so like the cactus, he had tossed that music into a trash bin of painful memories. He suddenly had an urge to hear it. He reached for his phone and hunted for the piece, hidden in his music collection. It was an aria from an opera—a tender, romantic soprano's song. He sat there quietly in the car, playing the tune, enchanted by the ideal of beauty and joy that it con-veyed. He leaned back, savoring the music and the heartening, uplifting feelings it unlocked.

His mind drifted to Laura. He thought of her passionate defense of Reed Miller. If the government's suit against Reed had been pursued, it could have severely weakened Miller News Network, the Taningers' most formidable competitor. Yet Laura had defended Reed repeatedly on her show. Laura had told Sean that her father had demanded she stop, but she refused. She'd said the lawsuit was unfair and that Taninger News shouldn't want to win that way, by means of a government cudgel over the head of its competitor. She'd warned her father that next time the Bureau of Fair Trade, or another agency, could find a reason to come after *his* businesses. *What happens to a country that punishes success?* she had asked, in editorials in *Taninger News* and in commentaries on her television show.

Sean had to admire her spirited stand in Reed Miller's case. He thought of the special relationship that Laura had with her ideals. She never backed down. She never cowered. She never let anyone's disapproval or mockery dissuade her from what she believed was right. She put her ideals on a pedestal, out of anyone else's reach.

As the music played, his phone chimed again, jogging him back to reality. It was another text message from Darcy:

Call me in the morning.

He glanced at the time on her message. Although it felt longer, only fifteen minutes had elapsed since her first message. Like a splash of cold water, Darcy's text was bracing. He turned off the music, straightened up, and drove away.

CHAPTER 3

Although her office door and blinds were open, Laura barely noticed the activity in the newsroom outside. She leaned forward in her chair, her body tense, her eyes focused on one of her wall monitors, which was broadcasting a live press conference. The Washington, DC, mayor and police chief were discussing the murder of James Spenser. With the seal of the city hung on the wall, the police chief stood behind a lectern addressing members of the press.

Five days ago, he explained, James Spenser was the victim of a beating and robbery by an armed assailant. When the victim resisted, the assailant fatally shot him, then fled. The police recovered a bullet from the crime scene, and they were hunting for the killer. They also were beefing up security in the neighborhood where the crime was committed. If anyone had information concerning this case, the chief gave a number to call. He then took questions from the reporters.

Taninger News' reporter, Vita Simpson, asked, "Is anyone investigating whether James Spenser, a high-level official in the president's administration, could have been specifically targeted?"

The mayor tapped the police chief on the shoulder. The chief moved aside to let his boss handle the question. The mayor waved his arm dismissively.

"There are some wild fillies out there that rear up and whinny about conspiracy theories, but we have no evidence of this being anything other than a random street robbery turned tragic," he said, smiling contemptuously. "Now if anybody else has a question—"

Vita, however, persisted. Like a small bird with a mighty song, her bellowing voice belied her petite frame. She asked, "Mr. Mayor, can you tell us if James Spenser was being monitored at work?"

The mayor laughed, saying, "We're not a police state, Ms. Simpson, despite some people's paranoia."

"Did anyone suspect James Spenser of being a whistleblower? Did anyone know who he was about to meet and what he was about to say when he was killed?"

"You'll have to ask the Feds that," the mayor replied.

Laura watched with pride as the unflappable Vita continued.

"I already have," she said. "I asked the people at Justice and the Bureau of Elections. They said this was a law-enforcement matter, and I should ask *you*."

"And you have your answer." He placed his arm around the police chief's shoulder protectively. "Now if you think our city's great men in blue aren't doing their job to your standards—"

"I was *not* attacking the police, Mr. Mayor."

"If you have a complaint about the city, you can take it up with the department of consumer affairs."

He looked away from Vita and called on another reporter.

Laura watched the officials field a few more questions before ending the meeting, but nothing of note was revealed.

She turned off the monitor and leaned back, mulling over the issue. In the five days since Spenser's death, she had tried to obtain more information about the matter, but to no avail.

After repeated calls to the director of the Bureau of Elections, she had succeeded in speaking only to an assistant.

"If you tell us what James Spenser wanted to meet with you about, maybe we can answer your questions," the staff member had said.

"I don't have to tell you anything," Laura replied in her calm but frank manner. "Your job is to give *me* information, not the other way around."

"Why do you want this information?" the assistant asked.

"I don't have to give you a reason."

"Did Spenser say anything to you before he died?"

"Did he say anything to *you*? Or to any of his co-workers?"

"I'll call you back after I speak to my supervisor."

The call never came.

Laura had sent Vita to question employees at the Bureau of Elections, but the agency's staff had been instructed not to speak to reporters.

In the weeks before her communication with Spenser, Laura had tried to get information about the $400 million discrepancy she had found. She had contacted the Department of the Budget, which listed the itemized expenses for various agencies, including the Bureau of Elections, and where she had found the $400 million line item for the development of the SafeVote system.

"You'll have to ask Elections about that," the person on the phone told her.

"But Elections doesn't list that item, and you do. It's in your posted report."

"We can't speak for it. If it's on our report, then we got it from Elections."

"But shouldn't *your* accounting and *their* accounting match?"

"You'll need to talk to them about that."

When she had inquired with the Bureau of Elections, she was told that someone would look into the matter and get back to her.

"Who? When?" she asked.

"We'll call you back," she was told.

The call never came.

She'd then turned the matter over to Samuel Quinn, the company's attorney, whom she was to meet with at that hour. Like clockwork, Sam appeared at her door.

"Ready for our meeting?" Sam asked.

"Yes, Sam, come in."

He closed the door behind him and sat down. A pin-striped suit and starched white shirt made the 60-year-old attorney look elegant. Wary eyes behind black-rimmed glasses on an unsmiling face made him look tough. Laura knew him as a fierce fighter for the Taninger companies. For decades, Sam was her father's and grandfather's trusted advisor, and he was the man she called to handle important legal matters for Taninger News.

"What do you have for me, Sam?"

"I sent inquiries to the director of the Bureau of Elections—by phone, email, special courier—but Sandra Frank is ignoring us. Because you have only a limited time to investigate this matter before Election Day, I'd say it's time we file a Public Disclosure Request."

"I figured it would come to that."

Every agency of the federal government was required by law to reply promptly to a Public Disclosure Request, which was a formal document submitted by a member of the media seeking information about a matter involving that department. The Public Disclosure Request was meant to show the government's commitment to full transparency, disclosure, and cooperation with the press and the public.

"I'll request information on the contractors being used by the Bureau of Elections for the planning, development, testing, and roll out of SafeVote," Sam Quinn explained. "I'll ask for the company names, addresses, key personnel, and complete contact information, as well as a description of the work that has been done, is being done, and will be done, as well as the payment for it. I'll request a full accounting of the $400 million item noted without a recipient in the Department of the Budget's list of Elections' expenditures in developing SafeVote."

"Okay, Sam. Maybe that will get them to respond, along with the segments I'll do on my show. I'll let my audience know that we're being stonewalled and that we're waiting for important information in this matter."

He nodded and rose to go. As he walked toward the door, he turned back to her with a final thought. "When your grandfather was attacked by his critics,

I remember him saying, 'The more important the truth of a matter is, the more likely you are to be shot down for exposing it.'"

"That sounds like something he would say."

"You still want to go ahead?"

"I'll wear a bullet-proof vest."

"Then we'll get to the bottom of this." The attorney with a reputation for being hard-boiled winked at her with the warmth of an uncle.

She smiled at him fondly in return.

CHAPTER 4

Early that evening, the lights were on in Kenneth Martin's office. A well-dressed, dark-haired man of fifty-eight, the president of the United States, was sitting on a sofa conversing with aides in the landmark mansion in which he lived and worked.

In the four years of Martin's first term, changes had been made to the building. Martin believed that the iconic house symbolizing the presidency should reflect what the country stood for in the current day, and not what it had stood for in the distant past. That required modernizing.

First, Martin changed the official name of the residence to the *People's Manor* in order to prompt Americans to think of the house as *theirs*, rather than as his. Then, he had the white exterior of the mansion painted gray. He thought the pure white color looked too unblemished and upstanding. The new gray color, he believed, was humbler, reflecting both America's flaws and virtues.

"Now the house is more realistic," he had said after the repainting. "No person is perfect, and no nation is either. The new gray color shows we're not beyond reproach, and we're not placing ourselves above any other country."

President Martin also had the towering marble columns outside the mansion modified. On the surface of each column, sculptors added in relief a larger-than-life, smooth, abstract human figure, with only the bare outlines of a head, torso, and limbs, all identical with one another. A blank oval served for a face with no eyes, nose, or mouth. A few curves served for the torso with no details to indicate gender. The arms and legs were in a dormant position.

"The columns are now the people. The people are now holding up this house," the president liked to say of the new look. "We're all alike, and we're all in this together."

Statues on the grounds that depicted great thinkers, war heroes, and past presidents were replaced by sculptures of humbler subjects: a woman with a tattered dress and disheveled hair, extending her hand as if looking for alms; a man hunched over, with his head down, looking dejected; a child rummaging through a trash bin, picking out a morsel of food.

"These figures represent everyday Americans who need our help," the president liked to say.

A critic once asked, "Are the most destitute and challenged people the ones you now consider as ordinary Americans?"

The president replied simply, "We're a country with a heart."

The critic persisted, asking, "Are you saying that those opposed to the changes you made don't have a heart?"

But the president gave no further comment.

Compared to the significant modifications made to the exterior, remarkably few alterations were made to the interior of the president's house. Inside, the mansion retained the stately, dignified, historical décor and sense of honor and stature that it had always possessed.

"Is the contrast between the inside and outside of this place supposed to make you folks in here feel good about yourselves and the people out there feel bad about themselves?" remarked an impertinent student on a tour, a young woman who had not yet been schooled in the art of communicating non-judgmentally.

Rather than taking offense, the tour guide, a member of the administration, replied with a hint of smugness, saying, "You know, a little humility in the masses can be a good thing."

President Martin did, however, make one significant change to his office. He removed from their honored place above the fireplace the portraits of two past presidents who were founders of the nation, and he had mounted in their spot two television monitors upon which he watched the news.

"If we're going to display important things on these walls, let's give a place to the one group in America who made our programs popular and our victory possible: *the media*," he'd said reverentially.

The television screens were turned off that Wednesday evening in August as President Martin met with his two closest aides, Darcy Egan and Zack Walker, who sat on a sofa across from him. Martin always kept the remote control nearby so that he could turn on the screens at a moment's notice. That evening the device sat on an antique coffee table between Martin and his two aides as they listened to reports from a briefer and a pollster standing nearby, presenting their findings.

The briefer, Sally Grant, was a young woman with a concerned expression. She read from notes on an electronic tablet she held, then said, "Mr. President, the stock market is tanking."

"And, Mr. President, your approval rating is tanking too," said the pollster, Arnold Larson, a man with a thin, forlorn face that added to the gloomy news.

The president sent a questioning glance to Darcy and Zack, who nodded, confirming the statements.

"The economy is shrinking, unemployment is up, and the national debt is rising," Grant added. She delivered her blunt words in a soft voice, as if she regretted having to convey such bad news. "Sir, more goods are now in short supply, and prices are reaching new highs."

"Mr. President, I'm afraid the public thinks your new programs aren't working. I'm not saying that's true, but it's what they believe. Every poll shows these programs are becoming less and less popular," said Larson.

"The ingrates!" Ken Martin whined. "After all I did for the people, they stab me in the back! I deserve better than this. How dare they turn on me? Why are they so disloyal?"

The full mouth that dominated Ken Martin's face when he flashed his trademark toothy grin looked just as imposing when he frowned, with downturned lips that almost touched his chin. With a compelling voice, a tall frame, short-cropped hair, and collegiate good looks, Ken Martin formed a charismatic presence. He had an athletic build without ever having made a sports team in school, and he had an intelligent-looking face without ever having made good grades. From this unleavened dough, he added the yeast of a persuasive personality to create the winning recipe for his rise to the highest office in the nation.

"People are closed-minded. They like to cling to their old ways. They need to give these programs a chance," Zack grumbled.

"And our political opponents poison the public's mind against the president's programs," added Darcy.

"Including retrograde journalists who oppose everything we're trying to do. They arouse the public's mistrust of us," Zack complained. "If I plant five favorable stories with our friends in the media, the one bad apple with her contrary story can undo all the good we're trying to accomplish." He did not elaborate on whom he was referring to or why he had used the female possessive pronoun.

"Mr. President, people are also angry about the tax increases," said Grant. Martin shook his head irritably.

"Folks want to keep their stuff and not help out their neighbors. That's not fair!" he lamented. His eyebrows arched in a plaintive appeal as he looked at the person he trusted most, the mentor who had coached him to the presidency. "What do we do now? Any ideas, Darcy?"

"It's our *messaging* that's the problem, not us, not our programs, and certainly not our ideas. No one could question our good intentions or our compassionate policies," said Darcy. Her voice carried through the room, making her statements sound like proclamations. "I think we need to explain our programs better to the people. We have to nudge people away from their parochial interests and onto a higher plane! But the problem is, we don't have much time. The election is only two-and-a-half months away!"

Darcy's face drooped. At sixty-six, Darcy Egan had a matronly look that was not a result of her age. Her below-the-knee skirt, suit jacket boxed over a squatty frame, and hair stiffened like a bird's nest around her face had defined her style since her youth. Standing just south of five feet tall, she was the shortest person in any group; but in defiance of nature's modest endowments, she was the most brightly dressed, with a multi-octave voice as loud and colorful as her clothes. That evening the chief advisor to the president wore hot pink.

"People are angry. We need to redirect that anger toward our political opponents, who are the *real* enemy of the people," Zack droned, his words like a mantra. His face formed its customary pose, with his mouth opened to a pie-hole O.

No one asked Zack to explain why the opposition party was an enemy of the people. Everyone simply nodded at the statement they had long ago accepted as an axiom.

The forty-five-year-old Zack Walker provided a tall, thin contrast to the short, stocky Darcy. While everyone who met Darcy remembered her, no one remembered Zack—until Ken Martin appointed him to be the senior strategist to the president. Zack's thinning hair, unbuttoned collar, tie askew, and pants in need of a hem gave the former journalist an Everyman appearance, which pleased his boss. "Zack looks harmless and not too bright, which means he can push envelopes that the rest of us can't," Martin had frequently said.

"Your party lost seats in the midterm elections two years ago, sir, and if the poll numbers remain the way they are now, I'm afraid you'll lose reelection," said Larson.

"Who did you poll for your survey?" asked Darcy. "Those who voted in the last election?"

"Yes."

"But that's only one-third of the voting-age population," said Darcy. "The rest of the citizens stayed home. A great many people are confused and discouraged, so they don't come out to the polls."

"That's our base, the ones who stayed home," added Zack, "and there are a lot more of them. We know they'd want us, if they didn't have such a hard time getting out to vote."

"There's our majority, the *non-voters*," Martin exclaimed. "The new voting law will get them out to the polls, and we'll win easily!"

"The people will love SafeVote. I'll keep playing up how great it is in our talking points to the media," said Zack.

Sally Grant straightened her shoulders. She looked reluctant to contradict her powerful client but determined to give a fair assessment.

"The people are suspicious of SafeVote," she said. "They think the law was passed for political reasons. They're afraid of what it might mean . . . mixing the voting process with . . . federal . . . power." The electronic tablet she held close to her chest looked like a bullet-proof shield, should her client want to shoot the messenger. "And the people's fears were magnified by a recent . . . troubling . . . event."

There was a pause in the conversation, the kind that suggested the staffers knew what the briefer meant, but no one was eager to talk about it.

"What event?" asked Martin.

"James Spenser's murder, sir. Our data shows . . . "

While Grant elaborated to the president on her remarks, Zack shot a nervous look at Darcy.

Zack leaned over and whispered in her ear, "What the hell happened with Spenser?"

"As I already told you," Darcy whispered back, "I was as shocked as you were."

"So you see, Mr. President," the briefer concluded, "the public's suspicions were magnified by James Spenser's untimely death."

"Accidents happen," observed Darcy, "and they shouldn't be a cause for alarm."

"Not unless rogue journalists stir up the people's fears," said Zack.

"Frankly, Mr. President, your poll numbers sank by *eight points* since James Spenser's murder," said Larson.

"And the D.C. police? What do they say?" Martin turned to his aides.

"Good news from their presser today," said Zack. "The mayor and police commissioner believe that the murder was the result of a random street robbery that escalated. That means they found *nothing* to connect Spenser's murder to his position at the Bureau of Elections."

"I spoke to the mayor, and he is totally on board," Darcy told Martin. "Right before this pivotal election, when it's so important for the country that you win another term, the mayor doesn't want to rouse people's fears."

"People's *unfounded* fears," added Martin. He glanced at his watch. "Prime-time news is about to start, so if there's nothing else," he glanced at Grant and Larson. "Thank you."

The two presenters said good night and exited the office, leaving Darcy and Zack alone with the president.

As soon as the presenters closed the door behind them, Martin turned to Darcy and asked, "And the mayor knows what we discussed?"

"I shared with him that he's on the short list for a major appointment at the Bureau of Justice in our second administration," Darcy replied. "Don't worry—he's solid."

"That's good," said Martin. "But we're still in a bind!"

He rose, walked around nervously, and then pounded his fist on the mantel, shaking the antique plate displayed there.

"After everything we've done, we're still on the verge of losing!" Martin complained. "The ungrateful public is turning on us!"

"We can't let a hundred years of progress go down the drain," Darcy remarked.

"We've made great inroads in reforming healthcare and education. We've been reining in business for the public good. Now we're reforming the voting process to give the neediest people—our voters—a fair shake. Yet we may still lose!" Martin's voice rose as he paced.

"Darcy's right," said Zack. "We absolutely *can't* undo a hundred years of progress. Our political enemies are trying to alarm the people with their doom-and-gloom talk about the debt, about out-of-control spending, about *every* new program we start."

"Our opponents scare the voters with budgets and figures. They're only concerned with money issues. We need to entice people with appeals to the heart," said Darcy.

"If we don't watch out, our opponent will take the presidency. We can't let this happen!" bellowed Ken Martin.

"Extreme times call for extreme measures," said Darcy. "We need to do what's necessary, even if it's . . . a bit . . . *unusual*."

"Do you think it's come down to that?" asked the president.

"Would that make us extremists, which we condemn our opponents for being?" asked Zack.

"This is different," replied Darcy. "Our ends are noble. Let's not forget that. Let's not dwell on the means. If we delay any longer, it could be too late."

"No one could doubt our good intentions. . . . Could they?" asked Zack. "We always do what's right. . . . Don't we? Our motives are pure. . . . Aren't they?"

"We do what's right for the country," confirmed Darcy.

"We do what we have to do!" said Martin, returning to his seat. His forehead wrinkled with worry lines, belying the conviction he put into his voice. He seemed like someone trying to convince himself to skate on thin ice.

Martin stared at the floor. Zack glanced vacantly out the window. Darcy slouched in her seat. They each looked reluctant to name something that was in their thoughts.

"It's time for *Operation Topcoat*," Darcy said finally, her voice low.

"Let's see how the media is covering the Spenser case," Martin said, ignoring Darcy's remark. He picked up the remote control, and turned on the two monitors, muting the sound.

One monitor was tuned to Miller News Network, the other to Taninger News, the two most popular channels. Martin turned on the sound just as *News and Views with Sean Browne* was beginning. The host opened his program with a clip from the mayor and police chief's press conference earlier that day.

"The police believe that James Spenser was murdered during an armed robbery. They beefed up security in the area, and they have a manhunt on to find the killer. In other news . . . "

"We can always count on Sean," said Darcy.

Martin turned off that monitor and raised the volume on the other one. The opening segment of *Just the Truth* was in progress. A close-up of Laura Taninger filled the screen. Her straight talk and calm manner had won her many fans, none of whom were in the president's office that evening.

"The subject of my Daily Memo tonight is: *Tools of Silence: Stalls and Delays*," she began. "One way in which governments try to silence their media critics is by ignoring and stonewalling journalists who attempt to get information. Even though administrative agencies are legally bound to release information about their activities for public scrutiny, they may oftentimes resist giving out material they think is harmful to them and their bosses. They hope their critics will grow weary of the effort to obtain the information and thereby go away, or the story will die down, or friendlier voices in the media will drown out the detractors. Administrations with something to hide count on their media friends to give a more favorable interpretation of a controversial issue or to distract the public by changing the subject.

"We have public disclosure laws in America to ensure transparency and to prevent agencies from concealing questionable activities. Although politicians and agency heads loudly voice their approval of these laws, their compliance with them is another matter.

"How does the Martin administration fare in complying with our public disclosure laws? We'll soon find out.

"*Just the Truth* has been trying for weeks to learn who is receiving $400 million from the Bureau of Elections for work being done on SafeVote's development. We know this money has been allocated, but Elections has failed to indicate who's getting it and for what purpose. So far, the agency has not responded to our phone calls, emails, and other requests for information. The agency's assistant director, James Spenser, had information for me—I believe it pertained to this $400 million that's unaccounted for—but he was murdered before he could reveal it.

"*Just the Truth* has now formally filed a Public Disclosure Request, petitioning the Bureau of Elections to release full information about all expenditures and contractors involved with SafeVote. Is Elections going to be open and above board, like an agency that has nothing to hide? Or is it going to be evasive and unresponsive, like an agency that has done something it doesn't want us to know about? We'll know soon. . . . "

"We have to do something about *that*," Martin growled, pointing an angry finger at the screen to punctuate his words.

"Good old Laura," Zack said, smirking. "She never changes! The *goddamn hack!*"

The sight of Laura on television took him back to a day six years ago, when he'd first called her a hack—and worse.

Zack Walker had worked for Laura at *Taninger News* when he was a seasoned journalist, and she a young executive just out of college, taking charge of the giant news corporation founded by her grandfather. There was a senatorial candidate that *Taninger News* was backing. In the belief that he was aiding his employer's efforts, Zack wrote an article on the *Taninger*-backed candidate's opponent, charging that he had falsified his military record. This blockbuster revelation, which ran just two days before the election, severely damaged the candidate. He had been leading in the polls, but he lost the election after Zack's exposé gained national attention. A week later, it was discovered that Zack's accusations were false.

"How could you not verify the charges you made? The story you wrote was a *lie*," Laura had said when she confronted him.

"I wouldn't characterize it in those terms. I reported something that I had heard certain sources mention."

"You mean, you reported a rumor as news?"

"I mean, I left it to our audience to make up their own minds about whether the story was true or not."

"You mean, the people who read our newspaper and watch our television network are supposed to petition the military for the candidate's records to verify the story for themselves? If that's the audience's job, then what's your job?" Laura asked hotly.

"I brought to light a story, a *narrative*, that was making the rounds."

"But it wasn't true."

"Not yet," Zack replied.

Laura looked exasperated. "It wasn't ever going to be true—because it was false."

"But that didn't come out until *after* the election," he said and smiled smugly.

"That makes what you did even worse."

"How can you say that, Laura? I was doing *Taninger News* a *favor.*"

"With an unsubstantiated hit piece?"

"The candidate you backed won, didn't he? What else matters?"

"You're fired."

Zack had been incredulous.

"Now wait, Laura, just wait! I know you're new at this, so let me give you some advice, since I've been working in the media from the time you were sitting on your grandpa's knee. You have no creds whatsoever in this business. It's *my* reporting that draws an audience and sells advertising for you. It's *my* tactics that get results."

"Not for me they don't." Her face, he sensed, held curiosity, even astonishment, but he could detect no sign of wavering. "Now clear out your desk and leave."

Six years later, watching Laura on the screen in President Ken Martin's office, Zack felt his indignation rise again. She had become an annoyingly strong voice against the president's historic voter-reform program. She looked so sure of herself that all he wanted to do was smash her!

Zack had settled some of the score already, he remembered with relish. His peculiar knack for using nefarious operatives to uncover dirt with which to bury his enemies had proven especially fruitful in Laura's case. Over a year ago it was *he* who had discovered her affair with Reed Miller. He had learned about the affair from a former colleague at *Taninger News,* who dated Laura's assistant. It was Zack who had exposed the affair through his media friends in order to embarrass Laura, to sow discord within her family, and to dilute the impact of her defense of Reed Miller. Zack later learned that Reed had jilted Laura. When he tossed that extra treat out, his media kennel barked excitedly and came running to devour it.

Now she was stirring up trouble again, but with his current job, he had more effective means to deal with her. Laura churned his anger. Or was it *fear* that was tightening his hands into fists? Fear of what? Before such a thought could fully form, he dismissed it. Zack was not inclined to question his feelings. He knew only that he had them and, given a chance, would act on them. As Zack watched that same implacable face he despised on the president's monitor, he could feel his own face reddening with indignation at the way he had been cast out, demeaned, humiliated six years ago—

"Arrogant bitch!" He had muttered then . . . and again now.

When Martin and Darcy suddenly turned to him, he realized he had spoken aloud.

"What do we do about her?" Martin asked, bristling. "She'd gladly destroy the nation's future for her ratings!"

"I'll take care of her," said Zack.

"Bigmouths like her are stirring up anger and distrust in our voters," Martin added.

"That's all the more reason to go ahead with *Operation Topcoat,*" said Darcy. There was no reply.

"Well?" Darcy persisted.

"Is he ready?" asked Martin.

"He's ready," said Darcy. "We've already announced in the Bureau of Elections that more programming will be done. We've described it as merely some patches and updates."

"Can he do it in time?"

"He assures us he can," she answered.

"Do we have the money set aside to pay for it?"

"We had budgeted for it," said Darcy.

"But it's . . . bolder . . . than anything we've ever done before," injected Zack.

"The upcoming election is a historic moment for our country. We're at a crossroads. Will we continue to make progress or will we regress?" Darcy asked insistently.

Her chin looked set in stone while Zack's lips looked loose and quivering.

"Can we trust him?" asked Martin.

"I hate to trust him. He's such a bastard," said Zack.

"We know his type. Money buys his soul," said Darcy confidently.

"He's got no soul to buy," said Zack.

"If anything goes wrong, we can smash him in a minute, and he knows it," said Darcy.

"If the plan backfires, you're sure *he'll* be the face of Operation Topcoat in the eyes of the world?" asked Martin.

"It *won't* backfire," said Darcy. "But if there's any question—any at all— he'll take the fall. That's as it should be," said Darcy. "What's wrong with sacrificing one rogue in service to the future of our party and our nation—"

"And of our place in history," added Martin, his face lifted, inspired by Darcy's words.

Zack said, laughing nervously, "But if anything goes wrong with him taking the fall—"

"We've been *very* careful. Nothing will go wrong," Darcy interrupted.

"Darcy, I know you're all in." Martin turned to Zack. "But I'm not sure about you."

Zack's face twitched nervously. The last thing he wanted was to lose the trust of the man who was now frowning at him.

"Are you sure you're on board, Zack? Can I count on you?"

"Remember," said Darcy, "the means are just the mechanics. We mustn't dwell on them because the end is so important, so great, so right. Just stay fixed on the goal! It justifies any means."

Zack rubbed his eyes as if to wipe away any doubts. Then, in a gesture fit for a barricade, with his arms outstretched, he announced, "By God, I'm all in!"

"Do we have your green light?" Darcy asked the president.

"Do whatever you need to do," said Martin, evading her direct glance.

"Including *Topcoat?*" she persisted.

Martin rubbed his chin, pondering the matter.

"This just in!" A news alert sounded from the monitor where Laura was continuing her broadcast. "A new Taninger News poll shows a shocking drop in President Martin's approval rating!"

Martin and his aides turned to the screen.

"The president is now polling at only 38 percent approval," said Laura, "and experts are warning that if this continues, Ken Martin will lose reelection . . . "

The president whirled to Darcy with a panicked look.

"Well?" she asked, waiting.

Ken Martin tried never to commit to anything definitively, especially to something that could go awry and be traced to him. His aides knew that they had come as close as they would get to his stamp of approval on Darcy's proposal when Martin smiled wryly and said, "It's showtime."

CHAPTER 5

Decades ago, in the heady days of its development, it was named Meadowlark Gardens. But there never were any meadowlarks in the Washington, DC, public housing project, only crows snaring mice that used the project for their playground. And there never were any gardens at Meadowlark Gardens. The city's ambitious landscaping plan to perfume the grounds with flowers and provide a parklike setting for residents fell victim to weed-whacking budget cuts before it could sprout. The only color splashes and aromatic whiffs to be found were in the bright orange dumpsters overflowing with uncollected trash in the alley.

Meadowlark Gardens had suffered the same fate as other city housing projects, the fate of high-sounding programs seeded in the hothouse of public agencies that ended up as hotbeds of corruption, crime, and despair. After drugs, gangs, and murders had overrun it, the Washington, DC, housing project was condemned and evacuated, its remains as lifeless as a cemetery.

A reporter doing a story on the city's bygone housing projects had described Meadowlark Gardens as a ghost town where a murder could occur without an echo, without a witness, without a sound escaping from the dusty walks and hollowed buildings.

As the standards for public officials changed, so did the places where they held their most important meetings. In keeping up with the times, two such officials found the abandoned Meadowlark Gardens useful.

That last Monday afternoon in August, Darcy Egan and Zack Walker exited a cab several blocks away and walked to the quiet ruins of Meadowlark Gardens. They walked past a stripped car, through a deserted alley strewn with empty beer cans, cigarette butts, and candy wrappers, and into a courtyard.

The alley formed one side of the rectangular courtyard, and the backs of three of the project's residential buildings formed the other sides. Darcy and

Zack arrived for a meeting that would have no cameras, no recorders, no written coverage, no electronic trail, no reporters, no entries in a visitor's log, and no other staff present.

"This is an historic moment in which you and I are called upon to secure America's future," said Darcy, stirred.

"Yeah," said Zack, distracted.

He turned full circle to observe the setting. It made him uncomfortable. In the center of the courtyard were the remains of what once had been a playground: a slide, a swing, and a covered bin containing soccer balls, jump ropes, and other equipment. Nearby, a picnic table with benches sat, rusted and neglected. To illuminate the area, the planners had splurged on several outdoor light posts with Mediterranean-styling, giving the cozy feel of lanterns. Now their glass panes were broken and the bulbs removed. Charred walls from old fires darkened the four-story buildings like wounds from past assaults. Outside one stood a discarded mattress, its inner springs protruding from a hole in the center. Another building's partially unhinged door stood ajar between two broken windows, one patched together with duct tape. A tool kit containing a roll of the duct tape still rested on the sill inside of one of the windows, either forgotten by the building's handyman or left there in anticipation of making further repairs.

To Zack, the buildings looked like scarred bodies. The broken windows and damaged doors were like glaring eyes and gaping mouths protesting his intrusion on their turf. He glanced nervously at the structures as if waiting for a boogey man to fly out from one of them.

He jumped at the sudden sound of an approaching car, his mouth opening to form its familiar O-shape. Then the engine stopped. The driver had evidently parked in front of one of the buildings, out of their sight.

"Don't be so jumpy!" warned Darcy.

"Is that him?"

"It's him."

"What if it's not?"

"You know he ignores our directions to park a safe distance away and walk here."

"If he insists on driving all the way, he could park in the alley, where we could see him, but he parks where we can't see him, just to freak us out," whined Zack.

"He gets his kicks out of getting on our nerves. Ignore it," Darcy said, looking derisively at Zack.

They waited for their visitor to walk from the front of the building where he parked to the courtyard in the back where they stood.

"Are you sure about this?" Zack asked his colleague.

"These are challenging times, and they call for innovative methods."

"I can't believe we're paying this creep $400 million."

"I'm no fan either, but you have to admit, he's an absolute programming genius. You know his background and credentials. He's indispensable to Topcoat."

"I don't trust him."

"You don't need to," said Darcy. "We have all the power in this situation. In the past, I would've said we shouldn't do this. But that was then. Societal norms have shifted, so now, we need to shift, too, Zack. We have a terrific cause. If we need to modify our approach to fulfill our destiny, so be it."

Zack sighed warily.

"Grow a spine, man!" Darcy's voice rose impatiently. "We're being called on to save democracy."

"You mean, you have to throw a monkey wrench into the spokes of democracy in order to save it?" asked their visitor. He'd overheard them as he slid through the partially unhinged door of the building with the broken windows and suddenly appeared, like the boogey man Zack had dreaded.

"You mean, we have to line *your* pockets to save democracy. That's the real outrage!" Zack charged.

"And so it is." The newcomer smiled, bowing slightly in greeting.

Wearing a polo shirt, baseball cap, and sunglasses, he approached his clients, who were dressed in business suits. He had the look of a young man in his twenties and spoke with the cynicism of someone in his fifties. His actual age was somewhere in between but toward the lower end of the range.

Intelligent eyes behind the sunglasses mocked them.

"Let's get on with our project," said Darcy.

"Yes, our project to preserve the gains of your party over decades of working for the people, who are about to spit you out at the ballot box. Isn't that what we're here to discuss?"

"You mock our ideals when you have none. You mock our public service when you give none. Why do we put up with you?" Zack said, annoyed.

"Because you need me. There are others who can do the job, but they have scruples. You need someone who can do the job and has no scruples. That narrows the field," said the man with the sunglasses, "and it raises the price."

"If you can wipe the smirk off your face, we can get down to business." Darcy snapped. "We decided to go ahead with Operation Topcoat."

"Of course, you did."

"There's still time, right?"

"Barely, but yes. I've been waiting to hear from you. What took so long?"

"We gave it careful consideration. Unlike you, we *do* have scruples," said Zack involuntarily. Somewhere on the edge of his awareness, he wondered why he needed to justify himself to this rogue.

"You had to deliberate, of course," said the man. "That makes you feel prudent. Besides, it takes a little time to convince yourselves that black is white."

"It's not that simple. The ends may be white, but in the real world, the means to reach them come in shades of gray," Zack replied.

The man smiled contemptuously.

"It's funny, you know. You think that you have the highest ends, and I have the lowest. You want a place in history, and I just want a big pay day. Yet our *means* are the same, aren't they? Here we are, sharing the same means to these wildly different ends. Odd, wouldn't you say?"

"We're here to engage your *services*, not your smart-ass mouth!" said Darcy.

"And Silk is in on this?" asked the man. For obvious reasons, his clients used code names. For reasons unknown, they chose fabrics for their designations. The one the man had mentioned referred to their boss.

"Silk is all in," said Darcy.

"When do I meet him to confirm that?"

"You'll work with us."

He glanced at Darcy, then at Zack. "I can't restrict myself to Velvet and Leather." Those were Darcy's and Zack's code names, respectively. "I also need Silk in my wardrobe."

"You'll deal with us, and you'll like it!" Darcy barked like a pit bull protecting its master.

"I'll have to meet Silk at some point."

"Do you want the business, or not?" Darcy demanded.

The man conceded. "Okay. Here's the deal."

His smile faded. The mockery disappeared. His eyes widened in intensity and his face acquired a serious look. It was as if a gear had turned on the power of a mighty engine. He paced. He gestured. He spoke in detail about his project while his customers listened. His words flowed unfalteringly as his mind flashed thoughts at the speed of spark plugs firing in high gear.

"First I'll do cosmetic upgrades. You told me you've already executed our first step by announcing to the top guns at the Bureau of Elections that upgrades and patches are coming. That will serve as a cover for you, should you ever be called out for having done additional programming after the certification." His self-assurance suggested he had done significant thinking about the matter. "I'll make various updates that will be useful, but not necessary. I'll streamline operations and give more detailed instructions to the programmers, to the users, to the people tabulating results. I'll make the program more user friendly.

"Then, after I do the window dressing, I'll get to the *heart* of the matter. I've already drawn up the plans. I'll concentrate on key undecided districts in swing states. There will be a minimum of adjustments, but they will profoundly affect the outcome. The interventions will be highly subtle, yet enormously effective. That's the beauty and brilliance of my plan!" His voice rang with pride, admiring his own work. "I've got it all mathematically worked out. I know exactly what to do, how to do it, and how to hide it in thousands of lines of computer code—no one will ever find out. With my fixes now and in future elections, you and your buddies will be in power for the next hundred years."

Darcy's eyes danced excitedly.

"Who knows about this at the Bureau of Elections?" asked the man.

Darcy replied, "People know that a company is coming in to do some minor updates and patches. There will be just one tech specialist on the inside who'll know more than that. You'll work with him."

Zack turned to Darcy. "What'll we do about the busybodies in Congress who have oversight of what we're doing and who ask too many questions? Like Senator Bret Taylor."

"Stall, stall, stall the eager beavers," the man answered for Darcy. "Then, after the election, when you won't have to face the voters again for a few years, you'll have the upper hand. Then, you can squash or ignore any attempted investigations."

"Is everything secure on your end?" asked Darcy.

"A leak can *only* come from your end, Velvet. Everything's tight on my side." The man spoke with supreme confidence. "If there are no leaks on your end, we have nothing to worry about."

"Certain members of the press like to pry and would love to upset the apple cart," Zack warned.

"Don't worry. I've anticipated that, and I've taken precautions. I'm handling the bulk of this myself. Any programming and technical expertise that I need from others is broken into small fractions of the total job. No one I work with could possibly know who the client is. No one on my end can possibly piece together the whole picture. It's only from *your* end that an outsider can learn anything. Is your side tight?"

"It's just me, Leather, and Silk in on this," Darcy said. "And the insider at the agency who will work with you as you install the program into our system."

"The importance of secrecy, accuracy, and on-time delivery is paramount," said Zack in a lecturing tone. The chance to assume the air of a superior dictating a work order to an underling was like a soothing salve that gave a temporary relief to his discomfort. "Are you sure you can pull this off?"

"I'm sure, Leather."

"You'll absolutely lay low. You'll be super careful and not let any of this get out. Right?" Zack said, persisting in his grilling.

"Of course," the man said coolly. "I burrow underground. I dig my den out of sight and out of shooting range. Foxes hide in foxholes, and I'm as cunning and sly as they are." He flashed a charming smile. "You don't call me the Fox for nothing."

Then, Frank Foxworth nodded to take his leave and walked out of the courtyard.

CHAPTER 6

After attorney Sam Quinn filed a Public Disclosure Request on behalf of *Just the Truth*, demanding a full list of SafeVote's contractors and expenditures, the friction between Laura Taninger and the Martin administration intensified.

Zack Walker tried to discredit Taninger News during his appearances on various news programs. His manner was calm and detached, like a reasonable person engaged in fair-minded reflections; his words, however, were an all-out attack on Laura—and on her grandfather. On one program, Zack pronounced, "No one can deny that old Julius Taninger was a bombastic loudmouth in yesterday's news industry. He lived during a time of bigotry, and he was a product of his age. He held disturbing views about voting that are now way out of the mainstream. His granddaughter Laura Taninger, who now runs Taninger News, has not gotten the message that times have changed and the public has moved on. She's said many times that her grandfather was her idol and mentor. What does that say about Laura Taninger?"

On another show, Zack remarked, "Laura Taninger is the granddaughter of that deceased news relic from a bygone era, Julius Taninger. She's taken over Grandpa Julius's company and adopted many of his anti-social, elitist views, which she pontificates on nightly through her show. And now this heiress to an unscrupulous tycoon's fortune has become the driving force behind a perverted scheme to stir up distrust and suspicion toward the Martin administration. She calls what she does reporting. I'm sad to say, it sure looks like fearmongering to me." Zack looked regretful at having to arrive at such negative conclusions about a fellow human being.

On a third show, he charged, "Taninger News is not a real news organization. It has a bias against our president, and it slants its stories to accommodate that. We try our best to work with them, but I can tell you that their president,

Laura Taninger, is so mercurial that it's hard to reason with them." Zack was the grieved party, shaking his head, bewildered by someone as wicked as Laura Taninger. His harmless, well-meaning, Everyman persona added to his aura of innocence.

Following Zack's appearances, the news outlets were buzzing:

Today the president's senior strategist, Zack Walker, called out the mercurial news commentator Laura Taninger.

The mercurial Laura Taninger today received a smackdown from the administration.

Well, I can't really blame the administration for coming out swinging at such a mercurial personality as Laura Taninger.

As Laura watched the interviews and the media's reactions, she shook her head in revulsion. Either a dozen newscasters had independently awakened that day intending to use the word *mercurial*, or they had simply parroted Zack Walker's characterization of her as a factual description.

Laura waited for the interviewers to press Zack on his accusations. She waited to hear probing questions, such as: *What does the deceased founder of* Taninger News *have to do with events occurring today? How does smearing him smear his granddaughter? How does smearing both of them erase the fact that an agency has been petitioned for information and has not been forthcoming about providing it? Why is the government not complying with the laws of full disclosure of its contractors and expenditures? What is it hiding? What's wrong with being "mercurial" in holding agencies accountable for their activities?*

But no such questions were asked of Zack. Merely making accusations about Laura was sufficient to switch the media's focus to *her* as the one who was misbehaving. Attacking the messenger, Laura thought, was so crude a dodge that everyone should see through it. Instead, most newscasters and viewers seemed to accept Zack's comments uncritically. His tie askew and deer-in-the-headlights gaze suggested he was not sophisticated enough for scheming; therefore, he must be trustworthy. Furthermore, Zack had compiled a list of treasured interviewers as meticulously as a museum curator collects masterpieces. Zack's list contained only those journalists friendly to the administration, who would be reluctant to grill the president's spokesman. Besides, Zack held the keys to the cabinet of top-shelf political power players, which his thirsty interviewers waited in line for him to open.

Four years ago, when the newly elected Ken Martin had named Zack Walker as the senior strategist to the president, many people wondered what the position entailed. Was Zack going to develop strategies on foreign policy to counteract the serious threats to national security posed by the country's enemies? Or was the president's senior strategist going to tackle urgent domestic problems to loosen the yoke of national debt, insolvent federal programs, regulations, or taxes that were choking the citizens?

Zack Walker, however, did none of the above. He used his sizable budget and staff to develop strategies to counteract the president's *critics*. When asked whether he was working for the people, or simply using taxpayers' money to run public relations for the president, he replied evasively, "The *president* works for the people. *I* work for the president."

The questioner scratched his head and uttered, "What does that mean? Don't you work for *us*? I mean, we citizens pay your salary, don't we?"

Zack provided no further explanation.

Four years ago, in his new post, Zack instituted a policy that he described as "a program that will set the new gold standard for administrative outreach and that will be studied by political operatives for decades to come." The program that was to assure his place in history consisted of arranging top-level job offers in the media for members of the president's administration, and conversely, offering key posts in the administration as a reward to helpful members of the media. Zack's adventures in recruitment paid dividends. He now had a cadre of journalists who were friends, former colleagues, or favor seekers whom he could depend on to advance the president's agenda. His strategy provided an especially high payout that week in his campaign against Laura with his talking points picked up by major print, online, television, and radio news outlets.

To aid him in his endeavor, Zack's researchers found a trove of old video clips featuring the feisty, straight-talking Julius Taninger commenting on the subject of elections. In one video JT had said, "Election Day is when people who don't pay taxes vote on how to raid the wallets of those who do." In another, he'd said, "If you don't know what you're doing, don't vote. If you don't know anything about politics or the candidates, your patriotic duty is to stay home." In another, he'd said, "It's a fool's dream to elect representatives who say they'll give you everything you want and someone else will pay the tab. It's a demagogue's dream that you'll believe it. Why do we let fools elect demagogues to enact pipe dreams?"

Zack forwarded the videos to his media contacts, along with a note:

> Hey, I thought you'd like to see these colorful clips. Along with them, we can make a few simple points: *Julius Taninger was a bigot who wanted to take away people's voting rights. His news organization worked against the interests of the poor and the working class. Laura Taninger follows in his footsteps. That's why she's trying to sabotage SafeVote, the fairest voting system ever designed that guarantees to all citizens their right to cast a ballot.* Just some suggestions. Thanks much! Zack

His "suggestions" were repeated verbatim by his many friends in the media. His curated list of friendly news personalities had grown so large that the clips were picked up by dozens of media outlets, making it seem as if there were a groundswell of public disapproval of Laura and Taninger News.

During this period, President Martin withdrew his offer to speak at the Pinnacle Awards ceremony, which was scheduled to air on the Taninger Entertainment channel. Zack Walker announced that President Martin had a scheduling conflict and would not appear. The press reported the announcement, people in the entertainment media parroted it, and the public accepted it without further probing.

One interviewer, however, was connecting dots. She asked Zack if the president's cancelation had anything to do with the charges being made by Laura Taninger against the administration.

"I'm not aware of any connection," Zack answered, his mouth forming its innocent O-shape, like a boy being wrongly accused of dipping into the cookie jar.

"But it's quite a coincidence, wouldn't you say, that the president suddenly cancels his appearance on Taninger Entertainment on the heels of Laura Taninger's Public Disclosure Request," the interviewer persisted.

"If the president had those misgivings about dealing with the Taningers, it just means he has a conscience and can't in good faith appear on the network of a corporation of . . . questionable . . . merit, one that's displayed hostility to voters, their voting rights, and fairness."

Zack's calm reply and courteous smile made him appear thoughtful, composed, and sensible.

The day after the president's appearance was canceled, another news item was leaked to a major media outlet. According to unnamed but reliable sources, the bill known as the Fairness Tax on Movie Theaters was about to be brought to a vote on the House floor. The sources further claimed that the president's party had the votes to pass it, and Ken Martin had decided to sign it.

The following day, just before the signing ceremony for the Pinnacle Awards that Irene Taninger had eagerly awaited, Mort Bennett, the president of Pinnacle, pulled out of his arrangement with Taninger Entertainment to broadcast the Awards ceremony. Pinnacle issued a statement regarding the pullout: "Because of certain ethical and humanitarian concerns that Pinnacle has about Taninger News, the sister company of Taninger Entertainment, we have decided that we will not engage this group as our broadcast partner for the Awards ceremony. Taninger News has been antagonistic to the new Safe-Vote program, which we wholeheartedly support as the means of ensuring universal voting rights and free elections. We at Pinnacle want to do our part to encourage everyone, even the poorest among us, to vote, and in our view, it's just wrong to oppose a program designed to do that. Pinnacle won't be a party to that."

Mort Bennett then signed on with another network to broadcast the Awards ceremony. To Irene's astonishment, Ken Martin was announced as the special guest of the event. His scheduling conflict had apparently been resolved. Irene's idea of arranging for President Martin to appear at the most popular awards ceremony in the entertainment industry would now set ratings records for her competitor.

The next day, buried deep within the print newspapers and on the less prominent areas of online news sites, another story surfaced: According to reliable sources, the Fairness Tax on Movie Theaters would *not* be taken up by Congress this year, after all. Ken Martin was said to have changed his mind about signing the bill, so Congress pulled it in order to avoid a presidential veto.

Ten days after Zack had told Darcy Egan and Ken Martin that he would take care of Laura Taninger, he met with them in the president's office to report on his progress.

"I shifted the media's attention from the alleged wrongdoing by the Bureau of Elections to the bias of a sinister reporter and her shady news organization," said Zack proudly.

"He's not my senior strategist for nothing," said the president, pleased.

Darcy beamed at Zack, as if he were a protégé who made her proud. She said, "Zack didn't merely defend us against an opponent's charges, he turned the tables on her, put *us* on offense, and made the top news story of the day about *her* corruption, not ours."

A smug, cocky Zack replied, "I just put into play what Darcy always says. 'Truth is what people believe it to be. Change their opinions, and you've changed the truth.'"

"That's it!" said Darcy. "And news is what the media reports. Control what they report, and you control the news. Control the news, and you control public opinion, which controls what's true. You get it, Zack!"

President Ken Martin flashed his oversized grin, saying, "Zack did what administrations have always dreamed of doing. He led the band, and the media played his tune."

Glowing in their praise, Zack quipped, "Next, I might try walking on water."

Martin laughed and slapped him on the back.

That same morning, Clark Taninger faced his four children around the conference table. Two of the wall monitors aired live broadcasts from Taninger Enterprises' television networks—Laura's Taninger News and Irene's Taninger Entertainment—the sounds of each station dueling for attention. With the twist of a gold-cufflinked wrist and the tap of a manicured finger, their father clicked a remote control and both screens went black.

Clark's assistant, Caroline Davis, sat ready to take notes, her fingers poised over the keyboard on her laptop computer, as her boss opened the session.

Clark said, "Friday, September 1, the executive management meeting of Taninger Enterprises will come to order."

"You've done it now!" Irene shot out of her chair, unable to contain herself until she was called on, and pointed her finger across the table at Laura. "When Ken Martin pulled out and the Pinnacle deal fell through, I lost a *fortune* in advertising. Not only did I lose all the sponsors of the Awards ceremony, but I lost a dozen more. They ran away from my network to make their self-righteous public statements to placate the nasty groups that swarmed around them like bees ready to sting. I've never been so humiliated! I've been disinvited to give the keynote speech at the Entertainment Expo in Las Vegas, and the medical charity I'm the spokesperson for dumped me! Imagine, a charity that I raised millions for and donated my time to for years just spit me out like that." She leaned over the table and snapped her fingers in Laura's face. "My network took big losses, I've been personally disgraced, and, little sister, *it's all your fault!*"

"I'm sorry, Irene, really I am," said Laura, with genuine sadness. "I'm sorry the president you admire and campaigned for is okay with his staff, his media friends, and his special interest groups ripping into *you* in his fight against *me*. What kind of man is Ken Martin if he's okay with waging vendettas not just against his political enemies but also against their innocent family members?"

"It's not Ken's fault. Politics is what it is. It's *your* fault for picking a fight with him."

"It's not about him personally. It's about a controversial new program." Laura said, correcting her.

"His *key* program! Why must you pick a fight on that?"

"Why did *his agency* pick a fight with *me*, instead of being forthright with the information I'm legally entitled to have?" asked Laura.

"*You're* responsible for the company's losses and for my humiliation!" Irene charged.

"And now we're seeing all kinds of unflattering clips from JT being dredged up," Billie complained. "He told citizens who have the same rights as he does not to vote. How nasty is that?"

"Now wait a minute—" began Kate.

"You keep out of this," Irene ordered. "You're an observer here!"

"I saw the clips," said Kate. "JT encouraged people not to vote *if* they didn't know anything about politics or the candidates, so they wouldn't do harm to all of us by casting an uninformed vote."

"But that's not how it's being reported," said Irene. "The media is saying he told people not to vote, period."

"But that's a distortion, Irene," said Laura.

"But it's the narrative we have to deal with!"

"What's going to drive us? A false accusation against our grandfather, or the truth?" Laura asked.

"JT also said that, for some people, voting is tantamount to raiding other people's wallets. That's a smackdown of the poor by an elitist!" said Billie.

"It's cringeworthy!" added Irene.

"But it's true, isn't it?" asked Laura. "People who don't pay taxes *do* get to vote on how other folks' tax money is used. Why are we afraid to speak the truth?"

"Who cares if it's true? It's the perception that counts," said Irene authoritatively. "JT made enemies every time he opened his mouth."

"He also made a lot of money that keeps you living in comfort!" Laura replied hotly.

Irene returned to her seat, folded her arms in a huff, and stared at Clark. "Father, what are you going to do to put a leash on Laura?"

Clark, who sat back in his chair, frowned as his children exchanged barbs. He leaned forward and glared at Laura, saying, "Why should *we* be the ones to stick our necks out? I already warned you, Laura. Cover other news. There are plenty of other stories to sink your teeth into."

"But Dad, this is important! This is a question of whether Martin and his staff are using a new voting system for . . . nefarious—"

"There you go. You have no grounds!" said Clark crossly.

"If they have nothing to hide, then why are they acting as if they do?" Laura asked.

"This sounds like another one of your headstrong crusades," Clark said, shaking his head disapprovingly. "Can't you be practical?"

"You do go off punch-drunk with your high-sounding ideals," said Irene. "In the past, that hasn't turn out so well, has it?"

"Irene, don't bring that up again!" said Kate.

"I don't think Laura's sleeping with our major competitor this time," Irene continued. "I guess we should be grateful for that."

"Even your lover was practical," Clark said to Laura, referring to Reed Miller. "He made an accommodation with the administration, and now, to the detriment of Taninger News, his network is thriving. When are *you* going to learn the art of compromise?"

"After the Bureau of Fair Trade dropped the suit against Reed, how long did he wait to dump you?" Irene peppered her sister. "One day? Or do we measure that timeframe in hours?"

Pained, Laura averted her sister's eyes and stared at a dust ball on the floor.

"The media had a field day with that, and Taninger Enterprises was a laughing stock!" Billie grumbled.

"Stop it, both of you!" Kate pleaded. "Dad, make them stop."

"A Taninger has an affair with our major competitor and defends his interests over ours," Irene said, pouting. "Then, when the threat to break up his company is gone—the threat that *she* used our network to help him fight—he spits her out and is back competing with us full throttle."

Rallying behind her principles, Laura said, "I was standing up for *us*, too. The Feds could just as easily have targeted us. Was it right for them to threaten to break up his company? Don't you care about that? Where's your integrity?"

Billie laughed wryly, dismissing the question, and said, "All I know is when *you* become the news, sis, and the media slaps you around, that doesn't work out too well for the rest of us. You're going to strike out again and lose another game for your teammates."

"And maybe get *kicked off* the team," added Irene, her voice a threat.

The group fell silent.

Slowly, all of them turned their heads toward their father for the final word. Clark looked at his children and stroked his chin thoughtfully.

"Irene has a point," he said. "Laura, we can't let you get us embroiled in another cause that backfires—like the Miller fiasco!" He bristled. "The board of directors wasn't happy with that."

"Dad, are you ever going to forgive Laura?" Kate asked indignantly. "I think she was right to side with Reed."

"And right to sleep with him, too?" needled Irene.

"A blunder she's yet to apologize for," said Clark. He looked at Laura pointedly, as if a belated apology might be forthcoming.

It wasn't.

Instead, Laura looked as if *her* patience was running out, too, as she replied to her accusers, "The issue before us now is that the Feds changed the entire election process. They took control of the presidential election away from the states and gave it to themselves. And things don't add up. Doesn't that bother you?"

"What things?" Clark asked. "If they made a few accounting errors or omissions, so what?"

"Just when the administration needs to be especially transparent, they're hiding things. What would JT think of a federal agency refusing to answer legitimate questions and the president's administration smearing *us* instead? Dad, where's your anger at this?"

Clark sighed.

"Why should I be angry? I can see why the administration had to put pressure on Pinnacle, and Pinnacle had to pull out of its deal with Irene. A savvy businessperson anticipates these conflicts and avoids them. It's part of doing business today. You get along with the people in power, you make accommodations for their needs—they have needs, too, you know—and you accept that," Clark said with finality. "It's time to drop your crusade, Laura, and move on to something else."

"But Dad," protested Kate, "what about JT's motto: *Find the truth wherever it hides?*"

"What about it?" said Clark indifferently. "That was then. Now's now."

"A better motto is: *Avoid becoming red meat for the media's barbecue*," offered Billie.

"It's better to be red meat than stale bread, which is what all of you wimps are," Kate snapped.

Her family looked annoyed at being dressed down by their youngest member—except for Laura, who laughed.

CHAPTER 7

"You can't go ahead with this, Laura! Your Daily Memo goes way too far," said Tom Shiner, the executive producer of *Just the Truth*. He stood by a flip chart detailing the night's lineup of stories, nervously rolling a marker in his hand. He and his two associates were trying to talk some sense into Laura.

"We're asking for trouble with this story," said Karen Doyle, the show's associate producer. Karen faced the group with keen eyes behind black-rimmed glasses on an unsmiling face.

"The president took a snipe at us at his news conference today," said senior producer Gill Barton. "It's time for us to back off." With a soft voice and conciliatory smile, Gill delivered the same appraisal as his colleague Karen.

"We can open with the Senate race that's heating up in New York," added Tom, pointing to an item on the flip chart. He brushed his hand across the other topics he had listed. "We have plenty of other news to cover."

The small meeting room off the set of *Just the Truth* felt stuffy to Laura that afternoon. She fanned herself with the printed copy of the Daily Memo she'd written to open the evening's show. After the combative encounter with her family that morning, she now faced the mutiny of her producers.

"The cyber world is burning you, Laura," said Gill.

Karen added, "The comments posted on our own website are overwhelmingly negative. Under our article about the Bureau of Elections, I'm reading comments like this: *What some people will do to get ratings! This is pretty far-fetched. Laura's been reading too many spy thrillers.*"

"There was even a thread panning our story on the back-to-school charity event you hosted to raise money to help kids buy school supplies. There are people accusing you of setting up that appearance and exploiting the kids just to improve your public image," added Gill.

"But I host that event every year," said Laura.

"The comments made it sound as if you've started hosting it just now to counteract your bad press."

"We know Martin's supporters troll our website with these comments. We know they lie. That never bothered us before," said Laura.

"This time, there's a petition circulating to take us off the air," said Gill.

"We need to kill this story and move on," Tom said in summary.

She had hired staff who were strong-willed and outspoken. Now she was experiencing the consequences.

"Since when do we back off?" she told her crew. "Why would we start now?"

"Because," said Tom, "your Daily Memo is as much as accusing the president of the United States of sabotaging Taninger Enterprises and even being involved in a *murder* in order to commit election fraud. We all have reservations about going that far."

The others nodded.

"And no other network has mentioned the Spenser murder for a week. It's old news," added Karen.

"The police said it was a street crime, not a political hit job. The *police*, Laura," said Gill.

"But our *viewers* are loyal," Laura replied. "They're onboard with our ideas. They want to see us investigate their leaders' suspicious activity, which the rest of the media largely ignores."

"Even if our fans agree with our perspective and will support us, our advertisers have no such loyalty, and they're starting to buckle. Their customer base is much wider than the viewers of one show," Tom said, delivering the ultimate admonition. "The Impartial Citizens for Responsible Media is demanding our sponsors pull out."

"That group is anything but impartial," said Laura. "We know they're a mouthpiece for the president's party."

"But they can put a lot of pressure on our sponsors because most people don't know who funds the group or what they stand for," said Tom. "If their attacks on you sound credible to the public, it's enough for skittish sponsors to bail."

"But the attacks aren't true."

"We can't afford to lose any sponsors," said Gill. "We could reach a tipping point, where the pressure on them becomes too great."

She listened, engaged and respectful. She let their shots fly until she received no more incoming fire and the smoke cleared. They looked at her anxiously, waiting for her reply.

"I hear you, and I recognize how much you care about the show," she said. "But here's how I see it. There are anomalies in a very important matter about which we're being kept in the dark. A powerful government agency is blowing us off. The administration is intervening to try to smear me and harm my family. An informant died moments before he could talk to me. It's our job to shed light on what's going on in the backrooms of power. If we cave, if we take the easy way out, if we don't do what it's our job and responsibility to do, then who will hold our elected officials accountable? If we give up, then . . . anything goes. Right?"

The crew listened.

"That's why I need to go ahead with the open as planned."

Thoughtful faces studied hers.

"A show called *Just the Truth* can't skirt the truth, the hard truth, the difficult stories that no one else wants to cover."

Her staff finally nodded, accepting her points. She had succeeded—at least for the moment—in tempering their misgivings.

That evening, a technician adjusted the lighting on Laura as she sat at her desk on the set of *Just the Truth*. An attendant refreshed her lipstick. Another adjusted the microphone pinned to her dress. Her Daily Memo was entered in the teleprompter. She saw Tom and other crew members in the control room. Their headsets were in place. She looked into the camera. Through her earpiece, she heard the countdown from the control room.

"Five, four, three, two, one—"

"Good evening and welcome to *Just the Truth*. I'm Laura Taninger. Tonight, we continue our series on how corrupt governments try to impede a free press, and we'll examine how the Martin administration fares in its treatment of the press. We already addressed how government agencies can delay giving out information the public has a right to know and stonewall those trying to get it. Now, we turn to other tactics. The subject of my Daily Memo tonight is: *Tools of Silence: Favors, Threats, and Smears.*"

A split screen showed Laura on one side and a graphic on the other displaying the title of her Daily Memo. Beneath the title, her key points would appear as she made them.

"A powerful politician can have a big impact on a company. If the politician makes an appearance at a business and endorses it, that can create lots of good publicity, which increases revenues. On the other hand, if the leader cancels an appearance, withdraws an endorsement, and says outright negative things about a business, that can create very bad publicity, which decreases revenues. Because powerful politicians can bestow or take away special favors from a business, it puts pressure on the owner of a company to agree with the politicians' policies and avoid attacking them.

"If you add to that the threat of levying taxes on businesses and industries whose executives don't get onboard with an administration's policies, you have a potent way of suppressing free speech.

"Would the Martin administration stoop to using favors, threats, and smears to keep political opponents from voicing objections to their policies? The answer is *yes*.

"As you, my viewers, know, *Just the Truth* has been trying to obtain information from the Bureau of Elections about the contractors used and the work performed in developing SafeVote. The agency is required to release this information so the public can feel confident that this unprecedented new election system is above board and beyond suspicion. However, the Bureau of Elections has not yet given us the information we petitioned for in our Public Disclosure Request.

"Instead, the Martin administration has chosen to attack me personally and to punish my family's corporation.

"Recently, President Martin granted a favor to our sister network, Taninger Entertainment, when he agreed to make a live appearance at the Pinnacle Awards ceremony, which Taninger Entertainment was going to broadcast. But after *Just the Truth* filed our Public Disclosure Request, President Martin suddenly had a scheduling conflict and canceled his appearance. The favor was pulled.

"Then came the threat. The Fairness Tax on Movie Theaters, a bill proposing a new levy that would hit the film industry hard, was suddenly pushed through committee by the president's party and scheduled for a House vote. Then, a spokesperson for the president announced that he would sign the bill, which reversed prior reports that he would oppose it. At that point—I believe for fear of this tax being enacted—Pinnacle pulled out of its arrangement with Taninger Entertainment to air the Awards ceremony, and the company decided instead to give another network this highly sought event. After Pinnacle broke ties with Taninger Entertainment, it went further. It issued a public denunciation of Taninger News for its probe into SafeVote. Then, lo and behold, the Fairness Tax on Movie Theaters lost the president's support and was withdrawn from this year's legislative agenda. And miraculously, the president no longer has a scheduling conflict, so he will appear at the Pinnacle Awards ceremony after all—but on another network.

"All of this has been accompanied by media stories smearing Taninger Enterprises, our founder, Julius Taninger, and me." She calmly made her case. "Why is a flurry of media stories suddenly appearing about a man who founded a newspaper seventy years ago? I suggest these stories were deliberately planted by the Martin administration to silence *Just the Truth*."

Laura smiled wryly.

"As Pinnacle Awards was manipulated to break ties with Taninger Entertainment and to say derogatory things about Taninger News, and as my family's corporation was manipulated to pressure me to drop my investigation of Safe-Vote, you too—the people—are being manipulated to receive only news approved by the government. Is that how we want to be treated—like puppets controlled by those in power?" She looked into the camera with resolve. "We're cutting our strings to get at the facts. So stay tuned."

At the same hour on the Miller News Network, *News and Views with Sean Browne* was airing. The handsome host addressed the same issue, not as the first item covered, but as one of the last.

"The Martin administration has been the target of charges made by a competing news network of strong-arm tactics to silence critics of the SafeVote system. Earlier today, we caught up with the president's chief advisor, Darcy Egan, and asked her about that. Here's what she had to say."

The next shot captured Darcy entering her office and pausing to address a team from Miller News that followed her. She stood beside an artificial tree, the foliage towering over her diminutive height. She formed a geometric pattern of a small sphere of face over a larger ellipse of body, held up by two cylinders of legs. A close-up of her face showed the pious poise of someone who bore no risk of being challenged.

"We welcome all inquiries into our activities," she said, "especially into Safe-Vote. No one is being silenced. We are complying with all disclosure requests."

The broadcast returned to Sean in the studio.

"Then, we interviewed the president's senior strategist, Zack Walker, about the charges."

The next shot featured Zack outside the People's Manor, the familiar O shaping his mouth to give his trademark look of innocence.

"We are the most transparent administration in history," Zack said. "Every expenditure is posted online and accounted for in SafeVote. We welcome all legitimate questions. This assumes the questions are sincere, and the questioner can be satisfied with reasonable answers. Of course, if some people, in an attempt to gain ratings for their shows, persist in attacking us, no matter how transparent we are and no matter how many of their questions we've already, tirelessly answered, then," he shrugged his shoulders, "there's really nothing more we can do."

Sean ended his show with a special programming note for his viewers.

"Remember to tune in this weekend for a Miller News Special Report, featuring my personal interview with President Ken Martin." Sean's smile held a hint of gloating. "You won't want to miss this chance to see Ken Martin, relaxed and candid, in this rare one-on-one interview, which he granted *exclusively* to Miller News."

CHAPTER 8

Since his interview with President Ken Martin had aired that past weekend, Sean's face had displayed a dreamy, drug-happy look. His drug of choice was public acclaim—it gave the best high of all. His interview was widely praised and quoted in the national and international press. Driving to pick up Laura for dinner, he dared to hope that she, too, had been impressed. This time it was *she* who had made the date with him. Was that a sign? Had his interview with the president opened a door? As he drove to Laura's row house, he not only basked in the praise he had received from the media orb that was his sun, but he also hoped Laura would echo their acclamations.

Replaying the interview in his mind, he marveled at how comfortable he had felt talking to the *president of the United States!* Having been the one chosen for this rare, in-depth look at the most important man in the world boosted his stature in the news industry. He'd met the challenge, he thought. He was fair— even tough—in his questioning. Prominent news anchors and television personalities had said as much. During his weekend special, ratings for his network had surged.

Laura, he thought, had been completely wrong about Darcy Egan. Far from being controlling, the president's chief confidante was a joy to work with. She politely offered a few suggestions. Might he find them useful? The questions Darcy had suggested were ones he had in mind anyway—or at least some of them—so why not let her believe he was accommodating the administration? Her request that he not ask certain questions, and the rationale she gave, sounded reasonable, so why not be as pleasant to work with as she was?

Later that evening, sitting across from Laura at The Waves, with its aquamarine glass walls creating a deep-sea backdrop for their rendezvous, Sean's fond musings about his triumph quickly vanished.

"Did you catch my interview this weekend, Laura?"

"I did," she replied, without further comment.

He paused, hoping she'd say more. With her silence, his confidence waned, and his defenses kicked in.

"I think it went pretty well!" he said.

"How could it *not* go well, when Darcy spoon-fed you the questions?"

With a wave of his hand, he dismissed the charge.

"Darcy made a few suggestions that were good, so why not incorporate them?"

"Did you really have to ask the president of the United States which baseball teams he thinks will win the league championships? And why did you need to know what his favorite barbecue food is? And whether his children had seen the new animated movie that's in the theaters this week? Those were Darcy's questions, weren't they?"

"The president has constituents who are interested in these topics, and they want to know how he weighs in. Those constituents are also an important demographic for my show."

"But no question about SafeVote or James Spenser?"

"Those are closed issues. You can't beat a dead horse, Laura."

"And no questions from you on why the president allows the Bureau of Elections, which is part of his administration, to drag its feet in answering a Public Disclosure Request?"

"You know, Laura, you're the only one who's not impressed," Sean said, wounded. "You and Reed. I asked him what he thought of my interview, and he said he hadn't seen it. A major coup for his network that sent our ratings into the stratosphere, and he didn't *watch* it! Now *you* give me flak? Why? The interview went as smooth as silk."

"JT always said, 'If an interview with a politician goes well, it means the reporter didn't ask the hard questions.'"

"*You* made this date with *me*," he said. "If it wasn't to congratulate me on my blockbuster interview, then why are we sitting here?"

Laura looked at him, her face displaying only a calm, unapologetic resolve.

She said, "I want you to get me more information about James Spenser from Senator Bret Taylor."

"Oh, no," Sean said, shaking his head. "What do you have, Laura? Not much of anything. You have a self-styled whistleblower, *maybe*, or maybe just a disgruntled high-level staffer who wanted to make trouble for his boss. And you have an unexplained line item on a budget. What are the chances it's a contract for a political donor? It could be a perfectly valid, qualified, vetted contractor who also happens to be a donor, which is why the administration doesn't want to go public with that and let you make hay with it. You don't have anything more than that."

"Even if I have nothing, I'm just asking you to get me a little more information from your source."

"No."

"I want to know if Senator Taylor ever heard James Spenser use the word *Fox*, or if he ever heard that word used in relation to SafeVote."

"Laura, I can't feed you information the way I used to."

"You *can't*—or you *won't*?"

"I can't."

"Why not?"

"I was offered the job of People's Manor Press Secretary. I accepted it."

Laura looked astonished.

"I hadn't yet mentioned it to you, Laura, but I'd been under consideration for weeks. My interview with Martin clinched it, and I got the offer. When I told Reed about it and tried to negotiate an early end to my contract, he told me to leave immediately. I said I'd have my lawyer contact his about the terms for breaking the contract, and he said there was no need—he'd cancel the contract and let me out." Sean continued, incredulous, "He didn't seem to care if *I* hosted his prime-time news program, or if a chimp took my place. So, I'll be starting my new gig right away."

Laura shrugged her shoulders in acceptance of the news.

"Okay, Sean, if you insist on working for those people—"

"Laura, it's the greatest opportunity of my life. It's a tremendous career move. You look as though I . . . should be . . . ashamed."

"So you'll take the job. That's your choice. You don't have to defend it to me."

"Laura, it's a golden opportunity!"

She tilted her head, assessing the news.

"Actually . . . this could be a good thing. You can get me even more information than before. You'll be a party to some very important conversations."

"Are you crazy? Absolutely not! Not even for you, Laura. I have to swear an oath that I'll keep the internal conversations of the administration completely confidential. I intend to honor my pledge. I can tell you for sure, I *won't* be giving you any more leads—none at all."

Laura stared at him with the hopelessness of having reached a dead end with nowhere else to go.

"Will you still want to see me, Laura? I'd feel . . . terrible . . . if this ended our friendship. We can still be friends, can't we? I mean, our relationship . . . it's not only about my giving you leads. Is it?"

Laura looked distant, trying to understand how she could possibly be alone in her search for the truth. First, she lost Reed. He caved in to the demands of the Feds. Then, he lost interest in her, and according to Sean's accounts, he lost interest in his business, too. *The purveyors of power,* she thought, *are like the Grim Reaper, except the powerful claim your spirit, not your body, leaving you lifeless, but still standing, a mere shell of your former self.*

Reed was no longer the person she had known. Now, in her view, Sean was acquiescing to corruption, and no more leads were to come from him. Her whistleblower was dead. Her Public Disclosure Request remained unanswered. And the election was only nine weeks away!

"Laura?" Sean squeezed her hand. "Our friendship? We still have it, don't we? . . . Laura?'

"Oh . . . sure."

The old clock hanging on the wall looked too large for the small meeting room off the set of *Just the Truth.* When Laura entered the room, the clock's face was the only one that met hers, its handles at nine o'clock. Three researchers sat heads down, weaving through documents. Stacks of papers swelled like hills from the plains of the table top. Empty containers from ordered-in dinners filled the waste basket. Having just completed her show that evening, Laura pulled up a chair, grabbed a stack of documents, and joined the others. The Bureau of Elections had responded to the Public Disclosure Request from *Just the Truth,* and every page of the documents it sent needed to be examined.

The old clock, a memento Laura had rescued from JT's office when it was dismantled after his death, hung next to a modern digital display: *THUR SEP 7. The continuity of the past and the present,* Laura had thought when she'd launched *Just the Truth* and placed the items in the meeting room two years ago. The technology may have changed, but in her hands, the mission of Taninger News remained as clear-cut and enduring as the old, round-faced clock. She would not notice the time again until well past midnight.

The next morning, she sat in her office with only one sheet of paper before her. In the reams of material the Bureau of Elections had sent, only one page had mentioned the item of prime interest to her: the $400 million expense entry for work on SafeVote, identified previously as *Other.* The document indicated that the entire expenditure was allotted to one contractor, a firm called IFT. She had never heard of the company. The Bureau of Elections had provided no indication of what the letters stood for, nor had the agency given any street address, phone numbers, names of key personnel, or contact information of any kind for this firm.

One of her researchers had performed a company search, which produced a furniture outlet in Tennessee, a trucking company in Florida, a food supplier in Indiana, and a few other firms—all with the initials IFT—but none of them remotely relevant to the development of SafeVote. Furthermore, the Bureau of

Elections had sent no documentation of a bidding process for the contract awarded to IFT, although the agency had included records on bidding for Safe-Vote's other major contracts.

She called the Bureau of Elections and spoke to its communications director, a woman with a perfunctory voice. Laura explained that the agency had sent her voluminous information on other SafeVote contractors, but nothing on IFT. She needed more information, a lot more.

"We need time to fulfill your request, Ms. Taninger."

"But you already had time. Why was this crucial information missing?"

"We don't have the staff. It could take months to get you all that you want," said the director. "Please try to understand—we're overburdened already."

"I hope *you* try to understand," said Laura. "The information I'm requesting belongs to the public, and we have a right to know."

"Yes, of course, but the public's right to know has to be balanced with what's practical for us to provide, unless you want the entire Bureau to come to a grinding halt to serve you, Ms. Taninger," said the monotoned voice on the phone. "Maybe we should postpone the election so that we can fulfill all of your requests of us."

Laura hung up in frustration.

She called her attorney, Sam Quinn, explaining the critical omissions in Elections' response.

"Can we sue them and get the missing information fast?" she asked.

"The words *government* and *fast* are not generally used in the same sentence," he quipped. "First, I'll need to file an *appeal* to our Public Disclosure Request, homing in on the company referred to as IFT, whose data is missing. We need to take that step before we can go to court."

Laura sighed wearily, saying, "Okay, Sam."

"I'll get on it right away."

Laura sat facing the lights, monitors, cameras, and technicians that formed the lively canvas of her show. She was ready to paint the evening's landscape. That night there would be a dark sky with growing storm clouds.

"Good evening and welcome to *Just the Truth*. I'm Laura Taninger. Tonight, we continue our examination of the tactics that unscrupulous governments use to impede the free press, and we examine whether the Martin administration is guilty of employing them. We've already addressed the tactics of stalling and delaying requests for information, and of using favors, threats, and smears to silence critics. Now, we turn to another tactic. The subject of my Daily Memo tonight is: *Tools of Silence: Fake Transparency.*

"Public officials love to proclaim they're in favor of transparency. They fall over each other in support of public disclosure laws. But do they really mean what they say, or do they try to skirt those laws when the disclosures could be unfavorable to their activities, policies, and programs? One way to skirt the public disclosure laws is for an agency to release only the material it wants you see and to withhold the rest. It may release reams of information about the contractors it uses and the work it assigns in areas that don't raise suspicions. That way, the government can say it complied with a request for information. Look at the enormous amount of material it produced. How can anyone find fault?

"However, if the most controversial of the contracts and payments is missing, is this honest, or is it an unscrupulous way for the government to pretend to be transparent when it really isn't?

"Now, let's turn to the Martin administration. Would it stoop to using these underhanded tactics to suppress its critics? Sadly, the answer is *yes.*

"The Martin administration has been skirting our Public Disclosure Request for the contractors being used, the work they're performing, and the payments they're receiving in the development of SafeVote. When Elections finally responded to our request, here's what it did: It overwhelmed us with information about the contractors and jobs that *didn't* raise our suspicions.

"But regarding the unexplained $400 million in expenditures, the item about which we *had* suspicions and questions, we received only the name—the initials, really—of a sole contractor who is receiving this payment, with no information whatever about the company or the work it's performing. This means that we have to file an *appeal* to our Public Disclosure Request and wait additional weeks for a response to information we should have already received.

"Is the Bureau of Elections deliberately running out the clock as it defies the disclosure laws by omitting crucial information? Will Elections be able to stall until after Election Day? We can't let that happen . . . "

In the office of the president, three people watched Laura's show.

Ken Martin swore at the television screen.

"I thought we took care of her!" he said, glaring at Zack Walker. "Laura Taninger is an enemy of the people. She wants to deny Americans their voting franchise. You gotta slam her harder, Zack!"

"She's a corporate elitist. She's one of the rich," Darcy sneered. "She and her fat-cat friends want to manipulate the election for themselves to suit their own interests and leave the rest of the country out."

"She's in bed with her advertisers, her investors, and her special interests who vote for our opponents. Are we going to let them run hog wild and destroy us?" Martin's oversized mouth looked ready to scream.

"No, we're not!" replied Zack.

Darcy and Martin turned to him.

"I'll crush her," Zack said, his eyes bright with a new scheme. Relishing its inception, his fingers tightened into a fist.

CHAPTER 9

Sean Browne sat in his office in the People's Manor, waiting for a visit from his new boss, Darcy Egan. Because the president's policies and communication about them were intertwined in the Martin administration, his chief advisor on policy also directed the communications staff as part of her expansive responsibilities. Later that day, Sean would conduct his first press conference. Although he had a staff that briefed him on the news, and he had specialists from key departments that also provided talking points, Darcy took a personal interest in grooming him for his job.

Sean left the door open—because he was expecting his visitor to arrive, he told himself. His repeated glances down the hall, however, suggested another motive. Smiling to himself, he had to admit that the real reason for the open door was to experience the thrill of seeing the entryway to the president's office just down the hall, with the country's—and the world's—most powerful political figures coming and going. Like a person who pinches himself to prove he's not dreaming, Sean kept his door open to see, hear, and almost touch the president of the United States, like a teammate whose locker was just down the hall from his own.

In the one heady week since his arrival, Sean had been given daily access to Ken Martin. The most powerful man in the world had whisked him, *Sean Browne*, onto the presidential jet for a tour of a military facility and a press event with its commander. Sean had also accompanied the president at a meeting with the world's wealthiest business leaders, at a formal dinner for visiting heads of state, and at a posh hotel for a fundraiser.

The announcement of Sean's new appointment received widespread coverage in the press. Rather than being a mere condiment to grace the plate of a sizzling steak, Sean found himself to be a juicy subject in his own right—for a magazine spread, a leading newspaper story, and an appearance on a popular late-night television show. He had received more invitations in one week than he had received in his entire pre-People's Manor life.

He had read the day's major newspapers piled on his desk and now turned to his computer to check the online news coverage. His appointment was still getting play, he noticed. As he clicked on Miller News Network, a dash of anger peppered his otherwise sanguine morning. Was it jealousy that fueled his visceral dislike of Reed Miller, the man who had been Laura's boyfriend, but who had never loved her? He, Sean, was the man who could so easily . . . so completely . . . love . . . Would Laura be more interested in him now with his commanding new stature? Would he finally be able to help her break free of what he sensed was Reed's lingering hold on her?

He thought of his last encounter with his former boss, when he had gone to Reed's office to negotiate a release from his contract so that he could accept the offer to become the press secretary. He had prepared a statement for the meeting about how grateful he was to Miller News Network for his big break in television, but that the opportunity to play a key role in a presidential administration may only come once in a lifetime. He wanted to be helpful, however, and would stay on until a replacement could be found.

Reed had studied him for a moment, then shrugged. "Pack up now. I release you from your contract effective after your show tonight," Reed had said indifferently.

"But you'll need time to find a replacement for me."

"Not a problem."

"What'll you do in the interim?"

"A guest host will do."

"Meaning I won't be missed?" Sean asked.

"Meaning you belong with them."

"I'm just curious, Reed. Where do *you* belong?"

Reed looked surprised at what sounded like an impertinence.

"We're not talking about me," he said.

"It's the prime-time news show on your network—don't you care about your company? Then again, with the way you treated Laura Taninger, I'm not sure you care about anything anymore."

Reed burst out laughing.

"I see you finally found your spine," he replied. "When you have nothing to lose, you suddenly speak up to me. That's brave of you."

Words that Sean had suppressed but always wanted to utter suddenly spewed out.

He said, "You used her and her show to defend you when the Feds were suing you, when your companies were in jeopardy, when the press was savagely smearing you, when your reputation was at its lowest point, when your fame and fortune were about to get knee-capped. That's when you toyed with her feelings. Then, when the crisis was over and you didn't need her anymore, you dropped her."

Reed's face showed no reaction, as if the man before him wasn't worth the bother of a strong emotion.

"If no one's ever told you, I will," Sean went on. "That was a goddamned, despicable thing you did, Reed! You'll rot in hell for it!"

"Maybe so," Reed said, agreeing with the assessment. "I may someday be standing on one of the lowest rungs in hell. But I'll still have to look down to see your new employers."

As Sean sat in his new office in the People's Manor, he felt indignant at Reed's indifference to him—and to Laura. A glance down the hallway changed his mood. He saw the President of Spain being escorted into Ken Martin's office, and Sean reclaimed his newfound sense of importance. He was now an insider to political events on the highest level. As he smiled, gloating over his new post, Darcy appeared for their meeting.

I respect Darcy, and she respects me, he thought. *Unlike Reed.*

"Hey, Darcy, come on in."

Darcy Egan closed the door behind her and sat down.

Sean smiled broadly, but Darcy barely cracked a grin.

"I'm having a great first week here. It's exciting—I'll tell you that!" Sean said, sitting back for a little small talk.

"Good," she answered perfunctorily, looking down at the papers she carried with her.

"I don't know if the buzz I get from having an office just down the hall from the president's will ever wear off—"

"Here are some notes I drew up for you," she said, handing him a few pages containing her thoughts.

Her manner toward him had changed, he observed. Gone were the warm greetings and courteous manner she had always employed when she called him at Miller News Network. Working as a journalist, he'd been accustomed to Darcy's diplomacy:

Oh, hello, Sean, dear. How are you today?

Would you mind if I mentioned a topic you might consider covering on your show tonight?

Might I share with you a different perspective on the issue than your guest discussed last night on your show?

Now, he was surprised to feel tense in her presence. He leaned forward and glanced at the papers.

"The notes run through what you need to say, especially how you'll handle questions you're sure to be asked," she said brusquely.

At least Reed never snapped orders at him, he thought. But in his new job, he was, after all, speaking for the *president*, so he would, of course, need to be under tight supervision, he reasoned.

"First, there's verbiage in the notes on how to address the item appearing in *The Daily Sun* that claims the chairman of the House Committee on Urban Development called the director of housing a moron—"

"But, Darcy, do you really think we need to address this in the *presidential* briefing? I mean, who cares about these petty squabbles except the inside-the-beltway crowd?"

"They're the ones we're talking to."

"I thought we were talking to the American people."

"But you always need to address inside-the-beltway stuff that the press eats up," she said, thumbing through her notes. "Let's see what else. Oh, yes. The Advocates for Peace and Democracy held a demonstration yesterday in Atlanta that got a little out of hand."

"I'll say. Ten people hospitalized, dozens of stores looted, police cars overturned, and a fire set in a shopping mall. Very few of the rioters and thugs were arrested, and they promise another round of street fighting tonight."

"Talking like that isn't helpful, Sean. You need to be careful. Our party's biggest donors fund that group, and the group campaigns for our candidates. We need to frame the coverage of *our* people in the most positive light. The Advocates for Peace and Democracy are a civil rights group addressing real grievances of people that society has forgotten. Yesterday, the advocates were engaged in a peaceful protest, when a few individuals in the crowd were provoked by rough police tactics, and they felt they had to . . . push back."

"I think even the sympathetic members of the press corps will challenge me on that rosy picture of the thugs," said Sean.

"Just say: *We call on all sides—the police and the demonstrators—to exercise restraint.*"

Sean hesitated. *What would Laura think of me if I equated the police with the rioters?* But reluctant to challenge his new boss, Sean conceded.

"Okay, Darcy, if that's what you want."

"And the tax proposal that the president submitted to Congress. We want to frame that as a tax cut."

"But it raises taxes."

"Not on the lowest bracket."

"It raises taxes on all the other brackets, which make up seventy percent of the taxpayers. So seventy percent of taxpayers will get an *increase* from the president's plan."

"Sean, we want to de-emphasize details that could undercut our proposal. I want you to frame it as a *sweeping tax cut that will help the neediest Americans.*"

Sean smiled nervously.

"Well, okay," he said. "The president's critics will no doubt have their say, and the truth will come out."

"You mean, the . . . *other aspects* . . . of the plan will come out," Darcy corrected. "Then there's the matter of Vita Simpson."

"What about her?" asked Sean. He knew *Taninger News'* fearless reporter and the confidence Laura placed in her.

"When it comes to Vita, never be afraid to use mockery, insinuations, and cutting remarks."

"But we need to be careful, don't we, Darcy? We don't want the president's office to appear defensive or . . . vicious . . . in responding to questions from the press."

"*Taninger News* isn't the *legitimate* press."

"You mean, they're not the press that agrees with our positions, don't you? I would think we don't want to stoke up Laura Taninger with cutting remarks at Vita."

"Do you think we're afraid to take that hack on?" Darcy asked heatedly.

Sean wanted to rush to Laura's defense, but instead he managed a nod and a smile.

"*Taninger News* is the enemy, Sean. We meet it head-on. That's how we deal with Vita . . . and her boss." Darcy irritably fanned herself with her notes. "When Vita peppers you about documents that *Taninger News* wants to obtain from the Bureau of Elections, the answer we give is: *All requests are handled by the agencies in question, which comply fully with the public disclosure laws.* When Vita accuses our administration of putting pressure on Laura Taninger and her family to thwart her investigation, the answer is: *We know nothing about any pressure to discourage members of the press from pursuing whatever they choose to pursue.* Then add a little putdown, like, *Of course, it's too bad that our simple explanations don't spike ratings.* Be cool when you say it, then move on to another questioner."

Sean's smile faded at the insults to Laura.

Darcy looked at him curiously.

"Are you uncomfortable with the talking points?"

"I guess your talking points are okay, Darcy, if you don't expect to speak the truth with them."

"Words can be used for *so* many other purposes."

Did he detect a note of condescension? He was prone to overreact, so he cautioned himself to check his impulses and not contradict his new boss.

"I don't mean to . . . challenge . . . anything, Darcy. I'm just asking questions to try to understand what you want."

"Words are flexible, Sean. Words are tools—asserting the truth is only one of their *many* uses, and not the most interesting one, either."

"I see. I . . . think I see."

"We make magic with words," said Darcy proudly.

"You mean, you pull them out of a hat to trick your audience?" he blurted involuntarily. "I mean, uh, I didn't mean to imply—"

Darcy smiled, unoffended.

"We *awe* an audience," she said. "That's what we do. We enthrall, mesmerize . . . even hypnotize."

Later that day Sean stood behind a lectern in the briefing room, with the nation's colors displayed at his side. The round seal of the People's Manor hung behind him on the wall like a halo with his face in its center. His first press conference had begun.

Rows of reporters took notes as he described the president's schedule of upcoming meetings and trips. Then he took questions. A few threw him softballs for his first day, which he easily fielded. No one asked probing questions or raised the slightest suspicions regarding the hot spots on which Laura had focused. How many of them were awaiting a position in the inner circle of the People's Manor—he wondered—a prestigious post like the one he had just obtained? A troubling thought flashed through his mind: *Am I a role model for their . . . compliance?* But his new job put him at the pinnacle of his career. How could he have misgivings during this, his finest moment? He hastily dismissed his qualms.

After the easy first round, he called on Vita Simpson.

She asked, "Will the Bureau of Elections respond *promptly* to the *second* request by *Just the Truth* for full public disclosure of the payments made and the contractors used in assembling SafeVote? Will Taninger News finally obtain the complete records, or will the administration stand by and allow Elections to keep stonewalling?"

There was only a moment's pause before Sean answered. What he said was the truth. He believed that. He had no evidence to controvert it.

"I assure you, Vita, no one is being stonewalled—in this matter or any other."

Arriving home after her show that evening, Laura sprawled across the couch and kicked off her shoes. As she waited for a food delivery, she had an idle moment. Her body lay limp and exhausted while her mind was still consumed with work. She grabbed her mobile phone and searched for the media's latest potshots at her, likely triggered by the president's sniper, Zack Walker. Since she had left the office, several new postings had appeared.

An article was published on a news site that had a reputation for pandering to the sensational and paying for stories. The piece was an interview with a former staff member of *Taninger News*, Ben Peters. The man expounded on how impossible it was to work for the explosive, out-of-control Laura Taninger. The assertions he made were unsubstantiated, and there were no corroborating witnesses named in the story. She remembered Ben Peters as a disgruntled employee who had been fired. The interview did not mention his dismissal. If he had received payment for his story, that, too, was not revealed.

Then there was the story on another news site of how Laura Taninger had once been arrested for drunk driving, but the matter was covered up due to her family's money and influence. An unnamed source was quoted as the only evidence for the claim. The charge was categorically false, but Laura knew the article's heading was sufficiently intriguing to lure tens of thousands to click on it to read the piece. She could join the fray and offer an absolute denial, backed up with public records showing she had never been arrested for anything, but she knew that even if the news site issued a correction, it would likely reach only a small fraction of the audience that saw the original piece. She could mention the matter on her show, but that would give the news site that attacked her substantial publicity and attract a greater audience to it.

The injustices stung. She jumped up. She paced. She tried to imagine it was someone else who was being attacked—someone else who was a monster, who was arrested, who was not to be trusted. She had to decide how to respond. She tried to quell the feelings that were playing within her—the anger, disappointment, revulsion, and pain.

Then the doorbell rang. It was her dinner delivery, and she remembered that she hadn't eaten all day.

CHAPTER 10

President Ken Martin's chief advisor and senior strategist were on their way to a meeting. No limousine or gaggle of press accompanied them as Darcy Egan and Zack Walker parked their car a distance away and walked through the alley leading into the dusty courtyard of Meadowlark Gardens. Nippy mid-September breezes tossed Zack's thinning hair and upset the bird's nest that was Darcy's do. Darcy and Zack's dip into the sinkhole of the abandoned housing project contrasted sharply with their climb to nosebleed heights in recent years.

Six years ago, Darcy had been a college teacher with a new book that had failed to break out of its small circle of academic readers, and Zack was an unemployed journalist, fired by Laura Taninger for violating company ethics in his coverage of a Senate campaign. As Darcy and Zack wandered along the backroads of their professions, their paths were soon to cross. When Senator and presidential aspirant Ken Martin discovered them, they received a jump-start onto a superhighway of dreams.

Just when Senator Martin had been searching for a route to the presidency, the headlight he'd found pointing the way was Darcy's book, *The New Leader*. According to the author, the world was awaiting a New Leader who would completely reshape it. To succeed in ways surpassing any predecessor, the New Leader, Darcy wrote, must possess three qualities. As Ken Martin read Darcy's book, he realized that he himself did not possess all three qualities needed for the New Leader's post. Nevertheless, he could compose a team that fulfilled each role and make himself the figurehead.

First, the New Leader needed a heart to form visionary policies that would best help the people, especially the ones Darcy alleged were victims of society's injustices and needed rescuing. Martin envisioned the heart of the New Leader not in himself, but in Darcy. What better heart could he find than the book's author herself, who would serve as a central pumping station for circulating the visions and policies that the Leader needed?

Darcy's assertions of caring about the people would form the moral basis of his campaign and the emotional appeal of his platform to the public. *Did Darcy really have a heart?* he had wondered. Then he told himself it didn't matter. It was the *alleged* caring that made her the heart. By the premises of her book, wasn't the *impression* all that counted?

Second, the New Leader needed a firm hand to topple the opposition. Nothing gets built up without tearing something else down, Darcy had asserted. The New Leader must have a strong will and an unusual talent to smash any opposition. To achieve noble ends, tactics such as dirty tricks, character assassination, ad hominem attacks, and outright falsities were a legitimate means. Martin had someone in mind for this task. He had taken notice of the *Taninger News* reporter who had caused the election loss of a favored senatorial candidate whom the newsman attacked with a brazen hit piece, replete with accusations later proven false. This behavior may have cost the reporter his job at *Taninger News*, but it had made Martin notice Zack Walker. *How much of a fist would Zack Walker be, with his wrinkled pants and confused look?* Martin had wondered. But Zack's venom-spitting pen rivaled the bite of any python in sapping his adversaries, and Martin's critics feared him, so he was the pick.

According to Darcy, the third quality essential to the New Leader was a charismatic personality to win over the public. The person who would transform society had to be charming enough to gain the citizens' trust and clever enough to articulate the vision in terms they would accept. The New Leader would convince the people that the cure for their ills was his own pervasive presence in their lives. The New Leader would masterfully win the voters' affections and motivate them to turn out at the polls. Thus, he would rise to power. For this quality, Martin's best fit was himself.

His handsome appearance and gift for oratory had turned his campaign into a cult of personality, with stories abounding about his family, his pets, his hobbies, and his famed chili recipes. He appeared on media where his base lived—on contemporary music, comedy, sports, and cooking programs. The entertainment industry was his booster rocket, and the media was his fuel in a campaign that catapulted him to the nation's highest office.

Some commentators had called Martin the *fortune cookie* president because he was given to making statements which were so vague that people could read into them whatever they wanted. Martin became the champion of their hopes and dreams. When Martin heard the fortune-cookie comment, he'd replied, "I always liked fortune cookies. Thank you."

One commentator had connected the Martin presidency to Darcy's theory of leadership, but in a triumvirate form. The observer noted that Martin alone did not possess the New Leader's three attributes, but in combination with his two closest aides, the three of them covered the ground well. Inferring from remarks Martin had made about the relationship of the three of them, the chronicler pinned Darcy Egan as the heart, Zack Walker as the fist, and Ken Martin as the mouth of a new order. When Martin heard the remarks, he was pleased that his ingenious strategy had been recognized by someone in the media.

"That pretty much summed us up," he'd proudly told his two aides.

"You mean, we have a heart, a fist, and a mouth?" Zack asked. He had not read Darcy's book and was unfamiliar with the traits of the New Leader. "Where's the brain? Who generates the ideas?"

"The ideas don't come from the brain. They come from the heart, and that's me," Darcy said.

"The ideas were spelled out long ago," added Martin. "It's just that the pathway to realize them has been cluttered with dead movements and defeated fighters who couldn't pull it off. We now have what it takes to put our own spin on the old notions."

Awed by thoughts over his head, Zack asked, "What notions?"

Martin explained, "Basically, we're here to fix whatever troubles the people. Whatever their problems are, we're the answer. Right, Darcy?"

"Right, Ken. Got it, Zack?"

Zack nodded.

Martin summed up, "We have to make the old slogans sound fresh and new, while we crush our political enemies and get our people to the polls. That's the ticket."

With this strategy, Martin had hoped to achieve a power beyond that which any past president had ever possessed, a tight-fisted power masked by the engaging, toothy grin of its wielder. As Darcy devised the new order and Zack brought the representatives of the old one to their knees, Martin rallied the people left standing—*his* people, the ones who worshiped at his altar—and a new country, they'd hoped, would be born.

In Martin's first term, the triumvirate had laid the foundation for the New Leader's America. But now a great threat had emerged. The president's economic advisors and pollsters had reported that the economy was tanking, his programs were ineffective, and suspicions were circulating about his administration's involvement in Spenser's death. These circumstances were causing the polls to turn against Martin in a reelection he had to win.

As they walked to their meeting in the Meadowlark Garden's complex, Darcy and Zack knew that Frank Foxworth, standing in the courtyard waiting for them, was integral to their success. With his hands in his pockets, wearing his trademark sunglasses, he watched them approach as he stood with a laptop bag dangling from his shoulder.

"Velvet," he said, bowing his head slightly to Darcy. He turned to Zack. "Leather." Foxworth had the air of a gentleman at a dinner party, except for the mocking grin.

"Think this is a joke?" Zack snapped.

"Do I rattle you?"

Ignoring their exchange, Darcy asked, "What've you got, Fox?"

The Fox gestured for them to follow as he walked a few steps toward the old picnic table in the courtyard. He sat on one of its benches and opened his laptop. His two companions took the bench opposite his, staring warily at him from across the rusted metal grid on the table's surface. Raising his sunglasses to his forehead for a few moments to enhance his view, the Fox called up various screens of a program. He turned the monitor so all three of them could see and demonstrated maneuvers as Zack and Darcy leaned forward to observe. The screens were polished, complete with visuals, tabs, instructions, and live links, ready for use by the administrators of the program and the public.

"Here's the administrators' home screen, and this is the user interface," the Fox explained. "So far, I've done a bunch of updates and revisions. For example, I made this function easier to use. In this section, I added a few more options that are beneficial to the administrators."

He demonstrated the program changes he had made. His audience listened and watched intently. When he was finished, the Fox closed his laptop and stared at them. Darcy stared back with a look as arrogant as that of their programmer, while Zack avoided his penetrating, mocking glare.

"The modifications I've made so far are to give you cover," said the Fox, returning his sunglasses to their proper position. "If my participation in this program is ever discovered, and you're called upon to explain the work I did, your tech guy inside the Bureau can point to the things I just showed you. They're all legitimate programing modifications."

"Okay," said Darcy.

"But from here on, nothing will be legit."

Darcy and Zack glanced at each other, a thrill of excitement in Darcy's eyes, a hint of ambivalence in Zack's.

"From here on, no one must know about anything I do. From here on, I'll alter the source code in subtle and hidden ways that nobody will be able to track down."

"Surely you've heard—we've got a crazy reporter breathing down our necks with Public Disclosure Requests about the $400 million payout that has no contractor information attached to it, and we've got a Senate oversight committee snooping around, asking questions," said Zack.

"Stall, stall, stall," advised the Fox. "Drag your feet on any disclosure requests. Give out as little information as possible. After the election, you can make documents disappear, and you can stack the Senate committee with more of your friends, who'll say there were no adverse findings and move on. After the election, you'll be home free."

"If you can pull it off," Zack mumbled.

The Fox laughed and said, "Isn't it a little late to have buyer's remorse?"

Darcy refocused the group, asking their technical expert, "What's next?"

"Operation Topcoat kicks in."

"Go on."

"I'll concentrate on crucial districts in swing states, districts that could go either way. I've done extensive studies of the polling data, and I know exactly where to intervene—and to what extent."

When the Fox talked about programming, the sarcasm vanished. His face grew serious, his manner more polished. As he explained his plan, he displayed a command of the technical details and an unwavering confidence that impressed his clients.

"I'll alter the program to randomly give votes to your guy in key districts in swing states that will ensure he has enough to win. On the screen, these randomly selected votes will have been cast for the opponent, and the voters will have no inkling that their choices will be redirected. But when it comes to tallying the results, a percentage of the votes cast for B will go to A, with A being your guy. The tally of the votes will show a different ratio than the actual votes cast, but everything will appear to match up perfectly in any checks done by the program administrators. I'll statistically work out everything, and I'll hide the new programming in thousands of lines of code."

Darcy nodded her approval, while Zack remained noncommittal.

The Fox went on, "Once you pull off this federal control of the presidential election, you can target Congress next. The new law allows you to oversee those races, too, in the coming years. That's when I can apply Operation Topcoat to key congressional contests. I can keep your party in power forever. That's why you can never think of hanging me out to dry. You need me too much, right now and in the future."

"Remember, our tech guy on the inside is keeping an eye on you for us, so you don't wander off the reservation," said Darcy.

"After I make the modifications, he can verify that the program works as I say it will," declared the Fox. "The whole operation will be as smooth as silk."

"It had better be," Zack said in a threatening voice.

"Speaking of silk, we're at the point where I need to meet *him*."

There was no response.

"That was part of our agreement. I meet Silk," the Fox added.

"We can't risk you two meeting. You'll work with us," said Darcy.

"I can't *only* deal with foot soldiers on this."

"You'll deal with us and like it," said Zack.

"I need to know that the general in the big tent has my back. I won't stick my neck out for some wild scheme that underlings cooked up. I need to be sure that Silk knows about Topcoat—and he's all in."

"You can't meet him. Absolutely not," Darcy said, shaking her head.

"No way," echoed Zack. "We shield him from swine like you."

The Fox laughed, saying, "What does it say about your project if it hinges on swine like me?"

"Listen to reason, Fox. You know it's way too dangerous for him to ever be seen with you," Darcy said.

"I won't go any further without a face-to-face."

CHAPTER 11

Clark Taninger took his seat at the head of the conference table.

"Friday, September 15, the executive management meeting of Taninger Enterprises will come to order," he said. At his side, Caroline Davis sat poised to take notes.

"Where's Billie?" Clark asked his three daughters, looking at his son's empty seat.

Suddenly, the door swung open, and Billie stormed in clutching a notice in his fist. He slammed the door behind him and threw the paper down on the table.

"We're screwed!"

Clark rose from his seat, picked up the notice, and read it. Then he dropped it on the table, stunned.

"What the hell—"

Irene, Laura, and Kate also stood up, leaning across the table to read the letter.

"Oh, no," Irene exclaimed.

"This can't be," Kate added.

"They can't do this!" cried Laura.

"They can, and they are," Billie snapped at Laura.

The notice bore the official stamp of the Federal Bureau of Building Safety, with the signature of its director at the bottom. It was titled: Report of Violation of Stadium Ordinance 472.01. It described how the new football stadium for the DC Slammers, owned by Taninger Sports, failed its most recent inspection. The production process for the plastic used in manufacturing the stadium's seats was found to have consumed too much energy, causing a detrimental environmental impact. Furthermore, the manufacturer of the seats, it was discovered, used less than the required amount of recycled plastic material. The single short paragraph of the notice ended with the directive: *Taninger Sports is prohibited from opening the new stadium until the non-compliant seating is replaced and the building is brought into full adherence with the Bureau's standards.*

"They just sprung this on me. There was no word of any of it in the previous inspections," Billie said, pacing the room. He looked at the others, who had returned to their seats. "That's eighty-thousand seats to rip out. It'll take me a good part of the season to fix this, and the cost will be astronomical." He loosened his tie. His shirt collar dampened with sweat. "Our old stadium was demolished two weeks ago, and the home opener is in *two days!*"

"You say this *wasn't* a problem before?" asked Clark incredulously.

"Everything was fine before. Now, they've sprung this regulation on me at the last minute."

"That's not fair!" said Kate indignantly.

"We'll take them to court," added Laura, her voice hot with anger.

"And risk antagonizing them even more?" Clark shook his head. "I wouldn't do that."

"JT would *never* let this slide," said Laura.

"That was then. Now's now. Times have changed," Clark replied.

"But right and wrong haven't changed, have they?" Laura persisted.

Clark rolled his eyes dismissively, then he turned to his son. "Billie, you'll have to act fast to line up another venue and put the opener there."

"If I change venues, thousands of our fans will complain. If I delay the opener, it'll cause disruptions for other teams, and the league will slap fines on us—and we'll still get fan complaints. What a mess!" said Billie.

"It doesn't make sense," said Laura. "The seats are already in. If the goal is to conserve plastic and energy, why would they want you to take the seats out? It'll use a whole lot more plastic and energy to rip the seats out and manufacture new ones. Why not just fine you?"

Billie shrugged, saying, "There's no recourse. It's all on the books. I checked. The regulation's been there for a few years. They'd never enforced it before, but now, it's suddenly *important.*"

"You have to *fight* this, Billie. I'll fight them with you!" said Laura. She looked up at him standing near her. She grabbed his arm and shook it.

"You're crazy," Billie replied, pulling his arm away.

"You can't let them win," Laura insisted.

"Look, I have to roll with the punches they throw at me and land on my feet."

"But it's not fair. They have no right—"

"Politics is *their* game, not mine. I'm a businessman."

"But, Billie, this is a *clear* abuse of power."

"What they can and can't do is for the people with the big ideas to weigh in on," Billie said.

"Why not *you*? Why can't the *victim* weigh in? Why can't you call them out for their strong-arm tactics?"

"No way! I have a business to run. I'm not a government watchdog."

"Why can't you show moral outrage?"

"I'm not a priest, either."

"Then what are you, Billie, if you don't fight back?"

"A realist."

"I'll say it if you won't. If we let this pass, we're *cowards*. All of us!" Now, Laura was on her feet, her arms gesticulating, her dark eyes flashing at her brother and the others.

Billie shook his head. He waved his hand to dismiss her, saying, "I'm not taking them on. No!"

Laura sighed. She sank back in her chair, silenced for the moment.

Kate asked, "Now that the agency that regulates building construction has started enforcing this law, what about all the other arenas that must be out of compliance? Do other stadiums have to rip out their seating?"

"Or is it just us?" asked Irene. "Why us?"

She looked pointedly at Laura.

The room fell silent. Slowly, the others turned to stare at Laura.

"Because we have a sister who has a penchant for useless causes and impractical crusades that tick people off," Irene charged.

"That occurred to me too. That has to be it," Billie said, pointing at Laura. "The last time you went on a crusade, it was *you* who got screwed! This time Irene got screwed, and now me." He whirled around to his father. "What are you going to do about this?"

Clark's face reddened, and he glared at Laura.

"First it was Irene losing the Pinnacle Awards," Clark said, his voice thundering. "Now this. Two big hits in the past few weeks. This isn't just a coincidence."

"No. I don't think it is, either," said Laura. "Billie, I would *never* do anything to hurt you or the Slammers. I'm outraged to think this . . . catastrophe . . . is their payback to me. How could they stoop so low?"

"Effective immediately," said her father sternly, "Laura will give up her crusade against the Martin administration."

"She was told to give it up after Pinnacle Awards pulled out of broadcasting with my network. But she's still at it!" Irene turned to Laura, saying, "You can't disregard a corporate directive and wreak havoc on the rest of us!"

"You'll drop your war against SafeVote. You'll drop it at once, Laura. That's an order!" demanded Clark. "With that chip in my pocket, I'll call Darcy and get her to lean on the agency to grandfather-in our stadium or let us install the new seating in the off-season—so we can goddamn open the place in time!"

"You'll give it up, Laura," Billie repeated. "You hear?"

Laura looked upset and regretful, but words of surrender would not come out. She was deeply saddened by the losses Taninger Enterprises had suffered in response to her investigation, but the cause of her feelings went beyond that. She regretted that her family had abandoned her values—JT's values—to find the truth where it hid, no matter the cost. They were family—yet they had become strangers to her.

"This isn't the first time, Laura," Irene reminded her sister. "Do you think we've forgotten that you slept with our major competitor? Do you think we've forgotten how your moronic behavior embarrassed us and damaged our reputation before? Do you think we've forgotten how wrong you were about *that* crusade?"

"Come on, Irene. Don't start that again," said Kate. "Laura defended what she believed was right."

"Yeah, she defended it from her bedroom," Irene said, persisting. "Laura *can't* be allowed to go off half-cocked again and cause a whole world of trouble, Dad!" She flashed eyes heavy with makeup at Clark. "You have to put a stop to her latest obsession."

Laura redoubled her efforts, saying, "JT would *not* want us to cave. He *never* caved. Let's fight this by exposing what they're doing to us, not by falling on the sword to accommodate their total abuse of power."

Except for Kate, the faces of her family were unmoved by her plea. Laura knew she was not the enemy, but her family circled around her, blaming her principles instead of confronting the real cause of their problems. Laura knew what she had to do.

"I'll expose them on my show," she said.

Without hesitation, Clark shouted, "No, you won't!"

"No way!" said Irene.

"You know, you can be *fired*," said Billie. His threat had a bracing effect on the others, who straighten in their chairs, as if a thought on all of their minds was suddenly named.

Irene smirked at the notion, which seemed to please her.

"Laura," she said, "you know full well that Dad, Billie, and I sit on the board of directors of Taninger Enterprises, and we have a say in who runs the divisions. You can't run Taninger News as if it were your personal kingdom."

"Laura has a vote, too," snapped Kate, "and so do I."

"A *proxy* votes for you, Katie, until you're twenty-one," Clark said, correcting his youngest. He turned to the others, shaking a finger in Laura's direction, underscoring the prospect now set loose to rumble through the room. "Irene's right—you're outnumbered, Laura. You'll give in and that's that."

The meeting adjourned early. Billie rushed out to handle his crisis. Kate headed to campus for a class. Irene closed her laptop and departed, leaving a whiff of perfume in her wake. Laura remained seated, still reeling from Billie's news and her family's admonishments. Darting a final vexed look at Laura, Clark left with his assistant. He closed the door behind him to leave her sitting in the conference room alone, isolated from the rest of the family.

The closing door sent a gust of air over Laura. Her father and older siblings hadn't rebuked her like that since they'd learned of her affair with Reed Miller. The thought of him made her look at the closed door and remember how he had shut her out, too.

He had appeared unexpectedly at her residence late that night of their last meeting. She'd sat on a couch while he remained standing, a coffee table between them.

"Laura, you'll hear news tomorrow that will upset you. It'll hurt you," he had said. "The sooner you grow to hate me, the better it'll be . . . for both of us."

He took the key he'd had to her apartment and stooped to drop it on the coffee table. Laura reached over to grab his hand and stop him.

"Reed, what on earth are you doing?"

"Divesting myself of things that matter. . . . You're part of that," he said sadly.

"What?"

He gently removed her hand. Then, he dropped the key on the table, and he left, smothering the fire he had ignited in her life. The sound of the key dropping and the door closing marked the end of their year together.

The next day Miller Communications announced that it was restructuring its news division to broaden its content. Miller News Network would become all-inclusive of other views. It would hire news reporters with differing perspectives on world events, and it would add programming to reflect its new diversity. The following day, the Bureau of Fair Trade announced that it would drop its suit against Miller Communications for its alleged monopolistic practices of bringing a slanted coverage of the news to its consumers, thereby robbing its customers of exposure to other views in the public forum.

Laura had met Reed a year before his run-in with the Bureau of Fair Trade, when he had made an offer to buy *Taninger News*. Clark and the other family members, including her, refused to sell. The asset of most interest to Reed had been the company's newly launched news program, *Just the Truth*. He had taken a special interest in it and in the feisty Taninger daughter who was the show's creator and host. Sensing more than just a professional interest from his chief competitor, Clark had told Reed Miller, "Laura's show is not for sale. Neither is she."

Although his business proposal was rejected, Reed's asset-acquisition plans had not ended there. He appeared outside the Taninger building one night as

Laura was about to hail a cab home after her show. His sandy hair, with its tight crop of curls, his translucent blue eyes, and his engaging grin gave a look of boyish openness to the man in his thirties who was a media mogul.

"How about dinner?" he'd asked simply. She had paused, stunned for a moment. A voice inside told her to refuse, but she ignored it. A smile and a nod gave her answer.

The media portrayed Reed as cutthroat and ruthless, but Laura had found no trace of those qualities in him. No scandal could ever be associated with him. He'd never paid off politicians or showed any interest in them. He'd never tried to smash his opponents with anything but good business practices that won customers in the marketplace. He'd never joined the groups of business-persons who cultivated political relationships in search of special favors they could harvest. With his boundless energy, his spectacular success, and his un-stained integrity, Reed reminded Laura of Julius Taninger. She'd found herself irresistibly drawn to a hero—and lover—who seasoned her life with exotic, bold flavors.

During the exhilarating year they spent together, they'd feasted on two pas-sions—their hunger for each other and their appetite for their work. She had listened to him talk eagerly about his plans to expand his company, bringing new devices and exciting changes to the world. He'd spoken with a lighthearted confidence, as if the world were a playground for him to explore.

When they could take a break from their work, they traveled. They would fly in his private jet to Europe, soaking in museums, artistic treasures, and con-certs. They'd walk, talk, and site-see for hours. Other times, they'd go for a weekend trip to the Caribbean, strolling on the beach, swimming, sailing, and sunbathing. Together, they'd experienced the world with curiosity, intelligence, and laughter. When they weren't in each other's arms, they were constantly talking—about themselves, each other, their work, their aspirations. Their re-lationship was one great banquet of love and conversation to feed their bodies and souls.

Then, things changed. Reed's businesses had gotten in the crosshairs of the Bureau of Fair Trade. Laura accused her father of instigating the agency to contain Reed, their major competitor, through Clark's many contacts in the administration. Clark denied any involvement. Whatever the cause, Reed had been the perfect subject for a takedown: he was self-made and successful.

Hit pieces began appearing in the news about Reed and his company. They quoted disgruntled former employees, anti-business groups, and anonymous sources. Nothing could be proved, but the media repeated the stories without verification. Reed was a monster to work for, the stories charged. He cheated his stockholders. He failed to pay his taxes. He paid his employees a pittance while he amassed a fortune. Reed was a menace to society. Reed was the fresh meat thrown to the clawed media and fanged politicians who hungered for their next prey.

Reed had dismissed them the way a thoroughbred with finish lines and wreaths of roses awaiting him would outrun those trying to catch him—until the lawsuit. The Bureau of Fair Trade sought to break up his company, claiming it was a monopoly that stifled its competition, which the government considered to be a crime.

"Customers *choose* me over my competitors," Reed had complained to Laura. "Is that what the people who don't accomplish anything can't stand? The success of others?"

Worst of all, Reed Miller's news division took positions unflattering to those in power. Reed had charged that *this* was the real reason behind the Bureau's action against him.

"It's our right at Miller Communications not only to report factually on news stories and events but to give our viewpoint of them," Reed had said in a televised appearance. "It's called free speech."

An advisor to President Martin who was facing off with Reed had answered, "The good of society is served by a diversity of viewpoints in the public forum."

"Why should *I* have to provide them?" Reed replied.

"A duty to serve the public interest supersedes any right to free speech that a monopolistic businessman thinks he has, especially when that businessman is making huge profits and having an untoward influence on society," Martin's advisor retorted.

"In other words, I'm effective. I'm persuasive. The picture I paint of those in power ain't pretty, so that's why they've got their pitchforks out for me," Reed responded.

The media had stoked the controversy, many of them giddy over the widespread attention and boosted ratings that Reed's problems brought to their work.

The lawsuit was like a hailstorm pelting the sunny grounds of Reed's world. He became introspective and melancholy. Defending himself was expensive, time-consuming, and stress-inducing. It drained his zeal for life that had so appealed to Laura. Through her show, she defended him fiercely, and he needed her more urgently than ever. Their passion for each other grew. Then came the day when Reed gave up the fight, the day he dropped her key on the table and closed the door behind him, leaving her blindsided with the suddenness of his retreat.

As she sat alone in the conference room after the meeting with her family, she realized that now the pressure was on *her* to give up. Her family demanded it. In contrast to what she had believed were the unfair charges the government lodged against Reed, her family, now, had legitimate claims against her. She had an obligation to the other members of the family business. She was causing them actual harm. Her crusade was a detriment to their interests, she reasoned. She felt a nerve throbbing at her temple. What should she do?

She gathered her things and left the conference room.

Later, as she sat in her office planning the evening's episode of *Just the Truth*, her thoughts lingered on the man she could not shake.

For what we once shared, Reed. For what we were, and what I still am . . .

As Laura waited for her show to begin, an assistant wiped the perspiration across her hairline and powdered over the shine on her nose. Then the assistant dashed off the set. The signal came from the control room. She was on the air.

"Good evening and welcome to *Just the Truth*. I'm Laura Taninger. Tonight, we continue to examine the tactics used by shady governments to suppress their critics and to examine whether the Martin administration is guilty of using them. The subject of my Daily Memo tonight is: *Tools of Silence: Selective Use of Rules and Regulations to Target Political Enemies*.

"Under the guise of public safety, governments enact an enormous number of rules to regulate businesses. Because they claim that these rules are essential to protect the public, hardly anyone has the temerity to object to them, unless he or she wants to be villainized by the government and its media supporters as being against public safety." She smiled wryly.

"What happens when reams of these rules are on the books, and there's no way to enforce all of them all the time? Enforcement becomes *selective*. Enforcement becomes a tool used by unscrupulous governments to crush political opponents. Would the Martin administration employ such a tool to suppress its critics? The answer is *yes*.

"The Martin administration recently showed its strong-arm inclinations in a matter involving football. Would anyone think it's fair if a football team were at the one-yard line, about to score, and someone suddenly moved the goal posts farther away, killing any chance of a touchdown? What happens when it's the *government* that cheats, and there's no one to call them out because the cheater is also the referee?

"The parent organization of Taninger News also owns the DC Slammers football team. The Slammers didn't expect the government to be its most dangerous opponent, an adversary that doesn't have to play by the rules, but instead can move the goal posts whenever it feels like it, leaving the Slammers no way to score.

"The agency involved here is the Federal Bureau of Building Safety, which just discovered a regulation on the books that for years had gone unenforced. It's an obscure rule hidden within hundreds of pages of a law having to do with requirements for stadiums.

"Just days before the opening of the Slammers' new stadium, the seats, which had passed all prior inspections, suddenly were unacceptable to the regulators at the Federal Bureau of Building Safety. It seems that too much of a controlled resource—energy—was expended in manufacturing the stadium's seats, and too little of another controlled resource—recycled plastic—was used.

The remedy the agency requires is to have all the seats ripped out and replaced, which means substantially *more* energy and plastic will be expended in the process. With a remedy that requires more use of the objected to practices and materials, we have to ask: Are these bureaucrats serious? Or is there another motive involved in the action against the Slammers?

"Can anyone tell me there's no connection between the reporting I've done at Taninger News of suspicious goings on at the Bureau of Elections and the flak over our sister company's stadium seats? Are we not supposed to connect the dots between a regulation against a football stadium and freedom of the press? With the Feds coming down hard on the Slammers for a rule that up to now has been unenforced, I believe they're retaliating in an attempt to silence *Just the Truth*.

"With the enormous power that today's government has over business, what's a company to do? Can business owners today afford to be free thinkers anymore? Is the government trying to regulate our stadiums, or our minds?"

CHAPTER 12

Guests in formal dress filled a parlor of the People's Manor. Servers weaving through the crowd with silver trays offered cocktails and hors d'oeuvres. The pinkish light of an approaching September sunset streamed in through the casement windows. Antique drapery, crystal chandeliers, and colonial sideboards completed the elegant setting of a cocktail party hosted by President Martin and his wife.

Although he was properly dressed in a tuxedo, the Fox looked out of place. He held a wine glass and stood on the margin of the room, observing rather than mingling. Perhaps it was the sunglasses, which he wore indoors, or the faint look of contempt on his face that invited no conversation and kept others at bay.

He saw Ken Martin, Darcy Egan, and Zack Walker scattered around the room. Martin smiled as he worked the crowd, taking no cocktail or hors d'oeuvres, keeping himself ready for handshakes and pats on the back. Like a tulip without a stem, Darcy looked plump and legless in her floor-length pink gown. Zack managed to look disheveled, even in a tuxedo. His pants, a bit too long, drooped. His bowtie, a bit too loose, tilted. He looked around, then spotted the man he was expecting: the Fox.

Zack approached Ken Martin and took him aside. The Fox observed Zack whispering in the presidential ear and discreetly tilting his head in his direction. Martin looked at the tech guru. The Fox raised his wine glass in greeting. The president did not return the gesture, but instead looked away.

Zack filtered through the room, taking his time to approach the Fox casually. "Wearing your sunglasses indoors? Did you expect to find skylights on the ceiling?"

"Why, no. I didn't expect that much transparency."

"Take them off, dude. You might call attention to yourself. Besides, it's disrespectful to the office of the president."

"Is it now? And what you, Velvet, and Silk are doing *isn't* disrespectful to the office of the president?"

Zack waited, but the glasses remained on.

"I'll escort you over. He'll have a few words with you. Then you'll *leave*. Got that?"

The Fox nodded.

The men walked to President Martin. No introductions were made, only a wary nod from Martin, which was returned by a grin from the Fox.

"In two days it'll be fall, Mr. President," said the Fox.

"That's right," replied Martin.

"I'd say there's a chill in the air," the Fox continued. "Wouldn't you?"

"I would," Martin said, trying to hide his perturbation.

"Time to get out the *Topcoat*?" asked the Fox.

There was a pause. The president seemed surprised at the bluntness. Then, he replied, "Yes, it's time."

"That should protect you from the changing winds and storm clouds."

"That's the idea," said Martin.

"So, you're *all in* on that?" the Fox persisted.

"I am." The president bowed his head to take leave and walked away.

CHAPTER 13

Kate Taninger sat at her desk in the office of the *Collier Voice*. Except for the modern computers and printers, the old office with its scuffed desks and dented file cabinets had hardly changed since Clark Taninger's tenure as editor-in-chief of the *Voice* a generation ago.

The window in Kate's work area overlooked the campus of Collier University and the streets and buildings of Washington, DC, surrounding it. Like its host city, the campus dated back to early America, but in recent times, it resembled an eclectic painting struggling to find its theme. A neo-classical library with Corinthian columns that resembled the Pantheon stood next to a modern student center, the facade of which included purple-trimmed beams supporting a wall of glass. A bronze statue of a Revolutionary War hero on horseback stood in a campus garden alongside a steel sculpture of what appeared to be construction girders fastened with iron screws. Some said this stylistic variety symbolized the university's diversity, while others said it reflected a trend toward disintegration and confusion. The dean liked to say that at Collier University all architectural and artistic styles were welcome—as were all viewpoints. Or were they? The third Taninger to head the *Collier Voice*, after Clark and Laura, would soon test that.

As Kate read an editorial published in the *Collier Dispatch*, the campus newspaper that competed with hers, the youthful sparkle that defined her—the eager face with the ready grin and lively eyes—vanished, replaced by a disillusioned frown and wary half-closed eyes. Kate suddenly looked older, her idealism wounded.

The *Collier Dispatch* titled its editorial, "Elites Don't Want You to Vote."

Laura Taninger's attacks on President Martin's SafeVote system are not so much about the voting program as they are about her bias against minorities, the poor, and other disadvantaged groups that the new law protects. Ms. Taninger comes from a family of wealth and privilege, so it's not surprising that she's against universal suffrage, wanting to keep the franchise restricted to her own class. Laura Taninger has a commitment to the welfare of only the top few.

What would Ms. Taninger know about a young mother who is struggling with screaming kids and no hot water in her tenement apartment, who loses the identification card that her state requires for her to vote, or misplaces her proof of citizenship, or forgets when Election Day is, or hasn't managed to sign up to vote, or can't read the ballot because her state refuses to publish it in her native language? What is this poor mother to do when state laws ignore her needs and put impediments in the way of her voting? What is this mother to do when she lives in a state that, in virtue of its requirements, denies her the right to vote? What does Ms. Taninger know about these grievances, hardships, and inequalities?

The disadvantaged deserve every chance, every reminder, every helping hand to get them to vote. Federal control of the process will remove discriminatory state-imposed obstacles and ensure that all people who choose to vote get to the ballot box and are counted. That's why we support President's Martin's new SafeVote program—and why we call out bigots like Laura Taninger.

Kate's face reddened with anger as she read the article. As soon as she finished reading, she turned to her computer and began to compose her next Editor's Column, a feature of the *Collier Voice*. It would be a rebuttal to "Elites Don't Want You to Vote." She titled it, "Bureaucrats Don't Want You to Know."

Does truth matter? Do facts matter? Does transparency in government matter? My sister, Laura Taninger, thinks so. *Taninger News* has always thought so. "Find the truth wherever it hides" was my grandfather's motto when he founded the newspaper that bears his name. There's a long tradition at *Taninger News* of holding the government accountable to the citizens. We believe that a free press protects all of our freedoms by exposing the wrongdoing of elected officials and putting a stop to corruption and unchecked power. My sister's news show, *Just the Truth*, and her investigative reporting proudly continue this tradition.

With its hit piece on Laura, "Elites Don't Want You to Vote," the *Collier Dispatch* is protecting a bureaucracy that hasn't been forthcoming with relevant facts. The *Dispatch* skirts any attempt to argue the substance of the actual issue but instead stoops to making malicious, false personal attacks on the messenger who's bringing you bad news about your government.

The *Dispatch* accuses Laura of being biased against minorities and the poor and against universal suffrage. Has anyone asked the *Dispatch* for evidence to back up its harsh claims? Has the *Dispatch* cited even one statement from any of Laura's broadcasts that lends credence to its smears? The *Dispatch* apparently didn't need any basis for its ugly accusations. It just tries to destroy people like Laura whose ideas it disagrees with, without ever trying to debate the substance of the issue. If Laura were guilty of all that the *Dispatch* claims, she wouldn't work so hard to protect our rights, including our right to transparency in our elections.

Let's interject some facts, so we're not left with only the *Dispatch*'s smear campaign. Here's the issue: The federal government is undertaking a complete overhaul of our election system. It's centralizing control of it. This represents a huge departure from the Constitution's intent that voting be controlled by the individual states. Court challenges have failed to stop the Feds, so we're going to have this new voting system, like it or not. At the very least, the federal government should be completely above board in exercising its newfound power, which starts with designing our nation's new voting system.

Laura Taninger has petitioned documents to see how the money is being spent in developing the new SafeVote system. But the Bureau of Elections has not been forthcoming. Why is this agency evading full disclosure? What is it hiding? The Bureau of Elections can simply release the requested documents as required by law. If all is in order, this would be the end of the matter. The public has a right to know how government agencies are spending its money—especially when it comes to transforming our election system. Everyone should thank Laura Taninger for her efforts to pull back the curtain on a powerful agency that is tasked with such an important assignment.

And let us not forget that James Spenser, the assistant director of the Bureau of Elections, was killed just moments before he was about to reveal something he believed was suspicious about the new program. The police have yet to identify a suspect in his murder.

Is it important to answer the legitimate concerns about SafeVote and to get justice for James Spenser? Or is it more important to protect the president and his party, which the *Dispatch* has long supported? Will partisanship at the *Dispatch* close its mind to the pursuit of truth—and close our minds, as well?

The skies were clear and there was little wind that late September day when Kate's column appeared in the print and online editions of the *Voice*. It was a perfect day for the outdoor activity Kate had planned. Walking along the campus in early morning, she carried a poster under her arm and wheeled a suitcase filled with reprints of her commentary. She headed to a display table in an area reserved for students who wanted to promote their causes. She had reserved this table to distribute her opinion piece and explain the issue to students. Her poster displayed a blown-up photo of President Martin with Sandra Frank, the director of the Bureau of Elections, and below it the message, "Stop Withholding Documents. Come Clean about SafeVote."

The staff of the *Voice* supported Kate's position and wanted to help, but Kate was hesitant to involve them. Because the matter involved her sister, it was in part personal, and there might be repercussions from students who promoted opposing views, some of whom could get . . . nasty. Thus, Kate published her rebuttal as a personal reflection in her weekly Editor's Column and alone manned the display table.

Soon after she set up her table, the first group of curious students arrived. They stopped to read her material and speak to her. They nodded thoughtfully and were receptive to her arguments. The young editor's optimism grew. Surely, she could persuade her classmates to see the logic of her position.

She did not notice a disapproving glare at her from a distance. It was the editor-in-chief of the *Dispatch*, observing her. He had read her column moments ago on his phone. He snapped a photo of his rival with her poster. Then, he transmitted the photo of Kate, along with her commentary, to a college friend who was interning at the People's Manor. He added a note:

Backlash to my pro-Martin piece from Taninger's sister.

The intern brought the information to someone on Zack Walker's staff, who passed it on to him. Zack's network of contacts—and his call to send him any material involving Laura Taninger or her family—were paying off.

Upon reading Kate's column, Zack's eyes flashed with excitement and the O-shaped resting position of his mouth expanded into a wide grin. Kate Taninger had unwittingly provided the kindling to ignite his imagination.

Through a private email account used for correspondences he did not want traceable to his position in the administration, Zack forwarded the information to Jack Anders, the director of the national organization Foundation to Enrich Student Life, an allegedly nonpartisan group that engaged in what it called charitable activities to help students cope with adult responsibilities—including signing them up to vote. This group had strong ties to the president, got out the vote for him, and in turn was itself enriched by becoming a line item in the budgets passed by Ken Martin and his party. The Foundation had the power to summon a cadre of young agitators on short notice to appear for what it called "spontaneous" demonstrations, protests, and even a little more . . . action . . . if necessary. Zack had the power to summon the Foundation, and when he forwarded the materials to its director, he wrote:

Hey Jack, can you do something BIG here?

Later that morning, a dozen exemplars of the Foundation's enrichment program confronted Kate.

They grabbed her materials out of the hands of students at her table. The students quietly backed away, looking intimidated by the sudden onslaught.

The Foundation's ringleader, whom the other disruptors called Sting, strutted up to Kate.

"We don't want you here. Get out, racist!" he ordered.

"I will not!"

She tried to call the police, but with a chop to her wrist, he knocked her phone to the ground.

"Who are you?" Kate demanded. "You don't go to school here! I never saw any of you before."

With a smirk, Sting turned to his minions. "Let's go!" he ordered. They ripped up her reprints and flung the torn sheets into the air, littering the campus while they knocked over her table and destroyed her poster.

One of the students who was standing at her table came to Kate's defense. "Hey, leave her alone," he said to Sting. "Ever heard of academic freedom?"

Sting, who looked ten years past college age, had cold eyes and a fiery voice. He bellowed, "We will *not* be guided by cardboard notions of civility! If we have to give up academic freedom in favor of justice, we have the guts to do it. Do you?" The leader drew near the boy and jabbed a finger in his chest.

The student backed off. He grabbed Kate's arm to pull her away. Kate resisted.

"There will be no freedom and no justice if you destroy my table and threaten me!" she shouted to the protestors.

The sympathetic student picked up Kate's phone and gave it to her. He continued tugging on her arm, until she finally backed away with him.

Alerted via their electronic media networks, Collier's most belligerent students soon joined forces with the growing throng of sympathizers from the Foundation to Enrich Student Life. By late afternoon, the protestors numbered two hundred. They blocked traffic on the main roadway of the campus and formed an encampment inside the administration building, up the stairs, and into the reception area outside the dean's office on the second floor. The Foundation's director, Jack Anders, hastily drew up a list of demands for the disrupters:

> We believe that uttering certain speech is tantamount to committing an act of violence. We believe that bigoted speech is violence and those who promote it are inherently oppressors. When a member of a university writes an article promoting or justifying bigotry and oppression, the administration must treat it like an act of violence and put a stop to it.
>
> Collier University must not permit speech that devalues people and makes students feel attacked. Our academic community must provide a calm environment for students, where people respect the feelings of others. In a world of growing controversy, the stamping out of bigoted and hateful views is justified.
>
> In her recent column in the *Collier Voice*, editor-in-chief Kate Taninger expressed ideas that are too offensive and harmful to allow on campus. She obviously opposes democracy and the right of all people to have their vote counted. This is why we demand that Kate Taninger retract her statement,

with a full-throated apology to the entire academic community—or else the administration needs to remove her from her post at the *Collier Voice*.

The protestors presented their demands to Ronda Pendleton, the associate dean of student affairs, whom Stewart Folner, the dean, sent out to face them. She received their demands and issued a statement:

> We regret the hurt we know the column in question caused people and their communities on this campus. We encourage everyone in our academic family to engage in speech that fosters healthy discussions, rather than sparks controversy.

With orders given to stand down, rather than to confront and evacuate the trespassers, security guards watched them passively. The guards' chief activity of the evening consisted of quietly shepherding the entrapped dean out of the building through a back stairwell and exit. In his sole communication with students since the encampment began, the dean summoned Kate Taninger to meet with him in the morning.

The stately administration building, a treasured landmark from the founding of the college, soon reeked of hamburgers and pizza as the protestors received food deliveries, courtesy of the Foundation that apparently supported their gastronomic, as well as their societal, enrichment. The occupiers lounged on the couches in the anteroom to the dean's office, eating what constituted their dinner. They tossed greasy food wrappers onto the high-gloss hardwood floor and plush oriental rug. They stacked pizza boxes on an antique side table, with sauce and cheese dripping onto a handsewn lace doily. They left water rings from their drinks on the heirloom furniture.

The Foundation to Enrich Student Life contacted reporters sympathetic to their causes, who arrived with cameras to interview the protestors and report from their encampment. Sting moved through the crowd like a supervisor, proudly surveying his group's work: intimidating students, blocking traffic, and setting wastebasket fires. Sought after for his comments, with microphones pushed toward his face, he recited the talking points given to him by the Foundation: "What you see here are students and their supporters who feel strongly about equality and justice. We spontaneously gathered here tonight because we're offended by our campus newspaper and its editor. We won't stand for oppression and injustice any longer. That's why we plan to spend the night here," he said with studied calm, as if employing the reasoned tone of the civilized was sufficient to be considered among their ranks.

When Laura learned of the protest, she sent a crew to the scene. She aired a different story on her show, told by the eyewitness whom her reporter interviewed: Kate.

"A group of bullies has attacked me, my campus newspaper, my sister, and the college," said the youngest of the Taningers.

After her program that evening, Laura sped down to the college, found Kate on the scene where the protests were continuing, and grabbed her shoulders in affection and concern. "Are you okay?"

"I'm fine," Kate said, sounding dejected but resolute.

"Why did you do this? You're not to get involved!" Laura said, her voice trembling with worry.

"It's a little late for that," Kate replied.

"You're to get yourself uninvolved fast!"

"Meaning what?" asked Kate.

"Meaning you'll retract what you said and go on with your education."

"Meaning I should side with the *Dispatch* . . . against you?"

"If it comes to that. It's not your time to make news. It's your time to do what it takes to graduate!"

"Graduate from this place?" she looked around with disgust.

"You'll swallow it now," ordered Laura.

"JT wouldn't swallow it."

"He would want you to."

"Is that what *I* want?" Kate said softly, posing the question to herself.

"Retract what you wrote. Say you didn't mean to imply any offense to anyone. Water it down. Say you regret your words were not better chosen, that they were misguided or misunderstood, or whatever. Just walk it back!"

"Why?'

"So you'll have something to give the dean, a concession. I'm sure you'll be hearing from him soon."

Kate did not mention that she had already been summoned to a meeting with the dean the next day.

By morning, the occupation of the administration building had turned uglier. A half-dozen glass panels in the casement windows had been broken. Antique tables had been keyed, causing jagged wounds in the varnished wood. Upholstery and drapery had been slashed. There were now 500 agitators. A placard-waving, foul-mouthed, angry throng gathered outside the administration building in support of the mob inside, some of whom had forced the lock and entered the dean's office. They declared in front of friendly cameras that they would not leave until their demands were met: Kate Taninger must be stopped. The placards read:

Stop the hate.

End oppression and privilege now.

Kate Taninger is a bigot.

Dean Folner received a report on the vandalism from his frantic head of security, who was ready and eager to put an end to the protest. The dean frowned, sighed, and paced indecisively. Then he concluded: "If we force them out, we'll be called oppressive elitists. Collier's reputation is more important than the property damage—and far harder to repair. We have to wait this out." Security guards and local police watched in dismay.

Campus guards escorted Kate to her meeting with the dean. With concerns for his safety, the guards had moved him to a temporary new location: a hall in the campus music center. He would have to be transplanted again the next day when the Collier Symphony Orchestra arrived for a rehearsal. Kate walked in to find a panel of three waiting for her. They sat in the center of the room on folding chairs in front of a grand piano—Dean Stewart Folner, faculty advisor to the *Voice*, Ellen George, and student council president, Gayle Polk. All glared at Kate, as if *she* were the cause of their problems.

The dean gestured for Kate to take a seat in a chair facing them. As she sat, Kate thought of the inquisitions of medieval times and wondered if there were a torture rack hidden among the kettle drums, harp, double bass, and cluster of music stands on the sides of the room.

The gray-haired dean had a distinguished look, except for a habit of nervously blinking. He spoke first.

"Now, Ms. Taninger," he said. "I'm sure you're aware of the gravity of the situation. Surely, you agree that something must be done."

Kate nodded. "Yes, sir. Of course, you have to do something."

"Oh, not *us*, Ms. Taninger. It's *you* who have to do something, wouldn't you say?"

"Do what?"

"Recant. Apologize, sincerely and at length, for what you wrote. Retract it, and hope the community is satisfied with that so we can all get back to normal."

"Why should *I* apologize?"

"Because your views have offended many people."

"I gave my views on a political issue. I didn't mean to offend anyone."

"Oh, but people *were* offended, whether you intended it or not."

"But, sir, it's not valid for them to be offended. I didn't say anything to warrant that reaction."

"People must be held accountable for the *disturbance* they create, Ms. Taninger, even if it's not what they meant to do."

"You mean, *I'm* to be held accountable for the feelings generated in the heads of rioters?" Kate replied. "But Dean Folner, *they're* in the wrong. Why don't *they* apologize?"

With a forced calm, the dean smiled cajolingly. "Look, this isn't about who's right and who's wrong. It's about curbing speech that offends the academic community—and yours does."

"But, sir, doesn't *rioting* offend the academic community? Isn't that what needs to be curbed?"

The dean folded his arms irritably. Ms. Taninger had a pesky way of bringing up things that made him feel . . . uncomfortable. He turned to the student council president, as if to say, *maybe you can talk some sense into her.*

"Look, Kate, you need to help us out here," said Gayle Polk. "We're asking nicely. We assume you didn't *intend* to offend anyone."

"I was thinking about what I was saying. The facts mattered, and I was thinking about them."

"Facts matter, of course. But feelings matter, too."

"You mean *power* matters, don't you, Gayle? Do vandals carry the day for us here at Collier?"

The panel of three glanced at each other, as if wondering what to try next. Kate presented a problem for them. She spoke directly—without anger, regret, or remorse—and the panel didn't seem to know how to handle someone who felt neither self-protective, nor apologetic, nor guilty.

"You know, Kate, we could hold a student council meeting and vote to defund your newspaper because it's provoked such a violent reaction. Then the *Voice*, the venerable newspaper that's part of Collier's history, would be shut down. Wouldn't you rather just walk back your column, so you don't bring down the whole paper?"

"It would be *you* bringing down the *Voice*, wouldn't it? Why should you do that over a column that speaks the truth, Gayle?"

"Because the student body may not want to hear what you perceive as the truth. They have other ideas about what their truth is. On the council, we'd have to go with the majority's decision."

"There are 500 people out there demonstrating. What about the other 10,000 students who aren't protesting my work? Aren't *they* the majority, the quiet ones, and why can't you go with *their* decision, which is to be unoffended by my views?"

"But the opinion of those 500 protestors is what'll sway the student council."

"Why?"

"Because *your* opinion represents privilege and discrimination. We can't support that."

"But what if my position is valid, and my views are *true*? Are you saying that an institution of higher education can't support the truth?"

"Now look, Kate." Ellen George, the *Voice*'s faculty advisor, chimed in. "Truth isn't the only factor we need to weigh. The *narrative* is important, too, even more important than the truth. There *is* discrimination and bigotry in our society."

"But not in this case. *I'm* not discriminating or being bigoted toward anyone. Neither is my sister. People have no right to accuse us of things we didn't do or say or imply."

"It doesn't really matter that you or your sister are not actually bigoted. Student protestors from poor backgrounds are complaining to me because you're causing them to feel as though you *are* discriminating against them," interjected Gayle Polk.

"But they're wrong to feel that way, Gayle. Why should I be responsible for how unfairly they reacted?"

"Sometimes impact outweighs intent, and when that happens people do need to be held accountable."

"Meaning the rioters," said Kate. "They need to be held accountable."

"Meaning *you*," the student council president persisted. "The narrative is there, and our students are concerned. They react to that bigger picture. You can't blame them."

"But half of the protestors aren't even students."

"That doesn't matter," replied Gayle Polk, shaking her head. "The demonstrators represent the wider community which our university serves."

"Let me get this straight." Kate looked at the panel thoughtfully. Being a Taninger and growing up under JT's tutelage, Kate had a way of not being awed by people in authority, and the three people she faced, by their nervous glances at each other, knew it. "The three of you don't blame *the protestors* for the damage they're causing? You blame *me*?" Her voice was incredulous. "You can't be serious."

Ellen George crossed her legs and fidgeted in her folding chair. "In my five years as faculty advisor, I never thought I'd have to protect the *Voice* from its editor-in-chief!" she charged, eager to wrap up the matter. "For the sake of the *Voice*, you need to retract what you said and apologize to your readers."

"You mean apologize to the people who shut down my table, threatened me, and trashed the dean's office?" Kate replied.

"Just say that you chose words that weren't the best, and now that you're more sensitized to the needs and feelings of the academic community, you regret having caused pain and you take back what you said."

"No one would believe that, and I'd be a coward for saying it."

Dean Folner, who had expressed no indignation toward the protestors, now bellowed at Kate, "Will you do as we ask, Ms. Taninger? Or will you push us to do something more . . . corrective?"

Kate's eyes held steady on his.

CHAPTER 14

Sean Browne sat in his office, listening to Darcy Egan prepare him for his daily press briefing. His eyes wandered from the sheet of talking points she had placed before him to the open door of his office and beyond it to the entryway to the president's office. He noticed that after a few weeks as the president's press secretary, the shimmer of being a sparkler so close to the biggest of the fireworks down the hall had dimmed. *That's expected,* he told himself. *You can't keep feeling the thrill of a new job after that job isn't new anymore. You have to come down to earth.*

Yes, he was privy to Ken Martin's important meetings, but like a favorite pet, he would sit quietly at Martin's side and be stroked occasionally when Martin turned toward him to make a comment. But he was never invited to contribute anything of substance to the discussions. *Why should you contribute? You're new to the job, and the president has lots of policy experts he needs to hear from,* Sean reasoned with himself.

"I don't have much time, so let's try not to ask too many questions," Darcy said, adding, "if that's okay with you."

"Okay, Darcy. Shoot."

"Regarding the education bill making its way through the House, the president has decided to support it," droned Darcy.

"But wasn't he against it last week?" Sean asked.

"He changed his mind."

"Why?"

"Just tell the media he supports the bill now. I thought you weren't going to ask so many questions."

"But, Darcy, the reporters will call me on that. They'll want to know why the president said he would veto that bill last week and now—"

"Then refer them to the House leadership."

Am I simply supposed to repeat the talking points like a parrot? he asked himself. *Darcy almost never explains. She never gives me reasons.* Then a more troubling thought occurred to him. *Maybe she . . . doesn't want to admit . . . why they do what they do.* He shrugged off his fears. *She's busy. She can't explain everything. My job is to make things easier, not harder, for her.*

"Then there's Vita Simpson." Darcy's tone became contemptuous at the mention of *Taninger News'* intrepid reporter. "Try to limit her questions."

"She'll ask about the Federal Bureau of Building Safety's recent action against the DC Slammers' new stadium," said Sean. "She'll want to know if that was done to pressure Laura Taninger to stop criticizing the Bureau of Elections. Vita will say we're trying to shut down free speech. I thought I'd speak to the folks at Building Safety to learn exactly what they did and why."

"*I'll* tell you what they did. That's all you need to know." Darcy glanced impatiently at her watch. "The government has to regulate businesses for the public safety and well-being. Building Safety enforced its regulations. Those are *economic* regulations, which have nothing at all to do with free speech. Tell Vita that, then call on someone else."

"What about the protests against Kate Taninger at Collier University? Vita will pepper me about that. Laura Taninger claims they were staged by an outside group that's tight with the president."

Darcy laughed contemptuously. "Tell Vita that sounds like the plot of a conspiracy novel. In the real world, apart from her employer's fantasies, the Martin administration has nothing whatsoever to do with Collier University and the activities of their students. Got that?"

Darcy rose to end the meeting.

Sean looked up at her with a wry half-smile. "I guess so."

The sepia walls, old wood booths, and brownish lighting made Annie's Alehouse look like a dive. A glance at the drink prices elevated its status to a Washington, DC, bar. Covering the walls were an array of blown-up photographs of celebrities; their salutations to the owner and signatures splashed across their pictures suggested they had come there to be seen. Two people in a booth at the end of a long row talked with their heads down and voices low, hoping to remain unseen.

There was a kind of anonymity established between Laura Taninger and Senator Bret Taylor in the back booth of Annie's. The bar was packed four-deep with D.C. types unwinding from a long day. Those standing around the bar formed a patchwork quilt of business shirts sewn together at the shoulders, with heads facing the center. No one paid attention to outliers in the booths.

"I agreed to meet with you this one time, Ms. Taninger, on the condition that you're not to call me or send me any more emails about this matter," said the senator, a distinguished gray-haired man with a perpetually worried look wrinkling his brow.

"I understand, Senator."

Laura liked Bret Taylor's honest eyes, which looked directly at her. The senator liked Laura's trustworthy face, which disarmed him.

He stirred his drink nervously, then took a generous slug. "For all I know, my office could be wiretapped!"

Laura's curiosity piqued. "Do you think you're being wiretapped? By the Martin administration?"

"No, no!" the senator said, retracting. "I didn't mean to imply that. I just want you to stop communicating with me about a sensitive issue that could potentially derail the president's—and my own—reelection campaign."

"Of course, Senator. I'll respect your wishes."

"When I gave Sean Browne permission to pass my lead to you, I didn't think you and I would have any direct contact."

"As I told you, Senator, Sean never revealed you as his source. I surmised you were the source, so I contacted you on my own hunch. You're the head of the Senate committee that oversees the Bureau of Elections, and you're the only senator in the president's party who has voiced misgivings about the new SafeVote program. So it wasn't hard to infer that James Spenser would've come to you with his concerns when he learned that Elections was bringing in a company to make additional, uncertified modifications, after the SafeVote programming had already been completed and certified."

"Okay," he said, acknowledging that her deduction was correct. "So how can I help you?"

"What else did Spenser tell you?"

"Only what you just said, that a new company was being brought in, under the radar, so to speak."

"He spoke to his boss, Sandra Frank, about that, didn't he?"

"He questioned Sandra."

"And she was evasive. She put him off, didn't she?"

"She told him not to worry, but he was suspicious. It was the only company whose name was being withheld from him, and no further programming was permitted to be done after certification. So he came to me with his concerns, and I passed him on to Sean and you."

"Did he ever find out the name of this company?"

"I don't know. I never spoke to him again after I passed on the lead."

"Did he mention anything at all about this company?"

"No."

"After he was shot, he could hardly talk, but he managed to whisper a word to me . . . he repeated it . . . it was somehow important that he tell me. It sounded like *Fox*. Do you know what he meant by that?"

"Fox? Why, no. I have no idea."

"Have you ever heard that word used in any of your dealings with Elections and the SafeVote program?"

"No, I haven't. I'm afraid I can't help you."

Laura sipped her wine, looking thoughtful. "Senator, could you inquire about this? Could you ask Sandra Frank at Elections some questions? Could you find out why her assistant director would've set up a meeting with me and uttered that word just before his death?"

The senator shook his head vigorously. "I can't get involved with this!"

"Why not? You head the oversight committee. Can't you get information from Elections? Can't you subpoena it, if necessary?"

"No, absolutely not!" He seemed to panic at Laura's suggestion. He said, "Forget it."

"But Senator, with all due respect, there are questions here. Someone was killed. It's your job to inquire!"

"Now's not the time. If I made waves for the president just before his reelection, the party would cut me off. They'd create some kind of scandal to get me off the ticket and bring in a new candidate—and they'd ruin my career in the process."

"But it's the right thing to do!"

"But it's the wrong thing to do politically."

"Surely your constituents won't desert you for pursuing this matter, for not wanting to brush this under the rug, for doing what's right and not what's expedient."

He shook his head regretfully. "Today, if you're on the right side of an issue, and you want to fight for it, you might be able to prove your case, but that doesn't really matter anymore outside of a courtroom." He bitterly looked away, as if there were disillusionments beyond the current issue that weighed on his conscience and compromised his standards long ago. "If you lose your case in the court of public opinion, you're doomed. Too often the public just hears snippets and half-truths, put out by partisans to advance their own causes. The media feeds off that, spins that stuff out, and the public sides with them."

"But, Senator, the truth needs to come out. It needs all hands on deck to battle the broadside attacks it gets from its enemies. It needs *you*. One sailor like me firing a single cannon isn't going to be enough."

"What good would I do, if I lost my seat? I can do more good in the long run by keeping my Senate seat and not being ousted. I can do more good by cooperating with my party."

"And losing your integrity? What good will that do?"

The senator sighed. "I have a different way of looking at things than you do."

Laura leaned back, studying the man across the table. She had to accept that Senator Bret Taylor had limitations.

"Okay, Senator, I won't take up any more of your time. If you think of anything else, you know how to reach me."

She finished her wine, pushed the glass aside, and signaled to the waiter for the bill.

"There *is* something else, Laura."

She looked at him curiously as he dropped formality to use her first name.

He emptied his drink, then he reached across the table to grab her by the arms, pulling her closer to him.

"I didn't just meet with you to say I'd be of no use to you."

"Oh?"

She could feel his fingers digging into her arms, pulling her even closer, until their faces almost touched. From a distance, he might have looked as if he were ready to kiss her, but Laura could see fear on his face and hear urgency in his voice. "*Don't let this go!* There's something wrong here. You have to keep at it, Laura. Everything rests on you."

"What rests on me?"

"The country."

They were unaware of someone breaking ranks with the line of bodies at the bar, turning toward them, aiming a phone in their direction, and taking their picture.

Sean Browne was double-parked outside Annie's Alehouse, waiting for Laura. He wondered why she had called him earlier that day and asked him to meet her for dinner.

"I'll pick you up at work," he had offered.

"I'm meeting someone at Annie's for a drink first. After that, I can meet you at the restaurant," she had replied.

Being ever the gentleman, doting on her, subliminally reaching for something romantic in their interactions, he'd insisted, "No, Laura, I'll pick you up at Annie's and take you to the restaurant."

As he waited, he saw Senator Bret Taylor leave the bar and get into a chauffeured car. Soon after, he saw Laura leave, find his car, wave at him, and approach. He got out to open the door for her, his broad smile a testament of how much he had missed her in the few weeks since their last meeting.

"This is our first time out together since you started your new job," she commented as she entered the car.

"Yes."

"I'm the big enemy of your bosses. Is it all right for you to be seen with me?"

"I don't know. I didn't think of that. Only that I miss you," he confessed.

"Tonight on my show, I'm airing an interview I conducted earlier today with the secretary of state about a few international hot spots, so I don't have to rush back for a live broadcast. I have the night off."

"Great!"

He drove to The Waves, and once they were seated at their usual table, he asked her about something that was bothering him. The mild annoyance in his voice was the closest he ever came to being angry with her. "I saw Senator Taylor leave the bar just before you did. You were meeting with him, weren't you?"

"I was."

"Why did you meet with him? Over James Spenser and the Bureau of Elections, right?"

"Right, Sean."

"Laura, I never gave you permission to meet with my source. I never revealed his name to you! Does he think I did?"

"No, he doesn't. I was perfectly clear that I guessed who the source was, and that you never revealed him. I wanted to ask him a few questions."

"And?"

"And he didn't have any answers for me."

"Surely, you don't expect me, in my new position, to have any more information for you."

"I don't expect that."

"So you asked me out tonight because you miss me?" he asked hopefully.

"No," she said curtly. "Because I saw your press briefing today."

"That's just an act, Laura. A dog-and-pony we do every day for the D.C. press corp."

"And for the public," added Laura.

"The public doesn't pay any attention to the briefing." Sean waved his hand dismissively.

"Oh, no? Your talking points—or rather your smears against my family—were repeated all over the TV news broadcasts, the talk shows, the radio, and the internet."

She looked at him with disappointment and anger, adding, "Vita confronted you with facts, and you dismissed them with lies. Why did Building Safety shut down *our* new stadium for faulty seating, when another sports arena that Vita cited has just installed the same seating, which Building Safety has allowed?"

"It's not my job to investigate federal agencies. I'm not a reporter."

I should have known this was coming, Sean thought. *The worst part about it is that I wanted to investigate further, but Darcy ordered me not to. I had to back off and not jeopardize my job, but if I told Laura that, she'd think I was a coward.*

"You didn't respond to Vita's question. You just said that Building Safety is enforcing its regulations. Yeah, they're enforcing them *selectively* to target my family and shut down my free speech."

"But those are just *economic* regulations. They have nothing at all to do with free speech. We're still an absolutely free country. There are no threats to that at all. Building Safety is a force for good; it regulates the private sector."

"Does that mean the private sector, which includes Taninger Enterprises, is a force for bad?" Laura asked.

"Now, I didn't say that, did I?"

"And Vita brought up facts about the demonstrations against my sister at Collier. It's a fact that they were started by the Foundation to Enrich Student Life. The head of it, Jack Anders, has been all over TV bragging about what he did. And it's a fact that that the Martin administration has given that group more funding from the government than it could have ever dreamed of raising on its own. It's a fact that the Foundation openly supports the president, even though it's supposed to be nonpartisan. When you ignore these facts and describe what Vita is saying as a plot in a conspiracy novel—are you proud of yourself? When you help vicious people eviscerate a kid in college for having an opinion on an issue—are you proud?"

"No one's trying to hurt Kate, or anyone else in your family. Laura, listen to yourself. You're wildly exaggerating."

Sean spoke loudly, as if the volume of his assertion could drown out any doubt that might be forming. He reached across the table to hold her hand, to console her, to soften her reaction. She pulled her hand away. Moved by her passion, he couldn't help but look at her affectionately. Even though *he* was the object of her wrath, she was so alive, so strong, so beautiful when she was fighting for what she believed. But like a viewer watching a stage play in which something heroic and important is happening, he felt distant from it. He saw someone who fascinated him, who was confident in her judgments and unhampered in expressing them, but who was also impractical, hyperbolic, far afield from what the world that he knew would accept. She belonged on the stage or on a pedestal.

"Sean, what's happening to you?" Her voice was softer. She sounded sadder and a bit hurt. "You used to care about accountability and the truth, even if you pursued them through me by giving me leads, and not through yourself. But now . . . "

"Laura, you're taking this to such an extreme. I'm still the same person. I sometimes have to say things for the president that I don't always agree with."

"You're working for people who want to destroy me and my family for the sake of their power."

"Now, really, Laura, you make them out to be monsters. They have good intentions. They're trying hard to accomplish worthy things in the long run, even if they sometimes have to . . . compromise . . . in the short term. There's an election coming up. They're doing what they need to do—what everybody does—to win."

"You mean, in order to win an election, they have to destroy my family?"

"Laura, you're so damn extreme!"

"Want me to tamp it down? To talk more like you and your bosses do? Let's see . . . " She straightened her shoulders, assumed a pompous air, and spoke affectedly. "Perhaps there might be a slight item omitted from the SafeVote accounting, a slight oversight of $400 million from the most well-meaning, well-intentioned, fine staff that run the Bureau of Elections and that do so much to uphold our democracy. Who are we to question them? But if it's not too much trouble, maybe they can spare a moment to reply to a humble reporter—"

Sean wasn't amused by her sarcasm. "You know full well that wouldn't be *you* anymore. You'd lose your fire. You'd lose those wild eyes that stare right through people. You'd lose your *soul!*"

Laura looked at him bewildered. "If you like what I am, then why don't *you* want to be this way, too? Where's *your* soul?"

The remark seemed to surprise—and hurt—him.

Sure, I've made some compromises. We all have to, everyone except you, that is. But look what it got me. My career is on fire, even if my . . . soul . . . isn't, he thought.

"I can give you a job at Taninger News if you're willing to quit a corrupt administration and fight this with me."

"Quit? Are you crazy? I mean, I'm delighted by your offer, but I can't do what you do, pick fights with everybody and open yourself up to constant attacks. Besides, I've got a job that everybody in the country would kill for."

"Who's *everybody?*"

"Every media person in the country, except you. My office is within spitting distance of *his* office—the most powerful man in the world! I'd love to work at Taninger News so I could see you every day, but any other job would be a big step down."

"You know, you sound more and more like them. They've got a hold on you—and it's tightening."

Hurt, but unwilling to continue the fight, Sean smiled wistfully at her and opened the menu.

Later, he drove her home. They walked past the gate at the entrance to her row house and up to the door.

"Goodnight, Sean," she said, as she opened the door and vanished into her home. There would be no small hug or kiss that night.

He returned to his car and sat. Although he had only rarely and briefly been inside Laura's home, he remembered every part of it. He watched various lights go on beyond the pulled drapery. Laura was in the kitchen, then in the living room, then the bedroom. He listened to a few opera pieces he had stored on his phone. He listened to the triumphal notes of a soaring chorus as an army returned home in victory. He listened to the tender duet of two lovers passionately declaring their love. He listened to the ringing aria of a rebel solemnly vowing to defeat a tyrant. He thought of Laura fighting at her own barricade. How was it that such violent emotions could be felt in life? How was it that the things they pursued resonated to the core in such people and that they would do anything to fight for them? Laura was the star in her own operatic life, he thought. She was among those whose lofty values would be considered impractical, naïve, and melodramatic in the world he inhabited, yet she was more exciting and full of life than anyone else.

When all the lights were out in Laura's house, Sean drove away.

CHAPTER 15

October began with the protests of the previous week continuing at Collier University. During the stand-off, a new normal was established. The protestors had set up their headquarters at the dean's office in the administration building, which they still occupied. The dean moved from his temporary quarters in the music building to a space in the science building with security to prevent entry by the protestors. A makeshift office with a desk and chairs had been hastily assembled for Dean Stewart Folner in one of the laboratories. Whereas his vacated office contained a niche with a curtained bay window and statuary on pedestals, the dean's new workplace had a niche for an exhaust hood with flasks and burners for mixing chemicals. Whereas his vacated office contained a marble-topped walnut sideboard holding two porcelain lamps, a crystal vase, and a gilded antique clock, his new workplace contained epoxy-resin countertops holding a spectrophotometer, microscope, digital scale, and other equipment, along with test tubes and bottles of solvents. As the setting of his life changed from regal to humble, he thought of the one student who could restore him to princely status—if she weren't so damn stubborn!

Before any school official could stop the staff of the *Voice*, the young reporters published a new edition of the newspaper. It contained an editorial supporting their beleaguered editor.

> Kate Taninger speaks for all of us. We will not be silenced. We will not be bullied. We support a citizen's right to question the new voting system and hold the government accountable, as Laura Taninger is doing. We also assert our own prerogative to express an opinion on the matter in our newspaper.
>
> This issue goes beyond any side's position on the new voting system. Whatever your views on that particular issue, all sides should be able to air their opinions without fear of intimidation. All sides should be willing to

present arguments, not invectives or threats. Some students have written to us with opposing arguments, which we have published as Letters to the Editor.

We will not let our voice be silenced. We urge our editor-in-chief, Kate Taninger, to continue to write her column, speak her mind, and respond to her critics.

In her Editor's Column, there was no apology from Kate Taninger. Guided by a keen intelligence and a maturity beyond her years, she penned her next piece, titled "Book Burning."

There was a time when humans didn't have the rule of law, which means they hadn't yet established an orderly, peaceful way to live together. A civil society was an achievement thousands of years in the making. Before societies had the rule of law, angry mobs dominated them. These mobs held brute power over people who were forced to comply with their orders. During these ugly times in history, a mob could be roused to a fever pitch in order to do the bidding of those in control, who ruthlessly tried to stamp out the things they felt threatened by, in the hope of relieving what must have been their chronic, overwhelming fear of losing their power.

Consider, for example, the Renaissance. Girolamo Savonarola resisted a new age of artistic, literary, and scientific freedom by smashing irreplaceable works of art and torching books with new ideas. Over a century later, Galileo Galilei was coerced to recant his innovative scientific theories by the pope. Most tragic of all, people who refused to conform were burned at the stake.

The campus bullies who are now occupying the administration building, damaging property, and threatening me and the *Collier Voice* are retrogressing to the dark times in history. They're trying to use their muscle to smash us and destroy our free minds. Dean Folner needs to stop their outrageous, bullying behavior. He must call in the police and have the protestors removed. He must notify the Collier students involved in the protest that if they don't end their disgraceful behavior now, they will be expelled.

We can't let a mob seize control of our university. It's the antithesis of what a university is supposed to stand for. The protestors pose a great danger—not only to me and the *Voice*, but to everyone. The rioters are staging a protest against thought itself. They are against anyone who doesn't think as they do. They want to smack down any students who think for themselves and reject being muscled by a mob.

Kate's editorial resulted in her being summoned for another meeting with the dean. She took a seat facing him as he sat at his new desk in the science building's laboratory. A goose-neck faucet from a workstation sink arched behind his left shoulder. A plastic skeleton of the human body hung eerily from a stand behind his right shoulder.

The latest edition of the *Voice* sat on his desk, opened to her column. "I assume there will be no retraction of your two columns, or will there?"

He looked at her half-hoping, even now, that she would give in to his demand, immediately print a retraction of both of her recent columns, and spare him from having to make the hard choice between his conscience and—no, he mustn't think of his conscience as having anything to do with this. *It's a clear-cut case of insubordination,* he told himself. *She's a reckless student defying me and her advisors.*

"Your new column makes it even harder to correct the situation, Ms. Taninger, but it's not too late to print a retraction. I'm giving you one last chance."

Kate did not reply.

"I'm bending over backward to be absolutely fair to you, Ms. Taninger."

"If you want to be fair to me, then I shouldn't be here in the first place."

"It's your choice. Either you print a retraction of your two ill-conceived columns and move on to other topics, or you will forfeit your position at the *Voice.*"

"That would be a choice between being true to my convictions and caving in to the bullies, Dean Folner."

His habit of incessantly blinking made him look nervous.

He said, "If that's what you think *your* choice is, you leave *me* no choice."

"But, Dean Folner, I think you *do* have a choice. Don't you? You can call in the police to remove the protestors, and you can punish them instead of me."

She sat calmly facing him while he cleared his throat and fidgeted in his chair. The dean apparently never had a JT in his life to guide his upbringing, as did Kate, who learned at an early age the importance of standing up for what she believed.

"It would make you a champion of free speech for the students at Collier and for students like me in other schools who are the victims of bullies like the rioters here. If you stop them, you can be a role model for all campuses, and you can be our hero."

The dean stared at her, astonished, as if equating his person with the term she used was like trying to mix water with oil. He chuffed. "You mean like in a fairy tale, I should be some kind of guardian angel?"

"I had in mind a *real-life* hero," Kate said, standing her ground.

He had the best advisors. None of them gave him this kind of advice. Who was *she*, a disorderly student, to council *him*?

"I've had enough of your impertinence! You Taningers know no bounds!"

"But Dean Folner, I don't mean to be impertinent," Kate said. Her manner was respectful, even if her advice was, at the least, unsolicited. "You see, my grandfather Julius Taninger stood up to *presidents* when he thought they were wrong. He taught me to be true to what I believe." The youngest of JT's grandchildren, who freely gave advice at executive meetings of her family's corporation, thought nothing of speaking her mind to the dean. "Why would we appease an angry mob that invaded our campus and think they run things? *You* run things, not them, sir! Don't give in to them!"

For an unguarded moment, the dean looked as if she might have reached him. His face softened at her plea. Honesty crept into his eyes. For the first time, the blinking slowed to a normal pace, and he looked directly at her.

"Look, Kate, I don't want to punish you."

He stood up as though he wanted to release some nervous energy. He walked to the lab's sole window. He glanced out worriedly.

"They're out there," he said. "They're growing in numbers." He walked back to his desk, grabbed a document, and waved it at her. "This is their latest communique. They demand that I place limits on free expression on campus when a student expresses views that violate the moral standards of the university and offend the academic community."

"But Dean Folner, those are just cheap shots by a couple of hundred students having a temper tantrum. They hardly even constitute a couple of percent of the student body. Exactly *who* is being offended by my views? *Why* wouldn't those who disagree simply avoid my column and read something else? *What* moral standards are they taking it upon themselves to enforce on the rest of us? The morality of storming buildings and damaging property? Their pathetic manifesto can be shot down so easily. Believe me, sir, their claims are so easy to debunk that you're in no danger at all if you shut them down! The protestors are only a small minority, so they have no right to claim they speak for the whole 'academic community.' And furthermore, it's absurd for them to claim that speech which offends someone must be shut down. Being offended isn't like having your wallet stolen or your leg broken. Speech is not physically harmful and can just be ignored. There is no such thing as a right to not be offended. For anything that anyone utters, you can surely find someone, somewhere, who will be offended by it. If that's their standard for shutting down speech—that it offends someone—then no one would be able to say anything. Think of it, sir! You can totally debunk their claims."

"But they *believe* their opinions, just as you believe yours," he said flatly, as if he were reciting something he had read in a text book and was expected to believe. "Who am I to take a side?"

"But occupying buildings and breaking windows aren't the expression of opinions, sir. Besides, you already have taken a side—theirs!"

The dean looked confused. Somehow Kate had knocked him off guard.

As he was considering how to reply, the door opened, and his assistant entered. "Excuse me, Dean Folner. I thought you should know that more protestors have just arrived in busloads. They're intent on blocking all the campus roads and entrances to the buildings so that no classes can take place today."

The dean's shoulders stiffened. He nodded to his assistant, who then left. Kate observed him as he fidgeted with his tie. Whatever vestige of character she might have reached, whatever honesty she thought she saw in his eyes, had now vanished. The blinking resumed and seemed to deflect from his sight the full meaning of his actions.

"I guess I have your answer, Ms. Taninger."

"I guess I have yours, sir."

"Effective immediately, you are removed as editor-in-chief of the *Voice*."

Despite Kate's dismissal from the *Voice* as the protestors demanded, they did not end their demonstrations.

"We kicked her out!" Sting, the ringleader, gloated on a phone call with the director of the Foundation to Enrich Student Life.

"You made it look easy!" Jack Anders replied, elated.

"We're on a roll!"

"Why stop now? Let's score some bonus points with our political friends. Let's give 'em more than they asked for."

"You bet!" said Sting. His voice soared beyond eagerness to the high octave of lust.

The next day, the protestors' numbers again increased. They prowled the campus grounds, shouting, waving placards, blocking traffic, and preventing students from entering buildings. Watching the chaos from his laboratory window, Dean Folner squirmed. *What the hell do they want now?* He had given them what they wanted, so why was he still surrounded by dirty test tubes and smelly solvents while they refused to leave his real office?

Presently, a new communique arrived. In the name of promoting justice, equality, and fairness, and putting an end to oppression, prejudice, and privilege, the protestors demanded that the university stop funding the *Voice*.

Although no one could trace their origin, new signs and posters appeared among the malcontents.

Defund Bigots! Defund the Voice*!*

No Money for Oppressors. Shut Down the Voice*!*

The signs were unavoidable—on lamp posts, at building entrances, in hallways, and in the waiting hands of the demonstrators as television cameras rolled.

The protestors' latest demand triggered a flurry of discussions among the dean, the associate dean of student affairs, the faculty advisor for the *Voice*, and others. The student council called an emergency meeting that afternoon.

One eager member of the student council opened the meeting. "Kate Taninger's columns are creating an unsafe learning environment on the Collier campus. Her views reflect a hatred of minorities and the poor, who are helped by the new election law that she speaks so forcefully against. So the question becomes, should the university be funding a publication that has now become an offensive symbol of privilege?"

After some discussion, the student council of Collier University took a vote on whether the *Voice*—Collier's oldest and highly popular student newspaper—should continue to exist. The *Voice* lost. The council passed a resolution to recommend that the administration defund the publication.

The dean and his administration approved the measure, and the *Voice* was silenced.

An administration spokesperson issued a statement: "It's not only, or even primarily, the editorial positions taken by the *Voice* that caused us to rethink our support. We've been planning for a long time to better allocate our student activity funds, and as a cost-cutting measure, even though we're a large university that wanted to encourage a diversity of opinions, we find that we really don't need two major college-funded newspapers to do that."

After the administration announced its decision, the council member who had initiated the vote against the *Voice* bragged to his friend, "See how easy it is to sway public opinion and make big changes?"

His friend replied, admiringly, "You know, you should go into politics. You have a knack for it."

"I know," replied the council member, who was the editor-in-chief of the *Dispatch*.

His gloating, however, was short-lived. Before the day was over, the *Voice* was back in business, stronger than ever before.

Laura Taninger heard the news and rescued the *Voice* by pledging a personal donation—with the condition that her money be earmarked only to support the *Voice*.

"We're now in this together," Laura explained to Kate. "I'm not giving charity to my sister, although there would be nothing wrong with doing that. But in this case, I'm giving to a cause we both believe in." In acceptance and appreciation, Kate wrapped her arms around Laura, as she had when she was a child, and Laura returned the embrace, pulling Kate close and stroking her hair.

"The *Voice* will continue to operate as we did before, with the same editor-in-chief and staff," the newspaper cheerfully announced. "Today's donation provides us with money to function independently of university funds, as well as to expand. We now have the resources for additional staffing, marketing, advertising, and distribution to increase our circulation and expand our readership on campus and in the Washington, DC, area beyond our university. The *Voice* is now stronger, and we will become more impactful on our community than ever before."

Upon hearing of this change in fortune, the director of the Foundation to Enrich Student Life called the ringleader of the Collier demonstrations.

"What the hell's goin' on there?" Jack Anders snapped.

"Big sister screwed us. Blame her!" said Sting.

"We need more action, more disruptions, more demands—and more violence, if it comes to that."

"We might be able to kick it up a notch," Sting teased. "Depends on what you're willing to pay."

That night the demonstrators expanded their reach beyond the Collier campus, into the heart of the nation's capital. They blocked roadways, overturned a police car, shattered car windows, set wastebasket fires, hurled epithets, and threw bottles at police.

Their ranks grew. Joining them were those students and local residents who uncritically accepted the vague slogans of the protestors and believed they were fighting for something worthy. Then there were those who joined the protestors because they needed to vent their undefined, yet powerful, frustrations by rebelling against something . . . anything. Others felt a driving need to release a pervasive, pent-up, dangerous lust for violence and were drawn to the protests as reflexively as a moth to light.

Even more people came because they were paid. As workers in the past would roam the country seeking jobs, this new breed of workers roamed the country seeking protests. These job applicants offered themselves as kindling to those who hired them to set raging fires from the embers of discontent. That the arsonist-employers paid them with funds from untraceable sources to harm innocent victims was of no concern to the kind of workers who sought this employment.

The ringleader at Collier passed his group's latest demand to Ronda Pendleton, the associate dean of student affairs, who passed it to Dean Folner. This demand excluded the group's previous grandiose claims about justice, equality, and other high-sounding terms. The communique was stripped to the essence of what the protestors wanted done, as if the recipient had already been softened up and did not need further rationalizations to be compliant. The communique amounted to an order contained in three handwritten words: *Expel Kate Taninger.*

The dean read it, slowly put down the paper, and shook his head. "I can't go that far. She hasn't done anything wrong," he said.

Ronda Pendleton looked surprised at Dean Folner's comment.

"I mean, she hasn't done anything to warrant going that far," he added, his tone more tentative. "Tell them I won't do it," Dean Folner replied to Pendleton, who passed his answer to the protestors.

That night, following the dean's refusal, the ringleader and a few from his squad bypassed the guards and surreptitiously entered the science building. In laboratories close to the dean's makeshift office, a shower was set off and a fire extinguisher activated. Thousands of dollars in property damage resulted. When he heard the news, Dean Folner went numb. His nervous blinking stopped, replaced by a blank stare that resembled the look of the doomed.

Laura Taninger blasted the rioters and the dean on *Just the Truth*.

"The subject of my Daily Memo tonight is: *Tools of Silence: The Mob*," she told her viewers.

"History teaches us that unscrupulous governments use many tactics to silence their greatest enemy: free speech. We've discussed several of the tactics and accused the Martin administration of employing them. The tactic I'm going to discuss tonight is in a class by itself. It crosses over a line and resorts to open violence.

"In America today, civility and the rule of law have been hampered, but they still exist and have a history of being the bedrock of our nation, so the government can't *itself* use open violence for fear of terrorizing the citizens and turning them against it. Rather than be so crude, the government can instead condone, excuse, and look the other way at violence used by supposedly private organizations, which are actually front groups that have close ties to the administration and receive handouts from it. These groups are the ones that crush their patron's enemies. Let the groups do the dirty work, so the government itself can look uninvolved to the unsuspecting and gullible among us.

"Paradoxically, this movement toward mob rule enjoys a footing in the institutions that are supposed to be developing the intellect: our universities. What better group can a government try to control than the young, impressionable, future generation? If you can teach the young that an angry mob is more powerful than an argument, you can control them for a lifetime.

"Colleges are becoming breeding grounds for belligerent organizations aligned with the government to advance the state's causes by bullying and force. Is the Martin administration onboard with these roughhouse tactics used against our most vulnerable young people? Sadly, the answer is, *yes*."

Laura showed pictures of Collier University with its stately buildings being overrun by protestors breaking windows, overturning cars, and setting fires in trash receptacles.

"Collier University was the recent subject of such a mob attack. This attack targeted my sister, Kate Taninger. She's a junior at Collier and editor of the school newspaper called the *Collier Voice*. Kate was targeted because she wrote an editorial supporting my investigation into SafeVote. She was attacked and denied her prerogative to express her point of view.

"Who's behind these disturbances? Many naïve or disingenuous journalists are reporting that these are spontaneous demonstrations by caring students troubled by injustices in society. Let's pour some cold facts over those claims. These demonstrations are not spontaneous. Busloads of professional protestors have been dropped in and are being paid.

"We've identified the hardcore demonstrators, and they are not students, but professional protestors. We see the same people appearing at other riots in other cities. Here, take a look." Images flashed, flagging some of the same people at the Collier protest as also being in the frontlines of other protests in other cities.

"Who sent them to Collier? An organization called the Foundation to Enrich Student Life. There's no need to guess about this. Although they've declined invitations to appear on this show, the Foundation's director and the ringleader of the protests at Collier have given joint interviews to other media outlets."

Laura looked into the camera, her face sober.

"Although it claims to be a nonpartisan charity so that it can receive government funding, the Foundation to Enrich Student Life actually gets out the vote on campuses around the country for President Martin's political party. It's *scandalous* that this group is funded by the taxpayers. The Foundation's involvement in the Collier protests makes us believe that the Martin administration elicited its help or is accepting it willingly and unethically."

Next, Laura showed a picture of Kate, a vibrant photo of her in a park, laughing, catching a volley ball, with the sun on her face.

"And my sister, Kate Taninger, who is an honor student at Collier and an up-and-coming journalist, has been fired from her post as editor-in-chief and her newspaper has been defunded in order to appease these thugs.

"I stepped in with a personal donation to keep the *Voice* afloat. However, the brave students who staff the newspaper are still vulnerable to verbal and physical attacks from the rioters. Do we want our beautiful young people—like my sister Kate—to be assailed by a mob while our universities abandon reason, arguments, and debates of ideas?"

During an evening meeting over wine and hors d'oeuvres in the president's office, Darcy Egan, Zack Walker, and Ken Martin watched Laura Taninger's broadcast. As Laura spoke, Martin downed a glass of wine and poured another, his face growing redder.

"How many heads does this hydra have? How many times do we need to cut her down before she's finally dead?"

Brooding, Zack observed Laura on television.

"It's time to take a new tack," he said, staring hatefully at the screen.

The next day, hit pieces appeared in the media about Dean Stewart Folner. The dean cheated on a high school exam, said an accuser who was in the same class and who suddenly surfaced thirty-five years later to make the accusation. The dean abused his wife, claimed another reporter, who had gotten that information from a source who was launching a legal action to release the twenty-year-old divorce records of the dean and his first wife.

The protestors became more virulent, their signs more vicious, their disruptions of students trying to enter campus buildings more numerous.

The discontents now called for the dean to resign. "It's you or Kate," they chanted from the sidewalk outside his laboratory window. The dean looked with horror at their latest placards:

Fire the Dean.
Dean Folner Must Resign.
End Bigotry or End Your Job.
Expel Kate or Get Out.

He heard the shouts of the rioters and watched them being interviewed by fawning reporters. No matter how powerful he was, they somehow had more power. What weapon did they have that was so potent against him? Fear paralyzed his mind before it could provide the answer. On a television news show, he saw the picture that Laura had released of Kate smiling in a park on a sunlit day, catching a volley ball, enjoying a moment worth living. His eyes lingered on the attractive, intelligent student of his university, whose face was filled with innocence and hope.

He felt like an ancient king being pressured to make a human sacrifice of a fair maiden to appease capricious, powerful gods. Would he?

CHAPTER 16

A gusty breeze lifted Laura's jacket and blew her hair as she approached the glass-and-steel headquarters of Taninger Enterprises. That first week in October, a restless autumn wind pushed through the city, sweeping out the warm temperatures from a lingering summer.

Laura felt impatient, too, as she walked through the arched entrance of Taninger Enterprises, glancing overhead at the stone engraving of her grandfather's motto: *Find the truth wherever it hides.* Almost another month had passed since attorney Sam Quinn had filed an appeal to her original Public Disclosure Request. Walking into the building through the revolving door, she felt as if she were on a kind of merry-go-round, stretching to grab a brass ring that was just out of reach.

She walked across the lobby, greeting the guard at the security desk. Behind the guard's station she saw the familiar portraits of her family members, who comprised the executive management of Taninger Enterprises. This day, however, the portraits struck her as sitting ducks to be shot down by a pernicious sniper. *How many of them have been hit now? Irene lost the Pinnacle contract and a chance at record ratings for her station. Billie is mired in re-dos and delays for the Slammers' new stadium. And now they're trying to pick off Kate!* The thought of her kid-sister as the victim of vicious attacks—a college student whose portrait had not yet even made it to the executives' wall—made Laura doubly impatient to get answers from the Bureau of Elections.

For what purpose were these cruel attacks unleashed on her family? And was James Spenser's murder the deadliest hit of all by the same sniper?

Her mind buzzed with unanswered questions as she headed toward the elevator. She was impatient to see all communications and documents relating to IFT, which the Bureau of Elections was required to provide in response to her appeal. On the elevator, her phone chimed. She found a text message from Sam:

Received BOE's response. It's on your desk.

She dashed out of the elevator and across the busy newsroom of *Taninger News* to her office.

She expected piles of paper. After all, this was a significant contract. Surely the trail of correspondences and documents would be massive. She would have to pull various members of her staff together to delve through it all.

She reached her office, saw her desk, and froze in her tracks. Sitting on her desk were not mounds of paper, or even a small collection of pages. There was just *one page*. She felt a shocking disappointment. *Is that it?*

She picked up the document and examined it. The paper was a memorandum written on official letterhead bearing the seal of the Bureau of Elections. The subject was: *IFT to Perform Updates and Patches on SafeVote.* Except for the first line, the rest of the text was redacted in heavy black marker. The name and signature of the official at the Bureau of Elections who signed the document was also redacted.

The unredacted first line was the whole of her mother lode. She carefully read and reread it. The sentence contained new information that identified the organization. IFT was a company based in Ireland whose full name was Integrated Foxworth Technologies. Its president was . . . she gasped . . . Frank Foxworth.

She slowly dropped the document on her desk. A memory from the caverns of her mind resurfaced to confront her. A mortally wounded man lay before her. She desperately tried to stop a tsunami of blood flowing from his chest, spilling onto her clothes, and staining the pavement red. He grabbed her collar, weakly pulled her closer, and tried to tell her something, but he could barely whisper one word before his eyes closed and his head fell with a sudden finality.

"Fox," he seemed to mouth to her in his last breath.

She now posed a question to the man who could no longer answer any inquiries: *James, did you mean Frank Foxworth?*

CHAPTER 17

"Your Honor, *Just the Truth* demands that the Bureau of Elections turn over all documents relating to its contractor Integrated Foxworth Technologies and the work it's been tasked with in the development of SafeVote. We have been trying for several months now to obtain information from this agency, first with informal inquiries, then with our Public Disclosure Request, then with an appeal to our request, but to no avail. That's why we're asking the court to intervene."

Attorney Sam Quinn stood before the judge's bench in the wood-paneled courtroom. On the wall behind the bench hung an oil painting of a scene from antiquity depicting the blindfolded Lady Justice in a diaphanous robe holding her scales, with attendants flanking her. The graceful beauty of the artist's rendition of the goddess of Justice contrasted sharply with the leather-tough features of the black-robed, unsmiling Judge Marianne Rogers, who opened her folder on the case, spread out the papers, and listened without expression. A white lace collar was the only touch of softness to contrast with her no-nonsense countenance.

A clerk at a small desk sat near the bench that morning when Sam Quinn filed a suit for *Just the Truth* and attorney Emmett Wallace filed a Motion to Dismiss on behalf of the Bureau of Elections. With no one present in the witness stand or jury box to absorb the sound, the lawyers' voices, full-throated and highly skilled in courtroom drama, echoed off the glossy wood walls.

Laura was the sole spectator at that hour, quietly observing from a pew in the public area beyond the balustrade. She listened as Sam related their saga with the Bureau of Elections to the judge.

" . . . So, Your Honor, after we filed an appeal specifically targeted to this one contractor, IFT, we received nothing more than a one-page response. *Only*

129

one page of documentation, Your Honor, for a $400 million contract. And the information contained on that single page was ninety-five percent redacted, giving us only the full name of the company and its president and stating that it's located in Ireland!"

Judge Rogers nodded, saying, "You have a point."

Then, she turned to Emmett Wallace, a young man with a dress-for-success pin-striped suit and carefully styled hair.

"Good morning, Your Honor," he said, smiling broadly.

His friendly salutation received no reply from the judge.

His smile fading, Counselor Wallace continued, "The Bureau of Elections has responded to both the original Public Disclosure Request and the appeal within a reasonable timeframe."

"But your response was incomplete. Wasn't it?" the judge interjected.

"We are cooperating as best we can. We have produced thousands of pages of information."

"But nothing on the contract that *Just the Truth* is most interested in, the IFT deal. Isn't that the problem?" Judge Rogers asked Wallace.

"With the rollout of SafeVote just weeks away, the Bureau of Elections is facing *exceptional circumstances*. The Bureau is responsible for our new national voting system, and the country's eyes are on us! We are unduly swamped with work and will be until this rollout is accomplished."

The judge nodded. "You have a point, too, Counselor."

"We can't postpone Election Day for the sake of providing the plaintiff with materials. We *are* complying, and we will *continue* to comply with the disclosure requests, without the court's involvement. We ask that the court grant our Motion to Dismiss and give us more time to work this out with the plaintiff."

Sam objected, saying, "Judge Rogers, we acknowledge that Elections replied, but as you point out, the response was incomplete. We've given Elections ample time. They are not complying with their transparency obligations. We need the court's prodding to get them to move on this."

"But, Judge," Wallace responded, "there are also serious national security issues at play here. We can't release technical material involving the new voting system for fear of breaching its security. We have to painstakingly go through every document to be sure that security-related information is redacted. This takes time, Your Honor. We can't pull our staff off of the SafeVote project to serve the plaintiff's television channel and shirk our responsibility to the nation to rollout the new voting system on time and without snags."

"How is a company profile and a general description of the contractor's tasks in layman's terms a breach of national security? We haven't even received that much," Quinn remarked. "Your Honor, this is nothing more than a lame excuse!"

The judge turned to the defendant. "What about it, Mr. Wallace? Why are you giving the plaintiff the runaround?"

"Short of halting the agency's work and devoting ourselves to serving *Just the Truth*, instead of the public, we are already giving them expedited treatment, and we're producing documents in a timely fashion."

"But you're not complying with the law," declared Quinn. "*Just the Truth* is engaged in disseminating information to the public, and this is an important matter that must not be hidden from public view. Elections must be transparent, and the public disclosure laws are supposed to ensure that they are, especially at this crucial time when a new voting system is rolling out. This matter now needs intervention from the court, not more stalls and delays!"

The judge's head swiveled from side to side as each contestant served his best shot and hoped it would score. Just as Wallace was about to retort, the judge held up her hands.

"Enough! I've heard enough." She gathered her papers and placed them back in her folder. "I will give you my answer on Monday."

"But, Your Honor," Sam Quinn implored, holding his notes in one hand and gesturing with the other, "Election Day is fast approaching. The SafeVote launch is imminent. There's an *urgency* to inform the public on this matter. We need the court to intervene *now* to prevent any more stalls, delays, dodges, and withholding by Elections."

"On *Monday*, Mr. Quinn."

"Thank you, Judge," said Emmett Wallace, his charming smile returning. "We're confident the court will recognize how reasonable we're trying to be and give us more time."

"Don't patronize me, Counselor."

Judge Marianne Rogers closed her folder and left the room.

With Sam headed to another appointment in the courthouse, Laura rode alone in a taxi on the trip back to her office.

She leaned her head back, trying to assess what had just transpired in the courtroom and how the judge would rule. She had to admit that she couldn't read the judge or venture a guess. She would have to wait until Monday to learn the fate of her lawsuit.

She grabbed her phone and skimmed through the latest postings on her news feed. One article that was just coming across the wires captured her interest. It reported that after ten days, the protests at Collier University had finally ended. At first, she was relieved. Then she read further.

"Oh, no!" she blurted out involuntarily.

The driver turned his head. "Hey, lady, are you okay?"

"Uh . . . yes." She managed an absent-minded reply as she continued reading.

The occupiers had finally left the administration building and campus, and the students were beginning their return to normalcy. All but Kate Taninger. She had been expelled.

CHAPTER 18

Clark Taninger took his seat at the head of the conference table. He glanced at his four children in their usual seats and his assistant Caroline Davis at his side.

"Friday, October 6, the executive management meeting of Taninger Enterprises will come to order," he said. "Hold the notes for a minute, Caroline. Our first matter is personal." Chagrined, he crossed his arms, elbows on the table, and turned to Kate. "Well?"

"I guess you all know what happened," said Kate. "I don't see why we should discuss it here."

"We'll fight this!" said Laura, sitting at the edge of her chair. "We'll get you back into Collier."

"Now the arsonist wants to put out the fire!" Clark bellowed, glaring at Laura.

"As usual, Laura makes a mess for our family, and *we* have to figure out how to clean it up!" Irene accused.

"That's not true, Irene, and you know it," said Kate.

"Laura, this has to stop. We can't keep being the hostages in wars you get yourself into!" Billie added, his voice peppered with anger. Then he turned to Kate. "And *you* have to go back to school!"

"I'm not going back."

"You have to finish your education," said her father.

"JT didn't go to college," she replied.

"Honey, Dad's right," said Laura. "That was okay in JT's day, but not today. I'll fight this with you! We'll take our case to Collier's alumni donors. We'll get them to withhold their contributions until you're reinstated, and this horrible injustice is fixed!"

"But I don't want to go back," Kate said calmly.

"How can you say that? You have to go back. They're not going to win!" Laura's hands curled into two fists ready to pound the table.

"It's not just that they're wrong," Kate spoke sadly. "It's that *they don't care if they're wrong*. They don't care what's right or wrong. They don't care if they're unfair to me. So why should I go back?"

Clark turned to Kate. "I want you back at Collier. I think I can pull some strings."

"None of you seem to understand," Kate said calmly. "I don't want to be in a place where I have to self-censor my every word, my every sentence, even my every *thought*, with the fear that I'll be slammed down. I don't want to live in . . . fear."

Clark didn't seem to hear his daughter's plea. "You'll go back to school, Katie. I have friends I can speak to on Collier's board of trustees. You may have to grovel a little, and maybe that's good for you!"

"Me? What do I have to grovel about?"

"If I do get you back in, you'll stay out of Laura's squabbles!" Clark ordered.

"A word of advice from your big brother, Katie. If Dad gets you back in, forget you even know Laura, and you'll be fine."

"Let Laura fight her own battles." Irene added.

Laura nodded sadly and said, "They're right, Kate. I absolutely *forbid* you to get involved in my affairs. I don't want to be the cause of you not finishing your education."

"If I can arrange it, you're going back to Collier. It's settled," Clark directed.

"Dad, Collier's not the same as it was when you went. You wouldn't recognize it now."

"We're Taningers. We adjust to changing times," her father insisted.

"You mean, we placate angry mobs? Is that how we adjust? No thanks!"

"You'll go back! No daughter of mine will be a dropout."

Kate stood up and held her arms out to quiet her family.

"You don't seem to get it," she said, her voice resolute. "They talk a foreign language at Collier. Oh, they use English words, but what do they mean by them? They use the same words we use, but these words don't mean the same thing to them." Her face lost its usual glow. She looked older.

"The protestors talk about wanting justice, but what they mean is they want their group to set the rules for the rest of us. They talk about fairness, but what they mean is they want their side to get away with crushing anybody who doesn't think like they do. They talk about ending bigotry, but they have the most horrible bigotry of all, the bigotry against ideas. They beat down people whose ideas don't click with theirs, and they get a sick thrill out of doing it. They talk about ending oppression but what they want is the power to oppress anyone who's an outlier, who doesn't hang with their crowd, who thinks differently."

Kate shook her head. "I feel so out of place there. I feel like I'm in a maze, where up is down, and right is left, and there's a different world outside, but nobody in the maze can see it. The protestors live in that maze, and they don't want to get out. *And the administration sides with them.*" She paused, incredulous at her own conclusions. "At Collier, it's *their* side that wins."

There was an awkward pause as the others realized how serious she was.

"You're sounding more and more like JT every day, even more than Laura!" Clark shook his head disapprovingly.

"But Katie, there are better people at Collier. Think of the *Voice.* Your staff stuck with you!" said Laura.

"And I'll stick with them. I'd like to continue publishing the *Voice,* if I can still use your funding, but redirect it to a new enterprise," Kate said, looking at Laura.

"Of course you can, if that's what you want. But I'd like to see you—"

"We'll drop 'Collier' from the newspaper's name," Kate said thoughtfully. "We'll just be an indie newspaper called the *Voice,* and we'll cultivate an audience outside of Collier, a young people's newspaper for the broader Washington, DC, area. I think students who worked on the *Voice* will join me in the new endeavor. That'll be enough for me to do right now."

"There have to be other schools that will take you, Kate," said Laura. "Not all colleges have deans like Collier's. I'll help you find a better place."

"No," said Kate.

"Okay, not now. You'll take a little time off now, and maybe in six months, you'll reconsider going back. Then we can work on getting you into another college to finish up." Laura persisted.

"Maybe," Kate said noncommittally.

Laura's head dropped. "I don't want my enemies to wreck your life—"

"It's not your fault, Laura! I'm glad all of this happened. Now I know what they're really like, those zombies who run Collier. With one editorial, JT would've smashed them!"

Kate took her seat, ending any further objections.

Unable to chip away at the iron will of his youngest, Clark sighed in frustration. "Okay. Let's move on," he said, looking at Caroline, whose hands moved to her keyboard, ready to start taking notes. "Laura first."

"Revenues, ratings, and readership are the highest they've ever been for Taninger News," said Laura. The others studied the financial figures that Laura transmitted from her laptop to one of the monitors on the wall. "As you can see, our print publications, online sites, and broadcast divisions are all doing well."

"And Laura's show is still rated number one in TV news!" Kate reminded them. "Laura's popularity shows you that the people are behind her."

"Yeah, but that doesn't make up for the damage she's done to the rest of the corporation," said Irene.

"I'm just curious about something, Irene," Laura commented. "When Ken Martin canceled his appearance at the Pinnacle Awards ceremony and your deal to broadcast it fell through, the president's people claimed that he had a scheduling conflict and that it had nothing to do with my opposition to SafeVote. When Billie's new stadium got smacked down by the regulators, the Martin administration categorically denied that it had anything to do with my opposition to SafeVote. When protestors stormed Collier, again the Martin administration claimed they were not in any way involved with the group that started the protests. If the president that you defend over me is to be believed—and his administration had nothing to do with any of these issues—then why are you blaming me?"

"Come on, Laura, we weren't born yesterday," said Billie. "We know there's retaliation going on."

"Then why aren't you blaming *them* for hurting us? Why aren't you joining me?" Her eyes scanned her critics. "Why don't you call them out for the abuse of power that we all acknowledge is going on?"

"Because it's *you* that goads them," Clark told Laura. "We have to accept their behavior, but we certainly don't have to accept yours."

Laura's shoulders braced at what sounded like a veiled threat.

"*Why* do we have to accept their behavior without pushing back?" she said. "Isn't accepting it the same as giving them permission to attack us?"

Clark ignored Laura's questions and pointed to his oldest daughter. "Let's move on. Irene?"

"Our ratings are up, too," said Irene. "Take a look at this." She pulled up a table of figures on her laptop and transmitted it to one of the large monitors in the room. The others studied the information as she read statistics and financial data for her network, Taninger Entertainment.

"That's impressive," Clark commented.

"Since you recovered from losing the Pinnacle Awards, maybe you can ease up on attacking Laura," suggested Kate. Irene frowned at Kate's admonition.

"No thanks to Laura, I recovered. It's the new celebrity cooking show we started. Our viewers love getting recipes from their favorite stars and watching them cook the dishes in their own gorgeous kitchens. I'll tell you, this show is off the charts! Sponsors are lined up to support it," Irene reported.

"Very nice, Irene. Very nice," said Clark. "And Billie?"

"We negotiated with the manufacturer and installers to share in the cost of replacing the seating in the new stadium. That project's coming along, and it should be finished ahead of schedule. Our temporary venue for the Slammers is working out well. It's larger than our old stadium, and it's bringing in some nice revenue. Here, I'll show you." Billie posted numbers for Taninger Sports on the wall monitor.

"I'm glad you're doing better, Billie," said Laura.

"These numbers are better than I expected," Clark said, smiling and leaning back in his chair. Contentment was rare of late. "Thanks to Irene and Billie, Entertainment and Sports are managing to overcome losses they suffered from their recent . . . challenges." He glanced at Laura, his smile fading for an instant. "Despite all that's happened, things are going well for our corporation."

The news was greeted with an awkward silence. Like earthquake survivors wondering if an aftershock were imminent, the group looked wary.

"So we should be happy, right?" Kate asked tentatively.

"We cannot afford to be blindsided by another blow. We've weathered all the calamities we can handle for one year," said Clark.

Like the others, Laura felt uneasy. Were there tremors rumbling underground and about to break the surface? As if to reassure herself that their footing was still steady, she pulled up the latest news on her laptop, hoping she and her family would not be a part of it.

Billie loosened his tie and fidgeted nervously. "Would they *dare* hit us again?" he asked. "I mean, most of the media support the administration, and the public isn't exactly tuned into our issues, so would the Feds squeeze us even tighter and think they can get away with it?"

The group had no answer, only worried expressions.

"Oh, no!" Laura gasped, breaking the silence. "I'm afraid they would. I'm looking at the feed, and Taninger News is making headlines."

"What kind of headlines?" Billie leaned forward.

Laura displayed her news feed on a wall monitor. All heads turned to read it.

"What the hell's going on?" Clark read the titles of the latest headlines.

Is Taninger News a Media Monopoly?

The Growing Empire of Taninger News.

Is Taninger Manipulating News for Agenda?

"Look at this one just coming on," said Billie, reading the latest posting. "'Are Monopoly Charges Looming for Taninger News?'" He looked stunned. "*Monopoly charges?*"

The headlines floated through the room like fumes ready to explode.

Clark's voice was heavy with worry. "Laura, what's the meaning of this?"

Laura looked at her family, shocked and dismayed. "I fear it means that the Martin administration knows I took the Bureau of Elections to court. I petitioned Elections for the information they're withholding about a company called Integrated Foxworth Technologies that they apparently brought in through a no-bid contract to modify SafeVote. There's no evidence that such a company ever existed prior to this contract. Don't you see how serious this is?" her voice rose in an urgent call for her family to understand.

Laura continued, "I think these articles mean that I'm getting damn close to learning something the Feds don't want me to know. I think someone in the

Martin administration triggered this, and their friends in the media—who happen to be our competitors—are more than happy to run with these hit pieces."

"Are they just rumors to rattle us?" Clark interjected.

"I don't know," Laura replied. "But I think we can assume there are huge ramifications to the story I'm investigating, and they're trying to stop me. It's the hottest story about the most dangerous abuse of power in our time. And a whistleblower involved with it has already been killed." Her voice pleaded. "This latest attack means I'm hot on the trail of something big, and I can't stop now."

Clark bristled at Laura. "It means, you *must* stop. *Now!*"

"The man who started this company, who built this corporation, and who gave all of us our jobs—that man would want us to pursue this story," Laura insisted.

"That was then. Now things are different," said Irene.

"I think we all need to calm down," said Kate. "I think Martin's people and their media friends are just spreading rumors to make us look bad, so the public will question our credibility. We need to stick by Laura with this story, or do you want the nation's voting to be rigged?"

"Quiet!" Clark whirled to Kate. "You're not a member of management, young lady. You shouldn't even be allowed in here!"

Undeterred, Kate continued. "I don't think the Martin administration can risk hitting us with anything else. The public could turn against them. Our ratings show that we have a big following. President Martin can't risk overplaying his hand."

The others were silent, ruminating, as Kate started a search on her phone, tapping the screen several times, and read a display.

"Listen," Kate continued. "I just opened one of these stories. It says things like, 'according to anonymous sources' . . . 'rumors have it' . . . 'Taninger News may be overextending its reach, according to some in government' . . . It's all smoke. The media has nothing tangible to report, only innuendoes and suppositions that make good click bait."

"Maybe she's right," said Billie. "Maybe we are being a little paranoid."

"If Laura drops her crusade *right now*, maybe we'll be home free," said Irene.

Clark looked thoughtful. "Maybe these commentaries are just warning shots. If the administration is contemplating any action against us, maybe they'll back off—if we back off first, which we will." He looked pointedly at Laura. "You hear?"

Laura didn't reply.

Clark continued, "Once we get out of the election business, we'll be on our way to record profits and one of the strongest growth periods in our history! I have to say, I'm pleased with the financials. The corporation is strong. Every branch is growing."

"Let's not let Laura screw it up," chided Irene.

Just then the door opened. An assistant entered and walked to Clark.

"Excuse me. This just came in. I thought you'd want to see it." The aide handed a document to Clark and left.

Clark's eyes darted across the page. His body tensed. "It's from the Bureau of Fair Trade."

The others glanced at each other, concerned.

Clark held out to them the document that bore the Bureau's official seal. "So they *do* dare to strike us again! This is a complaint filed by the Bureau of Fair Trade against Taninger News. We are under investigation for having a disproportionate share of the media market, which they claim is in violation of federal anti-monopoly statutes."

"What!" Irene gasped.

"Hell, no!" Billie said, incredulous.

Kate closed her eyes for a moment in horrified disbelief.

Clark continued, "The Bureau says that the public is being harmed by our undue influence on the nation's media. I quote, 'On a monthly basis, Taninger News' national television station and expansive network of online sites and print publications reach over two-thirds of the American population, exposing the public to news from the biased perspective of one company. The media overreach from the company's broadcast, online, and print divisions hinders competition, which harms our democracy.'"

Clark held the document in one hand and wiped the sweat off his forehead with the other. He quickly read the rest to himself, put the document down, and addressed the others. "The Bureau of Fair Trade claims that in order for us to correct our allegedly unlawful dominance of the news media, Taninger News must divest itself of one or more of its divisions." Everyone looked mortified. "They say that having our three venues—television, print newspapers, and online news—constitutes a monopolistic threat to the public!"

Billie's face looked caught in a vise, with his eyes bulging and his jaw tight. "They can't get away with this! . . . Can they?"

"Damned if I know," Clark said with a shrug. "But I'll spend a few years of my life and millions in legal fees to find out!"

Irene grimaced with a sudden realization. "They *can* get away with it, and they *will*. It's just like what the Bureau of Fair Trade did to . . . Reed Miller."

"This is exactly what you deserve, the three of you!" Kate said, glaring at her father, Billie, and Irene.

"Shut up!" snapped Clark.

"You didn't want Laura to defend Reed. He was the competition. You wanted him to be crushed. Laura told all of you that someday it could happen to us, but you were so short-sighted, so totally unprincipled that you wouldn't stand with her. JT would've been ashamed of you!"

"One more word out of you and I'll ban you from these meetings!" Clark thundered, pointing at Kate. Then he turned to Laura. "Your show *has to end!*" he demanded.

"It's about time we pulled the plug on her!" said Irene.

Laura shot up and leaned across the table toward her critics.

"Dad, Irene, Billie," she said, taking a moment to look each of them in the eye, "I feel *terrible* about this. I feel horrible about how the Martin crowd's hatred of me is hurting you. But I'd feel a whole lot worse if we not only had to suffer these hits, but we gave up the fight. We have to expose whatever it is they're hell-bent on us not finding out. We can't stop now! I plead with you to stand by me and fight this." She looked at three faces that remained unmoved. "What have we always been at our core? A news organization whose mission is to find the truth and to hold those in power accountable! If we quit now, it means we've lost our core."

Clark stroked his chin. Irene pushed back a strand of hair. Billie looked blank. Only Kate showed an intensity in her eyes, as if she'd heard something important.

"Frankly, I couldn't care less about some lofty, la-di-da truth if it brings about the demise of our enterprise," said Clark. "Does anyone else care about Laura's crusade?"

"Not me," said Irene. "Billie?"

"It's gone way too far," Billie said to Laura. "Remember, we're in *business.* We need to leave the big issues and grandiose truths to others."

Clark stood up and leaned in to address Laura face-to-face across the table. "*Just the Truth* is going off the air, and *you're* going off with it!"

Irene chimed in, saying, "Tonight, you can tell your audience that it's your last appearance on *Just the Truth.* You're moving on to exciting new activities, so you'll be passing the baton to a new host with a fresh, new show. Make it all sound nice. Then get a guest host for a couple of weeks till you assemble the new programming, and you're all set."

"That's absurd, Irene. No one would believe it. Everyone would know we sold our souls and caved to political pressure!" Laura insisted.

"You'll do it nonetheless," Clark demanded. "You'll replace *Just the Truth* with a news show that has balanced programming and a non-polarizing host. *That's an order.*"

Laura stared at her father, speechless.

"That'll be the peace offering I'll take to the Feds. And we'll hope to hell I can persuade them to drop their plans to break us up!"

Then Clark grabbed the document from the agency charged with upholding fairness, and he stormed out.

That day, Laura remained in her office, deep in thought, leaving the show preparation to her staff. When they came in with questions—*We want Senator Frank to come on for a segment on stopping crime, okay? . . . Ed Smith can do a live report from the Capitol on the education bill coming up for a vote tonight, okay?*—Laura gave brief answers with the detachment of a sleepwalker.

The pain that gripped her since the executive management meeting that morning had only grown sharper. Was it right to continue her crusade? After her management partners—her family—were adamantly against it? Was it right to risk the breakup of Taninger News? Should she relent to her family's wishes? If she gave up the SafeVote matter, the Feds would probably drop the suit against Taninger News. That was exactly what Reed Miller did, he gave in to the pressure. He averted the breakup of his company, and he ended his problems with the Feds. Look at him today; he's still wealthy and successful. . . . *But is he happy?* she wondered.

Her concerned staff brought her lunch. She ate a few bites, then pushed the food aside.

"Laura, when will we get the opening?" Tom Shiner asked.

"It's coming," she replied.

What would she say in her Daily Memo? Her staff was waiting to load it into the teleprompter. She felt like someone trying to decide on her means of execution. Would she face the firing squad head-on, or jump off the roof and hit the pavement facedown?

She thought of all the people she was hurting. Even Katie! She painfully recalled the incredulity she saw on that sweet face. Then she thought of JT. He had told her that a company was like a person. To be the best that it could be, a business, like a person, had to have a purpose it aimed to achieve and the character to achieve it honorably. The purpose, he insisted, had to be something important, worthy . . . noble. She missed the proud tilt of his head when he said things like that to her. The newspaper business for him was a calling, a profound expression of both the goals he dedicated his life to and of his character—his honesty and valor—in achieving them.

Finally, she made her decision. In the breathless pace of a high speed train, she wrote her opening monologue, the words screeching and clanging from her thoughts to her keyboard.

Soon her words were stretching across the airwaves as she began the show.

"Good evening and welcome to *Just the Truth*. I'm Laura Taninger. Previously, we've discussed methods that we believe the Martin administration is using to suppress free speech. These methods have been largely *indirect*—delaying the release of information harmful to the government, and using favors, threats, smears, and regulations to harm the government's critics and businesses connected with them. Then, we discussed how the administration, in effect, condones violence when it hides behind organizations tied to its ideology and policies as these groups stage riots to bully and shut down political opponents. Now, the government is taking off the mask, dispensing with the friendly face, and bypassing the use of surrogates. Now, the government is doing its dirty work in full public view.

"The subject of my Daily Memo tonight is: *Tools of Silence: Shutting Down the Free Press.*" The camera moved in closer to her face. Her expression was solemn, her tone serious.

"In a flagrant abuse of power, the Bureau of Fair Trade has opened an investigation into Taninger News to determine whether it finds us to be a monopoly that needs to be broken up—due to our expansive audience reach through our electronic, print, and broadcast components. Funny, we've been in business for decades, yet Fair Trade has just now taken an interest in us. This is an attack on a successful company that serves *you*, our audience, and delivers its content through different modes so that you can decide how you want to receive your news. Because you select us as your news source, it's also an attack on your freedom and an attempt to hide the truth from you."

She spoke with a growing intensity. "This latest attack of the Martin administration on Taninger Enterprises is the most dangerous because it's a direct attempt to regulate a news organization. It's an explicit attack on freedom of the press."

She paused a moment to let the audience absorb her words.

"To silence Taninger News, the administration is arbitrarily enforcing antitrust laws, claiming that Taninger News does not serve the public good due to monopolistic practices. So you see, it's the government, not you the public, that gets to decide which companies are and are not serving what it deems to be your interest. All I know is, we're serving you, our audience, who freely choose us over our competitors, and we have not committed any crimes.

"Since the administration is accusing us of what they say are violations of the law, I have a few things that I accuse them of, as well.

"I accuse the Martin administration of intentionally delaying, stalling, and ignoring valid requests for information about its new voting program because it has something to hide.

"I accuse the administration of instigating media smears against me and my family in order to discredit me and destroy my reputation simply because I'm a political watchdog.

"I accuse the Martin administration of pressuring a would-be client of Taninger Entertainment—the Pinnacle Awards—and causing the cancelation of a lucrative contract.

"I accuse the administration of using unfair and capriciously enforced building regulations to thwart the opening of the new stadium for the DC Slammers, thereby causing financial losses and a public relations nightmare for Taninger Sports.

"I accuse the administration of being the secret instigator behind the recent riots at Collier University, which led to the expulsion of my sister, an honor student, who did nothing more than voice her opinion defending me in a student publication.

"I accuse the Martin administration of doing great harm to my family as a prelude to its most brazen move yet, which is to subvert our news organization and achieve its real goal: *the control of political speech.*

"I accuse the administration of engineering all of these abuses in order to silence me in my investigation of suspicious activities surrounding the SafeVote program.

"I accuse the administration of hiding from public view a major contractor—IFT—and the nature of that contractor's work on SafeVote."

She raised her head and took a deep breath, like someone bracing to land a final knock-out punch—or to receive one.

"I accuse the Martin administration of tampering with the upcoming presidential election."

Her staff in the control room looked at one other in shock. This line was not in the teleprompter. They did not know it was coming.

"If I'm wrong, then let the administration release the documents I've petitioned, which *you*, the people, are entitled to have. We want those documents. We want to see what's going on during this federal takeover of our election system."

She shook her head regretfully, like someone saddened by a weighty burden that she never wanted to carry. Her voice softened as she said, "There was once a temple called America. She stood proudly on her great pillars of freedom. Now, a corrupt and power-hungry administration is chipping away at those pillars, leaving America swaying." For a moment, she looked younger and more vulnerable as she led her viewers into her confidence. "I'm caught between the survival of my family's businesses and my controversy with the Martin administration. But as long as I'm here and you're here, my loyal audience, we'll do our own chipping away—at corruption and deceit—until we finally get to the bottom of this."

CHAPTER 19

Attorneys Sam Quinn and Emmett Wallace stood before the judge's bench in the wood-paneled courtroom. From the canvas on the wall, Lady Justice oversaw the scene. It was Monday morning, and the judge was about to give her decision in *Just the Truth* versus the Bureau of Elections.

Laura Taninger sat in the spectators' section of the quiet courtroom, her auburn hair fanned over her shoulders, her brown eyes wide and intelligent, her face serious.

The voluminous gown of Judge Marianne Rogers rustled as she entered carrying a folder.

"Good morning, Counselors." She took her seat and opened her file on the case. "I have decided that the plaintiff's claim is just and should be fulfilled expeditiously."

Sam Quinn's face brightened.

"However, the Bureau of Elections does indeed have exceptional circumstances for its delay, granted its unusual workload in getting the new voting system ready in time for Election Day," the judge continued.

Emmett Wallace's face brightened.

"I, therefore, rule that *Just the Truth* has not yet exhausted its administrative remedies."

Wallace broke into a smile while Quinn frowned.

"I'm going to give the Bureau of Elections more time to hand over the requested documents to *Just the Truth*. With that, I'm dismissing the case *without prejudice*. If Elections is not forthcoming with the requested documents within the next ten working days, I recommend that *Just the Truth* seek judicial review at that time."

Laura closed her eyes in defeat. The strike of Judge Rogers's gavel sounded like a door slamming in her face.

Later that day, Laura watched Sean Browne's daily presidential briefing on her office monitor. He faced an array of microphones at his lectern, a cluster of camera operators hovering on one side of the room, and rows of reporters with pads on their laps sitting before him.

After reviewing the president's itinerary and various news items of the day, he opened the briefing up for questions. He looked as if he dreaded it, but knew he had to call on Vita Simpson.

"Sean," Vita began in her spirited tone and self-confident manner, "as you know, the Bureau of Fair Trade has opened an investigation of Taninger News as a monopoly. The activities of Taninger News have been going on for years, yet just now, when Laura Taninger has voiced persistent criticism of SafeVote, Fair Trade decides to take this action. How can this not be meant to intimidate the free press? How can this not be a serious abuse of power?"

"Let me put your mind at rest, Vita," he said in a patronizing tone, smiling as he spoke. "The People's Manor categorically denies any association or interface with the investigative activities at the Bureau of Fair Trade." He periodically glanced down at his notes as if referring to his pre-assigned talking points. "You have to realize that the Bureau of Fair Trade has thousands of attorneys that handle a multitude of cases every year. If the practices at Taninger News are among their many inquiries, you'll have to ask Fair Trade about that. We would have no knowledge at all of their investigations."

Laura fumed.

The day seemed longer than usual for Laura as she turned off her computer, rose from her chair, and swung the strap of her purse over her shoulder. Her show was over for the night, and her staff was leaving. She waved to her producer Tom Shiner as he headed out of the control room. Still feeling the pain that had gripped her three days ago—when she had learned that the Bureau of Fair Trade was suing Taninger News—she closed the door of her office and slowly, dejectedly walked to the elevator.

She hailed a cab and gave the driver her home address. Leaning back in her seat, she opened the news feed on her phone and entered James Spenser's name in a search. She could find no new information from law enforcement on his killer, who remained at large and unidentified. The media had lost interest in the case, with nary a news item about it appearing in weeks. The *Taninger News* reporter that she had following the case also had nothing more to report about the investigation since the first news conference the police had held shortly after Spenser's death.

It occurred to Laura that there had been no news coverage of Kate or Collier University in the four days since the protestors had disbanded. She was relieved that Kate was no longer the target of rioters and their enablers, but the media had been *almost too quiet* about this issue. The People's Manor, she knew, fed their cadre of sympathetic journalists daily talking points, virtually writing these journalists' stories for them, so the administration had also gone silent on the matter. Her suspicions heightened.

She searched the news feed for articles relating to Kate, the protests at Collier University, and the Foundation that had spearheaded the demonstrations, but she found no mentions in the main news stories of the day. Then, she looked deeper, and a small piece caught her attention.

In an obscure section of the news feed that hardly anyone would read, Laura found a terse announcement from the People's Manor: Jack Anders, the director of the Foundation to Enrich Student Life, had been appointed the Assistant Secretary of Education for the Martin Administration.

The next day, the airport bustled with people. Many were traveling for business that weekday in early October, walking briskly along the terminal with attaché cases or working on laptops at the gates as they waited to board. Laura headed toward her gate. When she approached it, she stopped in mid-stride, surprised to see someone holding one of those attaché cases, a man she hadn't expected to be there.

"Sam, you're *not* coming!" Laura declared.

The attorney for Taninger Enterprises looked odd without his suit and tie, dressed in jeans and ready for a long flight. Outside the terminal window, the transatlantic jetliner that Laura was about to board sat at the gate.

"How could Sharon book you a seat without clearing it with me?"

"Easy. I told her you authorized it," Sam Quinn replied. "And I got the seat next to yours."

Someone listening to them argue would not have been able to determine who was the boss and who the subordinate. The combination of bluntness and affection in their voices made their argument sound more like a family squabble between a father and daughter.

"Sam, my father has already threatened to fire you for helping me. If he finds out you went to Ireland with me, *you'll be creamed for sure.*"

"I'm *not* letting you go there alone. Someone involved in this matter has already been *killed.* You're not to forget that!"

Despite her anger, she smiled. For one disarming moment, she felt like an abandoned child who had found a protector.

After Judge Rogers gave the Bureau of Elections more time to turn over documents, stalling the probe of Integrated Foxworth Technologies once again, Laura had arranged for a guest host to fill in for her on *Just the Truth*.

That way she could travel to Ireland to continue her investigation in the country where the contractor's business was registered.

When she had informed her father of her plans, he'd still been reeling from the shock of her Daily Memo on the previous Friday.

Clark had said, "If your guest host works out, that can be our new prime-time anchor. You can stay in Ireland, marry a nice Irishman, and write me a letter now and then!"

Only the childless Sam showed her any paternal fondness and concern.

"Besides, uncovering information about the elusive IFT could be easier if you have an attorney with you," Sam observed.

"I'll hire a lawyer there if I need one."

"You have one."

"But I don't want you to come with me."

"JT would've wanted me to."

"JT's been gone for two years. He's no longer your boss."

"For thirty years before that, he was."

With pursed lips and crossed arms, she faced the man self-appointed as her guardian and grandfather incarnate. "Sam, I'm not getting on this plane unless you leave the airport right now!"

Shortly thereafter, Sam was sipping a cocktail onboard, and Laura was sitting next to him, reading reports from her management staff. The plane took off with the sun setting behind them. After handling a few business matters, Laura strategized throughout the flight. She had a lot to do when she arrived. Then she slept briefly before the pilot announced that they were approaching Dublin. The plane landed with the sun rising ahead of them on a new day.

After checking into their hotel, they ventured out into the city's medley of steel buildings and stone castles, cable bridges and cobblestone streets, loud pubs and age-old cathedrals. They took a taxi to Dublin's civic center, where its administrative offices were located.

Their steps echoed on the tiled lobby of a modern office building as they walked across the entryway and down a corridor to a door marked Office of Business Registry. After giving their business cards to a clerk behind one of the counters, someone was sent to escort them into an office, where Laura and Sam were greeted by a cheerful, bow-tied man. With a sprightly step he rose from his desk and walked up to them.

"I'm Adam McCarthy, the Director of the Registry. How'd you do?" he said, bowing slightly.

Laura and Sam shook hands with him.

"Nice to meet you, Mr. McCarthy," said Laura.

"Thank you for seeing us," added Sam.

"Please, have a seat." He gestured for them to sit on the couch in a small sitting area of the office while he closed the door and sat on an easy chair facing them. "I've heard of you, Ms. Taninger. Your broadcasts reach us, and our tabloids carry stories of your political intrigues," he said with a chuckle.

I always wanted to be the queen of the tabloids, Laura thought as she smiled politely.

Sam began, "We were hoping you could help us with a matter—"

"I say, when we recently updated our systems, our office made news *here*, but to have us checked out by the *American press*, well, that's a bit of a surprise," he said excitedly. "With our new procedures, businesses can now register in Ireland in record time. Americans who form businesses here say it's a lot easier, and there are many other advantages to setting up here rather than in the States. So we open our doors to coverage by your press to attract more businesses our way—"

"Mr. McCarthy, I'm afraid we're here about another matter," interjected Sam.

"Oh?" His exuberance tempered.

"We're here to find out all we can about a company registered here called Integrated Foxworth Technologies," Laura added.

"Oh." Their host frowned disappointedly. Then he shrugged, seeming to make the best of it. "Of course, we can help you with that."

"We looked the company up in your public records, but the information there was limited. So we came in person to see if there was anything more you could tell us," said Sam.

"We can call up a complete file on a business in a matter of seconds. What did you say the name was?"

Laura repeated the name as the official rose and opened the door. He called to an assistant outside. "See what we have on Integrated Foxworth Technologies for our American visitors."

The assistant soon appeared, handed her boss a document of several pages, then left the room.

"Have a look," Adam McCarthy said, offering the information to his guests.

Laura took the material and read the first page. "The company name is Integrated Foxworth Technologies, and the president's name is Frank Foxworth, which we already know. He's an American. The business was registered here six months ago. There's a street address and phone number for the headquarters in Dublin." She thumbed through the subsequent pages, then looked up. "But Mr. McCarthy, there's nothing else here."

She handed the material to Sam, who examined it.

"I see that most of the information asked for on the form was left blank," Sam said. The face of their host reddened. "Mr. McCarthy, there are no names of any other principals, no board members, no company description, no profile, and no operating documents. No bank accounts or mortgages are listed—nothing."

"That can't be!" said McCarthy.

"See for yourself," Sam said, handing him the document.

The official thumbed through the pages in disbelief.

"This is bloody unacceptable!"

"I'd like to try the phone number, if I may," said Laura. McCarthy showed her the number on the form. She took out her phone and dialed.

"Oh, no," she said. "There's an announcement. The phone number is not in service."

McCarthy rolled the report into a cylinder and nervously tapped it against the palm of his hand. "This Mr. Foxworth, whoever he is, fancies he can just do as he pleases. Well, I shan't let him get away with this. His company will be removed from our list for failure to comply with the requirements of this agency! He'll be enjoying no corporate liability protection or any other benefits from us!"

"Mr. McCarthy?" Sam spoke softly, testing whether the official was finished.

"I need more money and staff to catch these rascals! They go to a St. Paddy's Day Parade in the States and—poof!—they pop in here and think we're all fun and games. I need more power!"

"Mr. McCarthy?" Sam tried again.

"Yes?"

"Is there anything else you can tell us about Integrated Foxworth Technologies?"

"I'll check."

He left the office to confer with his assistant. When he returned, he said, "Unfortunately, there's nothing more we have on them!"

"Well, then, thank you for your time," Laura said, as she and Sam rose to go.

"Is *this* where you want to be dropped?" the taxi driver asked skeptically.

Sam consulted the map he had pulled up on his phone and said, "This is the address all right." He looked at Laura and shrugged.

The two of them exited the taxi in a run-down area of the city and walked toward the building that was listed as the corporate headquarters of Integrated Foxworth Technologies. It was an abandoned office building.

Laura and Sam paused to observe the blighted site. The concrete steps at the entrance were cracked and littered with debris. The white stone facade was covered with layers of soot. The three stories of windows contained many panels that were cracked, missing, or boarded.

"This can't be it," said Laura.

"But it is," said Sam.

Laura took pictures with her phone throughout their visit, so she had evidence to present back home.

They walked through a gaping hole under an arch that once held a door. Inside there was a wide expanse of emptiness, with cubicle dividers tossed aside, along with smudged chairs, dented file cabinets, dilapidated desks, and more debris—all of it forming obstacles in their path. Laura and Sam looked around dumbfounded. A trip up the stairway displayed empty offices, paint peeling off the walls, mounds of dust, and more discarded furniture. They opened desk drawers and file cabinets but found nothing.

When they returned to the main floor, their voices echoed in the hollow cavity of the building.

"Looks like no one's inhabited this place in years," said Laura. "Since IFT is only six months old, we can be sure it's *never* done any business from here."

"Right," said Sam. "This is just a front."

"This is a *huge* story!"

"It is." Sam nodded, his face a mixture of anger and disgust.

"What are the Feds covering up?"

"We'll find out."

"Let's call up the property records on this place," said Laura, as they stood outside, waiting for a taxi they had called to pick them up.

With her phone, she searched for the records on the abandoned building. "The local Property Deeds Authority has a public record on it," she said. Answering a few prompts, she found the title information. "It was purchased six months ago by Integrated Foxworth Technologies in a cash transaction. The seller was a real estate developer named Gallagher Properties. I have their address. I'll call for an appointment."

"How'd you do?" Keith Gallagher, the president of Gallagher Properties, greeted Laura and Sam. "Please, have a seat."

"Thank you for seeing us on such short notice," said Laura.

"Not every day that a major figure in the American press pops in for a chat, Ms. Taninger."

Gallagher had the cool blue eyes of a savvy businessman and the unsmiling face of a cautious one. His trim body held the vigor of youth, while his graying hair suggested years of business experience.

"What can I do for you?" Gallagher asked, sitting behind his desk, facing the visitors.

Sam explained, "We're looking for information about the buyer of a building you sold about six months ago." Sam gave him the buyer's name and the street address of the property.

Gallagher sat at his desk, looking at them with a tinge of suspicion. He made no attempt to look up any records on his computer or consult a staff member about the matter.

"Do you remember the transaction, Mr. Gallagher?" asked Laura.

"All the details are with the public deeds office, so I'm afraid I have to refer you there to look it up."

"We already have. We wondered if you had anything more you could tell us about the buyer," said Sam.

"I never met the buyer. The transaction was handled by my solicitor."

"And that would be Rebecca Doyle, whose name is on the record?"

"Quite right."

"Mr. Gallagher," said Sam, "the company that bought that abandoned building from you and claims that address as its headquarters is now doing a big job for the United States government. We visited the building and saw that it's been long abandoned. The Foxworth firm has not set up shop there at all." Sam leaned forward, trying to reach the detached Keith Gallagher. "Do you have any idea what Integrated Foxworth Technologies was going to do with that building? Why they were buying it? Who they are? Or where we might find them?"

"None at all."

"The sale price was listed at several times the amount you paid for the property just a short time earlier," said Laura. "So I thought you might remember some details of what was such a good deal for you."

What Laura intended as a benign comment had unwittingly hit a hot button. Keith Gallagher's eyebrows arched, and his voice became testy.

"You want to know, do you? Right, I made a killing on that piece of crap of a building. The previous owner was desperate to sell it, and I squeezed him for quite a good deal. Then, when I went to flip it, along comes a buyer with no business head at all, who pays my first, outrageous asking price. That's what I do." He flashed a gloating smile. "I buy low and sell high, and I'm brilliant at it." He cocked his head, observing his guests curiously. "Tell me, why does the media slam me for what I do? I'll never understand it. I've been called greedy, callous, unfeeling, anti-social—everything but *successful.*"

"Not by me, you haven't," said Laura. "I'm in business, too. I'm not here to do a story on you or slam you in any way."

"But you media types have a nasty way of spinning things."

"Our business here has *nothing* to do with you," Sam said forcefully. "It's all about Foxworth. That's who we're focused on."

"Regardless, you're still *the press,* and while I'm obliged to deal with you newspeople because I'm in business, I rather try to dodge your inquiries whenever

I can." He smiled pleasantly to soften the dressing-down. Then he rose to end the meeting. "Frankly, I don't know anything about the buyer, so I really can't help you even if I wanted to."

As Laura and Sam were leaving, Gallagher made a final comment. "If you do find the purchaser, I hope you won't give him a dose of buyer's remorse. I have a no-returns policy."

The next taxi took them to a modern business section of the city, where they entered a building and located the office of Ryan, Byrne, and Doyle, Solicitors. They entered a carpeted, well-furnished waiting area, and gave their cards to the receptionist behind the counter.

Laura's name and company once again were recognized—and this time warmly received.

"You're Laura Taninger!" said the receptionist. "I watch your show all the time! Many of us keep up with your investigations. It's lovely to meet you."

The receptionist vanished into an inner sanctum; then she reappeared, saying, "Erin Smith will be out to see you straight away, Ms. Taninger." Poor Sam remained unnoticed.

Soon an attractive woman in a business suit approached them, extending her hand.

"I'm Erin Smith," she said, "the legal secretary to Ms. Doyle."

She escorted them into her small but well-organized office. "Keith Gallagher rang us, so I know why you're here. He wishes us to keep the details of his property deals confidential, which we would do anyway. Ms. Doyle asked me to tell you that regrettably she can't meet with you or provide any more information."

Laura and Sam prodded, but Erin Smith stood her ground. "I'm sure you understand, we respect our client's confidentiality."

After the legal secretary escorted them back to the lobby, Laura and Sam lingered in the reception area until Ms. Smith returned to her office.

Laura walked to the receptionist's desk, where she received a broad smile from the young woman manning it.

"Say, what's your name?" Laura asked the receptionist.

"Anna," she said cheerfully. She appeared to be in her early twenties, with the unjaded look of someone who expects life to be an exciting adventure. Her silky hair, intelligent eyes, and animated face reminded Laura of Kate.

"I'm so happy you watch my show, Anna!"

Sam took a seat in the room, leaving the two women to converse.

"You're the reporter who gets in trouble," Anna said admiringly.

"Is that what your press says about me?"

"And a bit more. They can be quite cheeky."

"But you like my show, don't you?"

"Love the way you stir things up. We need some of that here."

"That's how a reporter thinks. Did you ever think of becoming a reporter?"

"Oh, that would be absolutely fantastic! I always wanted to do something big with my life. Instead, here I am stuck working the front desk for my aunt, Ms. Doyle, and her partners."

"Ah, working with family. I certainly can relate," said Laura.

"I appreciate the job, but Aunt Rebecca knows I'm only biding time here until I find something more . . . exciting."

"Anna, maybe you can help us with some reporting. We're just trying to get a little basic information about how you do things here."

"Sure."

"We're interested in how foreign real estate deals work."

"We do quite a lot of them here."

"For example, we have this deal your firm did with Integrated Foxworth Technologies, a company set up by an American named Frank Foxworth. The firm bought a building from your client, Gallagher Properties."

Anna immediately keyed the information into her computer, and a screen of data came up.

"Yes," she said. "I have the record here. This part of the transaction is public information, so I'm sure there's no harm in explaining it to you."

"How do these deals work?"

"When we represent the seller in a property sale to a foreign buyer, we rarely ever meet the other party. We talk on the phone and send documents for signing electronically. We represent our client, transact the sale, provide the buyer with the deed, and collect our fee. In this case, our client, Gallagher Properties, received a cash payment from the buyer, Integrated Foxworth Technologies, so there was even less interaction, with no mortgage involved."

"Anna, we tried to get information on the solicitor that the Foxworth firm used in the transaction, but we could track down nothing other than his name. Can you tell us anything about the buyer's solicitor?"

"Most probably. I have a directory of solicitors," Anna said eagerly. "The buyer's solicitor is indicated right here in the transaction record . . . a Peter J. Sullivan and Company."

She typed the name on her keyboard, and a table of solicitors appeared on her computer screen.

"That's odd," said Anna. She looked at Laura, puzzled. "There's no listing in the data base for any Peter J. Sullivan and Company. There's no address, no phone number, no record of any kind. I've never seen that before. Here, let me look further." She did another search. "Funny, there's no website for him, either."

Another dead end! thought Laura. *The abandoned building, the fake phone number, and now the phantom solicitor.*

"This is quite peculiar, Ms. Taninger. It's like a mystery is at work here."

"Yes," said Laura.

"I wish I could help you unravel it."

Laura smiled fondly at the eager young woman. She took out a business card. "Anna, if you think the news business might be a field with the excitement you're looking for, contact me. *Taninger News* has a team of international reporters, some of whom are based here, and I'd love to help a woman who is clearly a journalist at heart."

Anna placed the card in her palm and peered at it as if it were a jewel. "Oh my, that would be too massive a payment for me for trying to help you, which I didn't succeed at anyway."

"It's not for helping me. It's for being smart and earnest and having a desire to unravel mysteries. Journalism needs what you have."

Anna looked as if she had just learned something about herself that she hadn't realized before, something important that lifted her face with pride.

"Email your resume to me," Laura suggested.

"I certainly will! Do you really think I could . . . do something important . . . like you do . . . someday?"

"I absolutely do think so."

Laura and Sam remained in Ireland another day, trying to find out more information about Frank Foxworth and Integrated Foxworth Technologies, but as in America, they uncovered no trace of the man, his company, or any business dealings in the country where the firm was registered.

On their flight back to America, they encountered turbulence. Their cabin was rocked by a capricious wind, while the massive engines prevailed in plying through the disturbance and keeping them safely on course. Fastened in her seat, Laura thought of the headwinds she would face when she returned with her incredible story. What was the engine driving *her* through the turmoil?

Even as a child, Laura had taken things seriously. She never remembered a time in her life when she had accepted injustice. Whether it was a school friend being bullied, her grandfather being falsely attacked, or . . . Reed Miller getting shafted by the government, she had always fought to right the wrongs she saw. Now, she was more determined than ever to stay the course.

When the air steadied, she and Sam ordered drinks and discussed the matter.

"So now we find out that Integrated Foxworth Technologies is a company that has no physical location, no phone number, no records of any kind in the country where it's registered or in America. And this company did updates and patches to SafeVote. This has to be the company that aroused James Spenser's suspicions," Laura said in summary.

"And James Spenser is now dead," Sam added.

"Sam, this is a huge scandal. When I go back and tell Irene, Billie, and my father what we uncovered, they've got to give me their support. They can't ignore this!" She sipped her drink, leaned back, and continued, "The untraceable contractor, the stalls, the attacks on me, the strong-arm tactics against my family—the unsolved murder of James Spenser—all point to something more sinister than a case of patronage or embezzlement. What we're up against is something else."

"Yeah, like a carefully calculated plan to . . . *rig* . . . the presidential election," Sam concluded.

She nodded grimly. "I'll call a special executive management meeting to let my family know what we discovered."

She took out her phone and was about to send a message to her father and siblings. "Wait, I have an email from headquarters that's marked 'urgent.'" She scrolled down the message, her face reflecting new shocks.

"What is it, Laura?" Sam seemed alarmed at the sudden dread on her face.

"Sam, I'm being notified that the board of directors is holding a meeting on Monday, and I'm required to appear to—*What?*" She reread the message. "I'm required to appear to *defend* myself." She dropped the phone into her lap and looked at Sam. "The topic is whether or not I should be removed as president of Taninger News."

CHAPTER 20

Clark Taninger sat at the head of a conference table with his assistant Caroline Davis at his side. The table was set for seven participants, with a water bottle, pad, and pen by each place. When everyone had arrived, Clark began.

"Monday, October 16, the meeting of the Taninger Enterprises Board of Directors will come to order. I thank you all for coming," he said, his tone solemn.

Clark continued, "We have in attendance the seven directors. They include the presidents of our three divisions—Irene Taninger of Taninger Entertainment, William Taninger of Taninger Sports, and Laura Taninger of Taninger News. Also joining us are the president of Longfield Investments and trustee for shareholder Kate Taninger, Erica Longfield; the legal counsel for Taninger Enterprises, Sam Quinn; and the vice president of Washington National Bank, Bert Franklin. As the chairman of the board and president of Taninger Enterprises, I will preside."

He gestured to his assistant. "Caroline Davis will record the minutes and assist us."

Clark turned his head to the sound of the door opening.

"Katie, you know you're *not* supposed to be here!" Clark said, scowling. "According to your grandfather's will, your shares are kept in trust until your twenty-first birthday with your trustee voting for you in the interim. You'll have to leave!"

"It's not in the will that I can't *sit here*, is it?" Within seconds, Kate had closed the door behind her, pulled an extra seat in the room up to the table next to her trustee, removed her jacket, sat, and opened her laptop. She was not going anywhere.

Clark huffed. He cleared his throat. He looked uneasy but determined to execute an unpleasant task.

Clark returned to his opening remarks, saying, "The reason for our meeting is to take a vote on whether Laura Taninger should be removed as president of Taninger News."

Clark eyed the grim faces around the table. He wondered why they sat where they did, as though a battle of wills were forming, with his ally and banker Bret Franklin sitting with Irene and Billie on one side of the table, and Laura, Sam Quinn, and Kate with her trustee Erica Longfield on the other side.

"Everyone should have received a folder of information that I had Caroline prepare describing our recent controversies with Laura, including the minutes of our executive management meetings and a transcript of the monologues from her show that we find objectionable. Laura and Sam Quinn also added a document to the folder that brings us up to speed on the latest developments in the investigation that's in question."

The directors nodded. They had all brought their folders and placed them on the table.

"Especially for Bert and Erica, who come from outside the company, this information was meant to brief you on the situation."

"I received the documents and read through them, Clark," said Bert Franklin. He was a banker who *looked* like a banker, mid-sixties with an expensive suit. His measured tone had always instilled confidence—and sometimes fear.

"Clark, I also read through everything you sent," added Erica Longfield, a handsome woman in her fifties with a serious yet kind face.

"First, those with charges against Laura will make their case," Clark continued. "Then, Laura and any other directors wishing to defend her will get their turn to speak on her behalf. Lastly, Caroline will distribute a confidential ballot and assist us with the vote-taking." He eyed the group. Everyone sat still and expressionless. "Who wants to start?"

"I will," said Irene.

Laura observed her older sister and first accuser from across the table. She and Irene had never been close. Growing up, the girls had chosen different kinds of friends, life styles, and priorities. Irene had numerous acquaintances that she calls "friends." On the other hand, Laura had a much smaller circle that included people she knew she could count on—people who were contemplative and discussed important issues and ideas. Irene barely noticed JT, whereas Laura spent a lot of time with him. Irene seemed too frivolous to Laura, and Laura seemed too serious to Irene. In the past, they had gone their separate ways, and Laura had considered Irene innocuous.

For the past two years, their business and financial interests had been intertwined by virtue of their grandfather's will. They had been thrust into dealing with each other. No longer a harmless sister, Irene had become a dangerous rival. To Laura, eyeing Irene across the conference table, her sister's long red nails looked like flesh-tearing claws. Her black outfit and stagy makeup added to her vampiric look.

Irene began, "Laura's war against Ken Martin and his signature program, SafeVote, caused Taninger Entertainment to lose the most lucrative and prestigious contract we've ever had—the Pinnacle Awards. I'd worked on that deal for months, and when it fell through, my network lost millions of dollars in sponsorships. But that isn't even the worst of it. Celebrities and public figures who are friends of the president now avoid me. I'm being excluded from their circles, whereas before I used to attend frequent parties here, in New York, and in Los Angeles. I was so popular! Everyone wanted me to attend their parties and speak at their events. Now, I'm avoided, ignored, and *shunned*. Laura's bias against our president has caused me public humiliation and harmed my business!"

With a fingernail tapping on the table, punctuating her words, Irene concluded, "In her obsession with SafeVote, Laura has turned Taninger News into a bash-Ken-Martin network. She says she only cares about getting at the truth in her investigation. I think the more important question is: *Do we want to alienate the most powerful and influential people in our country, and what will that get us?*"

Irene was at the edge of her chair, almost standing. When finished, she sank back into her seat. Billie looked at his father and raised a finger to be called on.

"Thank you, Irene," said Clark. "Billie, you're next."

The loose-tied, athletic-looking businessman sighed deeply, then began, saying, "I don't want to talk against Laura, so this isn't easy. But we're at a point where it's necessary." His voice held sadness, with no sign of anger or malice. "In a sudden move that can't be explained except as a retaliation against Laura, one of President Martin's agencies made huge trouble for us at Taninger Sports. Building Safety's eleventh-hour decision to smack a regulatory violation on us that delayed the opening of the Slammers' new stadium cost us plenty. The financial damage and the scramble to find a new venue was bad enough, but that wasn't all. The public relations hit was hell. We were demonized as a shady, greedy corporation, just out to make a quick buck and public safety be damned. That's the kind of smear campaign we've had to battle."

He looked at Laura with a fondness he couldn't hide, and the gesture brought her back to their childhood, when he was her big brother, sometimes teasing, oftentimes protective, always making her laugh.

"Even our little sister Kate has been the victim of vicious attacks that also can only be traced to retaliation against Laura," Billie said. "Kate was expelled from college, with her future in turmoil. I'm sorry, Laura, but the trouble doesn't end—it just gets worse. This can't stand!"

He looked directly at Laura, his face sincere.

Billie continued, "We need to *narrow* our focus, stick to day-by-day business matters, stay out of the limelight, and not try to cure all the injustices in society. Laura's crusade conflicts with the interests of the other divisions and even with her own news organization. If only she'd adopt a more balanced way to report the news, we wouldn't seem so single-minded. If only she'd avoid the shocks and scandals, as we've asked her to do repeatedly, we wouldn't be a target for her political enemies. But she won't. That's not her. Laura is Laura, and business is business. Business needs to be pragmatic and not so high-minded and idealistic." Wrapping up, he looked at his father and said, "That's my view."

"Thank you, Billie. Now, I'll add my thoughts." Clark took a sip of water, surveyed his attentive audience, and began.

"Since our company was founded by my father, Julius Taninger, times have radically changed. In his day, when JT smelled misdeeds, corruption, and wrongdoing by the people in power, he eviscerated them with impunity. The most powerful politicians in the country—up to and including the president of the United States—feared his editorials. He was quoted widely and had tremendous impact. Many hated him, smeared him, and tried to destroy him, but none could. In JT's day, the private sector enjoyed more freedom, a greater influence with the people, a higher standing in public opinion, and less control from the state.

"But now, there's significantly more control over our businesses that we have to deal with. Look at what the Martin administration can do to us! They can get their congressional allies to influence Irene's clients and sponsors by dangling the threat of new laws and taxes on their industry; they can shut down our new stadium; they can force the expulsion of our Katie from college; and now . . . " His face reddened. Veins appeared across the taut skin on his forehead. "Now, they can invoke some rule or other about monopolistic practices to literally break up our company. They can force us to spend millions of dollars defending ourselves in the courts. They can profoundly influence the media and turn public opinion against us. All the tools are in their hands—federal agencies, media competitors, and academia. We can't win."

He shook his head in despair. He rose from his seat, paced, and raised his voice to the group.

"Today, *we're* perceived as bad. Companies are the villains, and the government is the savior. So many people now accept this viewpoint that these perceptions become their reality." He turned to Laura and said, "Even your idol, Reed Miller, gave in. And today, he's one of the richest men in the world. So here's the choice we face: Either we compromise, engage in give-and-take, and go silent on this investigation, or Taninger Enterprises will be *destroyed*."

The directors listened intently. Their eyes followed Clark as he paced.

"Laura was told multiple times to drop the investigation that's giving the administration heartburn. But she has steadfastly refused."

He paused to invite an apology from Laura, but she volunteered none.

"So there's no alternative but to relieve Laura of her control of Taninger News. That's my position."

Clark sank into his chair and said, "Before we hear from Laura, does anyone else want to speak?"

Kate stood up to address the group.

"Not you!" her father scolded. "You're *not* a director, and your trustee has no obligation to vote according to your wishes! Erica votes for your best *interest*, which might not be the same as your *wishes*. As we well know from your recent problems at Collier, your inclinations can be self-destructive."

Kate waited for Clark's reproach to end. Then, undeterred, she said, "JT gave me equal shares with every other family member, so he must've wanted me to have my say." Her hair was tied in a pony tail that swayed with her movements, giving her a youthful look, while her poise and self-confidence suggested a formidable future executive.

"Ever since mom died when I was nine, Laura has been like a mother to me. Laura was nineteen and the closest to me in age. She was still in school and had the most time to spend with me, while Billie and Irene were already working in the company. Laura instilled in me a lot of confidence. Whenever I was facing something hard, like a challenge in sports or a subject I thought I wasn't good at in school, she boosted my spirits. She was always sure I could do whatever I set my mind to, if I worked hard at it, and she made me believe it, too. This trust in myself spilled into everything I did and into my thoughts and opinions, too. Laura taught me not to shy away from doing tough things or taking tough stands.

"My editorials in the *Collier Voice* were my way of standing up for what I believe. I was shocked when bullies tried to shut me down. But I was even more shocked when the school administration didn't defend me. They totally caved.

"Now bullying tactics are being used against our company. Threats, intimidation, and downright thuggish maneuvers are being used to shut us down. Are we going to throw away everything a news organization stands for in fear of those in power?

"Are we going to buckle to this? If you fire Laura, you'll be acting like Collier did when it expelled me. *You'll be cowards, all of you!*"

Kate sat down. The group stared at her poker-faced. Only Laura looked proud of the words Kate uttered—and the person she was.

"Anyone else?" asked Clark.

"I'd like to speak," said Sam Quinn, his baritone voice a contrast to Kate's high notes. "I was the legal counsel for JT and Taninger Enterprises for thirty years. JT was always so alive. His face was always so animated. He had an inexhaustible energy. He thrived on his work. I can tell you that to JT journalism was not just a job. It was a holy quest. JT spoke truth to power just as routinely as he brushed his teeth. That, to him, was a noble cause. The way he practiced journalism took courage and independence. He always told me, 'We don't swim with the tide.' JT was the David at whose feet many a Goliath fell.

"In the report Laura and I provided, you can see that Laura is onto something big. What could be more important than the integrity of our election process? There's fraud going on in SafeVote—with a sham contractor working in the shadows and getting a huge payment—and the administration is pulling out all the stops to prevent us from finding out what's going on! The stakes couldn't be higher."

Sam's eyes scanned the room, stopping to look directly at each one of the participants. "If we betray Taninger News—by firing its heart and soul, which is what Laura is—we won't be a news organization any more. Not according to JT's definition. We'll not only swim with the tide, we'll sink with it, too."

Sam nodded to Clark, signaling he was finished.

"Thank you. Would anyone else like to speak?" Clark paused to survey the group. No one took the offer. "Okay, Laura, it's your turn."

Laura stood and faced her accusers.

"I'm heartbroken that I'm being used as a weapon to harm our company and family," she said. "I never would want to hurt any of you or Taninger Enterprises. But I have to respond to the reasons you gave for firing me.

"First, Taninger News has various straight news programs without opinion. My show, *Just the Truth*, is labeled as commentary, although a lot of what I cover *is* straight news, *before* I give my opinion of it. So it's not the case that we give biased, partisan, or slanted coverage—meaning coverage not rooted in reality. We present commentary based on facts. We evaluate evidence from the standpoint that we value liberty and strive to keep government in check. This is all totally valid for a news organization to do; indeed, it's our job to do this.

"The Bureau of Fair Trade charges that what we're doing is not in the public interest. What public are we talking about? The public that doesn't want factual reporting and evidence-based opinion? What our accusers really mean is that our reporting is not in the interest of the powerful people we're criticizing. We have to call them out on that. We need to fight back!" said Laura.

She looked around the room. Most of the directors did not look eager to take on the mighty Bureau of Fair Trade.

"Next, I'll turn to the other issues raised against me," Laura said, looking at her older sister. "It can't be right, Irene, that we should make getting along with powerful and influential people a higher goal than our obligation to report and comment on the news. All of our divisions should accept the importance of this sacred trust. Our audience expects Taninger News to investigate and report on important issues, regardless of whose feathers that ruffles.

"And it can't be right, Billie, that we should shy away from moral issues and silo ourselves into day-to-day business matters. Moral issues profoundly affect our day-to-day business. We're under attack, and we have a right and an obligation to defend ourselves. We can't leave it to the academics or the clergy, and hope they'll defend us. Questions of what's honest and fair and true and right are everybody's concern.

"And Dad, it can't be right to say that times have changed, so we must adjust or die. Why do we have to adjust to corruption, smears, and strong-arm tactics used against us in a flagrant abuse of power? The opposite is true. If we cave, we'll die. If we don't fight this, we'll lose our souls.

"And it's not just our company that's on the chopping block. There's a huge scandal and cover-up going on regarding SafeVote. I believe—and Sam agrees—that an attempt is being made to rig the presidential election. Our country—our right to vote in a free and honest election, which safeguards all of our rights—is on the chopping block."

"We've been through this, Laura," Clark said, interrupting her. "Even if there was some truth to your charges, why should we be the ones to stick our necks out?"

"Because we're a news organization!" Laura said hotly.

"We're not," said Irene.

"And we're not," echoed Billie.

"I'm in a terrible situation," said Laura, her voice low, her face troubled. "I don't want to hurt the company, and yet *I can't give up this case!*" She looked at Sam, who nodded sympathetically. "So, I'd like you to consider spinning off Taninger News. I mean, allowing me to buy the news division from the parent company."

She saw surprised looks on some of the faces, but not her father's, as if he had contemplated the proposition she now raised.

Clark shook his head. "I'm sorry to inform you that what you're proposing won't work."

"Why not?" Laura asked suspiciously. "You've already discussed it with the Feds. Haven't you?"

"I have to admit," said Clark, "that I thought of the idea myself. I thought of Laura changing the name of Taninger News and starting a completely new media organization of her own, with no association to our family. That way, Taninger Enterprises would be rid of its biggest problem. I've had . . . private conversations with . . . people . . . in the highest places. But that won't stop them. They believe that having Taninger News untethered to the other family businesses would make Laura even more . . . unmanageable."

"So now it's the Feds' job to *manage* me?" Laura hotly.

The group listened soberly.

"Laura," Clark continued, "they'd only go after your new company with the same charges they brought against Taninger News, so you wouldn't be out of the woods. It would be nonsense, of course, but they'd tie you up in court for as long as it took to ruin you. Millions of dollars, just up in smoke. And they'd find powerful inducements for Taninger Enterprises not to do the spin-off. You see, I know what they really want. I know what spawned this lawsuit to break up our news division, and I know how to make it go away."

"How?" asked Bert Franklin.

"They want Laura out of the news business. They want new programming on our network without her influencing it."

"You mean, you went to Martin's people, and you found out they'll leave us alone if you *destroy* your daughter?" Laura charged.

"You'll never understand, will you?" Clark pointed an angry finger at Laura. "You never get into *their* motivation and *their* point of view."

"You mean their need to break up *our* family and *our* business? That's what you want to accommodate?"

"I have a company to run, and that's getting harder and harder to do with you in it!" Clark charged.

"You know," Laura commented, "we're all operating on the premise that *the administration* will win in bullying us. What if that's wrong? What if *we'll* win? All of our divisions are profitable right now, and my show is still number one in TV news. The pressure is real, but the support I'm receiving from my audience is just as potent, and it needs to be recognized. What if we get to the bottom of what's going on at Elections and bring it the public? If we're right, and we can expose the corruption, we'll save the country. Did you ever think of that?"

"Yes!" Kate was jumping out of her seat in affirmation, a hot flame in the midst of cooler embers. The others were more circumspect, their faces skeptical.

"Are we journalists? Are we an independent and free press?" asked Laura. "Or are we the lackeys of those in power?"

"All right," said Clark. "We've all had our say. If there's nothing more, I'd like to take the vote and be done with it."

No one argued.

"Okay, Caroline," said Clark, turning to his assistant. "Kate, you will please move away from the table, so only the seven directors are seated here."

As Kate obliged, she turned to her trustee, saying, "Erica, you know what I want done with my shares."

"And don't browbeat Erica!" Clark admonished.

Erica smiled at Kate but gave no hint of how she would vote.

Caroline placed a small card and envelope in front of each of the directors. The card contained one simple question, with an option to check Yes or No under it: *Should Laura Taninger be removed as president of Taninger News?*

"This is a secret ballot," Clark explained. "Please answer the question on the card in front of you, then place it in the envelope and seal it."

When everyone was finished, Caroline collected the seven sealed envelopes and brought them to her place.

"Should Laura be removed?" Caroline said, restating the question and opening the first envelope. It made a loud tearing sound in the silent room. Then, she removed the card.

"Yes," Caroline reported.

She placed the card on the table; then, she opened the second envelope.

"No." She placed that card next to the other, starting separate stacks for the yesses and nos.

She opened the third envelope. "Yes."

Then the fourth one. "Yes. We have three yesses and one no," she reported.

She opened the fifth one. "No."

Then, the sixth one. "No. That's three yesses and three nos."

The tension in the room mirrored a high-stakes poker game that was coming down to the final card. Everyone stared at Caroline as she picked up the last sealed envelope.

Caroline broke the seal and repeated the question: "Should Laura be removed as president of Taninger News?" She removed the final card. With a hint of sadness, she gave the result that sealed Laura's fate.

"Yes."

Clark sighed in relief. "The yesses have it, four to three."

Laura's face went white. She sat in mannequin-like stillness. She tried to force her mind to focus on one goal: to get through this meeting with dignity.

Nevertheless, her thoughts wandered. While other children had to read books to find tales of adventure, Laura's childhood was filled with real-life excitements, courtesy of JT and the family business. She remembered when she was five years old, and JT took her through the paper mills. She watched in awe as newspapers were printed at breakneck speed. When she was six years old, she loved to play on the floor in JT's office while he sat working at his desk. "You're going to be sitting here in my chair one day," he had told her. Could she? The child wondered at something unimaginable. If JT thought she could do his job, then maybe . . . just maybe . . .

She loved being around him, loved the excitement of the newsroom, loved the lively phone conversations, the people coming and going with questions to ask, decisions to be made—all of it making her childhood one thrilling roller-coaster ride. When she was old enough, she began working at *Taninger News*, first in the mailroom, then as a beat reporter, then in the television studio. She learned every job. The family business became inseparably meshed with her life.

She mustn't think back. Not now! She had to get through this meeting.

"In accordance with our bylaws," said Clark, "I will take over the management of Taninger News until a new president is appointed."

When she'd written her first editorials, given her first news reports, had her first editing job at the television network, and then, produced her first program, JT had been proud of her. He'd given her the confidence to take on more and more responsibility. When she'd won a prestigious award for investigative journalism, he'd had the certificate framed and hung it on the wall behind his desk. Every visitor to his office was regaled with the story of his brilliant granddaughter's achievement.

"The first decision I'm making as acting president of Taninger News is this: I hereby cancel the program *Just the Truth*. Its host, Laura Taninger, will not appear on the network again or have any say in its programming or operations. Laura is relieved of her responsibilities," Clark announced.

JT had lived to see his protégée rise to become president of Taninger News. When JT was bedridden in his old age, Laura remembered how he smiled at her with the boyish optimism of youth. "I'm leaving the company in good hands," he'd said, clutching her hands in his.

"I thank Laura for her many years of hard work and company loyalty," said Clark with a forced pleasantness.

The directors looked wooden, their eyes avoiding Laura, except for Irene, who gloated with satisfaction, and Kate, whose eyes became two basins filling with water and whose body stiffened, resolved not to let any of the tears fall.

"We will work out a generous severance package," Clark said, smiling at Laura. He raised his eyebrows hopefully, as if anticipating acknowledgment of a fair deal, but she did not smile in return.

CHAPTER 21

Is the Martin Administration Rigging the Election?

Laura posed the question in the title of her explosive new commentary, detailing her findings and conclusions about SafeVote, its mysterious contractor, and the upcoming presidential election. She contacted the major national news outlets, seeking a place that would publish her piece, but other forces were already in play to defeat her.

Following Laura's dismissal, Taninger Enterprises issued a brief statement: "Laura Taninger is no longer the president of Taninger News. Clark Taninger will take over as the acting head of the network until a new president is appointed. Taninger News will be announcing new programming to replace *Just the Truth*, the show Ms. Taninger hosted."

Zack Walker and Darcy Egan quickly released their own talking points to the media. "We understand that Laura Taninger was voted out by the company's board of directors. We've heard from our sources that the board had serious reservations about her volatile temperament, which they deemed as unsuitable for running a news organization and hosting a prime-time program. Some at the company may have also suspected that mental-health issues and psychological instability were at play."

Zack and Darcy fed these talking points to their friends in the media. They also fed them to partisan organizations that supported the president, yet had vague, nonpartisan-sounding names like the Alliance for Democracy, Citizens for Universal Justice, and the Center for Voting Equality. These organizations communicated the same content as was expressed in the talking points to members of the media, creating the appearance that there were multiple, independent sources for the allegations against Laura, other than the mothership at the People's Manor.

The news stories followed: "Reliable, anonymous sources cite mental instability as the cause of Laura Taninger's dismissal." No one called Laura for her side of the story. Due to the influence of Zack and others like him, it was becoming more and more common for people to be mischaracterized by faulty reporting, with the subjects, themselves, never interviewed to obtain their comments. One reporter was too lazy to verify independently the facts assumed in the story, so he uncritically posted the talking points he received. Another reporter, eager to get ahead, and wanting to please her boss, who had a merger pending that required federal approval, welcomed any story favorable to the Martin administration or unfavorable to its critics. A third reporter was a fanatical supporter of the president and gleefully eager to smash his enemies, not with arguments and policy positions, but with character assassinations and smears.

With rumors spreading that Laura had mental-health problems, and anger-control challenges, her credibility was undercut. Editors presented with Laura's article had heard those stories and had them in the back of their minds when they politely declined to publish Laura's work. No major outlet dealing in the national news media would take on the article.

She tried to run her commentary as a full-page paid advertisement in leading newspapers, but they refused to accept it. She tried getting her story out as a press release, but the news agencies handling them declined her submission. It's too divisive, she was told. It doesn't conform to our editorial standards, she was told repeatedly by people who refused to answer when she asked what standard she had failed to meet.

Implicitly, Laura knew the real reason for her ostracism. Everyone knew, she thought, but no one would admit it. No other outlet wanted the repercussions that Taninger Enterprises had faced from powerful forces that could cause a world of trouble for businesses that they considered to be adversaries. All of the major news outlets had vulnerabilities with which they could be manipulated— taxes, employment regulations, environmental audits, etc. Behind all the rejections, Laura sensed fear.

She was now radioactive.

During the week after she was fired, Laura discovered that a change in fortune was occurring at her family's corporation.

In a piece published on a popular online site called Entertainment News Today, she read that Irene Taninger was awarded an exclusive interview with President Ken Martin and his wife. A rare, behind-the-scenes look at their private quarters at the People's Manor would air on Taninger Entertainment. The program was expected to draw record ratings for the network.

On the sports pages of a local newspaper, Laura found an article describing how the Federal Bureau of Building Safety was relaxing its action against the DC Slammers' new stadium. The agency decided to allow Taninger Sports to delay installation of its replacement seating until after the season was over so that the DC Slammers' new stadium could open without further delay. The reason the article gave for the agency's relenting was that it was sensitive to the undue hardship on the fans.

Buried on one of the back pages of another newspaper, Laura read that the Bureau of Fair Trade had dropped its action against Taninger News. This reversal at Fair Trade came about just as Clark was transforming the company's news practices. He had replaced Laura's hard-hitting, prime-time news hour with a program that offered just a mere few minutes of news, before it turned to less somber subjects, such as fashion, sports, movies, and what it called human-interest stories. A preliminary investigation was completed by Fair Trade, showing no cause to pursue further any charges of monopolistic activities against Taninger News. The practices at the company were found to be properly serving the public interest.

Even Kate Taninger was offered a pathway to reenter Collier University, according to an article Laura saw as she perused the recent online issue of the *Collier Dispatch*. Concerned about the future of a wayward former student, Dean Folner reached out to Kate with a generous opportunity to rejoin the Collier community, the article stated, but Kate declined.

Of his own accord, Sam Quinn quietly continued to provide legal help to Laura in her quest for documents from the Bureau of Elections. Two weeks after Judge Marianne Rogers had dismissed the case against the Bureau of Elections—strongly advising the agency to hasten its release of the petitioned documents, or else Laura Taninger could refile the suit—the agency had not complied. Now, on behalf of Laura as a freelance journalist, Sam sued Elections again.

A week after her firing, she and Sam had been successful in court. A new judge assigned to the case, Garrett Davidson, had allowed the suit. He reprimanded Elections for its stalling and ordered the agency to release the documents Laura requested within—yet another!—five working days.

"That means we'll get the documents next Monday or Tuesday, at the earliest. That brings us to October 31—just a week before Election Day!" Laura said. "It gives us almost no time at all, especially if Elections finds more ways to stall or only partially comply."

"We'll do what we can," Sam replied, sounding as frustrated as she was.

She recollected the week's events as she stood on the street outside her row house. She looked down the block, waiting for Sean Browne's car to pull up. She had called him that day and arranged to have dinner with him.

Lately, she had the uneasy feeling that she was being followed. The other day, she saw a man behind the wheel of a parked car near where she stood to hail a cab. When she got into the taxi, she noticed that the car started out after them. She thought she noticed the same car stopping down the street, behind where the cab was dropping her off. But it was dark, traffic was heavy, and the black car she suspected resembled many others on the road, so she couldn't be sure. Now, waiting for Sean, she wondered if the man who seemed to be talking on his phone in a black car parked near her home was the same man whom she thought was following her the other day. He was parked in one of the several residential driveways on her block that saw little activity, making them ideal places for watching people. When Sean arrived, she strained to see the man in the parked car behind them. She saw the car pulling out. Was it following them? The vehicle soon merged with other traffic before she could be sure it was tailing her.

When they were seated in their usual table at The Waves, Sean kept his menu closed, leaned back, and savored the sight of her sleek auburn hair falling onto a pink sweater, the soft curves of her body under her clothes, and the translucent brown eyes looking at him.

"It's been a while since we've done this," he said, his pleasure at their meeting obvious.

"I guess it has."

"It was about a month ago when you had cocktails with Senator Taylor, and I picked you up at the bar afterwards and took you here. We used to get together for dinner more often than that."

"We did."

"Laura, I know you're going through a terrible time."

"I am."

"I wasn't sure if I should call you, granted my new position."

"Do you feel your work for the president is . . . compromised . . . by seeing me?"

"Darcy hasn't yet said anything about my dinner dates. So I guess I'm still on my own for that." At the mention of his supervisor, he looked down worriedly. Then he looked across the table at Laura, and his doubts vanished. "I have to say, I was glad you called and suggested this. It seems like old times."

"Except we're not the same people we once were, are we, Sean?"

"My feelings haven't changed."

"Things have changed radically for me, as you no doubt know."

"I'm very sorry about your job," he said, reaching across the table to squeeze her hand sympathetically. "How are you holding up?"

"I'm . . . desperate," she whispered. She took her hand away from his to open her purse and pull out a document. "This is my latest commentary. It covers the shocking discoveries I made on my trip to Ireland to track down the elusive contractor that Elections is trying to hide from public scrutiny."

She unfolded the article and gave it to him.

As the waiter took their drink order and then served cocktails, Sean sipped his and read the material thoughtfully. Then he looked up at her.

"That's quite a report, Laura, but why are you bringing it to me?"

"Sean, as you may realize, the Martin administration has launched an all-out war against my family. The Bureau of Fair Trade's threats to break up Taninger News not only caused my own family to sever business ties with me, but it's caused other news outlets to want nothing whatever to do with me or my story."

"You're too good for them anyway," he said.

"Then you like the piece?" Laura asked hopefully.

"I didn't say that. I just meant that you, with your crazy, free spirit . . . There's something very much alive about you that makes everyone else seem like the living dead."

"I think I'm on to something very real and dangerous. I'll get right to the point, Sean. I'd like you to help me get this piece published."

"What?"

"The commentary I wrote is simple investigative journalism. It can be published as something from an 'anonymous source' and not be associated with me at all. Anyone could have done that research in Ireland. It didn't have to be me. I'd like you to pass the piece on to someone you know in the press to publish it. I'm looking for a wide reach with this story, and you know all the media players on the national scene. They'll take something from you without revealing—or even knowing—your source, while they won't even give me a hearing."

"That would violate everything my position requires of me. I'd be guilty of highly unethical conduct."

"More unethical than rigging an election?"

Sean shook his head, unwilling to believe that the administration would go that far. "Laura, come on. This company you're so worried about, Integrated Foxworth Technologies, could just be a new subsidiary of a well-known company in the election programming field. It could be that this IFT entity isn't on the radar screen yet. Companies set up new subsidiaries all the time. Maybe a known company set this one up and didn't have a chance yet to get moved in and running with its location—the vacant building you mention in your piece. There can be other reasons to explain what you've uncovered. You don't have to think the worst of everybody in the federal government, you know."

"Did you forget someone died with the word *Fox* on his lips? How could that not refer to Frank Foxworth, who's listed as the president of this totally bogus company?"

"That's pure supposition on your part, Laura."

"And the attacks on my family and on Taninger News? Is all of that supposition? Or can we finally say that someone is trying to intimidate me into dropping this issue?"

"The people I work for totally deny that they had a hand in any of that, and you can't prove they did. You don't even have a scintilla of evidence to implicate the People's Manor in your family's business challenges."

"And I suspect someone's following me. There was a parked car outside my house that pulled out just as you picked me up and we came here."

"Laura, honestly, I didn't notice any car following us. Are you suggesting the government is keeping tabs on you?"

"Are you suggesting all of these things are a coincidence?"

"Why don't you try to relax? Do you think we can spend this evening together without talking about politics? It might be good for you."

"And the so-called reports that I'm mentally unhinged—which the media are repeating like their newest blood sport—come from where?"

"I don't know. But what I do know is that you're incredibly passionate, and when you believe something, you'll go to the rack for it, even if your crusade is totally ill-advised." He gazed at her admiringly, as at the heroine of a fantasy story that could bear no relationship to real life.

"Sean, can't you infer anything? Don't you ever use critical thinking anymore? Or do you just inhale the talking points they give you like an anesthesia that makes your mind go numb?" Seeing the hurt look on his face, she regretted blurting out her thoughts. "I'm sorry, Sean, but you're working for liars whose lust for power makes them extremely dangerous."

"I don't think they're liars. Misguided sometimes, perhaps. But they're not lying to me—or to anyone."

Laura sighed in frustration. "I came to you because I'm at the end of my rope. You've always admired my idealism. I can't help but think that, deep inside, you want to be idealistic, too. To be different than you are. To stand up for what's right."

"But the way I am has skyrocketed my career, while the way you are has, well . . . tanked yours," he replied.

"Can't I reach you, Sean? Won't you join me to help save our country, instead of working for its destroyers?"

"That's so melodramatic! Give it up, Laura. You're at a dead end. You have no platform for disseminating your theories. And the election is just two weeks away."

"Sean, is there any way you can find to help me? Could you just give the article to someone who'd give it to someone else, and it'd never get traced back to you?"

"I can't!" He sighed, weary from their argument. He opened his menu, inviting no further discussion.

"I'm sorry, Sean. I lost my appetite." She looked at him disgustedly and pushed her chair away from the table, about to leave.

"Laura, don't go! Please! We've always argued, then we've had dinner."

"This is different, Sean. You're working for liars and crooks who are hell-bent on destroying me."

"If I believed that the administration were deliberately lying and trying to harm you, do you really think I could continue working for them?"

"I don't know, Sean," she said bluntly. "Do *you* think you could?"

He seemed taken aback, as if he were weighing the question himself, unsure of what he would do.

"I'm giving them the benefit of the doubt," he said. "In my mind, the corruption you're accusing them of is unproven. Please understand, Laura."

She sighed in resignation, pulled her chair back to the table, and opened her menu.

CHAPTER 22

The next day, the sky was a brilliant blue when Laura left her row house to hail a cab. As she waited on the sidewalk for one to come along, she checked the news on her phone. The media reports on her firing seemed gleeful.

Laura Taninger Thrown Out.

Just the Truth *Gets the Boot.*

Headstrong Laura Taninger Canned.

She thought of the blood sports of the ancients and wondered about the motives of those who reveled in someone else's destruction. Was it an outlet for venting their own perverted resentments and jealousies toward the world? For the modern-day media, spearing her was also a sure way to draw an audience.

Scrolling down the news feed, she saw that some stories mentioned her past scandal, as they called it, meaning her affair with Reed. Her eyes lingered on one report, which included a picture of her and Reed. The photo had been taken in an unguarded moment, when they were walking in a park, and Reed had stopped to buy a bouquet of balloons for her. The photo had captured one of her happiest moments, in which she looked at Reed with unqualified admiration. He was so boyishly handsome, so confident, so incredibly desirable. When he'd given her the balloons, her face had illustrated the whole of what she felt. Returning to the present, Laura read the headline, "From Tawdry Past to Stormy Present: The Fall of Laura Taninger." She glanced at the picture one more time. After their breakup, she had resolved never to look at Reed again as she had that day.

A taxi stopped for her. Upon entering, she turned to peer out the rear window. She saw a parked car pull out down the street. It was a black, ordinary looking sedan that had been parked in a driveway close enough to have a view of her residence yet far enough away to be inconspicuous. She momentarily caught a glimpse of the man behind the wheel before the car entered her lane of traffic with several cars in between them blocking her view. *Is he following me?* she wondered. She could not see the man's face or positively identify the car as the same one she had previously noticed parked on her block.

Then, she forgot about the possible tail, her attention focusing on an . . . unpleasant . . . task ahead.

The cab let her out in front of one of the city's most attractive modern office buildings. Its blue glass facade blended with the sky and looked like a part of it, a light structure floating in space rather than anchored to the ground. Thin steel beams completed the elegant, simple design, without even a name on the building to add ornamentation. As Laura looked up at the building from the curb, she couldn't help thinking of how it reflected the man inside—understated, unpretentious, and unmoored from the mundane.

She took the elevator to the executive floor where she could find that man, who owned the company headquartered in the building. She had not made an appointment. Would he be in? Would he see her? She entered an outer office, where an assistant looked up from her desk and smiled in recognition.

"Hi, Laura."

"Hi, Kelly," Laura said, returning the smile. "Is he in?"

"He is."

The assistant gestured to a half-opened door, inviting Laura to enter the inner office. *Is it that easy?* Laura wondered. *Is Kelly not even going to announce me?*

She walked into an office of cool neutral colors and closed the door behind her. Slanted, tinted glass panels separated by vertical steel beams formed a wall of windows. Lighted shelves with glass doors, holding books and other objects, formed another wall. The desk, a smooth slab of stone on a thick steel base, held a computer screen and a few papers. Light flooded in to give the room an immense clarity, a modern space uncluttered by past traditions, where new thoughts could form and innovations arise.

Despite her intention to remain stoic, she couldn't help but smile at the man she had not seen in a year, the man who had brought so much turmoil to her life but also so much unbridled joy.

"Hello, Reed."

"Laura." He pronounced her name as he always had—softness and affection in his tone.

As he gestured for her to take a seat, he smiled broadly, then seemed to check himself, as if he wanted to be cooler; however, a genuine pleasure in seeing her refused to remain hidden. He cocked his head, observing her fondly as she sat and faced him across the desk.

Laura assessed him as the sunlight from the windows sent blond sparkles into the light-brown curls of his hair. He looked fit and trim in a silk shirt that showed the contours of his arms and chest.

She sat in a dark leather chair that formed a backdrop for her slender body, clad in a white blouse and gray business suit. She intentionally did not dress provocatively, but now, under the scrutiny of a gaze he didn't try to hide, she felt keenly aware of her crossed legs and her high heels against his pale wood floor.

"Reed . . . " she began, her voice suddenly breaking.

She stopped, demanding that she not feel anything. *Just get through the assignment, Laura*, she told herself.

She tried again, "I'm coming to you because I have nowhere else to turn." She spoke just the truth, without self-pity or pleading.

"I know," he said softly. He leaned forward in his chair, his hands clasped, his elbows on the desk. "I know what you're going to say—and ask. But say it and ask it anyway, so you'll know you tried everything, even stooping so low as to come to me."

"How would you know why I came here?"

"Because I watch your show—at least, I did until Clark pulled the plug on it."

"Did you?"

"Every night."

"Don't you watch your own prime-time news?"

"You mean that cartoon show your silly friend Sean hosted? Why would I watch that clown when I could watch a real news show instead?"

Her eyes fell to the floor as she redirected her thoughts. She mustn't be distracted. Reed was confusing her, making her feel as though he . . . still . . . She would not think of that! She raised her eyes to meet his and to change the subject, but he wasn't through.

"Under your control, *Taninger News* spoke truth to power. Under your father's control, it speaks weather to homebodies."

"Like Miller News does?" She instantly regretted what sounded like a rebuke, but he showed no sign of being offended.

"I provide the model," he admitted.

"Reed, I didn't come here to rehash the past—only to discuss the present. You see, I not only lost my job, but I'm being ostracized by the national news media. I'm sitting on a story of immense importance, and I need a news outlet to get it released. It has to come out. Certain people in the highest positions of power have to be stopped before they do irreparable harm! If you've been following my show, you already know the story I've been investigating, but there are shocking new developments. Will you hear me out?"

"I'm listening."

She told him about her trip to Ireland and the discovery that the contractor the Bureau of Elections was trying to conceal was a totally bogus company.

"At first, I thought Elections might be merely trying to cover up a waste of taxpayer money or a political friend of the administration getting a lucrative contract. Now, I think there's much more to it than that."

"Of course there's more," Reed replied.

"What makes you think so?"

"They are who they are."

"Do you know something I don't? Something that can help my investigation?"

"I don't have to be privy to any special information. Isn't it obvious to anyone who can still think?" His tone was a mixture of cynicism and sadness. "Ken Martin assumes power, and the first thing he does is create a major crisis around our voting system. Sure, there have always been cases of fraud, but the cure Martin proposed is worse than the disease. Suddenly, the country has to have an entirely new voting system—controlled, of course, by his administration. That was the first thing to raise eyebrows. Then, an insider at Elections, a high-level staffer, comes forward with problems he detects in the new voting system."

"James Spenser," Laura interjected.

He nodded. "Funny, isn't it? A whistleblower they fear is about to meet a journalist they hate, and just like that, he's murdered." Reed snapped his fingers. "Then, you uncover this phony company that's a front for whatever it is they're doing."

"So you get it, Reed. *They're rigging a presidential election!*"

He stared at her, the statement hanging heavy in the air.

"Except for my lawyer, Sam Quinn, and my sister, Kate, no one else I know believes that."

"I do."

"Reed, you're in a position to make the difference. It's down to *you* to expose them."

"Sure, I'll expose them," he said sarcastically. "I actually love being sued and having my company chopped up by the Feds. Is that what you want me to say?"

"This time it's different. If we can uncover their plan and foil it, Ken Martin will lose the election. Once he's out of power, no one will touch you, Reed."

"And all this is to happen with the election just two weeks away?"

"If you give me airtime to expose this, and we get to the bottom of it, we have a chance to stop it. If we do, we'll be national heroes. I know you don't care about that, but we will have done something incredibly . . . noble. That's something you once cared about."

"That was in another life."

"But it's a *presidential* election. That has to remain honest."

"Nothing in their hands remains honest."

"But we have to do something about it!"

"It's too dangerous."

"You'd give them . . . absolute power? I can't believe you're saying that."

"Why can't you believe it, Laura?" He smiled wistfully. "I've changed. Now it's your turn. I did what everyone said was the right thing to do. I *reached out*. I *partnered* with the people suing me—aren't those the words they use? I listened to all the calls for me to be a *responsible* businessman, to recognize my duty to serve the public. So I gave the public what its self-proclaimed mouthpiece, the government, demanded of me—no red-hot news that would cause anyone heartburn. If I put you on the air, that would all change. The Feds would re-open the case against me tomorrow and Miller Communications would be back on their chopping block."

"But my investigation would crush Martin. I won't stop till I find out what he's doing."

"If you find out after the election, it'll be too late. If you find out before the election, you could wind up dead."

"Whether it's now, after the election, or into the future, I will not quit until I find out. And when I do, it will be the end for Ken Martin! Besides, if I raise enough questions before the election, the rest of the president's party can be defeated at the ballot box. The other elections aren't yet part of SafeVote, so even if Martin wins a rigged election, he would be impotent if the opposing party gains a majority in Congress. My investigation can do a great deal of harm to Ken Martin."

"If he doesn't destroy you first," he said. His words sounded low and ominous, like a death sentence.

Fortified with her own plan for winning, she didn't seem to hear his admonition. "So that's why I came here. To apply for Sean's job. You haven't filled it yet, have you? You've had several guest hosts, but no permanent new host has yet been assigned. You wanted me to join Miller News once, before . . . "

"Before I sold out."

"I didn't come here to throw that in your face."

"What choice did I have? I was declared a threat to the public and ordered by our great leaders to divest myself of my most prized values. With the re-structuring of Miller Communications came the restructuring of Reed Miller's Life. You were part of that."

Laura looked confused. If she were important to him, then why would he . . . She quickly refocused.

"Reed . . . about my investigation?"

"Investigative journalism is dead."

"Then we have to resuscitate it."

"Why?"

"What else is there that stands between us and—"

"No one cares about things like that anymore. Give it up, Laura. Martin and his people can play hardball, I tell you. Don't be a fool! You're acting like James Spenser didn't die right before your eyes."

Reed's insinuation hit a nerve. She thought of Spenser, and then she suddenly remembered the tail she believed was following her. She stood and walked to the windows. Could she spot him from Reed's office, outside waiting for her?

She remembered that Reed, who guarded his privacy, had installed treated windows so that he could look out, but no one could see in.

"These windows are one-way viewing, aren't they?"

"They are."

Reed rose from his seat and walked next to her, looking out with her. "What are you looking for?"

"I think they have an investigator tailing me. I wonder if I can spot someone who might be lurking around, watching your building. I have a general idea of his appearance and car. I've got to figure out who he is, then find a way to shake him."

"Don't even think of doing that."

"Why not?"

"*They* aren't having you followed. *I* am."

"*You?* Why the hell—"

"To protect you."

"*You're* trying to protect *me?*"

"Didn't *you* try to protect *me* once?" he asked fondly.

Laura looked at him curiously. "Actually, it felt too easy to get in here, and both you and Kelly didn't seem surprised to see me."

Reed took out his mobile phone. "Let's see." He scrolled through a group of text messages. "According to my man, you were entering this building ten minutes ago. Earlier this morning, you went to the gym. Yesterday, you had dinner at The Waves with that pretzel, Sean Browne. Shall I continue?"

"You really *are* watching me!"

"Someone has to protect you from yourself."

"Why you?"

"I may be a bastard, but there's one thing I can't do—I can't sit and watch you put yourself in danger, especially without backup."

"I most definitely don't want you knowing my every move! I *demand* you call off the tail."

"When you give up your investigation, I'll call off the tail."

"I won't cave!"

"As I did?" His face showed no guilt, just a touch of sadness. "And I won't call off the private eye."

For a moment, he took her in with his eyes. She made eye contact, daring him—daring them both—to feel a spark of their once wild fire.

"Don't try to shake that tail. He's there for your protection! If you insist on pursuing this story, a time could come when you need him!"

"I don't want you to know my business. What makes you think you have that right?"

"I don't think I do."

"Then call off the tail."

"No."

He took her arms and moved closer. "Laura, don't push them. Remember what happened to Spenser. They can play hardball. I'm afraid for you."

With his hands squeezing her arms, and his lips almost touching her face, she hardly heard his words. She thought of the picture of them together that she had seen in the morning's news feed, and the vow she had made never to look at him with such admiration again. But now, she was going beyond that limit to look at him with a longing she couldn't hide from herself or from him.

Reed went on, "They're desperate, Laura. They're losing. They can't stand it. They're not open to reason in any way. They'll win at any cost, use any means, to achieve their perverted goals. They're crazed. I know. I've dealt with them. Your life, my life—mean nothing to them. That's what power does to people who crave it, and they will stop at nothing to get it and keep it. That's what you're up against."

"What's the choice? To keep quiet about this outrage? I can't do that."

"Look," he said, taking a different tack. "Why don't you leave the country till after the election? I can arrange to fly you to a faraway place, where you'll be safe."

"And you? Will you join me there?" Against her resolve, she dared to make this advance. Her question sounded not like a degrading plea to a man who had jilted her but like an honest question from a woman strong enough to ask it.

For one disarming moment, she saw temptation break through the tight features of his face.

"Laura, you're a rare wine, a beautiful vintage. A man has to have a special reason for having such a fine drink. He has to have a reason to celebrate life, and I have none."

"We can still celebrate our lives. They can't take that away from us."

"They already have. The last thing I have left is to keep you safe." His hands moved softly along her arms like a caress. "Laura, the tail is there for your benefit. Think of it as your bodyguard."

"And if I'm in danger, you'll be there?"

"Don't seek out danger. *Don't!* Give it up!"

He closed his eyes for a moment, and the subtle, painful sign of an inner struggle did not escape her. Then he dropped her arms and stepped back. He returned to his desk, regaining his calm, his face composed, cool, and resolute. He sat down and looked at her dispassionately.

"I'm not putting you on the air. You came, you tried, and you have your answer."

She picked up her purse and left.

CHAPTER 23

Laura felt like a soldier sitting on an explosive device meant to detonate on an enemy—but how would she reach her target? She had been stripped of her powerful news platform. Her character was the subject of public ridicule. Her attempts to elicit help from Sean and Reed had failed. As she pondered her next move, feeling exiled from the media, maligned with the public, and alienated from her family, an ally appeared.

After being expelled from Collier University and moving out of her dormitory, Kate had accepted Laura's offer to stay at her row house. Then, Kate made an offer to Laura—and insisted that she accept it.

"Look, Laura, here's how I see it," Kate explained. "If a bogus company got a $400 million contract to do undisclosed, uncertified work on SafeVote, and Elections is doing everything they can to hide it from the public, we have to get this story out. And we've only got two weeks before the election."

Laura shook her head. "I don't want you to get involved."

"I want to help."

"It could be dangerous! I want to protect you."

"I can't just stand by and watch this corruption play out. I want to fight it!"

Looking at Kate, Laura saw a similarity to herself that went beyond their striking physical resemblance. *Hadn't I told Reed the same thing, when he urged me to drop the investigation because of the danger?* she asked herself.

As Kate spoke, her ponytail swayed youthfully, while her resolve remained steadfast. "It's like a tonic for me to support something I believe in, like a dose of fresh air after the smothering atmosphere at Collier. So let's get started!"

The two of them worked tirelessly. Each sister's energy and passion spurred on their mission and welded even tighter the bond between them. They were not only sisters thrown together by birth, but allies standing together by choice.

They decided to take Laura's story to local news outlets across the country. Compared to the national news services, these subsidiaries had a reduced circulation and audience, but they were not part of Zack Walker's inner circle and therefore not subject to the complex, behind-the-scenes network of favors and fears that too often determined what news stories were selected and emphasized in the major media outlets. Laura and Kate reached out to communities, many of which still believed that biased stories planted by the politically powerful and passed off as news were something that should never occur in America. The sisters contacted these smaller newspapers, television and radio shows, and online news sources. From her row house, Laura gave radio interviews. From a nearby studio, she broadcast interviews with television newscasters around the country. From her computer, she sent her investigative report to numerous print and online journals in towns, cities, and counties across the country. She also posted her findings on her own social media sites, where her loyal fans could read them.

At first, Laura wondered how she would fare. Having to *answer* questions was a radical shift from her customary journalist's role as the interviewer. To her surprise, she discovered that she could field even unfriendly, skeptical, or hostile questions and win over audiences.

In one interview, Laura faced off with Sheri Hale, the television anchor of the *Seattle Evening News*. "Are you really implying that the Martin administration is rigging an election?" asked Hale in disbelief.

"Yes! That's *exactly* what I'm implying," said Laura confidently. "And I'm not just implying it. There is evidence of foul play."

"But do you realize how fanatical and desperate that charge sounds from you, a known critic of the administration?" Hale continued.

"I call it as I see it, Sheri." Laura said calmly. "The people who are covering up the truth are the ones who are fanatical and desperate. They're in the fight of their lives to stay in power. If they can rig this election, then our freedom is lost. Don't we need to get to the bottom of why Elections invented a bogus contractor, did last-minute programming, didn't certify it, paid a fortune for it, and are hiding all of this from public scrutiny?"

Sheri Hale continued trying to make a dent in the body armor that seemed to cover Laura Taninger. The television anchor scanned a computer screen on her desk. "Our interview is generating quite a reaction from our viewers. They're asking, how can you be so sure?"

"I trust the facts. I've laid them out for your viewers. Now, I ask them," she leaned forward and clasped her hands, "with the intense effort of the Bureau of Elections to keep work they did on SafeVote a secret, can *you* be sure your vote will be counted as you cast it?"

Laura's interviews generated intense interest from audiences, provoked discussions on social media, and boosted ratings. Armed with evidence and the moral courage to stick to her convictions, her uncompromising style persuaded thousands of people.

Kate arranged a heavy booking schedule, and Laura gave the interviews. After a few eighteen-hour work days, momentum was building around their cause. Where public comments on Laura's story were posted, the sisters read things like:

"We all need to know about this!"

"Could this be happening? Everyone has to hear Laura Taninger's story."

"This is shocking news that needs to reach every voter."

"If what Laura says is true, Martin has to be thrown out of office."

The tables were turning, and news outlets started calling the sisters to ask for interviews. But was it too late?

An enemy she could not fight, which moved forward inexorably, needing no rest and stopping for no one, was *time*. The Bureau of Elections had stalled for months in turning over documents she had petitioned in her Public Information Request. Now, a week before Election Day, the agency, under court order, produced some of those documents.

Laura received a stack of papers pertaining to the Bureau of Elections' work with the elusive Integrated Foxworth Technologies. She scanned through the material, finding every page heavily redacted. Messages and memos appeared with the sender and recipient's names blacked out. Elections maintained that it had to protect the security of SafeVote as a rationale for many of the redactions. Despite so much missing information, the documents did give a rudimentary description of the programming that was done by the contractor.

Laura gave the material to Nan Evans, a technical expert on electronic voting systems. Soon she reported her findings to Laura and Sam: The Bureau of Elections' documents gave an account of work done by Integrated Foxworth Technologies *only* up to the third week of September. This work consisted of a variety of patches and updates. Revisions were made to various screen images, instructions, and live links so that the program would be easier to use by the election officials and the public.

Nan Evans concluded, "The modifications appear to be all legitimate programming changes to provide more options and clearer instructions for the administrators and a better organized user interface for the voters. But the changes were relatively minor. This work would *never* merit a fee of $400 million or anything close to that."

Laura and Sam looked at each other, perplexed. Could Elections have overpaid the contractor so flagrantly as to open themselves up to charges of misuse of public funds? Or did Integrated Foxworth Technologies do more work than

Elections is revealing? Did the contractor's work extend into the month of October? If so, what else had this company done to merit its fee? If the documents the agency released are incomplete, where are the rest of them?

The following day, Sam Quinn once again stood next to attorney Emmett Wallace, representing the Bureau of Elections, before the bench of Judge Garrett Davidson. Laura sat behind the balustrade in the empty courtroom, observing the proceedings. The judge's intelligent eyes and no-nonsense expression gave her hope, but the date on her watch—Thursday, November 2nd—dashed it.

Sam began his argument, saying, "Your Honor, it's unconscionable that Elections is still dodging! We believe they defied your court order by releasing incomplete documents that only go up to the third week in September. Furthermore, our technical expert, Nan Evans, informs us that the work described in the materials we received doesn't even come close to warranting the fee paid to the contractor. Your Honor, there is an urgency to inform the public concerning this issue. To do so, we must have expedited processing of the missing documents so that we receive them *today*."

The judge turned to Wallace, saying, "How about it, Counselor? Where's the rest of the material?"

"Your Honor," said Wallace, "In order to respond to Mr. Quinn's request, which we as public servants are most willing to do—"

"Spare me the blather about your good intentions," quipped the man in the black robe.

"Well, Judge, I have to consult with Ted Burns, our director of technology, who's responsible for the programming of SafeVote. It would be up to him to tell us if more programming work was done by the contractor in question and what that work was. And right now, he and his entire staff are totally unavailable. They're working with the states on rolling out SafeVote, and they have to be around to answer any last-minute questions and handle any glitches."

"Your Honor," Sam said with a huff, "the Bureau of Elections could have prevented this last-minute squeeze if they had turned over the documents two-and-a-half months ago, when we first filed a Public Disclosure Request for them. Election Day is Tuesday. We're running out of time to inform the public!"

Annoyed, the judge said, "Mr. Wallace, enough is enough. I want Ted Burns to appear here and be prepared to answer all of the plaintiff's questions regarding how much information was released, up to what date, how long the contractor's work continued, and what's still missing. And I want you to come prepared to hand over the missing documents to the plaintiff. Tomorrow morning."

Wallace gasped, his eyes bulged from their sockets, and his hands pressed against his chest in what could pass for the dramatization of a heart attack.

"Oh, please, your honor! Tomorrow we're having a complete *dress rehearsal* of the SafeVote rollout. All hands are on deck for this, and Ted is the one in charge of the dry run. We can't possibly spare him tomorrow!"

The judge sighed.

Wallace continued, "We can't compromise our monumental public mission for the sake of one reporter, who doesn't even have a national platform anymore to get the information to the public."

"But she *does* have a national platform, Your Honor. She's found a new way to reach the entire country through her extensive interfaces with local media," replied Sam Quinn.

"The smooth rollout of SafeVote is vital to the country. The integrity of our nation's voting process depends on it. Respectfully, Your Honor, we can't make a court date tomorrow," Wallace insisted.

"Then Monday—and no more delays," the judge said and banged his gavel. His assistant recorded the matter, and the attorneys slipped their files into their briefcases.

Across town that day, the sprawling grounds of the People's Manor were ablaze with fall colors. Crimson and gold leaves tugged on the trees to break free and fall to the ground in a final bow to the impending winter frosts. Zack Walker was about to feel a chill in the air inside, as well.

When he had awoken that morning, the president's senior strategist showered to his favorite music. When he shaved, he gave a thumbs-up to the man in the mirror. When he headed to the president's office for a meeting, his steps were spry, his expectations high.

He had defeated the great Laura Taninger, who had once fired him. He had shut her out of national media coverage. Not only did he taste sweet revenge, but he also looked forward to a banquet of praise at the dais of Ken and Darcy. Oh, sure, Laura was having some success, but her wings would soon melt in the sunshine of Ken's victory at the polls in four days. Walking through the halls of the People's Manor, where very important people engaged in high-stakes politics, he couldn't help but feel that *his* achievements had surpassed them all. He was the prime mover in a series of events that had leveled multiple injuries on Laura's family and mortally wounded her reputation and career. The ramifications to Ken, to the party—and to Zack's own future—of erasing an enemy like Laura could not be overstated.

Zack thought of a painting he had seen in which the artist depicted the commanding figure of God in the act of creating the earth and the heavens. He envisioned himself as the deity, no longer with his drooping trousers and thinning hair, no longer subservient to a world of immutable facts and events, but as a creator of his own universe. Not only had he orchestrated the demise of a political enemy, but he did so also by creating his own news. In a cosmic shift worthy of a deity, he expunged from the headlines stories harmful to his aims and replaced them with stories created and shepherded by *him*. God may have had his Commandments, but he, Zack Walker, had his *talking points*. And look how readily he was able to form a stable of media figures and harness them to run with those talking points!

Yes, he gloated, *I have made it to the winner's circle*. Surely, he was being called to a meeting with Darcy Egan and Ken Martin to receive their verbal bouquets for his first-place finish.

When he walked into the president's office and saw their faces, he knew that was not the case.

He sat on a sofa next to Darcy, facing the president.

"Our new internal polling just came in," Martin said grimly, handing Zack a report.

"The polls have us trailing," said Darcy. "They show an eight-point decline in Ken's ratings in just one week."

Zack glanced through the report.

"The polls show me losing the election by a wide margin," said Martin.

Zack's smug look vanish. A hint of panic replaced it.

"It's Laura Taninger," said Darcy.

"You may have wounded her," the president said to Zack, "but she's back on her feet. She started a media blitz eight days ago on the local level, and now she's gaining momentum."

Zack shrugged and said, "She has no audience of any size. People think she's full of hot air."

"Really? Have you seen the new public polling just released this morning?" asked Darcy.

"Not yet," Zack replied.

"It confirms what our internals are showing," said Martin.

Darcy handed him a news clipping. He read it.

"How the hell can she have this much traction?" Zack said in disbelief. "I thought I flattened her!"

"The polls ask if voters believe her story," Martin commented. "And *sixty percent* say yes!"

"I've seen some of her interviews, and I have to tell you, she's very compelling," Darcy observed.

"She's the underdog," Ken said, sneering. "She won't quit, damn her. People find that appealing."

"And she continues to press her Public Disclosure Request, so she's still in the ballgame," Darcy said, looking at Zack reproachfully. "With four days left till Election Day, she's still causing trouble."

The grave tone of their comments stunned Zack. His mouth formed its familiar O-shape, and his eyes gaped with a deer-in-the-headlights look.

"If Ken is trailing by a wide margin going into the election, his victory will add credence to Laura's charge that the election was fixed," Darcy noted. "If Ken wins, but our party loses substantial seats in Congress, that, too, will add weight to Laura's charges. After all, only the presidential election is managed through SafeVote. The other elections are still on the old voting system. If they tell a very different story, and there's no reason to doubt their accuracy, that calls into question whether SafeVote is above board."

Ken added, "And even if my win avoids suspicion about SafeVote, the party could still lose enough seats in Congress to render my entire second term ineffective!" He rose from his seat and paced nervously. "This bitch is trying to incite the people against me. She's got a vendetta to take me down. She's poisoning my people. I need to smash her," thundered the man who wielded the police power of the state against the words of a private citizen. "I won't let her get away with this. The people will believe what *I* tell them to believe---not what *she* tells them!"

His rage swelled. His anger was mixed with fear, a fear whose object seemed greater than Laura or the election. What weapons could Laura—unarmed, unemployed, and stripped of her national platform—wield against Ken Martin? He controlled the full arsenal of the state, while she had only a pepper spray to spread the truth. The president seemed to sense and fear that weapon, not in any words he uttered, but by the hatred in his voice and the panic on his face.

"We need something more on Laura Taninger," Darcy pronounced. "The techniques we've tried haven't dissuaded her. She's obsessed with her fanatical drive to destroy us."

"Going after her and her family professionally didn't do it," added Ken. "Questioning her mental health and temperament didn't work. We need something else."

Darcy and Ken looked pointedly at Zack. His initial frozen stare upon hearing the news of Laura's gaining ground had now tempered, and a calculating look replaced it.

"I have just the thing," Zack said, his confidence recovered.

"What?" Ken said skeptically.

"I have something that *always* works."

"Oh?" Darcy mused skeptically.

"A *sex scandal*," declared Zack.

"Oh, please," said Darcy. "Not Reed again."

"No," Zack said. "This is an ace I've been saving just for such an occasion."

"What's up your sleeve?" asked Ken, his rage giving way to hope.

Zack squared his shoulders and resumed his role of teaching the others how to mastermind a successful sabotage.

He said, "I know what we need. A juicy, salacious, personal attack. What we used wasn't scandalous enough. We haven't tried this yet, but it's just the thing we need." He stroked his chin as he formulated a plan. "How about an attack on Laura that also attacks somebody else we'd like to put a leash on?"

"What do you mean?" A calmer Ken Martin returned to his seat, waiting to learn of a new plot twist in an ongoing saga.

"I mean, Senator Bret Taylor and Laura Taninger," Zack said.

"Go on," said Darcy, her interest aroused.

Ken leaned forward, listening attentively.

Zack crossed his legs, more relaxed, back in their good graces.

"I've been, well, sort of, *spying* on Senator Bret Taylor." He looked at Darcy and Martin tentatively, wondering if he had overstepped his bounds, but neither one seemed disturbed by his declaration. "There's a key aide on his staff who's a great supporter of SafeVote, and this aide wasn't happy when Senator Taylor opposed it. The more vocal the senator got about his reservations, the more upset this aide became. After all, the senator should back his party and its signature program, right? That's what the aide told me one night when I took him out for drinks.

"So I befriended this aide and hinted at a possible position in the People's Manor in your second administration, seeing as there certainly would be some changeover of personnel after the election."

"Very clever!" said Ken.

"One day, the aide alerted me that the senator was going to meet Laura Taninger for a drink in a bar."

"Really?" Darcy's eyebrows raised in anticipation of new possibilities.

"And he arranged to have a photo taken of them together," Zack continued.

"What do you mean *together*?" asked Ken.

"Well, they look pretty tight in the photo. It could be construed as . . . well . . . "

"Are they having an *affair*?" asked Darcy hopefully.

"Who knows or cares?" Zack replied. "I mean, in the picture, they *look like* they could be. That's all I need. I can create a whole scenario around that. I can leak the photo and attribute some comments to anonymous sources to embellish it, and the press will run with that."

"So what's the scenario?" asked Ken.

"It's shocking, headline news. Senator Bret Taylor, a married man with five children, is having an affair with Laura Taninger. They're both plotting to undermine the new voting system by turning the people against it. The senator is a vocal critic of SafeVote. But he finds that his position doesn't play with our party's base. We've painted that position as anti-minority, racist, anti-poor, you name it.

"Then, he joins forces with his lover, Laura Taninger, who's also against SafeVote. Together, they try to defeat the program and help him win reelection. If he can get enough votes from our party, which is pro-SafeVote, and steal some additional votes from the opposition, where Laura's anti-SafeVote message resonates, then he can win. That's their scheme. Lust and power are what drives them."

"So Laura Taninger has a lover, and that's been her motive in smearing SafeVote?" Ken Martin weighed the scheme. "To bolster her lover's reelection bid she reinforces his reservations about SafeVote with her own bogus criticisms? Who's gonna buy that?"

"Even if the public doesn't buy that they conspired in a scheme to derail SafeVote, we still have the *affair* to discredit them with. That should be enough to take the wind out of Laura's sails right before Election Day."

"That just might play," said Darcy. "But what about Bret Taylor? He could lose enough votes from our party that his opponent will unseat him, thanks to us, if we smear him with this affair. Bret's not always drinking from the same trough, but he is in our party. We'd much rather have *him* in that Senate seat than his opponent."

Martin dismissed Darcy's concern, saying, "I don't really care if Bret loses his Senate seat on Tuesday. What's one casualty? In future elections, we'll include the Senate in Operation Topcoat, so we'll gain the seat back handily and then some."

Zack shot up from his seat, galvanized. "I'll get everything in place. I'll be sure our favorite reporters are briefed. The story will break tomorrow and get heavy media coverage through the weekend. There's still time to change the final polls before the election next Tuesday and turn public opinion against Laura Taninger and in your favor!"

"Go for it!" Ken exclaimed.

"Agreed," said Darcy.

Admiration for Zack had returned to their faces.

Zack gave them a thumbs-up and left to take care of the business he did so well, the business of creation, just as it was depicted in the painting he found so appealing.

CHAPTER 24

"Yes, Your Honor, Integrated Foxworth Technologies did work for our agency throughout the month of October." The Bureau of Elections' director of technology, Ted Burns, stood before Judge Garrett Davidson's bench. Alongside him were his agency's attorney, Emmett Wallace, and the plaintiff's, Sam Quinn. Laura observed the proceeding from the visitors' bench.

"And what work did they do?" asked the judge.

"More of the same jobs they had been tasked with earlier, Judge."

"Then, why weren't those documents handed over to the plaintiff?" the judge asked sharply. "Why are we still arguing this on the day before the election? And where are they now?"

Burns and Wallace pleaded with the judge that it was an oversight, that Laura Taninger would receive the remaining documents as surely as the sun will shine, that they just needed a tiny bit more time, just a few days . . . or a week or two at the most. But on this day—of all days!—the Bureau of Elections could not possibly gather the missing documents and review them for security issues before releasing them. The agency's entire technical staff was either in the field, working hand-in-hand with state voting officials across the country, or manning phone banks to answer last-minute questions from voters and state administrators. Everyone was working overtime to fix the remaining glitches in SafeVote's interface with the states. Ted Burns insisted that he had to get back to his job right then. There wasn't a moment to spare.

Counselor Emmett Wallace added, "*With all due respect*, Your Honor, because Laura Taninger lost her job and is not employed by any media organization at the moment, she's no longer primarily engaged in disseminating information to the public, thereby diluting her need for the petitioned information. Besides, the time she would need to process a stack of new documents before Election Day has now essentially run out. I hope the court will weigh these facts along with our agency's urgent need to concentrate on the SafeVote rollout."

Sam Quinn argued strenuously that Laura, as a freelance journalist, was every bit as engaged as she ever had been in disseminating information to the public and that it was egregious to give Elections any more time to flout the law. "Ms. Taninger's interviews have created a public outcry, and confidence in SafeVote is at an all-time low. In order to restore public confidence, her questions need to be answered immediately."

The judge weighed the matter and rendered his decision. "I hereby reprimand the Bureau of Elections for its tardiness and cavalier disregard of the public disclosure laws," he said. "Nevertheless, in view of the new national election system being rolled out tomorrow, I will give the agency a final two-week delay. But there will be no further delays under any circumstances. Do you understand that, Mr. Wallace?"

"Yes, Your Honor," said Wallace.

"Laura Taninger will still receive the information and be free to disseminate it to the public, albeit after Election Day," said Judge Davidson.

As the judge struck his gavel, Laura's head dropped. She would have no further information to give the voters before they cast their ballots the following day.

Nearby at the People's Manor, Sean Browne banged his fist on his desk and swore. Sprawled across his desk in print news stories and flashed across his computer screen were accounts of an alleged secret love affair between Laura Taninger and Senator Bret Taylor. Sean's face reddened in anger.

Laura Taninger Affair with Bret Taylor Unmasked.

Taninger-Taylor Sex Scandal and Conspiracy to Derail SafeVote Revealed.

Laura Taninger Sex Scandal Sheds Light on SafeVote Attacks.

The articles repeated the same talking points, using virtually identical words, as if they had all been cast from the same mold. One article read:

> According to anonymous sources, controversial journalist and leading critic of SafeVote, Laura Taninger, was having an affair with Senator Bret Taylor, the SafeVote critic from the president's own political party. Through both the Senate Oversight Committee on Elections, which Bret Taylor heads, and Laura Taninger's repeated media attacks on the new voting system, the two lovers conspired to denigrate the signature achievement of President Martin's first term and help Senator Taylor win reelection by appealing to SafeVote skeptics across party lines.

As evidence of the wild allegations, the articles included a photograph of Laura Taninger and Brett Taylor together. They were having drinks in a booth of a bar. The senator was leaning across the table, gripping her arms to pull her close to him as he looked straight into her eyes. She was returning the intense look in what could have passed for a moment of passionate desire between them. One article's caption on the photo was typical of all the rest: "Laura Taninger and Bret Taylor spotted getting friendly in a bar. According to sources, they later left the bar together, and he spent the night at her row house."

Sean knew instantly where the picture had been taken and the context surrounding it, which the writers had failed to investigate. *Is their false reporting due to laziness, incompetence, or malice?* he wondered.

On his monitor, Sean pulled up the website Laura used for her postings. He saw that she had issued a statement on the matter, which all of the articles omitted:

> I categorically deny having any personal relationship with Senator Bret Taylor. Not one so-called journalist called to interview *me* for my side of the story. The senator agreed to have a single, brief meeting with me on a current issue. The picture of us together was taken during that meeting in which we were having an intense discussion about a political subject in a public place. That is the extent of my contact with the senator. The rumors of an affair are nothing more than carefully orchestrated, anonymous claims of uncorroborated, defamatory information intended to smear the senator and me and to hurt his family. The aim of these slanderous lies is to discredit the president's critics, so they won't be taken seriously.

Sean slammed a fist of one hand into the open palm of the other, once, then again, and again. A knock at his half-open door stopped his outburst.

"Ready for the final press briefing before the election?" Without waiting to be invited in, Darcy entered with notes in hand, closed the door, and sat opposite Sean.

"Boy, am I ready! I'm ready to set the record straight!" Sean replied.

"It's very important to leave the voters with impactful final points to remember when they cast their ballots tomorrow," Darcy said.

"That's right, and one point they should know is we don't condone vicious lies."

"What do you mean?"

"I mean the stories that just broke about Laura Taninger and Senator Taylor. That picture of them was taken at Annie's Alehouse, where Laura met the senator for a drink. I remember that night. I recognize the dress she wore, and I know the booths at Annie's. I know for sure where and when that picture was taken because I was parked outside of Annie's that very night! I was waiting for Laura's meeting with the senator to end, so I could take her out to dinner. *I* was with Laura that evening. She and I are old friends. After she met with the senator at Annie's, he went his way, and she and I went to dinner, then later that night I drove her home. I had occasion to remain parked outside of her row house that night. I was . . . er . . . checking my phone messages. I saw the lights go out in her home, which meant she was turning in for the night. No one came or left her row house. I know because I was outside of it on that particular evening. I can verify that nothing happened between Bret Taylor and Laura, so the stories about them being lovers and spending the night together are totally false. When I'm asked about it, as I will be, I intend to say that a highly reliable source refutes the reports."

"Oh, but we intend to *confirm* the reports," Darcy said. "I've written out your talking points." She read from her notes. "You'll say, 'We have reason to believe that the sources are credible, and the stories are true. It appears likely that Senator Taylor will be stripped of his committee chair.'"

"But, Darcy, I *know* the allegations are false. I can't smear Laura and the senator when they've done nothing wrong."

"Why not?"

Sean looked at her incredulously. He replied, choosing his words carefully, "I understand I speak for the president and not for myself. I understand I communicate his views and policies to the press. But this is different, Darcy. This is an outright lie that wrecks people's lives, and it has nothing to do with any policies."

Darcy shrugged her shoulders, untroubled by the matter. "Just say that a credible reporter has come forward with documentation of the affair that was made available only to that reporter from an unidentified person said to be a close aide to the senator."

"How can you expect me to go with that, Darcy? Where's the credibility? There's not a kernel of fact to hang on to!"

"After you give these talking points at your press conference, there will be at least a dozen major news outlets that will pick them up—"

"Without any independent verification!"

"Doesn't matter," Darcy said, shaking her head. "The scandal will be intoxicating. It'll give the media so many clicks and page views and print papers sold that they'll go with it. It'll spread through sheer shock value."

"But it's not true!"

"But it *is* true that senators and media celebrities have affairs, isn't it?"

"So?"

"So, the *narrative* is true. In a wider sense it's true."

"But not in *this* case! I know Laura. I've known her a long time. She's not having any affair with a married man with five kids."

Darcy curled her notes into a cylinder and tapped it in the palm of her hand like a billy club. "The story gets the public's focus off of Laura's investigation, and it puts all eyes on her personal life and her outrageous behavior." She smirked. "Don't you appreciate the beauty of this, Sean? If you shame the messenger, you don't have to discredit the message."

"But, Darcy, I can't spread stories about Laura that are simply not true."

"Nobody cares whether the stories are true or false. People like the scandal. Laura will spend a few weeks trying to defend herself. Maybe that will tire her, and she'll give up her attacks on Ken. Besides, it's for a good cause. Are you forgetting that, Sean? An obnoxious reporter needs to be cut down a notch for the sake of the greater good."

"And do you care if you take down the profession of journalism along with her?"

"Isn't that a bit melodramatic? Why do you have to be so grandiose? Why don't you just do what works? Isn't the end worth it?"

"Is it?" Sean whispered, as if he was posing the question to himself, rather than to Darcy.

"Our goal is a great society with everyone voting, everyone franchised, equality for all—that's the noble end we've worked our butts off to accomplish. Getting to that end includes confirming today's headline story at your press briefing. What's the life of one journalist in the face of all we have to gain?"

Sean studied her critically. His face bore no trace of the admiration he had once felt for her.

"It's for the greater good, the far greater good," she continued. "The people need to trust the election process, and Laura makes them feel uneasy and distrustful. So we need to neutralize her."

"With a lie?"

"I said it's a *narrative*, and if you tell a narrative enough times it becomes the truth."

Sean looked taken aback as if he were seeing her naked.

"If you say something with full conviction," Darcy added, "how many people will take the time to find out if it's true or not? It'll stand. You'll make a new truth. You'll put Laura on the defensive, instead of us playing defense against her. Let her prove she's not a family wrecker and a conniving bitch. And if anyone challenges you, be sarcastic. Say something like, 'Is anybody here naïve enough to think these things don't happen?' Trivialize the question and make the questioner feel small."

Sean's astonishment had vanished, and his face was tightening into an expression he had never allowed himself to display toward the president's closest advisor: contempt.

"So remember your talking point: 'We have every reason to believe that the stories of an affair between Laura Taninger and Senator Bret Taylor are true.' Now, let's move on. I haven't got all day." Darcy skimmed her notes. "When you're asked about the new education bill our opponents are pushing, scratch your head and pause a minute. Make it sound as though your answer is extemporaneous and unrehearsed. Then say that the president opposes it because it involves spending cuts, and he wants to protect our children, not callously abandon them like our opponents want to do. Got that?"

Sean nodded absently.

"And when you talk about the recent stock market declines, don't frown. That makes it seem like we're worried about the market. Going into the election, we certainly don't want to appear worried. . . . "

Darcy's voice droned on until she reached the end of her notes.

"That about covers it. Take a look at these, Sean." She tossed her notes to him across the desk. He made no attempt to reach for them. "If you have any other questions, I'll be in my office."

She walked out, leaving Sean alone with the talking points that would destroy two people's characters and careers, one of whom he was especially protective.

Deep in thought, he slouched over his desk, his head down and arms crossed.

He had aspired to be in the inner circle of the people in power, and he had accomplished his dream. He held a prestigious job in the administration, making him the envy of his former media colleagues. But he had no power. He only parroted Darcy's talking points. If he squawked too much, Darcy, Zack, or Ken could knock him off his perch with a single swat.

The thought of losing the most significant job he'd ever had upset him. But now his job was on a collision course with the other important force in his life.

He looked back on his interactions with Darcy. He had to admit that previously she had asked him to stretch the truth about a number of issues, but he had convinced himself that there was a kernel of truth in those cases and that he wasn't outright lying. Besides, he had told himself, they were good causes, and Darcy meant well. He had believed that the president and all of his aides had good intentions. They were kind, generous people who had striven to do good for the people they served. But now, he wondered if his rationale had merely been pablum he swallowed to help him digest their bitter falsehoods.

If they were well-intentioned, what could explain their behavior toward Laura, a private citizen with no weapon to wield against them other than her single voice of protest? In crushing Laura, did they expect to crush the logic of her arguments? Were they trying to kill an even greater enemy—*the truth*?

His face flushed with anger. He felt a pressing need to defend Laura. He knew that his attraction to her went deeper than just his physical desire. It was her honesty, her integrity, and her inexhaustible principles that also captivated him. She never lost her ideals. She held onto them, no matter the price she had to pay, while he had found it necessary to . . . compromise . . . those traits in the course of his life, especially in his current job.

The chair screeched as he abruptly pushed back from the desk. He grabbed Darcy's notes and left his office. He curled the papers club-like in his hand as he walked down the hall to Darcy's office. He wanted to throw the talking points in her face!

But is that going too far? he asked himself. His old fear of taking a stand against his courted authorities returned. *What should I do?* he worried. *I can't be sure!*

His body tensed in panic. He felt trapped between two charged polar opposites—Laura and his job—each repelling the other and jolting him with their sparks.

Darcy's door was closed. A visitor was inside. He could hear murmurs of a conversation.

Whew! I need time to cool down and better plan my next move, he thought. He waited in the corridor outside, the back of his head touching the wall, his eyes staring at the ceiling, trying to decide what to do.

Then, the door opened a few inches. Darcy's visitor was about to leave. Sean saw a man's arm holding the door handle.

"Remember, we have a meeting today at three." Sean heard Darcy's voice through the open door. "Has he confirmed it yet?"

"No." Sean recognized Zack Walker's voice. "He's not skipping out on us, is he?"

"He'd better not try," Darcy replied.

A chime sounded. "That's my phone," Zack said. He dropped the door handle and removed his phone from a pocket. The office door remained open a few inches, the voices drifting out to Sean.

"He just texted me: 'Meet you at three. Meadowlark Gardens courtyard. Your humble servant, the Fox.'"

The Fox?

The last word rattled in Sean's mind, shaking off any lingering indecisiveness. Suddenly, he knew what he had to do. He quickly returned to his office before he was spotted.

CHAPTER 25

Kate Taninger enjoyed living in Laura's row house, where she had the constant companionship of her favorite sister, who was also her best friend. She liked the character of the house, as well, a renovated modern interior embraced by a classic Victorian exterior. It reminded her of *Taninger News*, an organization that offered the day's headline news proudly wrapped in the traditions and standards of its founder—or at least it did when Laura ran it.

Kate sat writing notes at a table on the airy second level of the row house, in the area between the kitchen and living room that had served as the dining room, but which she had commandeered as her office. Her laptop was open, with papers strewn across the glass-topped table and onto the sideboard by the wall. On that first Monday of November, sunlight streamed across the open living space, from the balcony off the kitchen and through the bay windows into the living room, making it seem like a spring day, while beyond the house, the bare tree branches shuddering in the wind were a reminder of impending winter.

Kate looked up from her work when she heard the front door open and Laura call up to her that she was home. Laura's steps sounded slow and heavy on the staircase to the second floor; then her face came into view, and Kate knew something was wrong.

"What happened in court?"

"The judge gave Elections more time. We won't be getting any more information from them for a few weeks."

Laura tossed her purse, jacket, and sunglasses onto the couch. The usual pep had vanished from her movements just as hope had vanished from her voice. She sunk into a seat at the table, facing her sister. No one could have guessed that there was a ten-year age difference between them. Kate's earnest expression made her look mature at nineteen, and Laura's trim figure in gold sweater and gray slacks displayed a teen's slenderness at twenty-nine.

Laura sighed and asked, "How are things going here?"

"All of today's interviews were canceled," Kate replied dejectedly.

"The scandal?"

"Right."

Since the story of Laura's alleged affair with Senator Taylor broke, news outlets that had scheduled interviews with her grew fearful of losing advertisers, so they canceled. Campaigns like the one being waged against Laura were often accompanied by pressure on advertisers from groups backing the Martin administration, and media outlets that ignored the threats knew the consequences.

"I can see Zack Walker's invisible fist at work in lining up organizations to hit the sponsors of the programs that were going to air interviews with me," Laura said. "Most of these programs would have announced their interview lists online. So anyone interviewing me would be easy to find and target."

"What do we do now?" Kate asked, despair in her voice.

"We've lost," Laura said, shrugging. "Election Day is tomorrow, and the Fox is as elusive now as he was when James Spenser first uttered his name to me with his last breath."

"Some creep's been hired to rig our election, and we can't stop him!" Kate said, frustrated.

"Ken Martin has to be in on this scheme. Instead of getting caught, that bastard will get another four years in power!"

Just then Laura's phone rang. She walked to the couch and took it out of her purse. "Hello? . . . Oh, Sean, hi. . . . *What?* . . . They're meeting . . . *the Fox?*"

Kate stood up. In rapt attention, she approached her sister.

"The Meadowlark Gardens courtyard?" Laura looked incredulous. "Yes, of course, I'm going. . . . Yes, yes, I'll be safe. I won't do anything dangerous. . . . Don't worry, Sean. Thanks!"

Laura ended the call and turned to Kate. "Sean overheard something at the People's Manor. *Darcy Egan and Zack Walker are meeting the Fox.*"

"No way! Seriously? Oh my God, Laura!"

"This is proof positive of the administration's involvement at the highest level in this scheme."

"It sure is."

"They're meeting him at three o'clock in the courtyard of Meadowlark Gardens. That's what Sean overheard Zack say."

"The abandoned housing project?"

"Must be."

Kate rushed back to her laptop. "Let me do a search." She tapped on the keyboard. "Let's see . . . " She scrolled through the results. "The only thing coming up for Meadowlark Gardens in this area is that old housing project."

"Now that I think of it, that's a perfect place for crooks to meet."

"So we'll go there and spy on them, right?" asked Kate.

"Wrong. You're not going."

"You can't go there alone, Laura. Maybe we should call the police."

"You mean the police who said Spenser's murder was a random street crime? The police who work for a mayor who's an ardent supporter of Ken Martin? We can't call them. I think that whatever story Darcy and Ken made up, the police would be pressured to take their side over mine."

"Then you and I will go and watch them meet without being seen."

"*I'll* go. I absolutely forbid you to go with me, Katie."

"What about Reed's tail on you? He'll follow you there. Can he protect you?"

"Oh, no! I can't let him follow me!" Laura started pacing the room, thinking. "The tail reports to Reed, and Reed wants me to give up this investigation. I definitely don't want Reed's private eye telling Reed where I'm going or who I'm spying on. I don't know how Reed would react. He could blow my cover and screw up everything."

"Do you think he would do that?"

"Maybe not intentionally. But even if he just wanted to protect me, he's a loose cannon. He or his private eye could unwittingly reveal my presence and totally botch up everything," said Laura. Then, she suddenly stopped pacing and whirled to Kate. "I have it!"

"What?"

"*You'll* dress in my clothes," she said to Kate. "You can walk down to Nifty Threads and pretend you're shopping. The tail will think you're me, and he'll follow you. Once he's off the block, I'll slip out and go to Meadowlark Gardens."

Kate sprung from her chair and walked toward her sister until they stood eye-to-eye like two fighters in the ring. "Laura, it's too dangerous for you to go there alone!"

"I'll be careful. I just want to get a few pictures of the Fox, especially a shot of him meeting with Martin's two senior aides."

"Swear you'll stay back, you'll keep a safe distance, you won't let them see you!" Kate demanded.

Laura grabbed Kate's arms affectionately. "Honey, I'll be safe."

Kate sighed, knowing her protests were futile.

Soon, Kate was wearing Laura's gold sweater and gray slacks, with her hair falling down her shoulders in Laura's style. Conveniently, Laura had worn sunglasses coming home from court that day, so Kate put them on, enhancing her impersonation.

When it came time to leave, Kate put on the jacket her sister had worn earlier.

"Let's see if the tail follows you," Laura said, giving Kate a reassuring hug.

Hidden by the drapery on the living room windows, Laura watched as Kate left the row house and walked down the street toward the shops a few blocks away. The tail, who was surveilling Laura's house from his parked car about five houses up the street, got out of the vehicle and followed Kate on foot. Success!

When they were out of sight, Laura left her home, walking in the opposite direction to hail a cab. She gave the driver a destination near Meadowlark Gardens. From there, she would walk the rest of the way.

Kate walked from the residential area of row houses to a street with retail shops. She paused to look in the window of their neighborhood clothing boutique, Nifty Threads. The private investigator who mistook her for Laura surveilled Kate from a distance. Neither of them realized that a man in a pickup truck slowly moving down the street was observing both of them.

The driver possessed the unwelcoming face of a creature that frowned excessively. Like a bear with a stockpile of fat and muscle tissue to keep him warm in the cold, the man was thickset with a generous body mass that seemed to make him sweat on that November day. Or was it the hot danger of his assignment that made him remove his jacket and open the window to cool down?

He observed his target, the woman in a gold sweater and gray slacks who was going into Nifty Threads. He had been told there was a tail on her. He recognized the surveillance detail from a time long ago when they both had worked for the same security company, before their lives took opposite turns. Soon, he saw the tail follow his target into the store. He grabbed his phone and made a call.

Down the street, Nicky, the young leader of a street gang, picked up his phone. He was on roller blades, directing two teenage boys, also on skates. The man in the pickup truck was pleased with himself for arranging a clever way of getting rid of the tail. Nicky and the two teens he commanded were happy to pick up some extra cash. Everything was set. The truck driver and the lead skater breathed audibly into their phones, waiting.

After a time spent browsing, Kate left the store and continued walking down the street. Soon after, the tail followed her lead.

"Now! That's him!" The man in the pickup truck told his accomplice over the phone.

Seemingly out of nowhere, a teenager careened down the street on roller blades. He collided with the tail and knocked him down. Just as the victim was getting up, a second skater collided with him and knocked him down again. Nicky then arrived on the scene. He scolded the two teens and told them to be more careful. The three of them apologized to the fallen man, helping him up and dusting him off.

Recovering, the tail shoved all three of the skaters out of his way and rushed toward Kate. But it was too late. The driver of the pickup truck had pulled close to the sidewalk, grabbed his target, shoved a gun in her side, and forced her into the vehicle and across the bench seat. With Kate at the wheel, the kidnapper told her to drive, keeping his gun at her waistline. The truck drove off before the tail could stop them.

Inside the truck, Kate's hands trembled on the steering wheel. The rancid sweat of the man sitting uncomfortably close nauseated her. She felt a stab of pain from the gun he jammed into her side. Then, she noticed something that made her mind race back to Laura's description of Spenser's killer. On the gunman's forearm, she saw a large tattoo—a human skull with black eye sockets and a full set of teeth smiling sadistically at her.

CHAPTER 26

By the time Laura reached Meadowlark Gardens, she had revised her plan. She no longer wanted merely to hide a distance away and photograph the Fox and his clients from afar. She wanted to get close enough to hear their conversation and make a video recording of them with her phone.

She walked through the deserted alley of the complex and into the courtyard. She grimly observed the rusted picnic table, and near it, the slide, swing, and covered bin of jump ropes and other gear that were the remains of a playground. She saw the lampposts with their broken lanterns and missing fixtures. She looked up at the dilapidated buildings lining the courtyard, which stood like the eerie gravestones of a failed project in which the hopes and dreams of the inhabitants were doomed.

She entered one of the buildings from which she hoped to hear the voices in the courtyard, and she crouched down under a broken window facing the playground. She paused at the eerie sight of a tool kit and a roll of duct tape left there, as if a handyman who had patched some of the windows had taken a break and would return any minute to make more repairs.

As she waited, she placed her phone in her jacket pocket, ready to pull out as soon as the meeting's participants arrived. With any luck, this recording would destroy Darcy Egan, Zack Walker, and the contractor who was making their diabolical scheme possible. This man would stop at nothing for money. He'd sell out a country, a once-great country, to enrich himself. As she crouched down and waited, she vowed to bring the Fox to justice for his unspeakable crimes against her country.

She heard a car approaching. Then, its engine stopped. She heard only one car door opening, so she concluded the person was alone. *It must be the Fox.* She heard footsteps coming through the building opposite to hers as the person headed toward the courtyard. She was about to see a monster who would extinguish the cherished liberty of America, a depraved individual who would destroy the people's right to elect their leaders at the ballot box. She was about to see a man who, for a load of money, would topple the hard-fought gains of human freedom that took millennia of human suffering to establish. She could feel her heart pounding against her chest as her face reddened and her hands shook. Every cell of her body was demanding the capture and punishment of the man she was about to see.

At first, she saw only glimpses of the man in the shadows of the building. She observed his baseball cap, his vest over a long-sleeved sweater without the benefit of a coat, and his sunglasses. He walked with a relaxed stroll that suggested to her a casual, devil-may-care attitude—a man without a conscience.

Then, he moved into the courtyard in full sight. She realized she knew that body all too well. The muscular arms, the tall build, the trim waist, the long legs, the tightly curled hair weaving out under the cap.

She forgot about hiding, about her safety, about the incredible story she was there to chronicle—a story that just became even more outrageous than she'd ever imagined.

She stepped out in the open to face him.

"Reed!"

CHAPTER 27

He whirled around to her, startled. How rare to see him caught off guard.

"What the hell are you doing here?" Reed asked. "You have to get out of here now. You're in great danger!"

She didn't recognize the voice that had dropped an octave.

"*You're* the Fox? *You*, Reed?"

"I just got a text. You're supposed to be out shopping. Who came out of your house and walked into a store? Wait, don't tell me—Kate."

"Reed, *you're* the traitor? How low can you go?"

"You lost the tail I put on you. You came alone—didn't you? To a place fraught with danger. That was very unwise and could cost us both our lives!"

"What the hell are you talking about, *Frank Foxworth*?"

"I can't explain. They'll be here any minute."

"What the hell's going on, Reed? You're working with Darcy Egan and Zack Walker to *rig* the election?"

"They think I am. It's complicated."

The reporter in her persisted. "Does it go all the way up to Ken Martin?"

His grim look told her the answer.

"Reed, if you have something to say, say it. Otherwise, know that I'll get you. I've hunted you down. Even you, Reed. I won't let you get away with this—"

"Okay!" He raised his hands in resignation to her will. "I'll tell you this much, and then you'll go. Last year, when the Bureau of Fair Trade dropped its plan to break up my company, more concessions than anyone knew were extracted from me. I met with Martin's closest aides and agreed to do a secret job for them. They were the ones who leaned on their partisan friends at Fair Trade to dismiss the lawsuit against me. It was Martin's closest aides who got them to

203

shelve the plans to destroy my company, and I, in turn, agreed to secretly help them with the reelection campaign."

"You mean, you saved your business by agreeing to destroy our country?"

"When I left you last year, it was to keep you from ever getting involved with this scheme. It was much too dangerous. That's why I had to leave you. I didn't count on you uncovering the whole thing on your own and throwing a monkey wrench in the gears I so carefully set in motion. You're too damn good a journalist, Laura, and it could cost you your life! Yes, you figured it out. Almost. But what you don't know is my *real* role here."

Just then his phone rang. "That's them. That's their ring." He slid his phone out of his vest pocket and answered it. "Yeah, Velvet. What's up? . . . Okay, I'll wait. Take your time." He ended the call and put his phone back.

"Your friend Sean is a no-show for his presser, so Darcy needs to rehearse another stooge to spit out the talking points. They'll be twenty minutes late." He grabbed her arms. "That gives you time to high-tail it out of here!"

"You said I don't know your *real* role in this thing. What would that be?"

"That will become clear to you later. But now, you have to go. As it is, I may not . . . This is my last meeting with them. It's very dangerous. If I didn't show up, that would raise their suspicions. So here I am, but I could be walking into a trap. Laura, I may not . . . If I don't . . . I want you to know . . . Oh, Laura . . ."

He pulled her close and kissed her. She felt the hunger of his mouth against hers, the urgency of his hands stroking her shoulders, the longing of his arms pulling her closer. Against her will, she felt her arms winding around him. She lifted his vest and felt the luscious folds of his back through his sweater. She felt the handle of a concealed gun tucked inside a waistband holster at his side. For a moment there was no investigation, no election, no country. Just the sudden release of a desire that had been repressed too long.

Suddenly, a man appeared behind Reed and dug a knife into his back, almost piercing his skin.

"Let her go!" the man demanded. "Let her go now, unless you want to be paralyzed for life."

Both of them recognized the voice. It was Sean Browne.

CHAPTER 28

Reed loosened his arms around Laura and raised his head. "Don't mangle my back the way you mangle the news."

"Reed!" Sean gasped in utter disbelief.

In a surprise move, Laura grabbed Reed's gun, stepped away from the men, and pointed the weapon at both of them.

"Drop the knife, Sean, and step back. You, too, Reed, step back."

The men looked astonished.

"Drop it, Sean!"

The seriousness of her tone made Sean obey. He dropped the knife. The men stepped back. She moved forward to stand by the knife as if guarding it.

"So now we know who the Fox is," said Sean. "The biggest bastard in the country is none other than Reed Miller. *He's* rigging the election. *He's* selling out our country for a pile of cash! I should've guessed it, Laura. We need to call the police and turn him in, along with his two accomplices, right now!" Sean reached into a shirt pocket for his phone.

"Not so fast," said Laura.

She stood about eight feet from the men. They stood about four feet apart, watching her as the gun in her hand moved slightly, leaning first toward one man, then the other, leaving them wondering where it would ultimately point.

"He's conning you again, Laura," Sean warned. "Remember how he used you and crushed your feelings without a care in the world?"

Sean raised his phone to begin dialing. "I'm calling the cops."

"Put that phone away, now!" Laura demanded, her gun pointing at Sean's chest.

"Okay, Laura. Don't do anything crazy. You hear?" Sean slid the phone back into his pocket.

Laura looked at Reed. "You said I don't know your *real* role here. Just what would that be?"

"Knowing the truth puts both of your lives in danger, and mine, too," said Reed, shaking his head. "But here goes." He turned to Laura while she continued to hold them at gunpoint. "Did you really think I'd roll over and play dead? Did you think I'd let Ken Martin's goons transform my company from something that served my beliefs and values, and served my customers, into something that served them? And would I *oversee* the SafeVote programming for them, as they so delicately put it, in exchange for them not destroying my company? What kind of a deal is that? A deal with a thief not to empty your house?"

Laura listened soberly while Sean sneered.

Reed continued, "I had no army to defeat them. I had no movement, no groundswell to stage an uprising. I had only myself. So I figured I had to play along with them in order to destroy them and their evil scheme. My weapon was a new high-tech video camera hidden within these lenses and frame, right here." He pointed to his sunglasses. "This was how I got video recordings of the commander-in-chief and his inner circle engaging in systematic, deliberate, unequivocal election fraud. I would be an army of one to bring them down. That was my thinking."

He glanced at his watch nervously and looked around the grounds to check that no one was yet approaching.

"Go on, Reed. I want to hear all of it," Laura ordered.

"Yes, I rigged SafeVote in a project called Operation Topcoat. I devised a program that would steal votes that were cast for Martin's opponent in the districts and counties of swing states, and I would give those votes to him. It was all mathematically arranged to give Ken Martin ballot wins in areas where he otherwise would have lost by a slim margin. Everything would appear to be plausible and no results would be so outlandish as to raise suspicions of rigging. That's the job I did as they know it. But there's more. I did more programming that no one knows anything about. You two will be the only ones who know what I'm going to say next."

He turned to Sean. "I trust Laura to know this. But *you?*" He glared distrustfully at Sean. "You can't say anything about this until after five o'clock tonight. This is of the gravest importance!"

"Come off it, Reed. You're spinning us to make yourself look innocent," Sean said.

"Shut up, Sean." Laura ordered. "Reed, you have to tell both of us. That's the way it is."

Reed shrugged and continued, "At five o'clock tonight, unknown to anyone, I've arranged for the SafeVote system to revert to the original certified program that was in place before I began Operation Topcoat. Also, at five o'clock tonight, a telecast will air on Miller News and be transmitted to news outlets across the country and the world. A pre-recorded video will play in which I'll explain everything to the public. I'll explain how I rigged the system, and I'll also explain how the changes I made are being reversed so that the original, legitimate program is being put back in operation as I speak. I'll tell the people that when they go to the polls tomorrow, they can rest assured that their votes will be counted as cast.

"Then I'll reveal to the world the amazing proof of my sting operation. I'll show the videos of me meeting with Darcy and Zack, explaining the vote-rigging, and getting their approval. The videos will also reveal my meeting with Ken Martin in which he shows he's aware of Operation Topcoat and gives me the green light to do it.

"I arranged my life, so there would be nothing they could threaten me with. I lost interest in my business and passively complied with their broadcast requirements. I also freed myself from other . . . entanglements." He looked at Laura and his voice softened. "I had to write you out of my life, so they would never know you were important to me, so they would never use you to manipulate me. I was willing to risk *my* life. But not *yours*."

Laura listened poker-faced, keeping her emotions in check, weighing the shocking things he told them.

"When my video is broadcast at five o'clock tonight—when the program I rigged is erased and the legitimate original program is re-activated—I'll be on my private plane headed to a remote spot outside the country where no one will find me."

Laura could tell that he was searching for her reaction, wondering if she believed his story. But she continued to fight off her emotions, trying hard to be objective and show no sign of either accepting his story or rejecting it until she had heard it all.

Reed continued, "No one can stop the reversion to the legitimate voting program, except me. Neither Darcy nor Zack can stop it. Ken Martin can't stop it. The tech stooge at Elections that's in on the scheme can't stop it. Everything is password protected and encrypted. No one must discover what's about to happen or be able to force me to halt it. The only thing that can stop me is if they somehow discover my plan and can get me to cancel it. I must have nothing here that they can use to force me! That means you, Laura. That's why you have to trust me and leave here now!" He finished speaking and glanced at his watch. "You have less than ten minutes before they arrive."

There was a pause as Laura and Sean absorbed the information.

Then, Sean broke the silence. "A one-man army! No one would ever do the crazy things you say you're doing."

"No one *you* know would," Reed replied.

"Why would Darcy and Zack trust *you* with this work?" Sean asked.

"I built a corporate empire on my own cutting-edge programming, so they knew I had the skill to do the job. With the lawsuit at the Bureau of Fair Trade to break up my company, they gave me the motive. They were holding my company hostage, and they thought I'd do what they wanted. Besides, they kicked in a hefty fee, figuring that would be an added inducement. They were right about my having the skill, but they didn't know that I don't pay ransom—and money-at-any-price is not what I'm after."

"You've been unreliable before, Reed," said Laura, the pain of the past resurfacing in her voice.

"You have to believe me, Laura. It's the reason I left you."

"How do I know you're telling the truth this time?" Laura asked.

"He's lying. Don't believe him," interjected Sean.

"You know, Sean, you don't have a good track record of grasping more than meets the eye and getting at the real truth," Reed said.

"There's one truth I know: *You're a traitor!*" Sean charged.

"*You're* the traitor. When you were in the news business, you betrayed your profession," said Reed, his voice heavy with contempt. "You know how much damage you've done with your clueless, sycophantic news stories that snow the public and perpetuate the power-grabbers? It's people like you who threw us to the wolves. And for what? So you wouldn't have to work too hard and verify the facts yourself, so you could swallow talking points somebody else fed you and go home for the day, so you could go along to get along and advance your career with a top job in the People's Manor? You're a bottom-feeder who got to the top!"

Laura tried to decide what to do. As her gun swayed from Reed to Sean, her feelings pulled her in one direction, but her mind nudged them back. She felt compelled to hear more, to stop her feelings from leading her in the wrong direction.

"Laura," Sean pleaded, "don't let him ramble on. He's not on your side. *I am.* I finally saw what you wanted me to see. When Darcy and Zack promoted that scandal about you and the senator, which I knew was false, I finally realized they had nothing resembling good intentions. I broke with them when they wanted me to spread vicious lies about you. But Reed knows about worse things that they're doing, and he's in bed with them. That's why you can count on me, not him. Now, I see the truth."

"*Now* you see the truth?" Reed remarked. "It's a little late—isn't it? I saw the truth from the time I could walk. I saw their types in school. They envy you when you get high grades. They resent your success. They hate when you do things better than they can. They're the ones who accomplish nothing and want to control everything. When they grow up, they gravitate to politics as their breeding grounds. They find useful stooges like you, who for whatever reason, help them along, who give them a moral sanction, which is the worst thing you can do."

"Laura," Sean pleaded, "he admits he rigged the election. You caught him. Now he's composing a wild lie to wiggle out of it." He turned to Reed. "Stop playing with her feelings. You don't deserve a hearing with her. You don't deserve her, period."

"You think *you* deserve her, man?" asked Reed. "When her family's businesses were being pummeled, you spit out the administration's moronic talking points. You said that they were only regulating *business* and not trying to influence Laura's *speech*. But if they control our property, they control everything else—what we say, what we do, our freedom—everything is theirs. So now, you finally wake up to what your bosses are really after. You're a little late to the party, Sean."

"That's enough! Both of you!" Laura said, still holding her gun on both men.

"Laura, we're out of time. You have to believe me," Reed said urgently.

"And be played again? Don't believe him, Laura!"

Sean and Reed stared at her, waiting. The gun pointed a little more toward Reed, then a little more toward Sean, then back and forth again.

"I've had enough of his lies." Sean reached for his phone. "I'm calling the cops."

"No, you're not!" Laura made her decision. She walked toward Sean and from close range aimed the revolver only at him.

Laura's move galvanized Reed. He picked up Sean's knife and lodged it in the back of his belt. He opened the bin in the playground and grabbed two jump ropes. Then, he pushed Sean down on the ground and went to tie his hands. Sean tried kicking and punching in protest, but Reed was too strong for him. He subdued Sean and managed to bind his hands behind him, then his ankles.

"Quit struggling, Sean," Laura said. "We don't have time for this."

Looking at Laura with defeat in his eyes, he stopped trying to break free. Reed trotted to the broken window and gingerly slipped his arm through to retrieve the roll of duct tape that had been left on the sill.

"Is that really necessary?" Sean asked, as Reed ripped a length of tape from the roll.

"It's to protect all of us, including you," Reed said, as he taped Sean's mouth with it.

Reed lifted Sean over his shoulder like a sack and lugged him to the front of the building where his car was parked. Laura followed. Reed opened the rear door of his sedan and laid Sean across the seat.

"You have to stay down, Sean. If you don't, we'll all be dead," Reed said. Then he turned to Laura.

"It's too late for you to run. They'll be here any minute. You have to hide here."

"Take this." She tried to give him back his gun.

"No! You keep it."

"You need it, Reed. I absolutely insist."

She held the gun out. He took it and dropped it in her purse.

"They play dirty, Laura. Nothing is beneath them. Use it if you have to."

He looked her over, drinking her in before embracing her.

"I'm supposed to give them the source code for Topcoat," he whispered into her hair as he held her. "It's reasonable for them to ask for a personal delivery of something that sensitive, so I have to comply. But I can't help thinking this could be a trap."

He pulled back and his face showed a grim resolve to accept the ultimate risk he was taking.

"If you see them leave, and I don't . . . come back. . . . If anything happens to me . . . hide until they're gone, then get out of here. Call in an anonymous tip to the cops to come and retrieve Sean but wait until after my video starts before you set him free."

"Reed, do you have to meet them? Can't you just leave the country now? Can't we go together?"

"You can't be part of this! If I don't show up, they'll suspect something. They could detain me before I'd ever get out of the private airport I use."

She pulled him close again. "Reed, be careful!" She kissed him passionately.

Their moment ended abruptly. They heard footsteps and voices nearby.

"Hide back here. Don't come any closer!" he whispered.

In a moment, he was gone.

CHAPTER 29

Reed walked into the courtyard and stood at the lamppost by the playground. At his side, the empty holster where his gun had sat now felt like a missing kidney. Sean's knife tucked into his pants provided some comfort.

Soon Darcy and Zack came into view, approaching as they usually did on foot through the alley. Zack carried a laptop case slung over his shoulder.

As they walked toward him, Reed nodded his head in greeting.

"Where is it?" said Zack.

Reed removed a thumb drive from his pocket and gave it to Zack. "Your tech guy at the Bureau will find all of the security information here to access the complete file sets of the source code."

Zack sat at the picnic table and removed his laptop from the case. He inserted Reed's thumb drive. "I'll transmit this under high security to Rayon to check it out." Rayon was the code name of the technical specialist inside the Bureau of Elections who was in on the scheme. He was none other than the director of technology, who had stood in Judge Davidson's courtroom, Ted Burns.

A few minutes passed before a reply came through. Zack reported, "Rayon verifies that everything is here."

The president's senior strategist looked pleased as he shut down the laptop, slipping it back in his case before he rejoined the others.

"Good," said Reed. "Operation Topcoat is completed and delivered. Now, if you'll excuse me, I'll see you again for the next election."

He turned and started to walk away.

"Wait just a minute," said Darcy.

Reed turned to the woman who was now pointing a gun at him.

"You're not going anywhere until after Election Day," explained Darcy.

Dread filled Reed. "Come again?"

"We've arranged for you to be taken to a pleasant place with everything you could possibly need provided."

"And what armed guards will keep me in there?"

Darcy huffed, and said reassuringly, "There are no guards. Really, now. There's just an associate of ours. He'll see to it that you're comfortable. You'll remain at our location until after the election is over."

"Why?"

"Because we want to keep you on our radar during the election."

"Then what?"

"Then, if all goes as planned, you'll be free to leave and do as you please," Darcy said pleasantly.

"If you think I'm a threat, you'll have to detain me forever—or kill me."

"After the election," said Darcy, "the deed would already be done, and you'd be guilty of doing it. Before the election, you could say you're innocent. You could say you're coming forward to reveal the scheme *before* it's carried out and leave me and Leather holding the bag."

"Come on, Velvet. You're protected by my involvement. That holds true before, during, and after the voting. *I'm* the one who did the work. Do you really think I'd expose you at the cost of incriminating myself?"

"We don't know what you'd do. We just want to be cautious." Her voice sounded benign while her eyes looked vicious. "Leather, do what we discussed. We need to get out of here *now*."

Zack reached into his briefcase and removed a pair of handcuffs. "Put your back against the lamppost, Fox."

Reed hesitated. Zack pushed him against the post.

"Leather will cuff you to the post, and we'll be on our way. You'll wait here for our associate to pick you up."

"You're okay with this?" Reed tried his case with Zack. "With her pointing a gun at me?"

Darcy answered for Zack, "We just want to be sure everything goes as planned, and you don't pull a fast one on us."

"That's why Velvet arranged for one of our people to escort you to a safe place, where you'll pass a day under our supervision. Then you can go," Zack said. He spoke in a monotone, as if he were one of Darcy's stooges, repeating her talking points.

"Are you trying to convince me or help yourself ignore what's actually happening?" Reed asked sharply.

Zack pulled Reed's arms behind him around the post and was about to cuff his hands.

"How much does she tell you?" Reed asked him. "Did she tell you about *Spenser*?"

Reed hit a nerve. Zack hesitated.

It had been a shock to Zack when Spenser was killed. Darcy had told him Spenser's death was an accident. Was he in for another . . . surprise?

"You're leaving me here for a hitman to get me. Are you okay with that, Leather? I know you're okay with *character* assassination. But now you're going far beyond that."

The cuffs dangled limply in Zack's hand. "What exactly is Denim gonna do, Darcy?" he asked.

"Oh *please*, Zack," she scolded him. "Get on with it."

Zack swallowed hard as if to dismiss his misgivings. "I'm cuffing you, Reed. That's all I'm doing, and that's all I know," he said.

"Hurry up, Zack," Darcy said. "Leave the handcuff key on the picnic table for Denim. We need to get out of here before he arrives."

As the tension mounted, they dispensed with their sartorial code names, except for their references to Denim, which seemed to be the man's actual name.

"Is Denim the same *associate* who killed Spenser?" Reed asked. "Were you an accessory to that murder, Zack, as you will be to mine?"

"Shut up!" Darcy bellowed. "Zack, cuff him *now!*"

"Oh, no you don't." Suddenly, from the shadows inside one of the buildings, a woman moved in close to the courtyard. She pointed Reed's gun at his two adversaries.

Laura said, "Drop the gun, Darcy."

Reed leaped into action. He grabbed Darcy's gun. He patted Zack down but found no weapon. Then, he walked to Laura and held them at gunpoint with her. He glanced at his ally with a mixture of affection for her and concern for her safety.

"You!" Darcy said, astonished. "Here? Then who's with—" She stopped short of finishing her sentence, looking as if she had gone too far.

"What the hell are you talking about?" Zack asked, suspiciously.

"Never mind!" Darcy replied.

A beep sounded from Reed's phone with a special tone that captured his attention. Holding Darcy's gun in one hand and lifting his phone out of his vest pocket with the other, Reed looked disturbed by the urgent message he'd received.

"I can tell you exactly what she's talking about," he said, as he scrolled down a text message with images that had been transmitted to his phone.

His private eye reported the kidnapping. He had recovered from his scuffle with the skaters quickly enough to capture photos of the event. Grimly, Reed held one of the images out to Laura.

"Oh my God!" Laura exclaimed, horrified at the sight of a monstrous man grabbing Kate and shoving her into a truck. Then Laura's eyes gravitated to the tattoo visible on the man's forearm, a marking she recognized. She whispered to Reed, "*That's Spenser's killer with Kate!*"

"Darcy was having Laura kidnapped, Zack. And someone got pictures of the whole thing." He held up his phone for Zack to see the image, then he slipped the phone back into his pocket. "You picked up the wrong woman!" Reed yelled at Darcy.

Zack looked mortified. "We didn't discuss any kidnapping, Darcy! We discussed taking Fox here into our custody for a day, and that's it."

Reed moved directly in front of Darcy with the barrel of his gun almost touching her chest. "Call your thug and have the woman you snared released. *Now!*" he shouted.

"It's too late," Darcy said. "They're coming here."

Reed quickly walked to Laura and whispered, "Keep your gun on them. I'll tie them up, then we'll hide here and surprise the thug."

"Reed, we can't leave here till we get Kate!" said Laura.

"Of course, we'll rescue Kate," Reed assured her.

Before they could execute their plan, a pickup truck pulled into the alley. The vehicle stopped abruptly, its brakes screeching. The man called Denim got out of the passenger's seat, dragging the driver behind him.

Reed and Laura froze in their places. They dared not shoot, fearing for Kate.

Terrorized, Kate Taninger could only move her eyes. She looked at Laura, knowing why her sister was there. Then she looked at Reed, utterly confused at his presence. Her shoulders were locked in the vise-grip of her assailant's arm, and a gun scraped against her temple. With her assailant twice her weight and almost a foot taller, she looked as if she could be crushed in his grasp.

Darcy sighed in relief. Her voice suddenly regained its vigor. "I thought you'd never get here!" She looked elated at the site of the stocky man pointing a gun at Kate's head. She turned to Laura and Reed. "Drop those guns and step back!" she ordered.

Laura and Reed complied.

Darcy peered at Kate, whose sunglasses had come off during her struggle. "It's Laura's sister, you moron!"

Denim did a double-take of his victim and the look-alike woman already in the courtyard. His face looked vicious and his voice was a snarl. "What the hell's goin' on? I don't never work with no audience watchin' me."

"I'll handle it," Darcy said. "Denim, keep your gun on the hostage! Zack, get my gun and give it to me." Darcy addressed the men like a general giving orders to foot soldiers. Zack handed Darcy the gun that Reed had dropped. "And take her gun." Zack picked up the gun Laura had dropped. "Pat them down."

Zack complied and found the knife Reed carried. For a moment, he paused, uncertain of what to do with it and utterly uncomfortable with the situation. Then, as if imitating the crime shows he'd watched on television, he assumed a cocky look and tucked the knife in his pants.

Reed, Laura, and Kate stood helpless, all held at gunpoint.

CHAPTER 30

"Get that Neanderthal off Kate!" Reed ordered.

"You're hardly in a position to give orders," Darcy said smugly, like a player who held all the aces. She turned to Denim. "Hold on to her."

Denim looked distressed. "I work *in private*. What the hell's goin' on?"

"Darcy, let the women go! I'll comply, but let them go," Reed demanded, but Darcy ignored him.

Zack glared at Darcy, a mounting fury on his face. "You never discussed any kidnapping with me! Are you crazy?"

"It's not just Reed that poses a danger. Laura does, too," Darcy explained to Zack, her tone patronizing. "I discovered she had a tail on her. We didn't put it there. *He* did. He still has a thing for her. Look at them here together. They're partners, and that's not good for us. She's as dangerous as he is."

"You and Ken planned this thing and left me out?" Zack sounded injured, as if he, the insider, were suddenly—shockingly—tossed out, just when he thought he'd reached the preeminent place to ply his trade. "I don't get it, Darcy!"

"I get it," Reed said to Zack. "You and Darcy were supposed to leave me here tied to the lamppost, so the kidnapper could swing by and grab me, too. You two were supposed to leave here before the hitman arrived, so you'd never see Darcy's *real* partner. Then, later on, you'd learn that Laura coincidentally disappeared, also. Then, she and I would never be heard from again. That would surely raise your suspicions, Zack. You'd know that something more was done than you were privy to. But to allay your conscience—what little of it there is—Darcy would spin it for you, so you could evade the fact that you were an *accessory to murder*."

Zack looked indignant. "What the hell were you thinking, Darcy? We have *nothing* on Laura. She's not our accomplice. She's committed no crime like he has. Why on earth would we take her? And now we have the other sister being kidnapped to add to our crimes? Are you stupid or what, Darcy?" Zack's face reddened with rage.

Denim, ignored in the heat of their argument, was growing impatient. "What the hell's goin' on?" Denim looked at Darcy, then Zack, searching for an answer.

Darcy spoke soothingly as if confronting a beast that might bite her. "Nothing to worry about, Denim. Tie the three of them up and take them away in the truck bed." There was a cap with dark tinted windows on the bed of the truck, convenient for concealing the contents. "We'll hold them at gunpoint until you're finished. Go on! . . . Denim?" She glared at the big man, who hesitated.

"I'm gettin' paid to do two. Not fer nothin' more," said Denim. "Not fer no crowd observin' my work."

"But you've already done something else, remember?" said Darcy. "We have that on you, so you'd better comply."

Becoming more agitated and out-of-control, Denim blurted out: "That wuz an accident 'cause the dude fought back. That wuz *self-defense*."

Zack shot an angry look at Darcy and said, "You told me we were just going to rough Spenser up, to scare him into keeping his mouth shut!"

"I was surprised it went that far, too," Darcy admitted. "But I've learned to appreciate the benefits. If there's no person, then the problem he posed is suddenly gone, too."

"You were spying on Spenser, weren't you?" Laura posed the question to Zack and Darcy. "You knew Spenser had found out something, and he was meeting me to reveal it. You sent *him*," she looked at Denim with disgust, "to beat up Spenser, which led to his death." She turned to the kidnapper. "Do you know we have a witness? When you killed Spenser, someone saw you jump the fence and got a good look at your tattoo. We'll nail you for that unless you let your hostage go and make a run for it now."

A profusion of sweat dripped down Denim's face.

"We can lean on the mayor, Denim. You see they've been soft on the Spenser investigation," Darcy coaxed.

"But now there's more evidence and more crimes," said Reed. "The police won't play politics with what I have, big man." Reed slowly pointed to his vest pocket. "I have pictures of the kidnapping on my phone. I'll show you."

"Shut up, Reed!" Darcy demanded.

"*You* shut up!" Denim overrode her. He momentary swiveled the gun to point at her. With a new coat of worry shellacking his leather face, he turned to Reed and demanded, "Let's see wut you got."

Gingerly, Reed reached for his phone and held it up to the kidnapper. Denim squinted to see the images. "Here you are shoving the woman into your car at gunpoint. Your face is in full view. So is your gun and your tattoo." He scrolled down to another image. "Here's a shot showing the license plate of your truck. Once the police magnify that plate, they'll identify you. Once they catch you, they'll match your gun to the bullet they recovered when you killed Spenser—"

"Shut up, Reed!" Darcy ordered.

"The private eye you knocked down took these pictures, and he's transmitting them to the police right now!" Reed added.

Panic gripped the big man's face.

Darcy softened her voice to plead with him, saying, "Now Denim, let's remain calm and focused. Do what I told you to do. We'll kick in extra for the sister. All you have to do is tie the three of them up and take them away in the truck bed."

"It's going to be a little hard to claim self-defense *four times*," Reed said.

"Your only chance is to *run now!*" Laura added.

Denim was shaking. His eyes bulged as if they were envisioning a scenario he had to avoid at all costs. Suddenly, he shoved Kate away roughly. With a cry, she fell to the ground. He ran to his truck and backed out of the alley at high speed, his wheels kicking up plumes of dust. Soon there was silence. Denim vanished behind the powdery cloud, like a monster retreating in the face of an attack.

But two guns still pointed at Reed, Laura, and Kate.

CHAPTER 31

With his arms raised to avoid provoking a shot from Darcy or Zack, Reed walked slowly to Kate and helped her up. His captors were too busy bickering with each other to stop him. In a brotherly way, Reed helped Kate dust off, and he comforted her with a hug.

"Reed, what are *you* doing here?" she whispered incredulously.

"I'm on your side," he replied.

Her face looked trusting, as if she were pleased to discover that someone she liked wasn't a villain after all.

She clung to him for a moment, welcoming the chance to compose herself. Then, she moved away and stood on her own, staring angrily at Darcy and Zack.

"There comes a time, Zack, when the New Leader's aides have to be willing to do extraordinary things in exceptional circumstances," said Darcy. "Did you read the last chapter of my book?"

Zack whined like a wayward pupil, saying, "I don't have time for idle academics."

"*I* read it," said Laura. "The last chapter is where she condones *any lengths* to achieve her end. I don't think she meant that as idle academics."

"We step over the norms. We create *new* norms for ourselves," Darcy said proudly. "There's been a change in plans, Zack. You need to come to grips with that and meet the challenge."

"What the hell are you talking about?"

"We're at war, and they're the enemy. You need to end the threat right here and now."

"Then, why doesn't *she* kill us?" Reed posed his question to Zack. "It's her cause, too. Why doesn't *she* get her hands dirty for it?"

"Yeah, why not?" Zack wanted to know.

"You're the *assistant* to Ken and me," Darcy said, sneering at Zack. "*You* take care of it. Dispense with them—now!"

"*What!*" Zack exclaimed in utter disbelief. "I write hit pieces. That's it."

"If you think this is just about word play, man, you're a piker," Reed said, taunting him.

Zack fidgeted. His sweat dripped on the gun.

Bulged eyes and a crazed smile dominated Darcy's face. "We'll stage it," she cried. "A double-murder committed by Reed Miller, and then, his own suicide."

Reed, the sisters, and even Zack gaped at Darcy. Everyone could tell she was becoming deranged.

"You'll do the talking points, Zack." Darcy continued, engrossed with her scheme. "We'll say that Reed was a lover to both sisters. They found out. They confronted him. He decided to kill them both, then himself!"

"I thought I was having an affair with the senator," said Laura.

"That was last week," Darcy insisted. Her eyes looked glassy, and her face looked dazed, unreachable. "This week we need a new spin, Zack. You'll put together a new narrative."

"*Are you crazy?*" Zack whispered, almost to himself.

"The truth is like clay, and we're the sculptors. We knead it. We work it. We mold it. We massage it to suit our ends. You're the expert at that, Zack."

"I can't massage three murders, Darcy."

"We'll use *their* gun and put it in his hands. That's the gun you're holding," Darcy continued in her delusion.

"Of course, it's the gun *you're* holding that does the job, Zack." Reed jibed. "Darcy never intended to kill us. That was the Neanderthal's job. Now that he's gone, it's *your* job."

"Go on, Zack. Do it!" Darcy's face lit up with a diabolical excitement for impending violence.

Zack hesitated as he held the gun on Kate, Laura, and Reed.

"Our ends are noble. We mustn't be timid," said Darcy.

"What's the noble end for Zack in this endeavor? A jail cell for the rest of his life?" Kate asked Darcy.

"I have news for you, Zack," Reed added. "The end isn't noble. It's *depraved*. The end is nothing more than feeding the raw lust for power of your handlers, a lust that totally breaks their ties to reality."

"You're a coward, Zack," Darcy said, disgusted. "You don't have the courage for what needs to be done."

"But Darcy," Zack pleaded, "remember when you, me, and Ken were labeled by the media as the heart, the fist, and the mouth of the presidency? You liked that. You said that fit in with the theories in your book. You're supposed to be the *heart*. Remember?"

"You're supposed to be the fist. Some fist you are!" Darcy complained.

"Some heart you are," said Zack.

Darcy sneered. Now, her gun wavered—first, pointing at Reed and the women, then pointing at Zack.

"Where's the heart?" Zack persisted. "We're supposed to have a heart and use non-violent means, like in a democracy, right?"

"Ironic from the man who was rigging an election," Laura mumbled to her companions.

"Democracy!" Darcy scoffed. "Such a sweet-sounding word, such a giddy fantasy. You want to ride the white horse, but you never want to see the underbelly of the beast." Darcy looked entranced by an inner vision, beyond the reach of any argument or plea. "You're like all the other self-fashioned devotees of great movements, Zack. When things out of your comfort zone have to be done, you recoil." Enraged, Darcy pointed her gun at Zack.

"If you're so comfortable with murder, then why don't you do it?" Zack asked combatively.

"I've shown my commitment to our great movement, our power, our place in history. If you want a share in that power, you need to do something bold to earn our respect."

The gun in Zack's hand was poised to do the job, if she could persuade him.

"After Ken and me, it'll be you, Zack. You'll be the third most powerful person *in the world!*" Consumed with an open, shameless, irrepressible craving for the power she desired, Darcy's eyes flashed excitedly.

Zack hesitated. He nervously shifted his weight from one leg to the other, the cuffs of his pants brushing the ground. The fate of the nation now rested on the man with the droopy pants.

"Shoot! That's an order!" Darcy charged, her gun now pointed at Zack's chest.

Zack's gun still pointed at Reed and the sisters, his finger on the trigger.

The victims had moved closer together. Laura and Kate held each other close. Reed stepped in front of them, his arms extended out to his sides to shield the sisters. Laura bent her head. Kate closed her eyes.

Then, suddenly, Zack looked as if a fog had finally lifted. His eyes widened in understanding and his body pivoted as he realized the answer to his own question. *"There is no heart."*

With a blast, Zack's gun fired. But the three captives remained standing. Darcy staggered. With a bullet wound to her chest, she struggled to raise her gun and aim it at Zack's heart. She pulled the trigger, but flinching in pain, she hit his midsection instead. They both hit the ground, and a shower of blood darkened the pavement.

Reed retrieved his gun, pushed Darcy's gun out of their reach, and then lingered for a moment over the conscious casualties. "You're not the last word on the human race!" He gestured to himself and the sisters, and he declared triumphantly, "We are!"

Laura felt tears pouring down her face, in relief, in elation, in admiration. *This* was the Reed she knew—a full-throated, tireless fighter for the ideas and values he ardently held. She knew that he had not lost any of his fire for the precious things in his life, including her. The tension of the afternoon and of his year-long ordeal suddenly drained from his face. The boyish grin that had charmed her in their glorious year together now returned. He flashed it at Laura.

CHAPTER 32

Reed drove away from Meadowlark Gardens.

In the car, the sisters recounted the story of the kidnapping and attempted murder to Sean, who was now untied and traveling with them. With Sean having played a pivotal role in foiling the scheme of his superiors and now repudiating them, the others welcomed him to join their group, and he decided to do so.

Reed called his pilot to report that three additional passengers were traveling with him. He made quick stops for them to get their passports, then he proceeded to the small airport where his private jet was waiting.

Reed spoke on the phone with the principals of the security firm he had hired to tail Laura. He related the story of what had just transpired at Meadowlark Gardens. The firm arranged for an ambulance to pick up Darcy Egan and Zack Walker, who were soon hospitalized and placed under police guard.

When the party arrived at the airport and boarded the plane, Reed transmitted the video of the entire courtyard scene recorded by the camera in his glasses to the security firm. The company would provide the police with Reed's video along with its own report and pictures of Kate's abduction so that Darcy, Zack, and Denim could be charged with a host of crimes, including election fraud, kidnapping, and the murder of James Spenser. Reed indicated that more evidence would be forthcoming at five o'clock—unassailable proof that Ken Martin, himself, along with his top two aides were engaged in massive election fraud.

Soon after the plane took off and cleared American airspace, it was time for Reed's five o'clock broadcast to begin. The travelers moved to the plane's lounge, where they could view the address on a large monitor. Sean sat next to Laura, but when Reed entered the cabin, he rose with a friendly smile.

"Perhaps you'd like to sit here, Reed," he said. Sean knew he had to accept what he could not change.

Reed bowed his head in a silent thank you, and the feud between them was buried.

With the plane headed for a small offshore island where Reed owned a villa, the four travelers watched intently as their host appeared on the screen. He sat at a desk in an unadorned studio with a blue backdrop, his sandy blond hair, solemn face, and pale shirt catching the light.

At the bottom of the screen, a graphic appeared: *A Special Report from Reed Miller*. Then Reed began his message.

"Good evening, fellow Americans. On the eve of this Election Day, I have information to share with you of grave concern. When the Martin administration launched a major campaign to turn voting over to the federal government and almost all of the national media backed it, the public was too quick to accept it. Hardly anyone objected to the unprecedented step of taking control over elections out of the hands of the states and giving it to the federal government, starting with this year's presidential contest. Now, one central program, SafeVote, governs that election for all voters in all states. Under the pretense of stopping voter fraud, SafeVote has opened the door to voter fraud on a massive, nationwide scale. Controlling the voting process is the dream of every dictator, and it was the dream of President Ken Martin to join their ranks.

"SafeVote gave Martin a tool to use when his programs failed and public opinion turned against him. When his chances to win a second term were in jeopardy, he and his top two aides enlisted me to rig the election for them in a secret project called Operation Topcoat. . . . "

Reed described the background he had that qualified him to do the job, the strong-arm tactics against his business that the administration had used to pressure him to do it, and the sting operation he had devised in order to catch them. He explained who had been involved with the scheme, their code names, and the places where he'd met with them. Most shocking of all, he showed videos of the conversations he had had with Darcy and Zack in which he explained the programming he would use to rig the voting in favor of Ken Martin—with their full approval. He also showed footage of his meetings with Ted Burns, the director of technology at the Bureau of Elections, who was also in on the scheme. Reed's series of videos culminated with a clip of his conversation with Ken Martin during a cocktail party at the People's Manor in which the president showed his awareness and approval of Operation Topcoat.

"As I speak to you now, my rigged program is being uninstalled, and the original, legitimate SafeVote program that had been in place before I touched it is being reinstalled. I can assure you, there will be a free and fair election tomorrow.

"This year, I made sure that the presidential election would have a fair vote. But in the future, we cannot allow the central authority—the federal government—to control voting. This is extremely dangerous. It gives the Feds too much power and makes elections vulnerable to corruption on a grand scale.

"I have set aside the money I accepted to do this work—$400 million that your government paid me to deny free elections to you. I am returning it to the government with the strong recommendation that SafeVote be repealed. I want this money to be used in disbanding SafeVote and returning all elections to the state and local authorities, as was originally intended by our laws.

"The Martin administration tried to break up my company because Miller News Network challenged its ideas and policies. Top officials in the Martin administration accused my network of being a danger to the public. But they are the ones who hold the power of force over all of us. They are the actual danger. The real reason they wanted to shut Miller News down was that we saw the truth about their growing power and our shrinking liberty, and we spoke out. Their real enemy is the truth we reveal when we expose their power grabs. That's what they know they have to destroy.

"When the media is on their side, dangerous public officials know they can get away with their power grabs. Regarding SafeVote, only one journalist had the integrity to probe into it. Only one journalist suspected wrongdoing and had the courage to investigate the matter. Only one journalist overcame all obstacles to uncover much of their scheme, and she never quit speaking out. She was vilified, her family's businesses were harmed, her sister was expelled from college, and she was fired—but she never gave up her quest for the truth. I'm here to tell you *Laura Taninger was right*."

In the plane, Laura's companions turned to smile at her with admiration. Reed squeezed her hand affectionately. Then, they turned back to the screen, where Reed's message continued.

"I embarked on my sting operation not just to protect my company, or even to protect the voting process. There is *much more* at stake here. Voting is intended to elect officials that will safeguard *all* of our liberties. If we elect the wrong people, we stand to lose everything. When politicians are brazen enough to try to rig an election, their power-lust is on full display. It's a confession that they're a threat not only to a fair vote, but to all of the underlying freedoms that they're entrusted to protect. That's the real danger they pose—to the gamut of our constitutional rights."

Reed paused, leaned forward, and with solemnity concluded. "You citizens have to be vigilant. You can't surrender your power to the government. The government isn't your friend. It's not your parent. It's not your helping hand. It's *force*, and that makes it a dangerous servant and a fearful master. When government takes more and more control away from our lives, it will eventually reach a point at which it will destroy the press. Journalism is the antidote to tyranny. Without it, the liberty we hold so dear will die."

When the address had concluded, Laura glanced at her phone's news service. She found that Reed's message had already gone viral. His shocking revelation, dramatically broadcast on the eve of Election Day, knocked all other stories out of the headlines in news outlets throughout the country and abroad.

By the end of the next day, the election results were in. Ken Martin had lost in a landslide.

In the following days, more shock waves rocked the nation as Laura used her social media sites to publish the incredible story of their final courtyard meeting on the day before Election Day, along with Reed's video recording of the events. The press immediately picked up the scandalous account. Darcy and Zack, who had been released from the hospital after receiving treatment for their wounds, were arrested, as were Ted Burns from the Bureau of Elections and Denim. Shortly thereafter, ballistic tests showed that Denim's gun had fired the shot that killed James Spenser.

The man at the head of the nefarious scheme, Ken Martin, who had tried never to get caught in an act of wrongdoing but instead let others take the fall, would also face criminal charges for authorizing Operation Topcoat and for his role in the other crimes committed. In current photos, his oversized smile and charismatic presence had vanished, and he looked hunched over, head down, disheveled, and grim.

The company that had certified SafeVote before Operation Topcoat began was brought back. It performed a thorough study and verified that the original program was indeed the one that was used on Election Day, ensuring all Americans who had cast ballots of the integrity of the vote.

The president-elect, who had defeated Ken Martin, commented publicly on the matter gripping the nation. He assured the offshore fugitives that once his administration took power, they would be welcomed back into the country as heroes. "This was a close call for America. We almost descended to a place from which we may not have been able to rise again. This incident shows that too much power has gone to the government, and my administration aims to begin a new epoch to reverse that dangerous trend. Our first priority will be the repeal of SafeVote." Reed and the others hoped he would follow-through with those plans.

As the four fugitives sat around the pool of Reed's villa, still shocked by the events they had experienced and elated with the results, Laura acknowledged the daring escapade of their host. "Reed waged a war, a kind of second revolution, for the same reason the first one was fought, and he won!"

The others clapped, their faces bright with admiration.

"All of you, it turned out, became soldiers in this war and played a vital role in its outcome!" Reed said as he smiled broadly. The past days had transformed him. He laughed easily and seemed more relaxed, light hearted, and happy.

"Now that the ordeal is over, it's time to plan for the future," he said. "When we return home, I'd like to revamp Miller News into what it used to be—and even make it much better—now that I expect to be free from government interference." He turned to the woman smiling at him. "I want *Laura* to head it."

Laura beamed, delighted with the idea. "Two years ago, you tried to lure me away from Taninger News, but I refused," she said. "Now, I'm ready to accept." Laura came alive. She looked like someone whose mind was firing ideas faster than she could express them. "We can make Miller News the premier place for in-depth news coverage, unsurpassed investigative journalism, and top-notch, trustworthy, objective reporting. We can also publish important commentary from our perspective as watchdogs of liberty."

"We need that kind of news coverage for people my age," Kate added. "College students and young professionals need a source of valid information about the important issues of the day, and they need an analysis of the news from people who value our freedoms. I'd love to incorporate the *Voice* into Miller News as a media format for my generation."

"I'd love to have you, honey," said Laura.

"Great ideas! Write up a proposal, and we'll get going," said Reed, his face as excited as theirs.

"Fabulous!" said Laura.

"I'm ready," said Kate.

Laura turned to their fourth companion, who had remained silent.

"What about you, Sean?" Laura asked. "What will you do when we go back?"

Sean paused to gather his thoughts, then he addressed the group, "First, let me say that I was wrong about you, Reed. I was wrong about a lot of things. My friendly, sympathetic feelings toward the Martin administration were totally misplaced." He shook his head as he re-evaluated his long-held beliefs.

"My naïve allegiance to the administration wasn't just a simple mistake. I always felt uncomfortable being different from others, not fitting in, not being part of the in-group. I always was quick to adopt other people's standards and to abandon my own." Involuntarily, his mind flashed back to the little cactus of his childhood, which he had thrown in the trash bin when others mocked him for favoring it. He smiled nervously at the memory. "I'm through leaving my integrity in the waste basket."

He laughed at himself, but the others did not laugh. They looked at him with compassion for what seemed like a painful admission.

"Looking back, I think a lot of my reporting reflected my own gullible perspective and my fears of being rejected by my pro-Martin colleagues in the media. The bias in my reporting wasn't conscious. It was almost subliminal, through the words I chose, the facts I included and the ones I omitted, the softball questions I asked on interviews with the politicians I liked and the hardball questions I failed to ask.

"After this incredible experience, I realize that public officials have to be kept in check," Sean concluded. "And there's a profession that does that." He smiled. "Yeah, I'm going back to journalism, maybe to discover it for the first time."

"If I have a say in personnel decisions," said Kate, "there might be a spot for a seasoned media guy who knows the ins and outs of D.C."

"A spot for someone who has now stopped carrying the water for corrupt public figures and admitted his mistakes," Laura added.

Sean beamed. The respect he had always sought from Laura now shone in her eyes.

Reed gave his endorsement, saying, "That's fine with me. These are new beginnings for all of us."

"In that case, I'm all in!" Sean replied with a renewed spirit.

The four of them relaxed, enjoyed one another's company, and looked forward to returning home. When Kate and Sean headed to the pool, Reed led Laura to the poolside bar. He took out a bottle of champagne and two glasses.

"At eleven o'clock in the morning? What's that for?" They were only casual drinkers, so Laura was surprised.

"I'm hoping I'll have something to celebrate," he teased.

Then his smile faded, his eyes grew intense, and his face looked earnest. He said, "The year without you was hell for me."

She closed her eyes as her own pain from the year without him resurfaced for a moment.

"I was thinking that as the president of Miller News, you should have some acknowledgment. It seems that your name also should be reflected in the company name, but it's not."

"Well, the name *Taninger News* is already taken," Laura said and laughed. Then she cocked her head as she studied the solemnity of Reed's manner more closely, and she wondered . . .

"The problem could be solved if your name were *Miller.*"

She paused for a moment, stunned. Then, she threw her arms around him in reply, in deliverance, in celebration of the happiest moment she had ever known.

"You accept?" he whispered.

"Yes!"

They kissed in a sacred bond that fervently sealed their future.

He popped open the bottle of champagne and filled their glasses.

IF YOU ENJOYED THIS BOOK

Independently published books like *Just the Truth* depend on word-of-mouth recommendations in order to succeed. Please take a moment to leave a few comments on Amazon's Customer Reviews and on your social media. *Thank you!*

And enjoy a copy of Gen LaGreca's other acclaimed novels, available in print and ebook editions.

ABOUT THE AUTHOR

Gen LaGreca writes novels with innovative plots, strong romance, and themes that celebrate individual freedom and independence.

Gen's debut novel is *Noble Vision*. This romantic medical thriller won four awards and garnered praise from magazine magnate Steve Forbes, Nobel laureate Milton Friedman, founder and CEO of BB&T Bank John Allison, and others. Gen also wrote the screenplay for *Noble Vision*.

Showing her talent in other genres, Gen's second offering is the historical novel *A Dream of Daring*. This antebellum murder mystery took six awards, including Finalist in the celebrated *Foreword* Book of the Year contest, and it received a coveted review and recommendation to buy from *Booklist*, the national journal for the American Library Association.

Gen's third novel is the science fiction adventure and romance, *Fugitive From Asteron*. Mixing a gripping plot with a heroic battle for freedom, this story won an Eric Hoffer Book Award.

Gen's most recent novel is the political thriller *Just the Truth,* which portrays a gripping issue of our times: truth in journalism and the threats to a free press. A member of the American Association of Community Theatre (AACT), Gen has written the stage play adaptation of *Just the Truth*.

In addition to fiction, Gen has also written social and political commentaries, which have appeared in *Forbes*, *The Orange County Register*, and other publications.

Prior to fiction writing, Gen worked as a pharmaceutical chemist, business consultant, and corporate writer. She holds an undergraduate degree in chemistry from Polytechnic Institute of New York and a graduate degree in philosophy from Columbia University.

Her variety of life experiences—in science and business, as well as in philosophy and writing—brings vibrant characters, urgent issues, thematic depth, and an outside-the-box approach to Gen's novels. Their sweeping themes of self-sovereignty and the triumph of the individual attract thoughtful readers across social, political, and cultural divides.

For more information, see: www.wingedvictorypress.com.
Gen may be reached at: genlagreca@hotmail.com.

Follow her on:
www.facebook.com/genlagreca
www.twitter.com/genlagreca

PRAISE FOR GEN LAGRECA'S FIRST NOVEL,

NOBLE VISION

"The novel deals with some of the most serious issues of the day, lending the story an immediacy and vibrancy. The author's prose is polished and professional."

—*Writer's Digest* magazine

". . . A well-researched . . . sensitively written . . . inherently captivating novel of suspense, *Noble Vision* is very highly recommended reading."

—*Midwest Book Review*

"This is a beautifully written book! . . . For a first novel, this is a marvelous achievement."

—Midwest Book Awards

"The mounting conflicts of this lovingly sculpted first novel will keep you turning pages late into the night."

—Laissez Faire Books

AWARDS FOR *NOBLE VISION*

Foreword magazine
Book of the Year Finalist in General Fiction

Writer's Digest 13th Annual International Book Awards
Honorable Mention in Mainstream Fiction

Midwest Book Awards
Finalist in General Fiction

Illinois Women's Press Association Fiction Contest
Second Place

PRAISE FOR GEN LAGRECA'S THIRD NOVEL,
FUGITIVE FROM ASTERON

"Exceptionally well written from beginning to end, *Fugitive from Asteron* is an impressive and original science fiction action/adventure story. Very highly recommended."

—Midwest Book Review

AWARDS FOR *FUGITIVE FROM ASTERON*

Eric Hoffer Book Award
Young Adult Fiction